The Guardians Trilogy: Rise of Vice

I0600089

Chance Fribbs

Between Realms Publishing

Published by Between Realms Publishing

ISBN: 979-8-9989025-1-2 (Paperback)

This is a work of fiction. Names, characters, places, and incidents either are the product of the author's imagination or are used fictitiously. Any resemblance to actual persons, living or dead, events, or locales is entirely coincidental.

For inquiries, please contact Between Realms Publishing at betweenrealmspublishing.com.

Acknowledgments: This book is a dream brought to life, and it would not have been possible without the incredible support of so many people who have shaped my journey.

To my family and friends: your unwavering encouragement, love, and belief in me have been my foundation. You've cheered me on through every draft, every doubt, and every triumph—thank you for being my biggest fans.

A special thank you to two remarkable teachers from my childhood, Todd Davidson and Kim George. Your passion for learning and storytelling ignited a spark in me that has burned brightly ever since. Your lessons extended far beyond the classroom, and I'm forever grateful for your guidance.

I owe an immense debt of gratitude to my extraordinary editors: Tammy Sayler, Alexandra Ott, and Ashley Emma. Your keen insights, meticulous care, and creative wisdom polished this story into something I'm proud to share with the world. Thank you for your dedication and for pushing me to make this book the best it could be.

Finally, to every reader who picks up this book: thank you for joining me on this adventure. Your time and imagination breathe life into these pages.

With all my gratitude,
Chance Fribbs

Contents

Prologue

In the dawn of Maeglover, a realm teeming with humans, elves, dwarves, and beastkin, a celestial figure descended upon the land. Saforus, an archangel of unparalleled power, bore a prophecy etched in the very fabric of the cosmos. His words, though incomplete, echoed through the ages, whispered in hushed tones by hearth and hall.

From realms beyond, a chosen few shall rise,
United by fate, their hearts a sacrifice.
A mortal world, by darkness bound, awaits their might.
To vanquish evil's princes, they must fight.

For from the shadows, aid may come,
From realms unseen, for their souls' home.
Guardians by sin, their hearts once astray,
May join the fight, come what may.

But heed this warning, lest you stray from the path,
For loss shall follow, deeper than the wrath.
If hearts remain true, and bonds unyielding stay,
A greater reward awaits beyond the fray.

Yet one among you shall pay the ultimate toll.
Descend to darkness, where their spirit's lost.
A sacrifice made for the world's salvation.
The price of victory, for mortals' sake.

And one whose soul is split shall mend and grow.
Two halves become one, stronger than before.
A guiding light, through the darkest hour,
Their journey complete, they'll find their power.

But know, the princes are not the only threat.

A hidden danger, lurking in the night.
Beware of friends that may deceive and bite.
Whereas a villain, their hand a way to the light.

Together they'll stand, their courage unfurled,
To save not just one world, but the entire mortal plane.
For in their triumph, horizons shall expand,
Knowledge and wisdom throughout the lands.

The prophecy, a cryptic riddle, left Maeglover's inhabitants both hopeful and apprehensive. Some saw it as a promise of salvation, while others feared the impending doom it foretold. But one thing was certain: the fate of the realm hung in the balance, waiting for the chosen to emerge and fulfill the ancient words.

Chapter 1: The Shadow and Light

The war room echoed with the thunderous footsteps of King Abraham and his retinue. Garthen, shrouded in the dim light, felt the air grow thick with anticipation, each step resonating like a drumbeat of doom.

"So, you find one person out of two entire strongholds?!" Abraham's voice boomed, his anger resonating. "What of my wife? My son?"

The heavy oak door swung open, revealing the king, his face flushed with fury. Behind him, Baron Ryoma Yasumoto, head of the magic guild, appeared, his expression grave.

"Sire, I'm still trying to re-establish communication across the land," Ryoma explained, his voice barely audible over the king's grumbling rage. "I found Garthen wandering in the White Pines Forest as I scouted with the soldiers I could muster."

"Garthen?" Abraham's eyes narrowed. "Where is he?"

Turning, he spotted Garthen sitting at the table, a map of the kingdom spread before him. Ryoma gestured silently towards Garthen, who stood, his stature a stark contrast to his former self.

Abraham's gaze narrowed on Garthen, his expression shifting from shock to disbelief. "You can't be Garthen. While you're wearing the seal for commander of Windmontley, someone I've known for my whole reign. You don't resemble him at all. You're ... broken. And why do you hide your face?"

Garthen stood, his voice steady but carrying the weight of his ordeal. "My liege, I swear I stand before you. I may be broken, but your loyal soldier is here." He inclined his body slightly, his eyes remaining locked with the king's.

Abraham's anger flared again. "You had the responsibility to keep my family safe! What could have happened?"

Garthen's blood felt as if it were boiling all over again. "You don't think I understand that? But you seem to have forgotten that I, too, have lost my family!" He pulled back his hood with a dramatic flair, revealing a face scarred and burned beyond recognition. His eyes, glowing an eerie red, pierced into Abraham. "I lost it all. The only thing left for me is to kill those damned demons that did this."

Abraham was speechless, his face a guise of horror. Ryoma nodded slowly. "I had my doubts that this was Garthen, but he was able to tell me about the secret security measures we'd started. Very few people knew about those plans." Garthen slipped his hood back on, stepping into the shadows, the place he now felt most comfortable.

Abraham buried his face in his hands, a single word escaping his lips, laden with despair: "Demons."

Garthen's voice echoed from the shadows, haunting and resolute. "I promise you, that's what did this. Nothing else explains the strange mages or the demonic Shadow Doom Guards. They were just like the stories, huge and armored, with inner shadows that seemed to have no end."

"How could they have overpowered you?" Abraham asked, his voice barely a whisper, tinged with fear.

"They were stronger than anything I've ever faced," Garthen replied, "and they seemed to have some kind of dark magic that held us in stasis. Before I understood what was happening, we were all in cages, stripped and in the dark. They came for us one at a time. That's when the screaming started."

A silence fell over the room, leaving only the sounds of crackling torches and the distant rumble of thunder outside, as if the world itself mourned with them.

"We must find my family," Abraham declared, voice filled with desperate determination. "At all costs."

Garthen shook his head, tone full with sorrow. "No one can help you, Your Majesty. I have seen their bodies alongside the broken form of my wife and hundreds of other citizens when they disposed of me."

Abraham slumped into a chair, all the determination and anger draining from him, an old man broken by grief. To Garthen, he looked just as shattered as he had felt waking to the carnage. Unlike the king, Garthen had long since moved past grief into a cold, resigned need to destroy whatever had brought this evil upon them.

With the opportune moment to persuade Abraham, Garthen moved back to the table, picking up a figure to represent a legion of the army. "Give me command again. I'll rain death upon those who would dare take our families."

Abraham stayed silent, staring at the map with an unfocused gaze, lost in thought. He was quiet for so long that the new footsteps entering the room felt like an intrusion. Duke Denither and Riversong Commander Wells stepped in, their expressions shocked and concerned as they took in the scene before them.

The chamber echoed with tension as Commander Wells strode forward, his gauntlet-clad hand clenching the hilt of the colossal sword slung across his back. His voice cut through the dim light. "Sire, who dares enter your presence at such a perilous hour?"

Abraham rose, his face a mask wrought of stone to conceal the fresh scars of grief. "Before us stands Commander Garthen—or what remains of the man I once called friend."

Garthen's jaw tightened, the sting of his king's words as sharp as any blade.

"Why venture here, Wells, with Denither at your side? I half-expected the Lawbringers to have barred your path," Abraham continued, his tone laced with suspicion.

Denither, ever dignified, stepped forward, his eyes darting between Garthen and the king. "Your Majesty," he began with a blend of urgency and fear, "reports flood in from the remnants of the magic guild. Cities, towns, all around Riversong, they're besieged—by the Blood Sail Pirates and the Black Crop Gang. The fall of Windmontley and Malgrave wasn't random; it was the prelude to this chaos."

Abraham turned his back, faced one of the narrow windows, and watched as lightning split the stormy night. He spoke without turning, voice low. "Do we discern a pattern in this madness? Can we thwart their advance?"

Wells approached the large, cluttered map of the realm. "The pirates strike north, towards Bridgeshire," he said, placing red markers with a forceful hand. "They're crippling our navy, severing supply lines to Commander Flavius in White Pines Forest."

Denither joined him, his fingers tracing lines on the map as he placed markers eastward. "The Black Crop Gang targets our east, pillaging farms and villages, cutting off Riversong's lifeblood. Swiftwallow and Lord Felix might soon be our only recourse for supplies."

"How has this storm gathered so swiftly?" Garthen muttered, shock etching his features.

Abraham returned to the table, his gaze hard as flint. "I left Windmontley on whispers of a revolt from the Black Crop. The only proof we had was from Tom Cabal and his Crimson Order. They're here, purportedly for a strategic advantage."

"And where is Cabal now when his information could staunch this bleeding?" Ryoma interjected, his voice tinged with accusation.

Abraham's response was a weary shake of his head. "Since arriving, those nobles have offered nothing of value. Their 'intelligence' seems but a pretense for their exodus from Windmontley."

Suddenly, an ethereal light bathed the war table, growing from a spark to an intense glow. Instinctively, Wells and Denither moved to shield their king, hands ready at their weapons. The light crescendoed, and a deep voice boomed, resonant and otherworldly, "I am the Watcher of Maeglover, here to bestow upon the Guardians their destined tools. May the prophecy guide you against the encroaching darkness."

A blinding flash engulfed the chamber. Garthen stumbled, the brilliance searing into his vision. The light extinguished just as quickly as it had appeared; darkness claimed the room, deeper than before. Garthen seized a torch, its flame casting jumping shadows, and hurried to ensure the king's safety, though Abraham and the others remained in place, blinking away the afterimages.

Garthen's gaze swept the room, only to settle back on the table where the map now bore six metallic slabs, each varying in size from a foot by half-foot to nearly triple, glowing softly with an internal light.

"The prophecy ... could this be the work of Archangel Saforus?" Ryoma's voice was a whisper, awed and trembling.

Garthen, skeptical, replied, "I've never given much credence to the church's tales." Yet his gaze remained fixed on the slabs.

Abraham, calm as he could muster, ordered, "Wells, summon a church official from the Seers. Now."

As Wells bowed and exited with haste, Abraham turned to Garthen. "Examine these artifacts. What do they signify?"

The torchlight danced on the reflective surfaces of the slabs. Ryoma pointed, his voice hushed. "Look, Garthen, your name ... It was there."

They all watched, mesmerized, as names and symbols shimmered into existence and faded: Rei, Ellena, Zenmore, Saphire, and Kriegon. Each name a whisper of fate, binding them to an ancient prophecy now unfolding before their very eyes.

Chapter 2: The Fall

The mugger's head hit the searing sidewalk with a sound like thunder in a narrow alley of Tucson—SMACK! Wayne, muscles tensed, stood over the fallen assailant, his knuckles smeared with the would-be thief's blood. Only moments before, the thug had made a grave miscalculation by brandishing a paltry pocketknife against Wayne. His military training had given the now bleeding man a harsh lesson to not mug a veteran.

"So, this is what you do with the freedom you've been given?" Wayne sneered at the prone figure. Ensuring the mugger was still breathing, Wayne concealed his bloodied hand in his pocket, the adrenaline now his only companion as he continued his journey home. He had left the 4th Avenue bars, where the night had offered him solace in the form of a light buzz, now rudely replaced by the sharp tang of combat.

He peered into another bar, its neon lights casting long shadows on the pavement. Inside, the place appeared nearly deserted, as it was too early for the night's full revelry. But then, the tranquility was shattered as a boisterous group of college students burst inside, their laughter slicing through the quiet. Wayne's solitude was officially over.

With a heavy sigh, he left the bar behind, the adrenaline fading, along with the metallic taste of blood and regret. The street grew busier, and amidst the growing crowd, he spotted a homeless veteran—a sharp reminder of his own lineage and potential future—accepting food from kind-hearted women. Wayne averted his gaze, taking a detour down a dim alley, the image stirring a tempest of pride and pain for his deceased military parents and comrades.

His parents, his heroes, had instilled in him a fervent patriotism, but their deaths on a distant battlefield had turned that love into a wound that refused to heal. The knife had been driven deeper recently with the news of the deaths of his former squad mates, his brothers. The only local hockey league kicked him off when someone made a military joke. He knew he'd overreacted, but the pride and pain surrounding the memory of his destroyed life were a spiral. Anyone caught in it did not come out unscathed. Now, he wandered, lost in thought, until he found himself at his apartment door.

Wayne entered; the space was modest, but it was his. He tossed his keys, which clattered against a stack of engineering reports meant for an upcoming class, scattering them over textbooks and a cherished photograph atop his Bible: a frozen moment of happiness with his parents before their final deployment. He left the mess for the morning, or perhaps later still.

He grabbed two beers from the fridge, seeking to wash away the night's bitterness. Plopping onto the couch, he flicked on the TV, intent on losing himself in the mindless escapism of YouTube. But a news segment caught his eye.

"That's correct, Dan! We witnessed it here!" A reporter's voice was urgent, the camera panning over a prison. "Just after our tour, a man vanished into the ground, right in the exercise yard!"

The broadcast cut back to the studio, the anchors' faces somber. "This marks one of twenty-five mysterious disappearances in recent days, all involving individuals with violent criminal records. If you have any information ..."

Wayne scoffed, dismissing the report. Criminals vanishing? Good riddance, he thought, switching to YouTube. "Welcome, Kriegon," the screen greeted, and he dove into a gaming channel, the world outside fading with each emptied beer can.

As the night deepened and the beer cans formed a metallic sculpture beside him, Wayne felt the pull of sleep. As he staggered up, the room seemed to spin from alcohol and fatigue. He shuffled towards the bathroom, his body on autopilot. His gaze caught the old shotgun his parents had left him, propped next to the doorway, a reminder of simpler times now tinged with neglect. Only two shots remained, one for each barrel, but he wondered if they would ever be used.

As he crossed into the tiled sanctuary, reality betrayed him. The ground was there, then suddenly, it wasn't. Wayne's arms windmilled in a desperate ballet, one hand instinctively reaching for the shotgun, fingers clawing at the void, his shout of surprise cut short as the dark engulfed him, an unwitting participant in the night's mysterious tapestry of disappearances.

The void was endless, a spiraling abyss where a sense of direction was a myth. Wayne plummeted, his limbs flailing in the darkness, until a pinpoint of light pierced the void. Like a moth to flame, Wayne contorted his body, seeking to orient himself toward the growing luminescence. His efforts were futile; the ground rushed up to greet him, slamming into his back with the force of a sledgehammer, his skull bouncing against the earth with a crack that echoed in his ears.

Stunned, Wayne curled into himself, gasping for air that seemed to dodge his lungs. His coughs echoed in what felt like a vast emptiness. Slowly, he uncurled, his vision swimming with star. Squinting against the harsh sunlight, he muttered in disbelief, "What bullshit is this? Daylight?"

Gone were Tucson's familiar desert vistas and urban sprawl. Instead, Wayne found himself laying on a verdant field, bordered on one side by a forest and on the other by a fortress that loomed high on a cliff, its walls blue and white like it was trying to blend into the sky.

He staggered to his feet, the world tilting around him as he fought against the disorientation. As he steadied himself, a figure detached itself from the cliff's silhouette, approaching with a deliberate pace. Wayne's voice cracked as he called, "Hey, where am I? What in the world is happening?"

His shout faded into the air as the figure drew closer, revealing itself not as a man but a creature of nightmare. Half of its face was the epitome of charm, the other a stark, grinning skull, bleached to an unnatural white. Wayne seemed to stop, his feet rooted to the spot in primal fear as his hands searched his waistband for the pistol that hadn't been there for weeks.

"Ah, this is more the reaction I've come to expect," the creature chortled, its voice a chilling melody of mirth and malice. "Run, little human, as your kind often does."

Wayne swallowed the desert dryness in his throat. "What ... what the hell are you?" he managed, his voice barely above a whisper.

The entity erupted in laughter that seemed to shake the very air. "You humans with your limited lore! Although, most do know me by my darker visage, my other half." Now near enough for Wayne to smell the faint scent of sulfur, the creature's human half was indeed handsome, almost deceptively so, dressed in a suit of midnight black with veins of fiery red that seemed to dance like living embers.

The creature stood just a breath away, its smile both inviting and terrifying. "I am Lucifer, the Morning Star, now the Prince of Pride before you!"

Wayne recoiled, his mind reeling. "You're not real. You're supposed to be ... down there, not here!" Then a terrifying thought hit him. "Or am I in Hell?"

Lucifer's smirk twisted into something far more sinister as he closed the small gap between them with a speed that belied his casual gait. "No, human, you are merely in a new world. One which I seek to take into a paradise that God has abandoned. How about it? Why not join me?" Lucifer paused, seeming to inhale deeply through the flesh half of his nose. "Soldier? Your pride, oh, it reeks delightfully of family, of brothers, of nation—such folly!" With a casual flick of his finger against Wayne's chest, Lucifer sent him hurtling backward as if he were no more than a rag doll.

Wayne's body tumbled through the air, an agonizing arc that ended with him crashing into the earth near the forest's edge. Consciousness flickered like a dying bulb. Through the haze of pain, Wayne witnessed a surreal vision—his own form, standing tall, smirking back at him with a look of mad glee. His doppelgänger, sharing a conspiratorial nod with Lucifer, turned away, sauntering back to the fortress as if they shared an old camaraderie.

With his last ounce of strength, Wayne attempted to rise, to chase this perverse reflection, but darkness swarmed his vision, his strength sapped by an unseen force. As consciousness slipped away, the last sound he heard was the echo of his own laughter, twisted and foreign, fading into the distance.

Chapter 3: Gathering

Garthen claimed his right, the slab of metal with his name sending lightning coursing through his veins as he touched it for the first time. The basic bar transformed before his eyes into a sleek, silver bow that lay gleaming upon the ancient, war-worn map table in the heart of the war room. Backed by the authority of the Cardinal from the Ever Watcher church, who stood solemnly behind him, Abraham proclaimed with a booming voice that Garthen would lead the Guardians.

However, no others were present yet, thus the king and the church granted assistance for Garthen's inaugural mission. Much to his displeasure, the mission to eradicate the notorious Black Crop Gang was to be completed before he could seek his vengeance on the demons who had besieged the Windmontley fortress.

He stood in the vast, cobblestone courtyard under the shadow of the castle's high battlements, facing a battalion of soldiers led by Lieutenant Artemin. Her voice, rough as gravel and tinged with the scent of stale smoke, resonated through the air. "It is an honor to serve, Commander Garthen. My brother has always spoken highly of you."

Garthen nodded in acknowledgment, his gaze steady. "Yes, Commander Flavius is indeed a great leader. I had the honor of co-leading the assault on the barbarians trying to establish a foothold west of Windmontley. I learned much from his tactics from Uthos."

Artemin returned the nod and moved aside, making way for the next two figures to approach. First stepped forward a young man, his eyes bright with zeal as he extended a hand. "Sir, it's an honor to be chosen to work with you. I am Coolgen Hero."

Garthen tried not to let his surprise show on his face. "A Hero family member graces us today?" he remarked, acknowledging the prestigious lineage led by Earl Vittel Hero of the Azure Alliance nobles.

Coolgen nodded eagerly. "Yes, though I am not from the main family line, I was pursuing the path to become a priest when both the church leadership and Uncle Vittel petitioned for me to serve you in this dark time."

After acknowledging the lively youngster, Garthen turned his attention to the last figure, a middle-aged woman with small glasses perched on a pinched face. "And you are?"

The lady straightened, her satchel clinking with what sounded like numerous tools. "Sir, I am Cabitha. I have served as Duke Denither's cartographer for years, and he bade me help you in your endeavors."

"That'll be good; I only have some terrain knowledge of southern Transcen—" Garthen's words were cut off by the sudden clatter of crashing armor and bodies. Turning, he saw in the midst of his troops two strange figures towering over the soldiers, some of whom were still scrambling away, swords drawn and spears at the ready.

The first to speak was a woman unlike any Garthen had seen before; her voice was sharp with venom, contrasting with her light blue skin and lively features. The two elegant horns curling from her forehead reminded him of the demon paintings displayed in the church. "What devilry have your shamans wrought, orc?" she spat.

The orc, muscles rippling like waves under his orange skin as he raised a menacing stone axe, retorted with a roar, "It was your kind's trap! Why do you badger me for answers you must carry!" His readiness for battle was palpable as the blue-skinned woman struck out with a large, fearsome, stone-headed mace.

The crash of the stone shattering as they met in midair stunned everyone; shards exploded like a storm of icy daggers. Several fragments struck Garthen's soldiers, causing cries of alarm and confusion. Before Garthen could call a halt to the bizarre events, one of his archers, driven by instinct, loosed an arrow. The shaft flew true, aimed at the blue-skinned woman, but was deftly intercepted by the orc with an outstretched, calloused hand.

He quickly bellowed towards the direction from which the arrow had come, his voice booming across the courtyard, "This is my fight! Who dares interrupt!" Garthen, his face set with determination, pushed through his troops, seeing on all their faces a mix of concern and bewilderment.

"Stop! Everyone calm down!" he shouted, breaking through the ring that had formed around the newcomers. "No more fighting from anyone here!"

The pair turned to Garthen, their expressions painted with rage and suspicion. The orc, his voice like thunder, spoke first. "So you dare tell me, Zenmore Ironjaw of the Forest Wolf clan, to not finish a challenge?"

The woman interjected, her voice sharp as the shards that had just scattered, "You think this was a challenge? I will end you!"

As the pair squared off again, Zenmore pulling the arrow from his hand with a grunt and tossing it aside, Garthen's voice cut through the tension like a blade. "ENOUGH!" His command startled both to look back at him. Garthen recognized Zenmore's name, etched on one of the metal slabs in the war room. "If I might be able to interrupt your pointless fight, I will tell you something important."

Artemin had come up behind Garthen, leaning in to whisper, "Wait, did you understand what those two are saying?"

Garthen now understood the confusion amidst the continued tension with weapons still raised. It seemed he alone could understand the pair standing tall before them. However, he pressed on, undeterred. "I have Zenmore's name. What of your name, miss?"

The lady looked genuinely shocked at being addressed so formally. "I am Saphire, defcore of the Antiptosis clan."

Garthen knew it then; both had their names on the metal slabs in the war room, marked as fellow Guardians chosen by Lord Saforus. Yet, he had never heard of defcore or orcs as a race within this realm. Surveying the still-tense soldiers, Garthen decided any further discussion would be better in private. "Thank you both for cooling off. How about we step inside to discuss your arrival and what it means?"

The orc grinned, his tusks gleaming in the sunlight. "Now you seek to give us orders?"

Garthen stepped forward; though nearly two feet shorter than the orc, he knew his gaze was that of a seasoned commander, one that had put many an insolent soldier back in line. "I am the commander here; if you want to find out why, we can do so after our talk." His voice grew deathly serious, the emphasis of his authority evident in the air.

Zenmore's grin fell, and Saphire took a cautious step back on her hooves. After a moment, Zenmore spoke again, his voice now dry and subdued. "O… okay, sir."

Nodding, Garthen turned back to Artemin, Coolgen, and Cabitha, all of whom wore expressions of shock at the sudden shift in atmosphere. His voice was firm, cutting through the lingering tension. "Artemin, get our soldiers ready for departure, then meet us in the war room. I will have orders for you then. Coolgen, Cabitha, with me."

He marched through the soldiers, who parted like waves before a ship, guiding the group into the castle. The war room was still with no one around, the tall windows casting beams of light like rays of hope into the dim, stone-walled chamber. Turning back to his companions, Garthen slapped the map table where the other five slabs still lay.

"Can you two find your names here or not?" His voice remained cold, ensuring Zenmore and Saphire understood the severity of the situation.

The pair approached cautiously, their eyes scanning over the map and the slabs. Saphire spoke first, her voice carrying a note of wonder. "Our names are written here? It'd be nice to see mine written down."

Zenmore agreed, his tone reflective. "Yes, never got to learn the shamans' letters before now."

Garthen closed his eyes, taking a deep breath to calm himself before he spoke. "You two don't know your own language?" When both merely shrugged, he sighed, contemplating how challenging it would be for them to do anything beyond fighting. "Here, Zenmore, touch this one; Saphire, touch that one."

With interest painted across their faces, they followed his instructions. As they touched their respective slabs, the largest in the group, a blinding light emanated, momentarily dazzling Garthen before dissipating. Where the slabs had been now lay two formidable weapons: one, a monstrous axe/mace hybrid; the other, a long, thin claymore with jagged teeth along one edge. Both appeared too hefty for any ordinary

20

human to wield, yet Zenmore and Saphire lifted them with ease.

Zenmore's wicked grin returned. He was eager for the promise of war. "This will make for amazing battles!"

Saphire whispered to herself, her eyes gleaming with resolve, "This will drive the orcs from our lands."

Behind Garthen, a gasp escaped Cabitha, and he turned to see both her and Coolgen staring in disbelief. "We can understand them now!" Coolgen quickly added, "They are Guardians?"

Zenmore turned, a look of confusion crossing his brow. "What's this about Guardians? I need to get back to my clan."

Garthen shook his head. "I'm sorry, I don't know where your clan is. You are on the land of Transcendent. Perhaps you are from around the elves' land in Asceriate or the dwarves' lands near the kingdom of Hammerforged?"

The pair exchanged a look, their previous hostility momentarily forgotten in their shared confusion. Saphire spoke up, her voice tinged with worry. "We have never heard those territory names before. Are you familiar with The Faye Orcacia lands? That's where we're from."

The realization struck Garthen like a physical blow. These two were not just from another part of Maeglover but possibly from an entirely different world. He posed the question to the group. Each reacted differently, with Saphire's voice rising above the others in urgency. "Send us back to our realm! We don't belong here."

Garthen shook his head, his expression one of deep sorrow. "I'm sorry, but no one in this world knows that kind of magic. We can ask the head of the Magic Guild, but I am sure he will confirm as much."

As he spoke, the heavy oak door to the war room creaked open, revealing Artemin stepping inside. Her boots echoed with authority against the stone floor, the clink of her armor adding a metallic cadence to the solemn atmosphere. With her entrance, the conversation shifted swiftly from the realm of the impossible to the immediate and grim reality of warfare against the Black Crop gang.

Garthen navigated the shadowy, ornate corridors of the mansion with a swift, determined pace, his steps echoing the urgency of his new role. The past two days had been a whirlwind of clandestine meetings with nobles draped in finery, stern church officials, and the enigmatic arrival of Zenmore and Saphire.

Pausing before the oak door of the office, Garthen took a moment to straighten his doublet, preparing for the scene he knew awaited inside. As he stepped in, the tension was profound; Zenmore, with his towering frame, and Saphire, her eyes a luminescent blue, were locked in yet another silent duel of wills.

Garthen, stepping between the two once more to dispel the brewing storm, announced with a strained patience, "I bring good tidings. King Abraham will not pursue charges of treason against Zenmore."

Zenmore's laughter rumbled like distant thunder, his eyes glinting with mischief. "Ah, so your king does have a sense of humor."

The tension in the room spiked as Saphire, her voice sharp enough to cut through steel, retorted, "Humor doesn't suit you, brute. Remember your place before you jest about forcefully taking leadership." Her words were like arrows, aimed to wound rather than warn.

Garthen could feel the familiar frustration boiling within him. Their constant bickering was like a squall that threatened to capsize their fragile alliance. He slammed his hand on the desk, the sound echoing through the chamber and silencing both Zenmore and Saphire. "Enough!" he barked, his voice a whip crack. "We have direr matters at hand than your petty squabbles!" His gaze shifted between them, oppressive with the burden of command. "We are to bring the fight to the demons, not tear each other apart. I need your skills, not your scorn."

Settling into the high-backed chair, the leather protesting under his bulk, Garthen shuffled through the reports. Each page was a grim reminder of his forces' futile chases. The Black Crop gang seemed like phantoms, always evanescing into the dense woodland east of Riversong.

Coolgen entered first, his youthful face bright with the eagerness of one yet untested by the true harshness of leadership. He carried a tray laden with a modest lunch, setting it down with a clink on a side table.

"Lord Garthen, the kitchen has sent up a meal. And I've brought some of the latest dispatches," Coolgen announced with a tone trying to mimic the gravity of a seasoned commander.

"Thank you, Coolgen," Garthen replied, his eyes not leaving the maps strewn across his desk. "What do these dispatches tell us?"

As Coolgen unpacked the scrolls, he ventured, "They speak of movements, or rather the lack thereof, in the eastern villages. It's as if the gang knows our every step. May I ask, how do you plan to counter this?"

Garthen looked up, appreciating the young noble's curiosity. "Strategy is not just about moving pieces on a board; it's about understanding the opponent's game. We need to predict where they will be, not just react to where they've been."

Coolgen nodded, absorbing every word. "So, we might consider setting traps? Or perhaps using smaller, more covert units?" he suggested, leaning over the map with interest.

"Exactly," Garthen affirmed, pointing to several locations on the map. "Here, and here. These areas could be choke points or perhaps bait for an ambush. We need to think like them, live off the land as they do. So to speak."

Not long after, Cabitha swept into the room, her presence like a breath of fresh air with her sharp intellect and detailed illustrations. She unrolled a new map, more detailed and annotated with recent scout reports.

"Apologies for the delay, Commander. I've marked all the sightings of the gang's activities," she said efficiently, her fingers tracing lines across the parchment.

Garthen leaned forward. "What patterns do you see, Cabitha?"

She pondered for a moment, her eyes scanning the map. "They're avoiding direct confrontation but are too large to be completely invisible. I believe they're using the old smuggler routes, here." She pointed. "Which would explain how they're evading our larger patrols."

Coolgen, not wanting to be left out, chimed in, "Could we not then predict their next move based on these routes? If we know where they can go, we can be there first."

Garthen smiled slightly, pleased with the collaborative spirit. "Yes, but remember, these routes are not just pathways but also their escape lines. We must be cautious not to push them into desperation. A cornered beast fights the hardest."

Cabitha added, "And there's the matter of the Sky Peak mountains. If they retreat there, we're dealing with not just terrain, but possibly new allies or threats. The scouts we sent there haven't reported back, which worries me."

"Could they have been intercepted?" Garthen mused aloud, his brow furrowing.

"Or perhaps they're taking longer due to the terrain," Coolgen offered, though his voice betrayed his uncertainty.

The strategic discussion was at its peak when the heavy tread of a Lawbringer's boots announced his arrival. The room's atmosphere shifted with his armored presence. Zenmore and Saphire, who had been quietly observing, now stood, their interest piqued by the potential for action.

"Commander, we've concluded the search within the city," the Lawbringer's voice boomed, slightly muffled by his helmet. "One candidate matched the names. They're being escorted to the castle now."

The promise of a new Guardian injected a fresh wave of energy into the room. Zenmore, his earlier frustration forgotten, was already moving, a grin spreading across his tusked face. "Finally, something to do," he exclaimed.

Saphire, ever his shadow in both rivalry and action, followed with a determined stride of clonking hooves, her earlier scowl replaced with focused intent. Trying not to lose his temper at the rushed action of the others, Garthen motioned the group to follow.

The mansion where Garthen and his newly formed cadre of Guardians had taken residence was none other than that of Earl Felix Zella, a noble whose presence was most needed in his duties at the kingdom's southern reaches. His daughter, Orris, the sole occupant of this grand estate, had graciously allowed its use as a makeshift headquarters. Nestled within the second tier of Riversong Keep, the mansion was one among the elite row of noble houses, shielded from the common bustle yet somewhat robbed of the panoramic views the higher tiers should have enjoyed by the twin walls on either side. This placement, however, afforded them swift access to the inner keep, a strategic advantage Garthen appreciated.

As they made their way from the mansion towards the keep, the usual disciplined air of the courtyard was replaced by an uproar. Soldiers, instead of training, were gaping skyward. Garthen followed their gazes, his hand instinctively reaching for his bow as he spotted the anomaly— a dark figure spiraling from the sky. His fingers tensed on the string, ready but not yet drawing.

The figure descended rapidly, revealing itself not as a bird, but as a woman, her features distinctly draconic with a lizard-like snout, shimmering black scales, and a powerful tail. Confusion and fear painted her expression as she landed, her voice trembling. "Where am I? Who are all of you?"

The soldiers exchanged bewildered looks, her language seemingly alien to their ears. Garthen, however, understood her perfectly, stepping forward through the crowd with a calming gesture. "You've been summoned, much like Zenmore and Saphire." He indicated the towering orc and the enigmatic defcore, both watching with keen interest from the sidelines. "You might be chosen as a Guardian."

Her eyes widened as she rapidly fired questions, but one stood paramount. "Can you send me back? I have an important ritual soon."

Garthen's expression was regretful. "We're as much in the dark about your arrival as you are. But let's start with introductions. I'm Garthen, commander of the Guardians. And you are?"

"Rei Blackwing," she responded, still processing her predicament. "Guardians? What does that mean?"

"Let's walk," Garthen suggested, signaling the soldiers to return to their duties, easing the tension. As they moved, he began to explain, "You are part of something bigger now, Rei. Your name, like ours, appeared on a metal slab gifted by the Seer Saforus."

Zenmore greeted Rei with a broad grin as they approached. "Is this our newest clan member?"

Saphire's retort was swift. "Clan? We're not forming some orcish clan here."

Garthen intervened before the banter could escalate. "Rei, meet Zenmore and Saphire. And yes, her name is on one of the slabs."

The Lawbringer, ever diligent, added, "There's also another we found inside."

"Two more! Our clan grows!" Zenmore's laughter boomed, echoing off the stone walls as they entered the castle. Garthen could hear Saphire protesting his use of forming a clan without her consent.

Rei, still grappling with her situation, touched Garthen's arm with a taloned finger, "Why can only you, that big guy, and the blue woman understand me?"

"It's these." Garthen tapped his bow. "Gifts from Archangel Saforus. These weapons, they're not just tools of war. They're imbued with a magic we're only beginning to understand. They allow us to speak across races, perhaps worlds, it seems."

Rei's eyes narrowed with academic interest. "Fascinating. In my studies, such artifacts would be inscribed with runes or glyphs. Do these have any visible markings?"

"None that we've recognized as runes," Garthen admitted, drawing his bow slightly from its quiver to show her. "But perhaps your eyes might see what ours could not."

She leaned in, her green draconic eyes scanning the bow's surface. "If I could examine it more closely, maybe I could identify the spell work. Perhaps we can see if the magic runes are universal and not subject to just one realm. Aw, but what am I saying? Only the top scholars of the university had theories of other realms. I guess by coming here I confirmed those theories." Rei seemed to be spinning off into her own musing around magic that he didn't have too much information on, but one person could give her the needed push.

Garthen nodded. "After we meet the others, we'll find Ryoma, the head of our magic guild. Your expertise could unlock secrets we've been blind to."

Rei's expression brightened at the prospect. "Yes, I'd like that. Understanding this magic might be key to finding my way back." Hope flickered in Rei's eyes as they quickened their pace to catch up with the others, the promise of understanding and, perhaps, a way back home.

The oak doors of the war room creaked open, revealing the solemn chamber where Saforus had once unveiled the mystical relics. Now, only three remained untouched upon the war table, their surfaces shimmering with the otherworldly glow. At the room's far end, King Abraham sat, his presence commanding, engaged in a hushed conversation with a striking woman whose raven-black hair cascaded like a dark waterfall. Her ears, pointed and tufted, marked her as a neko, a beastkin rarely seen in these halls. A silent Lawbringer stood like a statue behind the king, his eyes vigilant.

Garthen's heart pounded as he led Rei closer to the conversation, his nerves alight with anticipation. Rei, with her exotic features, eyed the room with curiosity and caution. Approaching the king, Garthen managed a steady voice. "Sire, I present Rei Blackwing, who has arrived as mysteriously as Zenmore and Saphire before her."

King Abraham rose, a warm smile breaking across his regal features. He placed a hand over his heart, bowing slightly. "It is an honor to meet you, Rei."

Rei's eyes widened in confusion, and she turned to Garthen for guidance. He quickly translated, smoothing over the moment of cultural discord. "The king welcomes you."

"Yes, let us not delay," Abraham interjected, his gaze shifting to the neko woman standing quietly to the side. "Rei should claim her relic. Communication should flow freely here."

Nodding, Garthen guided Rei to the relics. "Here, Rei, is the gift from the archangel. Can you find your name among these?"

Rei's fingers traced the air above the relics, her eyes reflecting their pulsating light. "Kriegon, Ellena ... and Rei," she announced, her voice a jumble of awe and certainty. As she touched her slab, a brilliant light erupted, enveloping her. Her majestic wings suddenly unfurled, catching Garthen with a sweeping arc that sent him stumbling backward. The light consumed the room, only to recede moments later, leaving in its wake a formidable scythe where the slab once lay. Rei lifted it, her expression one of cautious reverence.

Abraham, stepping forward once more, reintroduced himself with a formal tone. "Lady Rei, welcome to our realm of Transcendent. I am King Abraham."

"Thank you, Your Majesty," Rei responded, her voice steadier now. "I did not anticipate the relic's magic would be so ... immediate."

Abraham chuckled. "Indeed, it was swift for your predecessors as well. Though, thankfully, you have yet to challenge me for my throne upon receiving your relic."

A booming laugh from Zenmore filled the room, breaking the tension. "Give it time, King! The day is still young!"

Turning the conversation, Abraham gestured to the neko. "Let me introduce Ellena Rona of Asceriate, whose parents once bridged the sea of discord between us and the beastkin realms."

Ellena, small yet with an aura of resilience, stepped forward as Saphire and Rei greeted her warmly. Garthen, meanwhile, leaned closer to Abraham, his voice low. "Where are her parents now?"

"Malgrave," Abraham murmured, his voice deep with sorrow. "Lost when the demons overran it."

Ellena, seeing her name on a slab, approached her relic. The familiar flare of light ensued, leaving behind a seemingly ordinary sword, its true uniqueness revealed only upon close inspection of the intricate grooves along the length.

The room buzzed with new dynamics as subgroups formed. Ryoma, joining in just after Ellena received her weapon, found an eager conversationalist in Rei, diving into discussions of magic and comparing notes about its function. Meanwhile, Zenmore's deep voice rumbled with plans of grand hunts with the king.

Ellena, now armed with her angelic blade, approached Garthen, who had been standing off to the side taking in his team. "I sense your reservations about working with a beastkin. Many here still remember the scars of war," she said with a forthright gaze.

Garthen sighed, his personal storm abating. "The Ravage War is long over; besides, I wasn't a part of it, as I defended against the barbarian hordes. My only grudge lies with those who took my family. If you're with me in this fight, then I welcome your alliance gladly."

Ellena's posture stiffened with resolve, a fire kindling in her eyes. "Then we share a common cause. Together, we'll avenge the fallen, including my own kin. Trust me, Garthen, our enemies will know our wrath."

"Yes, and then perhaps we could find our way home," Saphire interjected, her voice tinged with hope and skepticism as she stepped closer, her hooves clicking softly against the stone floor. "By the way, Garthen, that king mentioned something about a prophecy. Are you keeping secrets from us?"

Garthen's face flushed, if it could, with embarrassment and urgency. He should have realized that these travelers from another realm wouldn't have grown up with the lore of Maeglover whispered in their ears each night. "My apologies," he began, his voice a solemn echo in the dimly lit chamber. "Let us gather everyone. It's time you all understand why destiny has woven our paths together."

He called out to Zenmore, urging him to come over from Abraham's side, who then left with a look of intense relief. Rei and Ryoma, still lost in their animated discussion about the intricacies of magic runes, barely noticed Ellena's approach. Only when she tapped Ryoma on the shoulder did they break from their trance, with Rei reluctantly leaving Ryoma to join the forming circle.

"Ellena knows of this, having been raised on Maeglover's tales," Garthen started, nodding towards her, "but for the rest of you, this prophecy is as ancient as the stones of this castle." He gestured towards Cabitha, who had unearthed an age-old tome from the dust-laden shelves. With a reverence that hushed the room, he opened the book to reveal pages that glowed faintly with the script of gold.

As Garthen began to recite, his voice took on the cadence of a bard, each word painting visions of destiny:

"From realms beyond, a chosen few shall rise,

United by fate, their hearts a sacrifice ..."

The prophecy unfurled like a tapestry, rich with imagery of trials, darkness, and redemption. Each line seemed to weigh heavier on the air, the prophecy's rhythm syncing with the heartbeat of those present.

Saphire paced to the window, her silhouette framed by the twilight, her mind visibly racing. Rei, lips moving silently, requested the prophecy be repeated, each word dissected as if it were a puzzle. After the third recitation, her brow furrowed in confusion. "Guardians by sin? What does that entail? I've led a good life, haven't I?"

Her question hung unanswered, more introspective than directed.

Saphire called from the window, "What possible sin could I be guilty of?" Again, the question hung in the air as each of the Guardians looked inward at the idea of being sinful.

Zenmore, lounging with a deceptive casualness, chimed in, "Sounds like we've got some princely figures to topple. Know any, Garthen?" His voice was light, yet his eyes betrayed a readiness for the battle ahead.

"The only prince known to this land perished when demons overran Windmontley and Malgrave merely a week ago," Garthen replied, his voice a fusion of sorrow and urgency.

The word "demons" snapped everyone to full alertness. Rei was the first to voice the collective shock. "Demons? In this world? We only

30

know them from terrifying tales, where they bred the monstrous wyverns."

"Wyverns?" Ellena and Saphire echoed in unison, their curiosity piqued by the mention of these creatures unknown to all the rest.

"Yes, wyverns," Rei continued, her voice lowering to the tone of campfire stories. "Beasts with wings where arms should be, driven by greed for shiny treasures or the flesh of the unwary. My parents warned me that too much desire for gold might one day lead them to my door."

The room fell into a contemplative silence, each member of the group absorbed in the seriousness of the prophecy and the revelation of demons, their minds wrestling with the intertwining of myth and their sudden, harsh reality.

Saphire broke the silence, her voice a blend of wonder and disbelief. "On Orcacia, we know of slimes, harpies, and the undead, creatures of decay and mindless hunger. But demons and wyverns? These are creatures of a different nightmare."

Zenmore nodded, his tusks catching the faint light as he spoke. "Yeah, slimes are more a nuisance than a threat, and undead are just ... remnants. But real, living threats like these? That's uncharted territory for us."

Garthen, his eyes nearly acting as the flickering torches, added, "Here in this land, Transcendent, the greatest foes we faced were shadow panthers. Beasts of stealth and darkness, not of flame or brimstone. They stalk the night, but they do not corrupt or conquer realms."

Ellena, who had been quietly absorbing the exchange, finally spoke up, her voice tinged with the tales of her own land. "On the Asceriate plains and in the forests, we've battled goblins. Small, yes, but in great numbers they swarm like locusts, pillaging and destroying with a cunning that belies their size. They're nothing like what you describe, yet they teach you to never underestimate a foe."

The group looked at each other, a new understanding dawning upon them. Here they were, each from worlds with their own unique threats,

31

now drawn together in a realm where shadows held more than just panthers and the night whispered of demons.

"This prophecy," Garthen continued, his gaze sweeping over his companions, "speaks of a united force from different worlds. It seems our diverse experiences with lesser evils might just prepare us for the greater darkness we must now face together."

Rei, her eyes alight with a scholar's excitement, leaned forward, eager to share her discovery. "While Ryoma and I were discussing earlier, we realized something astonishing. The runes we use for magic in Aerondrake, my world, are identical to those found here in Maeglover. It's as if the language of magic transcends our worlds."

Ryoma nodded, his fingers tracing invisible patterns in the air. "Indeed, the runes for protection, fire, healing—they all match. This could mean that our magic systems stem from a common source, or perhaps there's been some form of ancient exchange between our realms."

"This could give us an edge," Rei continued, her voice bubbling with possibilities. "If our magic is the same, then the spells I know, the patterns Ryoma has developed, they should work here without any alterations. We could combine our knowledge to amplify our capabilities."

"It might also imply that someone, or something, once bridged our worlds before," Saphire mused, tapping her chin thoughtfully. "Maybe the Archangel Saforus or some other entity has been weaving these connections for eons."

Garthen looked intrigued, his earlier embarrassment forgotten. "This unity in magic could indeed be part of the prophecy's design. Our combined strength might be greater than we assumed."

Ellena, who had been quietly sketching random runes in the dust on the table, looked up. "If magic is our common language, then we must all learn it. This could be crucial in battles to come. But I don't even know the first thing about how to use it."

The group pondered this revelation, the implications of their shared magical heritage slowly sinking in, binding them closer in their shared quest.

Then, Garthen shifted the conversation, his tone becoming more urgent. "There's still one matter we must address. Among the relics bestowed by Saforus, one remains unclaimed. Another needs to be found. They could provide even further insight to what we are facing, maybe even some information about these princes."

The room's atmosphere shifted once again, from the wonder of shared magic to the anticipation of greeting another Guardian. Zenmore smiled as he leaned in. "While it'll be great to have a bigger clan, do we have to wait for the latecomer?"

Chapter 4: A New Beginning

Wayne's mind was a turbulent sea, where memories bobbed like wreckage from the depths of his past. Scenes long submerged resurfaced with a vengeance, only to sink back into oblivion. However, the truly painful ones clung to his consciousness with a bitter aftertaste.

In the dreamscape of his mind, high school replayed in muted tones—his existence had been one of solitude, marked by moves throughout the world. The sweet relief of final exams should have come, but instead, there was only the knock that came to his temporary home, sharp and foreboding.

They stood there when he opened the door, two military officers, their uniforms impeccably somber, their expressions even more so. What followed was a whirlwind of revelations: his parents, gone in what was supposed to be a safe deployment—a statistical anomaly turned tragic. Documents, funeral arrangements, and the vulture-like circling of distant relatives, feigning solace while eyeing the scant inheritance. Wayne, in his grief, had lashed out, his pride a double-edged sword that severed ties and diminished spirits, including his own.

After the somber military officers left, Wayne's graduation felt like a hollow victory. The cap and gown were just costumes in a play where he felt like an understudy who never wanted the lead role. What felt right in the moment was to join the service and seek to make his parents' memory proud.

When that came to life, a band of brothers reminded him why this was important. Their lives became linked together in those four short years, even to the point of their wives knowing Wayne well enough to urge him to get his degree. They would always tell him he saw things more clearly than most and college would be easy.

However, the stink of college was a poor taste for Wayne. Teachers and other students besmirching his military training and his brothers tasted like acid, but he kept his head down. All of that was shattered with a single call. His new brothers had all been killed. Killed by a family in some random nation they were sent to protect.

The days that followed blurred into one another, each indistinguishable from the last. Wayne found himself adrift in a sea of tears and funeral flags. The teachers and students who once mocked his friends now found their lives nearly threatened by a broken man. His social circle dwindled as he withdrew into himself, unable to find comfort in companionship when his mind replayed the ring of the phone, the four draped flags, the news that broke his world.

Nights were no better. Where once there might have been dreams or even nightmares, now there was only the numbing embrace of alcohol. Each drink was an attempt to dilute the pain, to wash away the persistent aftertaste of loss. Whiskey, beer, whatever was at hand, became his nightly companions. The alcohol didn't ask questions, didn't offer empty condolences, and for a few hours, it dulled the sharpness of reality.

Wayne's apartment became his sanctuary. Bottles lined the shelves where books and accolades should have been. The television flickered with shows he didn't watch, its noise a poor substitute for conversation. His life, once on the cusp of beginning, now seemed stuck in an endless loop of sorrow and solace sought at the bottom of a glass.

This cycle of drinking away the pain was not just about mourning his parents; it was about mourning the life he was supposed to have, the normalcy that had been snatched away. Each day was a battle between the urge to move on and the gravitational pull of his grief, with liquor the only mediator he knew.

As the oppressive shroud of sleep began to lift, the pain of reality faded into something else entirely: relief. Afraid of losing those important to him, Wayne clawed at the fading memories, but they slipped away like sand through his fingers. Blinking against a harsh glare, his eyes adjusted to an unexpected view—a thatched roof above, not the sterile white of his apartment ceiling.

Confusion dawning, he sat up with a groan, half-expecting the familiar confines of his room. Instead, he was greeted by the rustic charm of what looked like a set from a medieval drama. Rough-hewn wooden furniture, a straw bed, and the coarse fabric of an itchy blanket that he hastily cast aside.

The agony in his leg brought reality crashing down. A makeshift splint held his broken leg, and with the pain came the memory—Lucifer had thrown him. "At least I'm alive," he muttered, relief and disbelief coloring his tone.

As if summoned by his whisper, the door creaked open, revealing a woman dressed in what could only be described as historical peasant attire, her clothes faded from years under the sun. She carried a bowl of soup, its aroma stirring his empty stomach. He reached out, managing a hoarse "Thank you," hoping the universal language of gratitude would suffice.

Communication was futile; her words were like a melody in an unknown key, no language he had ever heard. Frustration built as Wayne struggled with the language barrier, finally pleading, "English? Do you know anyone who speaks English?"

Her confusion was unmistakable before she hurried out, leaving Wayne to ponder his bizarre predicament. He sipped the watery soup, his mind racing. "Am I actually in another world?" The evidence was mounting: the fall through that abyss, meeting Lucifer, his clothes torn as if by claws, yet his skin mostly unscathed beneath the tattered fabric. "It would explain this soup; it's barely better than an MRE."

Driven by necessity, he hobbled to the door, his leg protesting with stabs of pain. Outside, the scene was even more surreal—the peasant woman conversing with a man clad in chainmail. The word "English" floated amidst their foreign dialogue.

Wayne called out, "Wait!" His voice echoed with desperation, the soldier pausing to look back. He waved at Wayne as if to say "stay put" before walking out of the house. Stunned by the appearance of the soldier, further solidifying the idea he was indeed in a different world, Wayne slowly turned back into the room.

The last remnants of the bland soup lingered in the wooden bowl, resting on the rough-hewn table. Hunger had driven Wayne to finish it, despite its lack of flavor. He leaned against the unforgiving back of the wooden chair, his mind a whirl of confusion and pain. The peasant woman returned only to clear the bowl and drop a few pieces of unfamiliar fruit, her eyes avoiding his, communication lost in the void of different tongues.

As the sun began its descent, casting long shadows through the small window, the sound of hooves clattered to a halt outside. Wayne's curiosity piqued, and with a grimace of pain, he maneuvered his splinted leg, hobbling into the main room just as the door swung open.

First to enter was a figure that made Wayne think of ninjas from old movies, garbed entirely in black leather, a harsh contrast to the rustic medieval setting. His face was obscured, save for eyes that glowed like embers in the dark, a silver bow gleaming on his back. Following him was a woman, her features distinctly Asian, which was not the most peculiar thing about her; it was the cat-like ears twitching atop her head and a matching tail that swished with each step. Her attire was pristine, a fine tunic with a silver sword that spoke of elegance and danger.

The soldier from before gestured towards Wayne as he spoke, but his words were cut short by the dark-clad man's crisp interruption. "Perhaps we should make that judgement ourselves?"

Wayne, still standing, felt a jolt of surprise. "I understood you," he said, his voice tinged with disbelief.

The feline-featured woman explained with a grace that matched her unique appearance, "It is good to meet you. I am Ellena Rona. It appears you have been summoned, like others before you, to become a Guardian in this world. Our weapons"—she indicated her sword—"enable us to communicate with the chosen."

Garthen, the shadowy figure, introduced himself with a tone of authority. "And I am Garthen Brus. Commander of the Guardians. Welcome to Maeglover and the Kingdom of Transcendent. Pray tell, which world do you hail from?"

Wayne's mind reeled. "How do you know I'm from another world?" he managed to ask, his hands gripping the chair for support.

Ellena's gaze swept over his tattered modern clothes, a silent answer. "Others have come before you, through the castle. But you … why here? And who did this to you?" Her questions were gentle yet probing.

Wayne's spine crawled, and the pain in his leg grew slightly as he formed the name. "Lucifer."

The name sent a visible ripple of tension through the room. Garthen's voice was sharp, laced with urgency. "Are you sure it was Lucifer? The ruler of hell?"

Wayne nodded, the memory of his encounter fresh and painful. "He announced himself. Who else could it be? And that appearance, it shouldn't be possible for someone alive to look like that. He announced himself as the Prince of Pride."

The revelation seemed to weigh heavily on his visitors, their expressions darkening. Ellena broke the silence. "That somewhat explains the prophecy for the evil princes."

Ellena's words hung in the air, filled with implications. The name Lucifer seemed to echo with a sinister ring, causing a ripple of whispers between the soldier and the peasant woman until Garthen's sharp glance silenced them.

Ellena and Garthen shared a look that spoke volumes of their shared knowledge and worries. Garthen shifted the conversation, his tone lighter but still probing. "We haven't caught your name amidst all this. Nor have you answered about your world."

Realizing he hadn't formally introduced himself, Wayne said, "Oh, right. I'm Wayne. Nice to meet you both, though the circumstances could be better. I'm from Earth."

Garthen's eyes narrowed slightly. "Wayne, huh? Not Kriegon?"

The mention of his online persona caught Wayne by surprise. "No, Wayne is my real name. Kriegon is just my gaming handle. How would you know about that?"

Ellena, stepping in before Garthen could answer, motioned gently towards Wayne's injured leg. "Let's not overwhelm him with too much at once. We should take you to the castle. Our healer, Rei, can tend to your leg, and we can explain more there."

Garthen sighed, the burden of leadership evident in his posture like Wayne's captains before as he stood. He handed some coins to the peasant woman and the soldier, a gesture of thanks or perhaps payment for silence, before leading the way into the deepening night. Ellena supported Wayne with an unexpected strength, guiding him as they followed Garthen. Her touch was reassuring, a small comfort in the vast unknown of this new, fantastical world he had been thrust into.

The night air was crisp, carrying with it the scents of pine and earth, foreign yet comforting in their familiarity. Garthen had arranged for another horse; Wayne was helped onto one, his leg throbbing with each movement, yet the prospect of answers urged him onward.

They rode through the countryside, the landscape slowly giving way to cobblestone paths as they approached the medieval city. The walls towered above, massive and imposing, built from stones that told tales of centuries past. Torches flickered at intervals, casting dancing shadows across the faces of guards who nodded at Garthen and Ellena with recognition and respect.

As they ascended the hill, the city unfolded below in a tapestry of flickering lights and shadowed rooftops. The transition from the common quarters to the noble district was marked by a large wall giving way to wide streets, cleaner air, and the grandeur of architecture that spoke of wealth and history. Here, the buildings were statements of power, adorned with banners and intricate stonework.

The mansion where the Guardians resided was nestled among these grand structures, less ostentatious but no less impressive. Its gates opened silently for them by posted guards, revealing a courtyard of immaculate landscaping.

Ellena helped Wayne dismount, his descent awkward but managed with her assistance. "Welcome to our base of operations," she said with a hint of pride.

Garthen led them inside, where the warmth of the interior was a pure distinction from the cool night. The halls were lined with artifacts and tapestries depicting heroic scenes that Wayne guessed were from this world's history or mythology.

They entered a room that breathed the essence of healing, with the gentle aroma of medicinal herbs pervading the air and the soft luminescence of enchanted lanterns casting a serene light. Here, they were greeted by Rei, who was unlike anyone Wayne had ever imagined.

Rei's appearance was striking; she had the sleek, black scales of a dragon, shimmering with an almost metallic sheen under the light. Her eyes were a vivid green, sharp and intelligent, set within a face framed by flaming red hair that seemed to flicker like living fire. When she stood to greet them, she had to duck her head so it did not scrap the roof. Despite her draconic features, there was an unmistakable warmth and kindness in her demeanor. She picked up a large shining scythe when she moved to greet them.

"Ah, the newcomer," Rei said, her voice soothing, like the whisper of a comforting mother on a quiet night. "Let me attend to that leg."

Wayne was guided to a plush seat, and Rei knelt before him. As she examined his injury, her hands, though clawed, moved with delicate precision. A soft, green light emanated from the back of her hand where what looked like a rune had been etched into her scales, the pain diminishing under her touch, replaced by a comforting heat. Garthen explained what they had done while she worked in short, informative sentences.

"Lucifer did this?" Rei inquired, her focus unwavering from her task, her question carrying a lightness of familiarity with such injuries.

"Yes," Wayne confirmed, still taking in Rei's extraordinary presence. "He was ... quite the introduction to this world."

Garthen, observing Rei's healing process, remarked, "There's much for you to understand about our world, Wayne. But for now, allow yourself to heal. Tomorrow, we delve into why you've been summoned here."

Ellena, standing close, offered reassurance. "And how you might aid us. Guardians aren't chosen by chance. I am sure you will fit in just fine."

As Rei's magic worked to mend his broken bone and soothe his battered body, Wayne felt a mingling of awe and trepidation.

With his leg now healed under Rei's expert care, Wayne followed along to a room within the mansion, one that whispered of comfort with its plush bed draped in silken sheets and walls adorned with tapestries that depicted heroic sagas. The exhaustion of his ordeal finally weighed upon him, and he sank into the bed, sleep claiming him almost instantly.

The sun had barely risen when a series of sharp knocks jolted Wayne from a dreamless slumber. Before he could fully shake off the remnants of sleep, the door swung open with enthusiasm, revealing Ellena and a figure that made Wayne sit up straight in bed.

"Morning, Wayne! I trust you've rested well. Zenmore here was dying to meet you," Ellena greeted with her cheery smile. Beside her stood Zenmore, an imposing giant with vibrant orange skin, his presence filling the room. His eyes, a playful shade of blue, twinkled with mischief, contrasting his intimidating size.

"By the Clan's honor, you look like you've been through a dragon's gullet and spat back out. I didn't think Rei would be so rough on you!" Zenmore boomed, his laughter echoing around the room, deep and infectious. Despite his jesting tone, there was a warmth in his voice that suggested camaraderie rather than mockery.

Wayne, still trying to reconcile his image of orcs from fantasy with this lively, orange-skinned giant, managed a nervous smile. "I guess I've had better days."

Ellena, sensing Wayne's initial discomfort, chuckled. "Don't let Zenmore scare you. He's like a big, orange teddy bear ... with a sense of humor as sharp as his axe." The mention of an axe drew Wayne's eyes to the massive silver axe and mace combo resting on his shoulder.

"Speaking of looks," Zenmore continued, leaning against the doorframe, "we need to get you out of those tattered clothes. Can't have a Guardian looking like he lost a fight with a flock of harpies, can we?"

No sooner had he spoken than Betty, a seamstress, bustled into the room with an air of purpose. Ellena's introduction was lost in the whirlwind of activity, her eyes critically scanning Wayne. "Hmm, yes, you'll do nicely for my work. I've just the thing to bring out the Guardian in you," she mused with Ellena translating for her, her fingers already threading through various pre-tailored fabrics.

She selected a set of dark blue spider silk shirt and pants, its texture fine yet with an undeniable strength when Wayne felt it. "This," she announced, "will not only complement your new status but also your ... intriguing hair."

Wayne reached up, touching his hair, then walked over to one of the mirrors, only to find it had turned a stark white. Not only that, but his eyes had gone from the original brown to a deep maroon. "When did ...?"

Ellena interjected with a grin, "Seems like crossing worlds has its side effects. You're looking more the part every moment with that odd look!"

Betty worked swiftly, her needles moving like quicksilver as she tailored the shirt directly onto Wayne, ensuring it fit like a second skin, the dark blue fabric catching the light with every movement.

"There," Betty said with a flourish. "Now you're not just dressed as a Guardian, you look like one."

With Wayne adorned in the finery of this new world, Ellena clapped her hands. "Perfect! Now, let's head to breakfast. Zenmore here eats enough for three, and we wouldn't want you to miss out on your first meal with the Clan."

Zenmore threw his arm around Wayne's shoulder, nearly lifting him off his feet. "Come, my white-haired friend! Let's fill our bellies and speak of tales and battles!" He felt like Zenmore would have fit in perfectly with his old brothers from before.

The trio made their way through the mansion's corridors, the smell of fresh bread and cooked meats wafting through the air and guiding them towards the dining hall, where the day's first meal waited for them.

The grand dining hall of the mansion buzzed with an energy that was almost tangible, filled to the brim with more people than Wayne had anticipated. At one end of the enormous mahogany table, Garthen and Rei were ensconced with a striking figure—a woman whose skin shimmered in shades of blue. Short, elegant, gazelle-like horns crowned her head, and her eyes, a luminescent blue, starkly contrasted against Garthen's fiery red gaze. The massive shinnying claymore with ragged teeth dug into the floor and leaned on one of her shoulders. This diverse assembly of characters fell silent as Wayne entered, announced with the pomp of royalty by Zenmore, whose voice boomed across the hall like a herald.

Flushing under the sudden attention, Wayne navigated through the sea of curious eyes to greet his companions. "Good morning," he managed, his voice steady despite the nerves, "and thank you again for the healing."

Rei dismissed his thanks with a grin that revealed sharp teeth, while Garthen, with a broad gesture, introduced the blue-skinned woman. "Wayne, meet Saphire, the last of the Guardians." His hand swept towards the other end of the table, where three more sat among the serving staff. "And there's Cabitha, our cartographer; Coolgen, a nobleman's son with connections to the church; and Lady Orris Zella, whose family owns this grand estate."

As Wayne took his seat, the trio at the table's far end offered what he assumed were warm greetings. A servant swiftly presented him with a plate heaped with exotic fruits, warm bread, and eggs. Saphire leaned in, her eyes curious. "Wayne, could you enlighten me about this 'gaming handle' you've spoken of with Garthen?"

With a mouthful, Wayne began, "A gaming handle, or gamertag, is essentially an alias I use in the fantasy realms of video games. Imagine it as a cloak of identity for when I step into worlds of make-believe, controlling characters in stories that unfold on screens. My handle was Kriegon."

Saphire's brow furrowed, her confusion mirrored by the others. "So, these worlds you enter, are they conjured by magic like Rei's or perhaps

Ryoma's?"

Shaking his head, Wayne explained, "No, there's no magic in my world. It's all technology—advanced, interactive, but ultimately just a simulation. Like watching a story through a window where you can also pull the strings of the characters inside."

The conversation was cut short by Garthen, who sensed the growing complexity. "Let's not delve deeper into this rabbit hole. Why 'Kriegon,' though?"

Wayne's gaze drifted, a shadow passing over his features. "My father chose it because he got overruled at my birth by my mother. It was his way of diving into fun worlds together and using the original name he had for me."

Ellena placed a comforting hand on his arm. Her touch was warm, her voice softer. "Don't worry, we'll strive to return you to your world, just as we seek passages home for Rei, Saphire, and Zenmore."

His response was a shake of the head, the words hanging heavy. "I have no family to return to. Their military career didn't agree with our life goal. I have nothing to go back to." The admission left a bitter taste, turning his meal bland as he mechanically continued eating.

The silence that followed was shattered by Zenmore, oblivious or perhaps indifferent to the somber mood. "So, Garthen, when do we arm our friend Wayne? I'm eager to test his mettle against mine."

A roll flew through the air, courtesy of Saphire, hitting Zenmore squarely on one of his tusks. "Can't you go a day without a challenge?"

Unfazed, Zenmore chuckled, the sound like distant canon fire. "Didn't challenge Lady Orris, did I? Wouldn't want to muss up her fine dress."

Orris, with a blush creeping up her neck, retorted in her native tongue, sparking another bout of laughter from Zenmore, his chair creaking ominously.

Wayne, bemused, glanced at Ellena, who only responded with a subtle shake of her head and a playful wink. As the meal concluded, with only Zenmore still indulging, the group readied to depart. Each

Guardian picked up their weapons without a second thought. Cabitha and Coolgen gathered their maps and notes, discussing with Garthen as they all moved towards the mansion exit, everyone else in tow.

Chapter 5: Understanding and Mission

The morning light cast long, dramatic shadows as Wayne and his companions navigated the noble district, hemmed in by two towering walls that seemed to touch the sky, separating this realm of wealth from the rest of the city. Each mansion they passed was a bastion of prestige, with golden relics that shone like beacons behind the intricate patterns of high wrought-iron fences.

Wayne, still adjusting to this strange new world, turned to Ellena, whose head was now obscured by a dark hood that merged seamlessly with her raven hair. "Is this entire country so prosperous? These homes boast treasures I didn't think possible."

Ellena, her voice tinged with indifference, replied, "I concern myself only with the now. The inner workings of this kingdom are of no interest to me."

Her detachment prompted Wayne to probe further. "You're not from here, then?"

Ellena's head shook slightly, her voice full of a sorrow that echoed Wayne's own. "My parents served as ambassadors between humans, beastkin, and elves after the wars. They perished in one of the fortresses during the demon invasion. Only Garthen survived that massacre ... Not even the king's own family made it out, nor Garthen's."

Wayne's gaze shifted forward to Garthen, who was deep in strategic conversation with Coolgen and Cabitha. "How long since the attack? How is he holding up after something like that?" he asked, his voice low, thinking of his own loss and how he wouldn't be that strong.

"Just over a week," Ellena whispered, her eyes distant. "Garthen has a purpose now, something to cling to. We dare not speak of anything that might shatter his resolve."

"And you?" Wayne hesitated, his hand hovering near her shoulder, wanting to offer comfort but unsure.

Ellena's smile was a ghost of itself. "I'm managing ... barely. Zenmore and Rei have been my anchors these past couple days. Before I joined this quest, my behavior wasn't ... fitting for the Rona lineage."

She quickened her pace, the massive gate looming ahead, opposite from the one they'd entered last night.

At the gate, two sentinels stood, their armor polished to a radiant glow, each piece meticulously crafted like legends come to life. These guardians, almost as tall as Zenmore but not as broad, wielded menacing poleaxes, their full helms nodding in recognition as Garthen led the group through.

Inside, the castle's magnificence was overwhelming. The walls were adorned with mosaics of white and blue marble, designed to mimic the flowing rivers, giving the illusion of movement. The courtyard was a hive of activity, with soldiers in rigorous training, their movements underscored by the sharp commands of their officers.

Garthen led them confidently through the ornate halls, past towering portraits of stoic ancestors, each frame whispering of centuries past. They arrived at a grand oak door, which Garthen pushed open to reveal a war room. The map on the table caught Wayne's eye—it resembled Italy but on a scale he couldn't quite comprehend.

But his attention was swiftly captured by a metallic slab on the table, its surface alight with glowing, shifting runes, at one point displaying Kriegon. Drawn to it, Wayne's touch triggered a brilliant light. His body felt charged, as if every atom were vibrating with energy, until the light dimmed.

In place of the slab now lay a staff, slender and metallic, impossibly light. As Wayne examined it, he was reminded of a college course, a particular lecture on material science where he'd seen electron microscope images of metallic grains. The staff's surface mirrored those images, displaying a dynamic array of microstructures, each grain telling a story of immense pressure and perhaps magic fused into metal. Here, in his hands, was a relic of power, and of strange knowledge, something he wanted to learn about and use to help others.

The air still buzzed with the residual energy of magic as Wayne held the staff, its plainness suddenly profound rather than disappointing. As Wayne watched, a sliver of the shifting metal looped around his small finger, making a permanent attachment to the magic. Garthen was the first to speak, his voice gruff yet curious. "Not what you expected, I gather?"

Wayne rotated the staff, feeling its balance. "I thought it might be ... I don't know, more ornate? But there's something about it. It feels ... right."

Ellena stepped closer, her eyes reflecting the staff's subtle glow. "Sometimes, the simplest forms hold the deepest power," she remarked, a knowing smile playing on her lips.

Rei, with her usual warmth, added, "Wayne, dear, it's not the weapon but the wielder. You will make it special."

Saphire, usually reserved thus far, simply nodded in agreement, her glowing eyes conveying silent support.

The conversation was cut short by the entrance of two imposing figures. The first, a man with a regal bearing and weary eyes, and the second, a stern-looking military man with an air of command.

Garthen quickly made introductions. "Wayne, this is King Abraham, ruler of this land, and Commander Wells, head of our military forces in the city and to the northern territory."

Wayne, taken aback by the sudden introduction to royalty and command, managed a nod. "Uh, nice to meet you both. I'm Wayne, but—"

King Abraham cut in, his voice resonant. "Wayne, is it? Or should I say Kriegon?"

Wayne felt a jolt at the name. "Kriegon was just my gaming alias. How does this fit here?"

Commander Wells stepped forward, his expression serious. "The slab bore the name Kriegon, and in this world, the inscription is tied to prophecy. If the nobles, especially those of the Crimson Order, learn that your real name doesn't match the written name ... well, it could undermine your position and our cause. It does not help they already seek to undermine the current Guardians before we have even officially announced your coming."

King Abraham nodded. "We propose you take the name Kriegon. It would solidify your role as a Guardian in the eyes of all who doubt."

Wayne pondered, his thoughts drifting back to childhood games with his father, where "Kriegon" was his avatar for justice and heroism. There was a symmetry to it, adopting this name in a world where those values might actually make a difference.

A smile crept onto his face. "Kriegon ... I used to be him when I wanted to stand for something good, make the right choices. Maybe here, I can truly be that person."

The king's expression softened. "Then, by royal decree, you shall be known as Kriegon. Let this name carry the importance of your destiny and our hopes."

Garthen clapped a hand on Wayne's shoulder, now Kriegon's. "Welcome to your new life, Kriegon. Let's see what you make of it with that staff of yours."

Kriegon, formerly Wayne, gripped his staff, feeling a surge of purpose. He turned to Garthen, for the first time seeing him up close. His burned, charred skin shocked Kriegon, but it also further cemented the thought that this world needed to be set right. "What can I do?"

Garthen led Kriegon to the far end of the dimly lit war room, where an ancient tome rested on the table, its thin, almost translucent pages fluttering slightly as if alive. At Kriegon's touch, the book reminded him of an old family Bible, sacred yet foreboding, but here the script flowed in luminous golden ink, unfamiliar and mystical. Kriegon leaned in, his eyes narrowing as he deciphered the text that should have been foreign to him, a semi poem that spoke in riddles of destiny and doom.

As he read, the hushed murmurs of strategy discussions filled the room, but Kriegon's focus was absolute. Upon finishing, he lifted his gaze to meet Garthen's, an assortment of realization and concern in his voice. "Is this the prophecy you've all been hinting at?"

Garthen gave a solemn nod, his expression grim. "Then what you said about Lucifer now makes more sense."

The name Lucifer echoed like a thunderclap, stilling the room into a tense silence. King Abraham, previously engrossed in conversation with Commander Wells across the vast map table, spun around, his voice resonant and filled with dread. "Lucifer?! What's this, Garthen?"

Garthen straightened, his posture stiffened by the significance of the revelation. "My apologies, sire. Kriegon was attacked by Lucifer upon his arrival in our world."

The color drained from King Abraham's face, his eyes wide with the enormity of the news. "So, it's not mere summoners we face, but the very legions of Hell itself." He turned sharply to Wells. "Double your efforts, Commander. The pirates must be dealt with; we need those reinforcements at the White Pines Forest!"

Wells saluted with a clang of metal, his gauntlet striking his chest plate, then swiftly exited to enact the king's command. King Abraham fixed his stern gaze back on Garthen. "Daily reports on the Black Crop Gangs, Garthen. In return, I will keep the nobles off your back for now, but if you withhold such dire news again ..." His threat lingered in the air as he exited, leaving behind a palpable tension.

The silence was broken when Coolgen approached hesitantly. "Sir, Lieutenant Artemin reports ... the village you sent her to investigate has been obliterated."

Garthen's fists clenched, his body trembling with suppressed fury. He turned away, struggling to compose himself, as Cabitha, with quiet efficiency, rearranged the markers on the strategic map. When he faced the room again, his eyes burned with a fierce light, his voice chillingly calm, he said, "We must deploy immediately. Our larger forces are too cumbersome, too slow."

Ellena, her voice cutting through the thick atmosphere, added, "It seems the gang predicts your moves, sir."

Amid this, Kriegon, still grappling with the whirlwind of revelations, inquired, "What exactly does this gang want?" The room exchanged uneasy glances, the question hanging unanswered, too complex or too terrifying to contemplate.

Kriegon pressed on, "Understanding their objectives could give us an edge."

With a heavy sigh, Garthen admitted, "We have no insiders, and the few we capture ... they don't survive to talk."

Coolgen, sifting through his scrolls, offered what little he knew. "The attacks intensified about five days ago. They're targeting food supplies—grain, meat—bound for Riversong and our troops. And there's more; people are vanishing after these raids."

Kriegon ran a hand through his hair, feeling the unfamiliar weight of the mission that the others had seemingly shouldered with ease. In this moment he felt something solidify in him, something he hadn't felt since serving with his brothers in arms before. Around him stood those who shared a mission he saw as just, and it was his time to pick back up the role of defender, even if it was in a different world.

"We need to gather more intelligence, and quickly," Garthen declared, his voice echoing slightly against the stone walls. Turning to Cabitha, whose eyes gleamed with resolve and apprehension, Garthen asked, "Cabitha, can you hold this ground? I need someone I can trust to coordinate our efforts from here while I venture out. Order Artemin to Noble Paris's main city. Perhaps they can assist us."

Cabitha, her posture stiffening with the responsibility, gave a firm nod. "I'll manage the fort, Garthen. You have my word."

Garthen gave a tight smile with his clothed mouth. "Good. Coolgen, you'll assist her, and you, Kriegon, as well. I need the three of you to mingle, to weave through the courts and barracks. Speak with nobles, guards, anyone who might unwittingly be a pawn or a player in this game. Sow seeds of doubt, or perhaps, harvest some truth. Kriegon, assist Coolgen where you can, learn about our world while acting as a servant to him and the Noble family."

Kriegon, whose brow furrowed in mild shock at being thrust below Coolgen and kept from potential fights, interjected, "But why not send Ellena or the others? They're versed in this world compared to me. I much prefer to fight with you all on the front lines."

With a weary sigh, Garthen, the seasoned strategist, explained, "The other Guardians are not human, Kriegon. Their faces, their races—all too recognizable. Sending them into meetings with nobles would raise flags brighter than the royal banners. No, it must be you three humans. You'll be less conspicuous, yet equally effective."

Garthen clapped a hand on Kriegon's shoulder, feeling the cool leather of his glove through the tunic. "This isn't just about fighting head-on; it's about blending in while standing out enough to shake some trees and see what falls. Us five will slip out under the guise of mercenaries or traders. It's risky, but it's our best shot at flushing out these gang members."

The room fell into silence, filled only with the distant call of birds through the open windows. Kriegon felt the importance of their mission; this was how he could help those who couldn't help themselves. Would this be what his parents or fellow soldiers would do if they were here?

Chapter 6: Gang Hunting

The carriage wheels transitioned from the cacophonic clatter over the cobbled streets to a smoother glide as they passed through the eastern gate of Riversong, the city's walls receding into the night. Garthen shifted uncomfortably beside Ellena, attempting to realign his spine, which had been battered by the journey's relentless jolts. He scanned the darkness, ensuring their solitude, and leaned toward the back of the carriage to whisper, "We're clear of the city, but let's put a few more miles behind us before we abandon this contraption."

A groan issued from Zenmore, too loud for the quiet escape. "It felt like being hurled off a mountainside."

"Keep it down," Saphire snapped from beneath her cover, her voice laced with irritation. "I can't wait to distance myself from you; I hadn't realized the full extent of your stench."

The pair had been concealed under layers of coarse blankets among the crates, their trader's disguise having sailed them through Riversong's vigilant checkpoints with ease.

Above, the silhouette of Rei cut through the moonlight, her wings briefly casting shadows that spooked the horses. She alighted with a grace that belied her predatory form, her talons gripping the tarpaulin before she maneuvered to squeeze beside Garthen and Ellena, making the seat even more cramped. "No followers in sight, and the road ahead is clear," she reported, her voice a low thrum.

A ripping of fabric preceded Saphire's head emerging through a new tear in the carriage's covering. "I was about to choke on that oaf's musk," she complained, her eyes reflecting a mix of relief and annoyance.

From within, Zenmore's chuckle rumbled, a stark contrast to the tense silence of their escape. The road, empty and silent, stretched before them, the magical lights of Riversong eventually dimming into nothingness. At Garthen's signal, they veered off the path, the team moving with efficiency. Zenmore, with his formidable strength, flipped the carriage aside as if it were no more than a child's toy.

The horses were quickly prepared; Zenmore swung onto the back of the sturdiest steed, while Garthen helped Saphire onto the other. Rei, with a powerful beat of her wings, took to the air, her talons gently but firmly clutching Ellena for the flight.

As they set off, the urgency of their mission fueled their pace. Days blended into nights, the landscape shifting starkly as they crossed from Duke Denither's well-kept lands into the neglected territories of Count Neil Paris. Here, the roads were unforgiving, the earth itself seeming to resent their passage, and the few people they glimpsed were as worn and weary as the land they trod.

Throughout their journey, Garthen's thoughts were on the horizon, on the answers that awaited, on the confrontation with their quarry. His connection with Cabitha through the magic scroll provided by Ryoma was their lifeline, updating them on troop movements or potential trails the gang members used.

The jagged silhouette of the Sky Peak Mountains clawed at the twilight sky as Garthen's band made camp on their third night out from Riversong. The air was crisp, carrying the chill of impending confrontation. Garthen unfurled the worn communication scroll and map beside a flickering campfire, its light dancing across his rugged features. His eyes, reflecting the flame, scanned the map that outlined their perilous journey.

"We're here." Garthen's finger stabbed at a spot on the map, his voice low and resolute. "This village was razed to the ground. It's where we'll pick up the trail."

Zenmore, skeptical, leaned in, his shadow merging with Garthen's on the map. "And why did your men leave without finding anything?"

"They're soldiers, not trackers," Garthen replied, his jaw set. "I instructed Cabitha to push them east, towards the mountains. Our goal is to herd the gang into our forces or catch them ourselves. Either outcome works."

Ellena's sharp gaze met Garthen's. "So, we're cleaning up their mess?"

"Yes," Garthen admitted with a sigh, "but look here." His finger traced pathways to nearby hamlets, isolated and vulnerable. "These villages haven't reported in. If the bandits struck, we're blind to it. Tracing their path from here could reveal their hideout."

Saphire's finger brushed over a larger settlement near the mountains. "And this place? It looks significant."

"That's Count Neil's domain," Garthen said dismissively. "Well-guarded. The gang wouldn't dare. And even if they did, Neil wouldn't impede us, not with the king's seal."

The mention of authority hung in the air, a reminder of the power backing their quest. The group fell silent, each contemplating the paths and perils ahead.

Rei, breaking the quiet voiced a thought that lingered like smoke. "Garthen, why not hunt the princes like Lucifer?"

Garthen's boots crunched over the carpet of dead leaves, each step a measured beat to his internal dialogue. "Direct orders from the king are one reason," he began, the words escaping his lips in a low, reflective growl. The night air was thick with the musk of pine and the faint, acrid scent of smoke from their dwindling fire. "But there's strategy too. Our military's stretched thin, possibly by design. Chasing these bandits might lead us to whoever's orchestrating these disruptions. Plus," he said, then paused, his gaze sweeping across the tense faces of his companions, the firelight dancing in his eyes, "the demons would be elusive, but human conspirators? They might just slip up."

Ellena, her face half-shadowed by her hood, nodded in agreement. Her voice, when she spoke, carried a note of caution. "And remember, the Crimson Order's already spinning tales that we aren't the Guardians from prophecy. We tread a fine line; we need the people's trust."

Saphire, skeptical, leaned forward, her horns catching the firelight. "Is that why you left Kriegon behind, to combat the Crimson Order?" Her question hung in the air like a challenge.

Garthen shook his head. "It's like I asked, I need someone to root out the potential rat informing on our movements. Kriegon is new to the scene and sounded like a smart guy. Plus, his parents have a military background. That indicates he is likely a noble from his world too."

Ellena shrugged, her expression doubtful. "I don't know about that. I did get the impression that he is smart but wasn't knowledgeable about noble life. You can only be smart at something you know."

The conversation paused as Garthen moved back to the fire, its warmth a stark contrast to the chill of the night. "I'm sure it'll be fine. Coolgen and Cabitha are with him too. Let's get some sleep. I'll take the first watch." His voice was firm, the decision final.

The fire crackled, casting long, eerie shadows that seemed to dance with the whispering leaves. Then Garthen's thoughts turned inward, lost in contemplation of their perilous mission. The significance of this task pressed upon him, as tangible as the darkness that surrounded their small circle of light. Again, with the silence of the watch, his mind wandered back to his lost family, his lost life, and rage flared in him anew.

As night deepened, Garthen stood at the edge of their camp, his silhouette a stark figure against the flickering orange glow. His eyes, sharp and vigilant, pierced through the veil of night, looking for a foe to strike down. Behind him, the rest of the group settled into their bedrolls.

With dawn's first light, they set out, soon coming to the destroyed village, Zenmore at the forefront. His keen eyes caught something new amidst the disturbed earth: signs of dragging, alongside the distinct marks of carriage wheels.

"They're taking people," Zenmore muttered, his voice low with realization. This discovery linked back to the reports they'd heard— people disappearing in the wake of attacks. The implications were grim, fueling their resolve.

"But why? Wouldn't that just slow them down?" Saphire's question went unanswered as they set off again.

The next day revealed two more hamlets, each as lifeless as the last, the air still carrying the scent of burnt wood. Here, the tracks were fresher, the drag marks more evident with the absence of the troops coming through. "They're still moving east," Zenmore confirmed, his tone laced with determination and dread.

Rei quickly soared ahead to scout at Garthen's request. Upon her return, her expression was one of confusion fused with urgency. "The trail doesn't just head towards Count Neil's town; it goes directly into it," she announced, her wings folding with a soft rustle.

"And our forces?" Garthen's query was quick, his mind racing with possibilities.

"Stationed south of the town, just as you ordered," Rei affirmed, her gaze steady on Garthen.

The group's discussion was fraught with speculation. Why would the Black Crop Gang, knowing of the military presence, proceed into what could easily become a trap? Was it sheer boldness, or was there an alliance with someone inside?

"We need to get to the northern side of town," Garthen decided, his leadership cutting through their indecision. "If they're planning something, we'll be in position to cut off their escape or uncover their scheme."

With their course set, they spurred their horses northward, the terrain growing more rugged as they skirted the town. Garthen was sure each member of the group felt the burden of the missing villagers on their shoulders, the silent hope that they might yet be saved fueling their haste.

As they approached the northern outskirts, the atmosphere around Neil's town seemed almost too calm, contrasting starkly with the chaos they'd anticipated.

As twilight draped over the landscape, Garthen and his companions found themselves at the northern edge of Count Neil's town, the tracks of the heavily laden carriages cutting deep into the earth, leading straight into the heart of the settlement. The eerie silence of the town, juxtaposed with the evidence of recent activity, set everyone on edge.

"These tracks are fresh," Zenmore noted, kneeling to inspect the marks. "They must have entered recently, perhaps even last night."

Saphire looked towards the town walls, her eyes narrowing. "If the town has fallen, or worse, is complicit, we need to know before we're caught in a trap set by the gang and Neil's forces."

Garthen nodded, his mind racing through scenarios. "We'll camp here, out of sight. Observe the gates, see who comes and goes. Meanwhile, I'll update Cabitha."

After Garthen unrolled the communication scroll, his quill danced across the parchment, detailing their findings and his instructions for Artemin's unit. The ink glowed faintly as his words were magically relayed.

By morning, a reply had etched itself onto the scroll. Cabitha's script was concise: Artemin prepares to move. Neil promises cooperation but shows reluctance.

The day passed with tense patience. They watched as the town's life unfolded, ordinary on the surface, but with an undercurrent of tension that only those looking for it would notice. As predicted, near dusk, several figures darted from the northern gate, their movements hurried and secretive.

Rei, with her aerial advantage, was the first to intercept. Garthen and Zenmore followed, cornering the runners before they could vanish into the surrounding forests.

"Hold!" Garthen commanded, his voice a blend of authority and urgency.

But as they closed in, a strange, pulsating rune appeared on the forehead of each runner, glowing with a malevolent light unfamiliar to Rei. Before any interrogation could begin, the runners collapsed, their life extinguished as the runes flared brightly and then faded into nothing.

"Suicide magic," Rei whispered, her wings twitching with unease. "I've never seen this rune before. It's designed to kill rather than betray secrets."

Frustration gnawed at Garthen. "This confirms someone powerful is behind this, perhaps even within the town."

The next morning, another message from Cabitha arrived: Artemin is at an impasse. Count Neil cites ancient rights, blocks thorough inspection. Suspects of internal collusion.

Garthen's jaw set. "We can't wait for diplomacy. We need to get inside, tonight."

The group prepared for stealth, their movements, except for Rei's, practiced and silent as shadows. Under the cover of a moonlit night, they approached the town walls. Zenmore, silent even with his bulky form, led them to a forgotten drainage grate at the base of the northern wall he had spotted earlier. Rei's tail dragging on the dirt put Garthen on edge and he glared at her, but she did not seem to understand the issue.

Ellena, with her sword, cut through the iron bars as if they weren't even there, making just enough space for the group to slip through, one by one, into the underbelly of the town. As Garthen and his companions moved through the dimly lit sewers of Count Neil's city, the air grew thick with an oppressive magic, the kind that reminded Garthen of the agony he had suffered not too long ago. Their path led them to a large chamber, the stone walls slick with moisture and something darker, more sinister.

The scene before them halted their breath: three figures in dark robes were huddled around a stone bench, their hands locked over complex patterns, etched glowing runes in the bench next to a thrashing figure. The person on the bench screamed, a sound so raw it echoed off the stone, reverberating with pain and terror. His body contorted grotesquely, limbs elongating, skin splitting to give way to scales, as wings sprouted where arms once were, and his feet twisted into talons.

"By the Archangels watch, they're creating a wyvern!" Rei hissed, her own draconic heritage making her recoil at the perversion of nature before them.

Without hesitation, Garthen signaled the attack. Ellena whispered movement and closed the distance on the rightmost figure, quickly cutting through him like the iron bars before. Zenmore charged with a roar, his massive form a blur as he brought down another with a crushing blow from his war hammer. Garthen, his bow singing, loosed two quick arrows into the last individual, one in the chest and the other in the temple.

But even as the cultists fell, the transformation of the man into a beast continued, accelerating with the absence of the casters' control. The creature, now more wyvern than human, let out a guttural screech, its eyes wild with confusion and agony.

Rei, understanding the threat, leapt into action. Her wings unfurled, and with a swift, unsteady move, she ended the creature's suffering with clean controlled removal of its head with her scythe. It slumped, the transformation stopping as life left its eyes.

The silence that followed was dense, laden with the implications of what they had witnessed. "This is why they're abducting people," Garthen murmured, his voice a blend of anger and sorrow. "It's just like before."

Determined to save any others, they pressed deeper into the underground complex. Not far from the chamber, they found what could only be described as a dungeon, cells lined with iron bars, the air stale with despair. Inside, huddled figures looked up with haunted eyes.

"It's alright, we're here to help," Ellena said softly. Yet the prisoners shrank back from Garthen's burned visage, Zenmore's imposing orc stature, Saphire's otherworldly blue skin, and Rei's draconic scales.

"How many were taken before us?" one of the captives managed to ask, his voice a hoarse whisper.

"At least twenty," another replied, her voice breaking. "They ... they took them for ... for those things. The screams ..."

Rei and Saphire quickly took charge, gently leading the survivors towards the surface. Rei's wings offered a protective canopy, while Saphire's calm demeanor soothed the traumatized group.

Meanwhile, Garthen, Ellena, and Zenmore prepared to ascend to the streets of the town. Their mission had grown even darker, the stakes higher. They needed to confront Count Neil for something far worse than collusion with the Black Crop gang: siding with the demonic forces like those that had taken Windmontley.

"We move for Neil's mansion," Garthen declared, his voice echoing through the tunnels. "This ends tonight."

Emerging into the cool air, they left the underground horror behind but carried its weight with them. The streets were eerily quiet, the townsfolk either complicit or intimidated into silence. The group moved like wraiths through the shadows, their resolve hardened by the atrocities they had uncovered.

Count Neil's mansion loomed in the distance, its windows lit from within, casting long shadows across the cobblestones. The structure was opulent, a plain difference to the suffering they had just witnessed. Garthen's mind raced with strategies, knowing well that what awaited them inside could be as twisted and dangerous as the dark magic they had just quelled.

They approached with caution, noting the absence of guards, which was either an oversight or a trap. Ellena scouted ahead, her keen senses attuned to any movement. Zenmore checked his weapon, his eyes scanning for any physical threats.

As they prepared to breach the mansion, Garthen ensured the other two were acutely aware that what they discovered was the start of their true mission and that this would set the groundwork for going forward. They needed knowledge and success here and now.

Inside the mansion, the silence was as thick as the shadows. Garthen, Ellena, and Zenmore moved with the grace of seasoned warriors, their steps barely whispering upon the luxurious carpets lining the hallways. Their first encounter was swift; a guard, unsuspecting, turned a corner only to be met by Garthen's arrow, which found its mark with a muted thwack. Before the guard could slump to the ground, Ellena was there, her sword uncoiling like a whip, slicing through the air to silence another guard who had barely registered the threat.

The trio paused over the fallen guards. Garthen, with a grim expression, rolled the man's sleeve back to reveal what he feared most—the mark of the Black Crop gang, a dark, intricate tattoo of a crow clutching a dagger, etched into the skin of his hand. "This is it," Garthen whispered, the confirmation of Neil's betrayal hardening his resolve. He looked to Ellena, watching her sword return to normal. "That's new."

She nodded. "I just … I don't know how I did that, really, but I needed it to happen to get there in time."

Garthen merely nodded, impressed with her new ability. They proceeded, guided by the faint light from ornate candelabras, until they heard the murmur of voices from behind a heavy door. Stealth was their ally as Garthen gently pushed the door open, revealing a grand chamber where Count Neil was encircled by ten figures, all armed, their postures tense with anticipation.

The moment the door creaked, the room erupted into chaos. The trio burst in, and the fight commenced with a ferocity that belied the room's opulent decor.

Zenmore, with his massive frame, became the eye of the storm. His war hammer swung in deadly arcs; the first swing caught a burly man off guard, sending him crashing into a marble statue, which shattered under the impact. The second and third met their fates with equally brutal efficiency; one tried to parry with a sword, only for the axe head to crash through the blade and into his chest, while the other was lifted off his feet, his attempt to charge cut short by a blow that left him lifeless against the wall.

Ellena's whip sword danced through the air, a blur of deadly grace. She engaged two adversaries at once. Her whip coiled around one's neck, tightening with a yank that sent the head falling to the carpet before she flicked the blade towards another, slicing through armor and flesh with equal ease, leaving both assailants in pools of their own blood.

Garthen's arrows flew true, each one singing a short, sharp song of death. His first arrow pierced through the eye of a woman charging with a spear, stopping her midstride. The second found the heart of a man who had managed to close the distance, his dagger inches from Garthen's throat when the arrow struck, felling him instantly.

As the clash of steel and the cries of combatants filled the air, two of

Neil's cohorts, a man and a woman, threw down their weapons in a sudden plea for mercy, their faces pale with the realization of their imminent defeat.

Neil, his face contorted with rage at this betrayal, drew a concealed blade, lunging at them. His last loyal guard followed suit, aiming for the man who had surrendered. Garthen's response was immediate: an arrow loosed from his bow with such precision it pinned Neil's hand to the wall, the arrowhead emerging from the other side of his palm, blood dripping down the ornate wallpaper.

Zenmore roared, surging forward to intervene, but even his speed was not enough to save the surrendering man. The last loyalist had already reached him, striking through the man's jaw with savage results. Zenmore's massive hand clamped on the attacker's skull, the sound of crushing bone echoing as he lifted the body away, but it was too late. The man on the ground gasped, his jaw destroyed, blood pooling rapidly from his ruined face.

The woman who had surrendered screamed, a sound raw with grief, as she crawled to the dying man, her hands trembling over his face, trying in vain to offer comfort in his last moments. Her sobs punctuated the sudden quiet of the room, save for the labored breathing of the combatants.

Garthen turned his attention back to Neil, whose face was a mask of pain and shock, the rune on his chest now visible through his torn shirt, glowing with an ominous light. Before Garthen could interrogate or secure him further, the rune's glow intensified, and Neil's body went slack, his life snuffed out by the same suicide magic that had claimed the runners. The arrow remained, pinning nothing but a corpse to the wall, as if the very magic that was meant to protect him from betrayal had instead ensured his silence.

The room fell silent, save for the woman's quiet weeping. The scent of blood combined with that of the wax of the burning candles, creating a somber atmosphere. Garthen, Ellena, and Zenmore exchanged looks, the weight of what they had uncovered settling upon them. Here was a clear sign of a conspiracy that reached deeper than mere banditry or local politics, into realms where dark magic intertwined with human greed and power.

"This is bigger than we thought," Garthen muttered, his voice low. "Neil was just another piece, not the head of this serpent."

Ellena nodded, her whip sword retracting with a flick of her wrist. "We need to find out who's truly pulling the strings. This ... this was just the beginning."

Zenmore, his chest heaving with the exertion of battle, looked down at the carnage. "And what of her?" he asked, nodding towards the woman still cradling the dead man's head in her lap.

"We'll take her with us," Garthen decided. "She might have answers, or be in danger if left here. And we need every clue we can get now. Plus, it's nice not to have someone who keels over once captured."

As the echoes of combat died down within the lavish confines of Count Neil's mansion, Garthen quickly unfurled his communication scroll. His quill danced across the parchment, ink bleeding into words of urgency. Cabitha, inform Artemin: Open the southern gates. Conduct a thorough search. Apprehend or eliminate any with the Black Crop mark. No quarter for the marked or those who shelter them. He rolled the scroll after watching as his words glow in a whisper of magic, sent on their way.

Garthen turned to Ellena, his voice firm. "Make your way to the southern gate. Open it to Artemin's forces. We can't risk any more surprises."

Ellena nodded, her beast kin agility promising a swift journey. "I'll see it done," she affirmed and disappeared into the mansion's shadows, her departure silent as the night itself.

With Ellena gone, Garthen faced Zenmore and the weeping woman. "We head north. And anyone who stands in our way ..." He didn't need to finish. The grim set of his jaw spoke volumes.

The journey through the mansion was a tense affair. Every corner hid potential threats; every shadow seemed to hold a blade. Garthen guided their way with purpose, his fingers tight on the string of his bow, but the mansion's layout was unfamiliar, leading them into a slight detour.

As they navigated the narrow corridors into the open air, figures emerged, their intentions clear in their aggressive stances. Garthen and Zenmore reacted with lethal efficiency. An arrow from Garthen's bow took down one before he could even shout, while Zenmore's hammer crushed another's attempt to flank them. These were not trained fighters but desperate individuals, perhaps coerced or corrupted by the dark promises of the Black Crop.

They encountered more resistance as they neared what appeared to be the path to the north gate. Each encounter was met with swift and decisive action; Garthen's arrows flew with deadly accuracy, and Zenmore's brute strength left no room for second chances. The woman they escorted, silent now except for her ragged breathing, seemed to understand the grim necessity of their actions, even if her eyes were wide with fear at the bloodshed.

Finally, after what felt like an eternity in the town's labyrinthine alleys, the trio found the north gate. The gate itself was unguarded, perhaps an oversight or a sign of the chaos within the town. Garthen pushed it open, the cool night air in contrast to the stifling atmosphere of betrayal inside.

They made their way back to the campsite where Saphire, Rei, and the rescued captives waited. The captives, though safe, were visibly shaken, their eyes haunted by what they had endured. Garthen approached, his expression softening ever so slightly at the sight of them.

"We've dealt with Neil," he began, his voice carrying the stress of the night's events. "But the problem goes beyond one man. Ellena has gone to open the gates for our forces. They'll scour the city, root out the gang's influence."

Just as he finished, the distant sounds of conflict reached them— shouts, the clash of steel, and the occasional scream. The city was indeed in turmoil, the night alive with the sounds of its reckoning.

Ellena emerged from the shadows shortly after, her form a blend of grace and urgency. "The city is in open warfare," she confirmed, her eyes reflecting the flicker of distant fires. "Artemin's troops are engaging. It's chaos, but it's necessary."

The group watched as the horizon glowed with the fires of conflict, the sounds of battle a grim symphony to their ears. Rei, rather motherly, tried to comfort the captives, her voice a soothing melody against the backdrop of violence. Saphire stood guard, her hooves tapping a rock softly as if itching to run back into the city, her glowing gaze piercing the darkness.

Garthen looked at his companions, each bearing the marks of the night's ordeal in different ways. "Tonight, we've started ourselves on the journey of the prophecy. This isn't just about a gang or a corrupt noble. It's about who is siding with hell's forces, and there will be a reckoning," he said, his voice low but filled with resolve.

The others nodded, understanding the depth of what lay ahead. They were no longer just hunters, soldiers, or scholars; they had become Guardians for the first time.

As the hints of dawn began to challenge the night, the group settled into a weary but vigilant rest. Garthen found in himself satisfaction at getting some revenge, but he knew this was just the start of the path that had been imposed upon him. Though forced, he was now determined to see it through, even through these fires of war showing above the battlements.

Chapter 7: Misunderstanding or Framing

In the absence of his fellow Guardians, Kriegon found the quiet, elongated days in this strange new world increasingly disorienting. His only solace was Coolgen, who served as his guide through the labyrinthine politics of Maeglover. Each conversation with Coolgen was a lesson in survival, as Kriegon wrestled with the minutiae of noble customs and decorum, acutely aware that his mission, assigned by Garthen, teetered on the brink of failure with every misstep. He had to avoid the hidden mines in the fields of conversation. To navigate these waters, Kriegon found himself adopting the guile of the political leaders he had once despised back on Earth, with Coolgen's adept leadership proving invaluable in these increasingly complex discussions.

The ring from his weapon, now a constant and light presence on his finger, granted him the ability to communicate with the denizens of Maeglover. Though this magical artifact also helped ground him in the overall mission at hand, it felt just as if he carried his rifle again.

Among the first nobles with whom they conversed was Baron Ryoma Yasumoto, a figure as enigmatic as his name, which hinted at distant, exotic origins yet was woven into this medieval fabric. At merely fifteen, Ryoma had not only mastered the arcane arts but had revolutionized them, crafting magical artifacts like the communication scrolls, once considered nothing but fantasy. His guild's influence surged like a relentless tide, but with growth came vulnerability; they were stretched thin, becoming both the creators and the backbone of a burgeoning communication network across the continent. Kriegon's encounters with Ryoma were fleeting, filled with elusive promises of magical tutelage that never quite materialized.

Seeking to embed himself within the societal fabric, Kriegon, the substantial significance of his ring moving him forward, followed Coolgen from one meeting to another. Each interaction with nobles was a learning opportunity, allowing him to absorb and adapt to the local customs and idioms.

Here, within the ornate halls where the Azure Alliance and the

Crimson Order convened, the air was thick with tension. These factions, rarely mingling except in fierce debate, presented a stark contrast in ideology. The Azure Alliance, staunch supporters of the crown, prided themselves on their military prowess. Their commitment, however, bordered on zealotry, with figures like the verbose Earl Vittel Hero, whose tales of battle were as endless as his conscription of local peasantry. They viewed the Guardians with disdain, especially their association with the beastkin.

Conversely, the Crimson Order, approached initially with caution by Kriegon—having been warned of their role in luring King Abraham and their escape from the doomed fortress city of Windmontley—revealed themselves to be astute in matters of commerce and diplomacy. Figures like the eloquent Baron Frank Tolas and the insightful Viscount Adelisa Cabal fascinated Kriegon. They were the architects of postwar reconciliation, reopening trade routes with former enemies, the beastkin and elves, and forging paths of peace through economic ties. The halls echoed with the clink of goblets and the murmur of negotiation, each word carefully chosen, each gesture laden with hidden meanings, as Kriegon learned the delicate dance of diplomacy, his ring a silent translator and facilitator in this land where magic and might intertwined.

Yet not all interactions were pleasant. On the seventh day of solitude from his Guardian companions, at a particularly opulent gathering, Kriegon stood by Coolgen's side with the calculating Earl Tom Cabal, Adelisa's brother, and the imposing Count Bracus.

As the evening wore on, the grand hall of Baron Tolas's estate buzzed with the murmur of noble intrigue. Kriegon found himself under the scrutinizing gaze of Earl Tom Cabal and Count Bracus. Cabal, with his vest reminiscent of old British redcoats, approached with a swagger that spoke of both confidence and skepticism. His thick mustache twitched as he spoke, his voice laced with curiosity and a challenging tone.

"So, Coolgen, you bring this underling to these noble halls?" Tom began, his skepticism plain. "Could this be a member of the rumored

Guardians? He does appear ... different from the church's other practitioners."

Kriegon, who had faced far more annoying confrontations in his original world, felt an unexpected calm envelop him. He met Tom's gaze squarely. "I follow Mister Coolgen in learning about the nobles' society for my own preparation to serve at the Guardians' sides. After all, they are to change this world for the better, as they are already doing." One of Kriegon's personal goals with all his meetings was to boost the Guardians' reputation within the nobles' circles.

Tom's sneer softened into a thoughtful frown. "Ah, the Guardians. Legends to some, but you speak as if they're as real as you and I. Do you know when might the king or church formally present these interesting folk? Yet, I must wonder if my distant cousin, our king, can truly bear the crown's burden without a proper lineage to back him. Perhaps they might be some freaks he has pulled together to appear strong."

Count Bracus, standing tall and gaunt beside Tom, his fingers adorned with rings, interjected with a smooth voice, "And these Guardians, what proof do we have of their effectiveness? The tales of their background are ... fantastical, to say the least."

Coolgen nodded, acknowledging the validity of their doubts. "The Guardians are as real as the peril that besets us. Their effectiveness will be proven in time. If they fail, or if they are but a myth, then indeed, it might be those with the most to lose, like yourselves, who will feel the sting of downfall first. Your lands, your wealth, your influence—all tied to the stability they seek to restore."

Tom's eyes narrowed as he considered Coolgen's words. "You speak with a certainty that borders on arrogance, yet there's truth in your analysis. If the economy falls, we stand to lose much. But know this: should your Guardians prove to be nothing more than a child's tale, it won't just be the economy that falls. The house of Hero has raised yet another smart lad; too bad you seek to serve the church. What money you might have made if you applied half the intelligence your uncle

71

wields."

Bracus chuckled dryly, his gaze distant. "In my experience, fortunes rise and fall with the tides of power. I've weathered worse storms. Whether by Guardians or by my own hand, I'll ensure what my house endures. But …" He paused, fixing the pair with an intense look. "I'm curious about the difference these Guardians could make. Are they truly capable of altering the course of our fate?"

Kriegon sensed the shift in the conversation, the probing for reassurance amidst the skepticism. "The Guardians bring not just might but wisdom. Their presence could herald a new era of prosperity and peace just as the prophecy hints at, or, if they are ineffective, we face a darker path. However, their success depends greatly on the unity and support of the nobles."

At this, Tom's interest piqued, his earlier hostility giving way to a more calculating demeanor. "Unity and support, you say? And what would such allegiance entail?"

"Support for the crown, belief in the Guardians' mission, and, perhaps most crucially, a united front against the chaos that threatens us," Kriegon stated, his voice steady. Perhaps this was the foothold they had been looking for to get the nobles' support in raising the Guardians' reputation and influence. "And in return, there could be stability, perhaps even advancement, for those who stand on the right side of history."

Bracus nodded slowly. "A gamble, then. But one with potentially high rewards. I'll consider your words, Kriegon. But remember, we are not men who back losing causes. Prove the Guardians' worth, and perhaps you'll find more than just skepticism at our tables."

As the conversation around the Guardians waned under the load of political maneuvering and noble intrigue, Coolgen and Kriegon found themselves at the heart of a delicate balance. The air was thick with the scent of ambition, veiled threats, and whispered alliances. Kriegon's mind, however, was a storm of pride, feeling almost invincible with the knowledge and power the Guardians represented, yet Coolgen's presence was a constant reminder of the need for humility. Every so often, he would lean into Kriegon's ear to remind him to back off some topic Kriegon had started to get heated about.

As the night deepened, the grandeur of the gathering began to wane, yet the undercurrents of politics and intrigue only grew stronger. Kriegon, feeling the evening's weight, managed to extricate himself and Coolgen from the encircling nobles, their questions and veiled propositions echoing in his mind.

They extracted themselves from the speculation and probing questions of Kriegon's background. Coolgen commented quietly, "You got the hang of dealing with this political ground quickly."

Kriegon shrugged. "It's a mix of watching similar interactions in my past and the ability to not rise to pointless jabs." He reflected again on his strange calm. Not too long ago, if someone had questioned him with such clear disdain, he would have gotten hot under the collar quickly. "And as always, thank you for catching me in those times I almost showed my hand."

Just as they found a quieter corner, away from the prying ears and speculative glances, Count Bracus reappeared, his approach silent as a shadow. His rings glinted under the chandelier's light, each one possibly a vessel of wealth or a token of some clandestine deal. "Coolgen, Kriegon," he started, his voice low, carrying a sly undertone, "let us speak more ... candidly. Financial backing for your Guardians could be arranged, should there be certain ... services rendered at my discretion. A mutual benefit, if you will."

Kriegon was about to respond, his instincts warning him against the entanglement Bracus suggested, when a disturbance cut through the subdued ambiance of the hall. Cabitha, one of the few allies Kriegon had come to trust implicitly, burst into the room. Her usual composure was shattered; she was breathless, her face etched with worry.

"Kriegon! It's urgent," she gasped, drawing the attention of nearby nobles whose curiosity was piqued by her disheveled state. "The Guardians, with their forces, they've uncovered something—Noble Neil

Paris, he's ... he's connected to the Black Crop Gang, and there's dark magic involved!"

Before she could delve into more detail, or before Kriegon could refuse Bracus's offer, he realized the need for discretion. He cut her off with a subtle gesture. "Let's discuss this away from here," he said, turning to excuse himself from Bracus. However, when he looked back, the Count had vanished, as if he were a specter of the court, leaving only the echo of his proposal.

The urgency of Cabitha's news propelled them from the party. Kriegon, Coolgen, and Cabitha made their way out, their departure unnoticed by most, who were too engrossed in their own politicking to care about yet another hushed conversation.

"Dark magic?" Kriegon pondered aloud, his voice laced with concern. He wished for what felt like the thousandth time that he was there with them, facing whatever might come.

Coolgen, his tone more worried than usual, responded, "This could be far worse than mere political intrigue. Dark magic, if true, suggests powers similar to those of demons. We need to consult with Ryoma. His knowledge in the arcane might shed some light on this."

Upon reaching the castle, they were met by Commander Wells, who had a grave look that matched the night's revelations. His posture was rigid, indicative of the tension within.

"Commander Wells," Kriegon greeted him, "we must speak with the king immediately regarding urgent matters uncovered by the Guardians."

Wells nodded, his expression unchanging. "The king has just concluded a council. He's expecting you, actually. He mentioned something about needing to discuss Garthen's daily report."

"Does he know about Neil Paris?" Cabitha interjected, still catching her breath.

"No, but he's aware something's amiss in the nobles' lands," Wells stated, leading them through the torch-lit corridors. "You'll find him in the throne room."

The throne room doors loomed before them, massive and ornate, crafted from wood that seemed as old as the kingdom itself. As they swung open, Kriegon beheld the throne room for the first time. The space was cavernous, with a ceiling that vaulted high above, lost in shadow where the light from the chandeliers dared not reach.

The eastern wall was dominated by enormous plate glass windows, offering an uninterrupted view over the darkened forest that stretched out like a sea at night, the two moons' light casting silver edges on the treetops. This room was a statement of power, designed to humble any who entered.

The throne itself was an amalgamation of opulence and austerity. Gold adorned its edges, catching the light in a display of wealth, yet its core was of stern, gray stone, unyielding and cold, symbolizing the enduring nature of the monarchy amidst the fleeting lives of men.

King Abraham sat upon this throne, not as a figure of distant majesty but as a man burdened by the crown's authority. His expression was contemplative, his eyes reflecting the flickering torches that lined the room, making them seem like windows to a soul wrestling with the darkness encroaching upon his realm.

Within the vast expanse of the throne room, the air was thick with an unspoken anticipation as Cabitha stepped forward, her posture reflecting the earnestness of her message. "Your Majesty, Commander Wells," she began with due deference, "Garthen has conveyed through the communication scroll that they've liberated a town formerly under the control of Neil Paris. They're currently searching for further evidence to implicate others in what appears to be a widespread conspiracy involving the Black Crop Gang, their hostages, and dark magic."

King Abraham, who had been unaware of these developments, leaned forward, his expression shifting from concern to profound seriousness. "And this mention of dark magic, what does Garthen say about it?"

Cabitha took a breath, choosing her words carefully. "Garthen didn't detail the nature of the dark magic in his message, preferring to discuss it in person. He believes it's critical enough to warrant a face-to-face explanation, perhaps something too sensitive or complex for the scroll."

"And the hostages?" Wells asked, showing his military leadership, needing to know each piece on an imagined chess board.

"Yes, there are signs that more hostages than those we've managed to save have been transported, likely to the Sky Peak Mountains," Cabitha continued. "Garthen and the other Guardians, along with our troops, are now mapping out the routes to these mountains, aiming to rescue the remaining captives and perhaps uncover more about this dark magic."

King Abraham absorbed this, his mind racing with the implications. "What, then, does Garthen plan to do next? And this dark magic, can Ryoma be of assistance in providing details?"

"He intends to secure the area, continue the search for hostages, and gather all possible intelligence on the dark magic and any connections to other nobles or factions," she elaborated. "As for the dark magic, I'm not sure, my lord."

The king's face was a canvas of contemplation, his previous unawareness now replaced with the burden of urgent decision-making. "The fall of a town under Paris's control and this mention of dark magic ... These are developments of profound significance. We've been blind to how deep the rot might go."

Wells, acting as a strategist, nodded gravely. "If Paris was involved with such forces, we're dealing with something that could further destabilize the entire kingdom. Garthen must return with haste; we need all the information consolidated here to strategize our response effectively."

"Indeed," agreed King Abraham, his decision firming up amidst the whirlwind of new information. "Send word for Garthen and the Guardians to return to Riversong at once. We must convene a council to discuss these revelations, assess our vulnerabilities, and plan our countermeasures in light of this ... dark magic and nobilities' connection to a lawless gang."

After a brief exchange on the logistics of their return, the king, his expression deeply concerned, inquired, "Who else is aware of this?"

Kriegon, who had remained silent, absorbing the unfolding crisis, spoke up. "Some nobles from the Crimson Order might have overheard Cabitha when she first relayed the information to Coolgen and myself. Their reactions were ... difficult to read."

A shadow fell over the king's face, his voice intense with implications. "This adds layers of complexity. Neil Paris isn't just a lone noble; he's tied to the Crimson Order. If his allies or enemies within the order know, we could be facing internal discord, or worse, they might attempt to manipulate this situation for their gain."

The king stood, his movement a physical manifestation of his restless thoughts. "The Crimson Order's involvement in trade and economy could mean this corruption has roots in our economic stability. We must act with caution but also with decisiveness."

Wells added, "I'll prepare our forces for any eventuality. We need to be ready for unrest, both from within and outside the court."

Cabitha, clearly feeling the import of her role in this pivotal moment, assured, "I'll ensure Garthen understands the urgency of his return and the need for secrecy regarding these findings until we can convene."

The trio, after paying their respects to King Abraham, exited the throne room with the weight of the kingdom's future on their shoulders. The castle's corridors, eerily quiet, echoed with their footsteps as they made their way into the night.

The journey back to the mansion was anything but tranquil. The darkness seemed denser, the shadows more pronounced. Kriegon, perceptiveness heightened, felt the prickling sensation of unseen eyes upon them, similar to patrols he had had when serving with his comrades before. "Eyes up," he whispered to Coolgen and Cabitha. "I feel we're not alone out here."

His companions, already on edge from the night's revelations, nodded silently, their hands not straying far from their weapons. Every rustle in the underbrush, every distant hoot of an owl, set their nerves jangling. The usually serene path through the royal city now felt like a gauntlet, with potential adversaries lurking in every shadow.

Upon arriving at the mansion, the group let out a sigh of relief as they passed through the gates. The mansion, a beacon of safety, loomed before them, yet even here, the night's events cast a long shadow over their refuge.

The next morning brought with it a semblance of normalcy, yet the air was thick with tension. At breakfast, Orris approached Kriegon. Her usual composed demeanor was replaced by a look of concern. "Kriegon, there are ... disturbing rumors spreading among the nobility," she began, her voice low, not wanting to be overheard by the servants.

Kriegon, his fork paused mid-air, met her gaze. "Rumors?"

"Yes," Orris continued. "They're saying the Guardians have turned against the Crown, that they've slain citizens ... even Neil Paris."

Kriegon's brow furrowed. "Neil Paris dead? That's news to me. I thought they had just captured him. How did this come to your attention?"

"My friend, Tom's daughter, came here early today, quite distraught. Earl Tom Cabal is in an uproar, spreading these tales like wildfire," Orris explained, her worry evident. "She fears what this might do to the balance of power, to her father's position."

Cabitha entered the dining hall just as Orris finished speaking, her arrival timely. Kriegon quickly relayed the information. "We need to send another message to Garthen," he said, urgency coloring his tone. "The political situation here is spiraling out of control. If they return without solid proof to clear these rumors, we're looking at potential chaos."

Cabitha, ever efficient, nodded. "I'll draft it immediately. We need Garthen to understand that his findings could be the linchpin in this growing crisis. Proof of Paris's dealings, of this dark magic, could either quell these rumors or ignite a full-blown conflict."

Orris, listening intently, added, "It's not just about proving the

Guardians' actions were justified. It's about showing there's a real threat that could corrupt from within. If the nobles start choosing sides based on misinformation, we're looking at a divide that could fracture the already weak kingdom."

Kriegon stood, pushing his chair back. "Then we act swiftly. Cabitha, get that message out. And Orris, perhaps it's time you leverage your connections. We need allies aware of the truth, ready to support the Crown's efforts against this conspiracy."

Orris nodded, her resolve hardening. "I'll speak with those I trust. But Kriegon, be careful. If you're right about being watched last night, then whoever is behind this might already see you as a threat."

The breakfast, which had started with the clink of cutlery and soft murmurs, ended with the urgent rustle of plans being set into motion.

In the shadowed corners of the city, where the river's murky waters whispered secrets of the underbelly, an ominous meeting was about to unfold. The air was thick with the stench of decay, a fitting backdrop for the assembly of the three hooded figures, their silhouettes barely discernable in the gloom of the dilapidated hut.

With a sound like the crack of a whip, the wooden door slammed shut, severing the last connection with the outside world and signaling the beginning of their dark council.

The tallest among them, a figure whose presence commanded the space with an eerie stillness, spoke first. His voice was calm, yet it carried the hint of a serpent's venom. "They've discovered the rituals far sooner than anticipated. We must adapt; half the wyverns will have to suffice for now."

Leaning against the rotting wall, another figure, whose posture suggested a casual disinterest yet whose eyes gleamed with sharp intelligence, retorted, "The numbers matter little. Once our trap springs, this kingdom will crumble into your grasp. Just ensure your part of the bargain holds."

A nod from the tall figure, his face obscured by the shadow of his hood, confirmed the agreement. "Indeed, a portion of my hoard shall finance your ... adventurous ambitions."

From the side, the third, a figure of nervous energy, couldn't contain his disdain. His voice was a sharp hiss. "You call us fools, yet it is your wealth we'll eclipse with the spoils of our victory."

The relaxed man, who had seemed almost amused by the bickering, now stood, his movement fluid, signaling an end to the squabble. "Enough. We've never been allies by choice, and harmony isn't required now." As he approached the exit, he paused, his hand on the doorframe, and turned back slightly. "I delivered the two you need to set the final piece in place. Do not obstruct him," he advised, with a dismissive wave towards his edgy companion.

He departed, leaving behind a silence filled with the substance of their conspiracy, only broken by the first figure's query, laced with impatience. "Do you know where your partner is to join us?"

The reply came with a sinister assurance. "She's positioned at the Orris mansion. From there, she'll extract the intelligence we need to keep one step ahead of the Guardians."

With these words, the two remaining figures fell into a contemplative silence.

Chapter 8: Alliance Shore Up

As the luxurious hall of the Zella mansion filled with the murmurs of the Azure Alliance nobles, Kriegon's heart thudded with the importance of the revelation he was about to unleash. The room, usually echoing with the laughter and music of high society, today bore the tension of a political chess game about to be played out in the open. He was going out on a limb without the king's or Garthen's input, so this was a time to show he could rise to the challenge, even if it was by revealing he had been a Guardian in disguise this whole time. However, he suspected some of the nobles might have known; after all, he did have strange hair and eyes, like Ellena had said.

Orris, the gracious host, navigated through the crowd with an ease that opposed her age. Her eyes, however, often flickered towards Kriegon, who sat to the side, his presence marked by the oversized cloak that hid more than it revealed. Kriegon's hands, though obscured beneath the fabric, clutched his staff, a symbol of his true identity, the power that Coolgen and the others had said could be felt on sight.

Coolgen approached Kriegon, his face etched with concern. "Is this going to be it?" he whispered. "Do you really think this a good idea? Shouldn't we wait for Garthen?"

Kriegon, counting the fourteen nobles present, most of whom were strangers to him, nodded. "Yes, if the rumors are this thick here, they're wildfire elsewhere. We need to act now before the Guardian name is ruined," he said, his voice betraying none of his inner turmoil.

Before Coolgen could press for details or dissuade him, Kriegon moved towards the small stage at the end of the hall, usually reserved for musicians during lighter gatherings. Orris and Cabitha quickly joined him, their expressions a mix of support and apprehension.

Cabitha leaned in, her voice low. "Garthen says Rei's on her way back with evidence of the dark magic. She'll explain everything."

Orris, with her characteristic calm, added, "You have my backing, but remember, these nobles respect Garthen more than the idea of non-human Guardians. Use his name; it should hold weight."

Kriegon acknowledged with a nod, his smile a mere shadow on his lips as he stepped onto the stage. The nobles, sensing something significant was about to unfold, slowly turned their attention towards him, their conversations dying into a tense silence.

"Thank you all for coming on such short notice," Kriegon began, his voice steady despite the storm of nerves within. "Orris Zella has been an exemplary host." His gaze swept across the room, meeting the eyes of the nobles, some curious, others skeptical. "Many of you know me as Kriegon, the assistant to Coolgen and a rising church official. However, today, I stand before you to confess a truth far greater than any church official could rise to."

The cloak fell away with a dramatic flourish, revealing the staff. Its simplicity contrasted with an aura of power, a silent testament to Kriegon's claim. The room gasped, the air charged with disbelief and intrigue.

"I am not a child of this world," Kriegon declared, his voice rising above the murmurs that threatened to drown his words. "I am a Guardian, a summoned soldier to aid Garthen and our companions in restoring peace."

The hall erupted into chaos, voices raised in disbelief, anger, and questions. Kriegon stood firm, his resolve unshaken, even as the cacophony threatened to overwhelm him. Then, silence fell like an oppressive cloak over the room as Vittel Hero, supported by his cane, made his way to the stage.

Vittel's voice, though weakened by age, carried a commanding presence. "Kriegon, you've admitted to deception. What proof do you offer now of your claim to be a Guardian?"

Kriegon met Vittel's gaze, the significance of his next words hanging heavily in the air. "The proof," he said, holding up the staff allowing the light to catch it, "is in this. Not just a weapon, but a beacon of our vow to protect this realm from threats far beyond mere human ambition. My name, etched into the slab of metal given to King Abraham by Archangel Saforus himself changed into this weapon under my touch."

The nobles watched, some leaning in, their skepticism warring with curiosity. Vittel, his face an unreadable facade, nodded slightly, signaling Kriegon to continue.

"Garthen, a name many of you respect, leads us. He has sent Rei with undeniable evidence of dark magic at play, a threat that endangers us all," Kriegon explained, his voice gaining strength. "This is not about power or thrones. It's about survival."

The room, once filled with the clamor of doubt, now buzzed with whispers of potential alliances and the implications of Kriegon's revelation. Vittel, leaning on his cane, addressed Kriegon for the assembly, his words slow but deliberate.

"What of the prophecy? We all know of it. How do you plan to defeat the unnamed evil princes? We don't even know if the Guardians are here for real if we don't know of any such princes."

As the murmurs settled into a tense silence, Kriegon stood at the forefront of the hall, his figure a lone beacon amidst the sea of doubt and suspicion. The nobles of the Azure Alliance watched him, their faces a mosaic of shock, skepticism, and curiosity. The burden of his words hung heavily in the air, each syllable a stone cast into the still waters of their collective consciousness.

Kriegon, feeling the significance of the moment, knew this was his chance to either solidify their support or lose it forever. His mind raced, but his voice remained steady. "The prophecy speaks of unnamed evil princes," he began, his tone deliberate, ensuring every word was heard. "But these are not ordinary princes. They are the princes of Hell, entities that require the might of not just one world, but all."

The hall erupted once more, but this time, Kriegon's voice cut through the chaos with a sharpness that demanded attention. "I have faced one such prince: Lucifer, the Prince of Pride. His very presence is a testament to the dark forces at play, forces that threaten the very fabric of our existence."

The revelation stunned the assembly into silence. Even Vittel Hero, with his years of experience and unflappable demeanor, showed a flicker of surprise. The air was thick with tension, each noble processing the implications of Kriegon's words.

Then, a question from within the crowd broke the silence. "And what of Noble Neil Paris? He was no prince."

Kriegon nodded, acknowledging the validity of the inquiry. "Neil Paris was indeed no prince, but he was a pawn in a much larger game. He betrayed not only the kingdom but also humanity by aligning with the Black Crop Gang and endorsing dark magic against his own people. Rei will bring forth evidence of this betrayal."

The mood in the room shifted palpably. Whispers of disbelief and accusations of madness filled the air, but Kriegon stood his ground. "I realize the gravity of what I'm asking you to believe. But consider this: the Azure Alliance has the strength and the will to stand with the Guardians and the king in seeking justice for the atrocities at Windmontley and Malgrave. Both the king and Garthen have lost everything to these demonic forces. This isn't just about power; it's about survival, about justice."

The nobles remained silent, their expressions unreadable. The tension was a living thing, a silent predator in the room. Then, Vittel Hero, with a gentleness that contradicted his reputation, placed a hand on Kriegon's arm. "Might you leave us to discuss the position the Azure Alliance will take?"

Kriegon nodded, stepping down from the stage with relief and apprehension. He had laid his cards on the table; now, it was up to the nobles to decide their next move. As he shuffled through the crowd, he could feel the weight of their gazes, an assortment of scrutiny and contemplation. The air was thick with the silent deliberation of the Azure Alliance, each noble weighing the implications of aligning with the Guardians against an unseen threat.

He found a quiet corner, his mind replaying the speech, analyzing every word, every reaction. The stakes were high for the other Guardians; he hoped this act to gain alliances would pay off. The mention of Lucifer had been a gamble, revealing the depth of the darkness they faced, but also potentially alienating those not ready to believe in such ancient evils.

As the nobles began to murmur among themselves, forming small groups to discuss, Kriegon caught snippets of conversation. Some dismissed his words as fantasy; others pondered the possibility of a world where ancient evils walked among them, and a few seemed genuinely concerned about the implications of dark magic and demonic princes.

Vittel Hero, still at the center, leaned heavily on his cane as he listened to the debates around him. His face, lined with age and wisdom, showed signs of deep thought, a man who had seen much but was now faced with the unimaginable.

Kriegon watched from his corner, his heart a jumble of hope and dread. The outcome of this meeting could very well determine the course of their fight against the encroaching darkness. He knew that some nobles might never accept the reality of the Guardians or the threat they spoke of, but he hoped that enough would see beyond their immediate disbelief.

The discussion grew heated, with voices rising in both support and opposition. Kriegon caught Orris's eye, who gave a subtle nod, signaling that the debate was going as well as could be expected under such extraordinary circumstances.

After what felt like an eternity, Vittel raised his hand, calling for silence. The room quieted, all eyes turning to him. "We have heard much today that challenges our understanding of the world," he began, his voice resonant despite its age. "The existence of Guardians, of dark magic, and of demonic princes. This is not a decision to be made lightly."

He paused, letting his words sink in. "However, the evidence of dark magic, as Kriegon promises, will be crucial. If what he says holds true, then we, the Azure Alliance, must consider our role in this unfolding drama. Are we to stand idly by, or will we rise to meet this challenge?"

The nobles exchanged looks, some nodding, others still skeptical, but the seed of unity had been planted. Vittel continued, "Let us reconvene once we have seen this evidence. Until then, let us ponder our next steps with care, for the fate of our world may well rest upon our decision."

Kriegon felt a surge of relief mingling with a persistent undercurrent of tension. The meeting had not ended in outright rejection, which was a small victory in itself. As the nobles began to disperse, some approached him, their curiosity piqued, others with hard questions still in their eyes.

Orris, moving gracefully through the crowd, approached Kriegon with a supportive nod. "You've given them much to think about," she said, her voice low but carrying a warmth that belied the importance of the situation. "Let's hope the evidence Rei brings will sway the doubters."

Kriegon managed a weary smile. "I hope so too. The truth is often difficult for those who don't have the stomach for it." He glanced around, ensuring no one was too close, and lowered his voice. "Did you notice Lord Helain's reaction? He seemed more than just skeptical."

Orris nodded thoughtfully. "Yes, and Lady Kristin seemed unusually attentive as well. Her interest could be pivotal, given her connections within the court. We might need to speak with her privately, see if we can turn her curiosity into support."

Kriegon agreed, feeling the consequence of each noble's reaction, each potential ally or adversary. "And what of the others? There's still too many doubting my status, I fear. I wish there was more than the staff to prove my claim."

"Indeed," Orris replied, her gaze scanning the thinning crowd. "But doubts can be eased, especially if Rei's evidence is compelling. We'll need to prepare for when Rei brings it."

As the last of the nobles left, Kriegon and Orris stood amidst the remnants of the gathering, the grandeur of the hall now feeling empty and echoing. Coolgen and Cabitha joined them as they made their way to the dining hall to eat, even though none had an appetite.

The morning sun did little to warm the chill that had settled over Riversong, nor did it ease the tension that wrapped around Kriegon like a cloak. After the tumultuous revelations of the previous day, he had hoped for a moment's respite. Instead, he found himself embroiled in a set of tense, private meetings with nobles from the Azure Alliance.

Helain Bold, the first to seek him out, was as skeptical as Kriegon had anticipated. His questions were pointed, his doubts evident. "Without concrete proof, your words are but wind," Helain had concluded, his tone dismissive as he departed, leaving a trail of skepticism in his wake.

Barely had Helain's figure receded before Lady Kristin Collin approached, her steps measured, her eyes sharp with curiosity rather than doubt. Unlike Helain, Kristin's inquiries delved not into the existence of the Guardians but into Kriegon's motives for concealment among the nobility.

Kriegon, with reluctance and necessity, revealed Garthen's initial strategy—to gather intelligence and allies from within, to understand the land's politics before revealing the true nature of their mission. Kristin listened, her expression unreadable, her mind clearly racing through the implications of such a strategy.

Their conversation was abruptly cut short by the arrival of a Lawbringer, one of the towering, armored figures that served as the king's personal guard. The Lawbringer's voice boomed, resonating through the hall. "Sire and Lady, the king has called for an assembly of the city's present nobles. Please see yourselves to the throne room with due haste."

The urgency in the Lawbringer's tone spurred them into action. Kristin and Kriegon, with Orris, Cabitha, and Coolgen following closely behind, made a brisk exit from the mansion. The air outside was crisp, carrying the scent of last night's rain, a stark contrast to the thick atmosphere within.

As they hurried towards the throne room, Kristin leaned into Orris, her voice low with concern. "It might be that our friend's pitch of unity

87

has come too late."

Orris, her face also etched with worry, glanced at Kriegon, who met her gaze with a determined look. "Perhaps," Orris replied, "but we must do our best with the hand we've been dealt."

Kristin offered a soft, somewhat sad smile at Orris's optimism, a quality Kriegon admired in these trying times. Their pace quickened as they approached the grand doors of the throne room, where Duke Denither was already striding forward. His presence was commanding, his expression one of stern resolve.

Inside, the throne room was a spectacle of power and tradition. The high ceilings adorned with banners of battles won and alliances forged, the throne itself a symbol of authority, yet today, it felt like a stage set for a confrontation rather than a place of judgment.

The room buzzed with nobles, each whispering, each speculating on the reason for this sudden assembly. Kriegon could feel the heft of their gazes as he entered, some curious, others hostile, but all aware of the shift in power dynamics his presence had sparked.

The king, seated upon his throne, exuded an air of authority with an undercurrent of tension. His eyes, sharp and calculating, swept over the assembly before settling on Kriegon. The room fell silent, awaiting the monarch's words, the air thick with anticipation.

"Your Majesty," Kriegon began, his voice hard as if addressing a superior back in the military, "we are here at your summons. What is the matter of such urgency?"

The king's response was measured, his gaze never wavering from Kriegon. "It seems, Guardian, that your presence has stirred not just the nobles but the very fabric of our kingdom. We gather today to discuss the future of this city, this continent, in light of your revelations and your candid attempts to gather allies to your side before we have even officially announced your arrival."

The assembly erupted in murmurs; the nobles' reactions were of fear, intrigue, and disbelief. Kriegon stood his ground, ears growing hot at the rebuke of the king before the entire assembly of nobles.

The tension in the throne room was unmistakable as the king's words hung in the air, a challenge and an invitation wrapped into one. Before Kriegon could respond, a figure clad in the dark red tunic of the Crimson Order stepped forward. Tom Cabal, his face nearly as red as his clothes, spoke with a voice that carried venom as much as authority.

"Your Majesty, we stand here under the guise of unity, yet we are fed tales spun from the mind of a charlatan. Kriegon claimed to be an official of the church, and now a Guardian from another world no less, yet where is the proof? Where are the signs of his supposed divine heritage or his powers, if any?"

The room erupted in whispers, the nobles turning their attention from Kriegon to Tom Cabal. Clearly, yesterday's speech had made its way around the nobles' circles quickly. Kriegon's hand tightened on his staff, and he bit back the retort on the tip of his tongue. Tom's accusation was bold, a direct challenge to the very foundation of Kriegon's identity and mission.

Kristin's voice cut through the growing unrest like a blade. "Tom Cabal, you dare label Kriegon a liar without proof, yet you ignore the dark truths that have come to light under your own noble order's watch. Neil Paris, a noble of the Crimson Order, was found to have underlings wielding dark magic, sanctioned by none other than himself. This is not mere coincidence with your exceptional timing to leave Windmontley before the invasion but a pattern, perhaps one that extends further than we know."

The indictment hung in the air, a direct challenge to the integrity of the Crimson Order. Tom Cabal's stance stiffened, his eyes narrowing as he prepared to rebut. However, before he could speak, Earl Vittel Hero supported Kristin's claim. "Indeed, the Azure Alliance has evidence of these dark practices. We've been too silent on matters that concern the very essence of our realm's safety."

Kriegon, seizing the moment, addressed the assembly, his voice firm yet carrying an undertone of urgency. "Let's be clear: my identity with the church was a guise, a means to an end. My true purpose is to unite us against greater evils. The dark magic we've uncovered, the demonic entities we face, these are the real threats. Threats I have encountered personally and seek to help destroy."

Tom raised an accusing finger at Kriegon. "Even if you are who you say you are, there is still no proof justifying the murder of a noble. Garthen and these supposed Guardians need to answer for his death."

The king, observing the exchange, leaned forward, his expression unreadable. "We are faced with accusations and counteraccusations. What we need now is not division but unity. If there is truth to these claims of dark magic or murder, it is our duty to investigate, to protect our realm, regardless of political allegiance. It is also true that the Guardians did not receive authorization to execute a noble without a proper hearing."

Tom Cabal, his voice cold and calculating, stepped forward once more. "Your Majesty, I propose a neutral inquiry, an investigation into both the claims of dark magic, the authenticity of these so-called Guardians, and their over stepping of authority. Only through impartial scrutiny can we hope to uncover the truth."

The proposal hung in the air, a challenge to Kriegon's credibility and a call for transparency that resonated with the assembly's growing unease. The nobles murmured among themselves, the idea of a trial appealing to those wary of unchecked power or deceit within their ranks.

The king, his gaze shifting from Tom Cabal to Kriegon, then to the assembled nobles, nodded slowly. "A fair request. I, however, have seen delivery of the weapons the Guardians carry from Archangel Saforus himself. I will not be a judge, since I side on one side of that inquiry. Instead, we will focus on the Guardians' tactics around gathering nobles to their cause and killing a noble without proper authority. Along with the corruption the Guardians and Azure Alliance have uncovered."

As the king's words settled the assembly's decision for a trial, a sudden commotion at the entrance of the throne room drew all eyes. The heavy doors swung open with a force that echoed through the grand hall, revealing a figure striding confidently towards the throne, her black scales shimmering in the light from the huge windows.

Rei, with a determined look in her eyes, approached the king, her steps echoing in the silent room. In one of her clawed hands, she carried not scrolls or artifacts but the severed head of a wyvern.

"Your Majesty, nobles of the realm," Rei began, her voice carrying the burden of her recent battle. "I present to you the evidence of the dark magic we face." She dropped the head at the foot of the throne, where it landed with a wet thud, the dark aura around it rising like steam from boiling water.

The assembly gasped, some in horror, others in fascination. The head, with its twisted features and still clear human eyes, was a grim reminder of the threats Kriegon had spoken of.

Rei, with a solemnity that filled the vastness of the throne room, continued, "This was once a peasant, someone who lived among us, now twisted and transformed into this horror under the dark arts of Neil Paris's mages. I watched as he was turned from man to monster, a testament to the evil magic that has been unleashed upon your world. More like him exist out there now, a terror I have known all my life in my world, now spreading its shadow over yours."

The revelation struck the assembly like a cold wind, the nobles recoiling at the thought of such dark transformations happening within their own lands, under their very noses. The severed head, a symbol of dark magic's perverted creation, lay as a dark warning of what was at stake.

King Abraham stood from his throne, his face a fusion of anger and resolve. "This ... this is an abomination," he declared, his voice resonating with authority. "The trial will proceed, but this evidence shifts our timetables. We are to swiftly run this ... inquiry I agreed to ground and proceed to proper action for this kingdom."

Tom Cabal, for once, was silent, his earlier skepticism replaced by a dawning realization of the depth of the evil they faced. Even he could not deny the physical proof of malevolence laid before them.

Kriegon, standing beside Rei, felt a surge of hope. "Your Majesty, with Rei's testimony and this grim evidence, let us unite against this common enemy. Perhaps we can forgo the inquiry to proceed with finding the depths of this evil."

Bracus rose from his seat along the far wall, the gold necklace and earrings shining in the light of the window, his voice cutting through the growing murmur of the assembly. "While this evidence is indeed shocking, we must not let our guard down so easily. The authenticity of this ... this head, and indeed, the claims of the Guardians, must be scrutinized. We cannot afford to be swayed by fear alone. The trial will proceed, and we will demand clear, irrefutable proof that the Guardians are who they claim to be. I along with many others here still find a trial is necessary for both fronts."

His words, though harsh, carried a emphasis of caution that resonated with many in the room. The nobles nodded, some reluctantly, acknowledging the need for thorough investigation before rallying to any cause, no matter how dire it seemed.

King Abraham, seeming to sense the shift in the room's atmosphere, stood tall, his decision firm. "Bracus speaks wisely. We will not rush into this without due process. The trial will examine all facets of this matter, from the depths of the Crimson Order's involvement in this corruption to the Guardians' seemingly overreaching actions."

Turning to his closest advisors, Abraham's voice softened but carried an urgency. "Denither, Tom, Vittel, Ryoma, join me in my private chambers. We must discuss the details of this trial, ensure it's conducted with the utmost fairness and scrutiny. Our realm's future depends on the quick outcome."

As the king and his chosen advisors moved towards the private chambers, the rest of the assembly dispersed, the stress of the day's revelations heavy on their minds. As the last of the nobles filtered out of the throne room, the doors groaning shut behind them, Rei and Kriegon lingered. The echo of footsteps and the murmur of voices faded, leaving a profound silence that seemed to press in on them from all sides. Kriegon glanced around, ensuring their privacy before nodding towards the exit, signaling Rei to follow.

They walked in silence at first, the weight of the meeting still hanging over them like a storm cloud. As they approached the mansion, Kriegon's curiosity got the better of him. "I didn't expect such a dramatic reveal of the evidence. Are the others okay?" he asked, his voice low, almost swallowed by the crunch of gravel underfoot as they entered the courtyard.

Rei, towering over Kriegon by nearly a foot, bent slightly at the knees to speak directly to him, her face set in a determined line. "They're holding up," she began, her voice carrying the substance of their recent trials. "We've been through much since heading out. Our journey took us into the dark side of Neil Paris's influence. His city was like nothing I've seen—a place where the air itself seemed tainted with dark and demonic magic."

Kriegon listened intently, his mind painting vivid images of their struggles. "And Garthen's attack on the nobles' mansion?" he prompted, needing to understand the full scope of what they had faced.

Rei's eyes hardened at the memory. "That was a night of fire and chaos. Garthen had a mingling need to prove something and defend those who couldn't save themselves. But in the end, a lot of people died that night. We do have one prisoner who didn't get killed by some suicide rune like most of the others."

Kriegon nodded, a sense of respect for his companions growing and the longing to have helped sinking in his stomach. "We need to prepare for the trial. The evidence, the testimonies, everything must be ironclad."

"As soon as we get back, I'll set up the teleportation stone," Rei assured him. "We'll bring the others here. They'll have more details, firsthand accounts that will strengthen our case."

The mansion loomed ahead, its silhouette against the dusk sky, the sanctuary they had turned into a fortress. Rei placed a reassuring hand on his shoulder. He must have shown the weight of how he was meant to pull off the trial, thinking through the steps they needed to take. "We're in this together, Kriegon. You're not alone."

Chapter 9: Confinement and Strategy

Rei's summoning of the remaining Guardians and some witnesses did not take long. After the witnesses were taken away, the one with the Black Crop gang in chains. However, when Kriegon finished listening to the accounts Zenmore was all too happy to trumpet, he had to relay what he had accomplished.

"So, you didn't find who could have been reporting to Neil. Or whomever Neil was conspiring with?" Garthen's voice was sharp, cutting through the thick air of the room. His eyes, once warm with camaraderie, now glinted with a cold scrutiny that Kriegon hadn't seen before.

Kriegon, stunned by the unexpected rebuke, scrambled for words. "But we did get the Azure Alliance on our side," he managed, his voice weaker than he'd intended.

Garthen sighed, a sound filled with disappointment or perhaps the burden of leadership. Without another word, he turned and strode towards the mansion's exit, his silver bow clinking softly with each step. Kriegon hurried after him, the echo of his own footsteps cloaking the movements of Garthen slightly ahead of him.

"Wait, where are you going?" Kriegon called, his voice echoing slightly in the expansive hallway.

Garthen didn't pause or look back, his pace unyielding as he approached the grand doors of the mansion. Just as they reached the threshold, a group of Lawbringers, imposing in their splendid armor, blocked their path, with Duke Denither at their forefront. The duke, his expression one of duty and regret, turned from conversing with the peacekeepers to address Garthen.

"Ah, I didn't expect to see you quite so soon. Must be that magic again that Ryoma crafted," Denither remarked, his tone light but his eyes serious. "However, I've come with orders. The Guardians are to be confined to the Felix Mansion for the duration of the investigation."

Garthen stopped dead in his tracks, his gaze hardening as he faced Denither. "Why?" The single word was laden with defiance and interrogation.

"It's been decided by King Abraham and the trial's overseers. We need you all in one place for questioning as required. And with that, I'll also require any communication scrolls you possess. Commander Wells will oversee operations with Artemin during this time."

Garthen turned without a word, quickly retreating into the mansion. Kriegon watched him go, a sense of unease settling in his stomach. He turned to Duke Denither, who stood with an air of someone accustomed to having his orders followed without question.

"Sorry, sire, he is ..." Kriegon began, trailing off, unsure how to explain Garthen's reaction or his own turmoil, having seemed to fail his leader's expectation.

"It's fine," Denither interjected, his voice soft but firm. "I understand. These are trying times for all involved." He stepped past Kriegon, gesturing towards the interior of the mansion. "Now, could you lead me to whoever oversees the scrolls and notes? We need to ensure all communication lines are secured."

Kriegon nodded, feeling the burden of failure pressing further on him as he led the duke inside. The halls of the Felix Mansion, once a place of strategic planning and hopeful alliances, now felt like a cage. Each step seemed heavier, the air thick with the anticipation of an uncertain future.

As they walked, Kriegon's mind raced. The confinement wasn't just a physical restriction; it was a strategic play, perhaps to isolate them from potential allies or to control the flow of information. He couldn't shake the feeling that their enemies were using this time to weave their dark web tighter around them.

Reaching the room where their communications were kept, Kriegon paused at the door and turned to Denither. "I need to understand, Duke Denither. What exactly are we looking at with this confinement? Is this merely about control, or is there a deeper game at play?"

Denither's eyes met his, a flicker of respect passing through the older man's gaze. "Kriegon, in times of war and trials, control is often the first casualty. But this confinement is not just about keeping you here. It's about ensuring that when the trial comes, the Guardians are seen as cooperative, not conspiratorial. It's about optics as much as reality."

Kriegon nodded, though the explanation did little to ease the knot of anxiety in his chest. When he had been a soldier before, he was the one to confine people when it was deemed necessary, but now the tables had turned on him and his new comrades so quickly. He opened the door, revealing stacks of scrolls and books scattered across tables, evidence of Cabitha and Coolgen's frantic efforts to gather information.

"Here are our communications," Kriegon said, gesturing to the mess. "But, Duke, with respect, being confined here makes us targets. We can't gather more evidence, nor can we defend ourselves effectively if we're to be kept in the dark."

Duke Denither surveyed the room, his expression unreadable. "I understand your concerns, Kriegon. But this is the king's decree. We must comply, for now. However, I assure you, Commander Wells and Earl Vittel will keep you informed as much as possible. And remember, confinement can also be a time for reflection, for strategy. Use it wisely."

Kriegon watched as Denither began to sift through the scrolls, his mind racing with possibilities. Confinement meant they had to rely on others outside, but it also gave them time to solidify their arguments and proof, to plan their next moves with precision. The duke left with a bundle of scrolls under his arm, promising to keep them in the loop.

Later that evening, as twilight cast its dim glow over the Felix Mansion, Kriegon and the other Guardians gathered in the dining hall, the atmosphere intense with the gravity of their confinement. Their conversation was interrupted by a firm knock at the door, which swung open to reveal Vittel Hero and Kristin, their expressions stern, their presence a hard reminder of the political machinations at play.

Vittel, his eyes scanning the room with a hint of suspicion, spoke first, his voice carrying an edge of authority. "We're here to strategize for the trial, but let's not forget the stakes. Our alliance holds, but trust is thin, especially with non-humans among us."

Kristin, with a diplomatic tone, followed, "We've brought new evidence, but we need to present it in a way that doesn't alienate potential allies."

Garthen, his frustration evident, leaned forward. "Why the patience with the trial? It's obvious the Crimson Order is behind the attacks. Neil's involvement, the timing of their move to bring the king to Riversong—it all points to them. Why play into their hands with legal games?"

Vittel's expression hardened. "It's not just about what we know, Garthen. It's about what we can prove in a way that the court will accept. We can't afford to be seen as rushing to judgment, not when the very legitimacy of your group is in question."

Kristin added, "And remember, this trial isn't just about proving the Crimson Order's guilt. It's about securing the future of our alliance and ensuring the stability of the kingdom. We must be thorough, methodical."

Garthen's gaze remained locked on Vittel, his expression unreadable but his eyes burning with a silent challenge. "Then what is it you suggest we do?" Garthen's voice was calm, yet it carried the authority of a leader burdened by the fate of his team.

Vittel, unfazed, responded with a strategist's cool detachment. "We have trusted operatives sifting through the communications, financials, and movements of Tom, Bracus, and their ilk in the Crimson Order. What we need from you, Garthen, from all of you, is patience. We'll bring you findings or queries as they arise. And I assure you, an Azure will oversee any interaction with Crimson members."

The silence that followed was almost oppressive. Garthen's stoic demeanor did not waver; his mind seemed to be racing through scenarios, strategies, and potential outcomes as Kriegon watched him closely. The quiet stretched on, a silent battle of wills, until Zenmore's voice pierced through, light and devoid of the room's somberness.

"When is dinner coming? I haven't had a proper meal since we left on that grand adventure!" His casual tone was jarring against the backdrop of tension, drawing skeptical looks from around the table.

Kriegon's eyebrow arched in surprise, his attention momentarily pulled from the weighty discussion. Kristin, with a hint of disbelief, addressed Zenmore directly. "Zenmore, is it? You seem remarkably at ease. Do you not grasp the severity of our predicament?"

Zenmore, unfazed by the scrutiny, offered a small, knowing smile. "Oh, I'm well aware, my lady. But maintaining one's strength, both physical and mental, is crucial in such times. After all, we can only prepare so much for what's to come."

Vittel, though visibly still on guard regarding Zenmore's demeanor, couldn't help but concede to the logic. "He's right. We must not let our concerns paralyze us. Physical strength is part of our readiness."

As the conversation drifted into lighter topics, the tension eased slightly, but not entirely. Everyone except Zenmore seemed to carry the stress of the trial on their shoulders. When Orris entered, signaling the approach of dinner, Zenmore seized the opportunity to engage her with an animated recount of their journey, his tales now seeming to Kriegon slightly embellished for effect.

The morning light was barely seeping through the curtains when Kriegon awoke, the feeling of confinement pressing down on him like a tangible mass. Even the air seemed to carry the scent of restriction, a reminder of their imposed seclusion within the Felix Mansion. As he descended for breakfast, the sight of the Lawbringers, statuesque at the gate, underscored their reality.

Breakfast was a quiet affair, the Guardians exchanging few words, each lost in thoughts of the trial ahead. It was Rei who broke the silence properly, her voice cutting through the morning's stillness. "Can we meet outside after this? There's something I've been pondering about our weapons."

Kriegon followed her with Ellena and Saphire, careful to maintain a respectful distance, mindful of her formidable presence and the literal tail she occasionally flicked around in thought. The back lawn was an outward reflection to the mansion's interior, adorned with rows of rose bushes, their blooms a defiant burst of color against the backdrop of their predicament.

Rei turned to them, her scythe in hand, the morning light catching on its blade and casting glints of light across the lawn. "I've been thinking about the capabilities of our weapons," she began, her voice steady despite the underlying tension. "Have we truly grasped their full potential?"

She held up her scythe for emphasis. "This weapon, for example, is just for combat. It's cumbersome to carry around, or in my case, to fly with." She paused, allowing her words to sink in, scanning their faces for acknowledgment.

"Even with the makeshift sheath that secures it to my back, maneuvering remains a challenge. During my flight, I wished the blade could fold against the shaft for easier transport." As if on cue, the blade of the scythe smoothly adjusted, folding along the shaft, transforming into a more compact form.

"The adaptability of our weapons isn't just physical; it requires psychic energy, similar to casting a spell," she explained, her eyes intense with the discovery.

Ellena, intrigued, chimed in, "That makes sense. I've used my sword like a whip in battle without realizing it. But afterwards, I felt unusually drained, probably because I'm not accustomed to magic."

Kriegon, eyeing his own staff with renewed curiosity, interjected again, "And consider Garthen's bow. It's made of metal, right? Normally, the tension needed to draw such a bow would be immense, yet it sounds like it functions as if it were wood. There's something more to these weapons than meets the eye."

Rei nodded, her gaze reflecting her excitement and resolve. "Exactly, Kriegon. If we can demonstrate this adaptability, this ... mystic flexibility of our weapons in court, it might help validate our claims about their origins, their power. It could be pivotal in showing that we're

100

not wielding ordinary weapons but are connected to something greater, something that could prove our legitimacy as Guardians. The first step to solidifying skeptical nobles."

Ellena, absorbing this information, quickly excused herself. "I need to relay this to Garthen and Cabitha. They should prepare to present this as evidence to the Azure Alliance. This could allow us to focus more heavily on the Crimson Order than proving our roles." With a determined stride, she left the group, her cat tail flicking around in excitement.

As Ellena departed, Kriegon's focus returned to his staff. Inspired by Rei's demonstration, he attempted to transform it into something more familiar to him—a katana. With a concentrated effort, the staff shimmered and reshaped, the metal twisting and condensing into the sleek, sharp form of a simple katana.

Encouraged by his success, Kriegon pushed further, envisioning a detailed gauntlet. The weapon began to morph again, but this time, the transformation was slower, more taxing. He could feel the psychic energy draining from him, a sensation akin to physical exhaustion but deeper, more profound.

Suddenly, the effort proved too much. Kriegon's knees buckled, and he fell to the ground, his vision blurring slightly from the exertion. The gauntlet, incomplete and unstable, seemed to melt off his hand, the metal pooling onto the grass before slowly, almost reluctantly, reforming back into his staff.

Rei was by his side in an instant, concern etched on her face. "Kriegon, are you alright? You've pushed too hard. The psychic energy required for the changes could be painful if you demand too much."

Kriegon, catching his breath, managed a weak smile. "I see that now. It's not just about the physical form; it's about understanding the detail and amount of change needed for the idea to take place."

As Kriegon sat on a nearby bench, still feeling the drain from his attempt, he rubbed the cool metal of his staff, a physical reminder of the power he had just tapped into. His mind, however, was already racing with the implications of what they had discovered. Possibilities of how to use this new power to help his team succeed flicked quickly by.

Rei, her concern for Kriegon momentarily set aside, turned her attention to Saphire, who had been watching the events unfold with keen interest. With her massive claymore, its blade distinct with sharp teeth on one side, she approached with a thoughtful expression. "Rei, I've always struggled with carrying my sword since receiving it. The sheaths are either too weak or are sliced through during regular walking. Could we perhaps try something different?"

Rei nodded, intrigued by the challenge. "What do you envision? Something that would allow for both protection and ease of movement?"

Saphire's eyes lit up as she explained her idea. "I was thinking of a wrap, something that could secure the sword to my back but also be part of the sword itself, so it wouldn't interfere with its sharpness or my movements."

Together, they discussed the design, Rei guiding Saphire through the mental visualization needed to manifest such a change. They settled on a concept: a thin, flexible strip of metal that would extend from the hilt to the tip of the sword, designed to wrap around her body from shoulder to waist, crossing between her ample figure without restricting her mobility.

Focusing deeply, Kriegon watched as Saphire channeled her intent into the claymore. It took a couple of minutes, but slowly the sword's metal began to shimmer, and from the hilt, a slender yet sturdy strip of metal began to form, extending along the length of the blade. It was smooth, unadorned, and served as the functional wrap they had discussed.

Rei watched, impressed. "You've done it, Saphire. Now try it on. It might be good to try and quickly detach the idea to wield your weapon quickly, then reform it as you want. Practice for a while; hopefully this can help in your future magic studies."

Saphire tested the new addition, swinging the claymore with ease onto her back, the strip securing it in place. "It feels right," she said, her voice full of relief and pride. "This could change how we fight, how we move."

Kriegon, now standing, observed the transformation and the mention of magic with a renewed sense of wonder. "Wait, Rei, how can this help with our magic studies?"

Rei turned back to Kriegon with a glint in her eye and a small smile. "To employ magic, you need to have a very clear image of what you want done." She held up her scythe, a new rune glowing with a faint green light on the blade. "For instance, I want a ball of wind to form." And just like that, a dense, turbulent ball of wind formed, only visible from the dust and leaves picked up by the force.

"Amazing. It's like something out of a dream," mumbled Kriegon.

"Maybe for now, but until you and the others can form proper shapes with my supervision, we will only focus on these weapons changing. Honestly, magic learning is going to be much safer than how we learned on Aerondrake." Rei looked off into the sky and pondered the change in her teaching method for a moment before turning back to Saphire and Kriegon. "Well, let us start there ..."

The training continued under Rei's guidance. Kriegon and Saphire practiced transforming their weapons into various forms, each change a lesson in control and intent. Ellena, returning from her discussions with the Azure Alliance, joined them, her curiosity piqued by the evolving dynamics of their abilities. While Ellena and Saphire had a harder time picturing the needed changes, resulting in strange shapes, they were bounds ahead of Kriegon when it came to speed of their psychic energy use and seeming reserves.

Days melded into one another, a cycle of practice, exhaustion, and recovery. "Psychic energy is like any other muscle," Rei would remind them as they lay panting on the ground. "You must work it to strengthen it." Her words became a mantra, pushing them further each day.

As the Guardians honed their skills, the mansion saw a steady stream of visitors from both factions. Some came with questions, others with updates on the investigation into the dark magic outbreaks, and a few simply to observe the Guardians' training sessions. Garthen and Zenmore, however, remained aloof, their involvement limited to sparring sessions or quiet discussions away from the group. Garthen's isolation grew more pronounced, his presence at meals becoming a rare occurrence, his mind seemingly elsewhere, burdened by thoughts unspoken to the others. On the other hand, Zenmore could be found talking fondly with Orris around the mansion, seeming to always drink in her attention.

One crisp morning, the routine was broken by the arrival of Kristin. Her steps were purposeful as she approached the training group, her expression that of urgency and relief. The Guardians paused, sensing the significance of her visit.

"The trial date has been set," Kristin announced, her voice cutting through the morning air. The words hung there, a moment of silence following as if the world itself was holding its breath.

Rei, her scythe now resting in her lap, met Kristin's gaze. "When?"

"Three days hence," Kristin replied. "The court wishes to expedite matters, given the stakes."

A murmur of tension ran through the group. Three days to prepare, to solidify their strategy, to ensure that their newfound understanding of their weapons—and perhaps their magic—could be leveraged in the courtroom.

Kriegon felt a surge of adrenaline, the change of their situation pushing him up like a pep talk. This wasn't just about proving their innocence; it was about demonstrating their worth, their role in the larger tapestry of this world's destiny.

Rei nodded, her expression resolute. "We'll be ready."

The following days were a whirlwind of preparation. The Guardians, under Rei's guidance, refined their weapon transformations, each change now imbued with a sense of urgency and purpose. They discussed strategies, potential questions from the Crimson Order, and how to present their case. Garthen, despite his earlier withdrawal, was pulled back into the fold, his tactical mind too valuable to ignore. Vittel and Kristin were ever-present now, going over the plans and testimony.

On the eve of the trial, the mansion was quiet, the usual sounds of training replaced by the soft rustle of papers being reviewed by Garthen, the low murmur of last-minute discussions. Kriegon sat with his staff, now a familiar heft in his hands, going over his testimony in his head. The biggest hinderance that he should have focused on was the written language of this world. Rei had mastered it quickly and often went over the information with Kriegon, Saphire, and an uninterested Zenmore.

As night fell, the Guardians gathered, a silent pact of support passing between them. They were more than just fighters now; they were becoming a family, bound by their shared trials to come. Tomorrow, they would step into the courtroom to defend themselves and to assert their place in this world.

The air was thick with anticipation as they retired for the night. Kriegon was sure the others were lost in their thoughts, each carrying the stress of what was to come just as it weighed on him. The trial loomed like a storm on the horizon, but within the Felix Mansion, there was a quiet strength, a readiness to face whatever challenges lay ahead.

Chapter 10: The Trial

Garthen slipped through the shadows, his movements as silent as the breath of the wind. Each step he took was a defiance of the king's decree, a personal mission cloaked in the darkness of the deep shadows. His nights were spent prowling the streets, gathering whispers, seeking truths that eluded him during the day. His frustration grew with each fruitless search, his determination hardened by the elusive feeling of being watched, yet never confronted.

It was only when the official date of the trial was announced that Garthen felt compelled to reintegrate himself into the group's activities at the mansion. His annoyance at what he perceived as the others' passivity and reliance on the Azure nobles was something he had to bury deep. If he was to regain the command the king had once entrusted to him, it would be through showing leadership now, not through solitary ventures.

The morning of the trial dawned like any other, yet there was an undercurrent of tension that even the serene beauty of the rising sun couldn't dispel. Zenmore, usually a fount of light-hearted banter, was uncharacteristically quiet. He ate his meal with a focus that seemed almost meditative, in contrast to the usual jovial atmosphere he cultivated.

Garthen, at the head of the table, felt the familiar power of leadership on his shoulders as he looked at his comrades. The other Guardians, close around him, looked to him for guidance, their faces etched with a blend of determination and anxiety. Rei, taking charge of the briefing, went over their strategy one last time.

"When the Crimson Order questions our evidence, our legitimacy as Guardians, we must be ready. Show them your weapon, explain the connection you felt when you first activated it from the slabs. If you can, demonstrate its adaptability," she instructed, her voice steady, her eyes scanning each of them for acknowledgment.

Ellena leaned forward, her concern evident. "And the bishop from the Ever Watcher? Is his presence confirmed? His testimony about our weapons' origins could sway the court in our favor."

Rei, flipping through her notes, responded without looking up, "A representative will be sent, as a witness and as a jury member. It's a good sign."

Kriegon, his voice hoarse with the tension of the moment, managed to ask, "And the others on the jury?"

Rei finally lifted her gaze from the notes, meeting each of their eyes in turn. "Lord Denither, Ryoma, Helain Bold, Adelisa Cabal, Frank Tolas, along with the unnamed church member. It's a diverse panel, which could work in our favor if we present our case correctly."

A murmur of contemplation passed through the group. Each name carried weight, influence, and potential biases. Garthen's mind raced, calculating the implications of each juror's presence. This was not just about proving their innocence; it was about convincing those in power of their worth, their destiny to pursue the monsters in the night that had taken everything he loved.

As they finished their meal, the atmosphere shifted subtly. The tension did not dissipate but morphed into a focused energy, a collective readiness. Garthen stood, his presence commanding even in silence. His mind, though still frustrated by his nocturnal failures, was sharp, his resolve unyielding.

"Let's make our preparations final. Today, we not only defend ourselves but take another step in defending this world," Garthen declared, his voice a blend of command and camaraderie. The others nodded, their agreement silent but profound.

As they rose to leave, Zenmore finally broke his stillness, his voice carrying a lightness that seemed to lift the mood slightly. "May the winds not betray us and the truth be in our favor," he said, a seemingly traditional blessing that felt oddly fitting for the day ahead.

The trial was set to take place in the castle's grand throne room, a space usually reserved for royal decrees and celebrations, now transformed for the magnitude of the legal proceedings. The room had been rearranged; to one side of the throne, a row of chairs awaited the jury, while on the opposite side, four imposing Lawbringers stood sentinel, their presence a stark reminder of the seriousness of the occasion. In the center, two distinct boxes had been constructed, one for the Guardians and their Azure Alliance supporters, and the other for the Crimson Order, ensuring a clear division in the room.

As the first to arrive, the Guardians took their places in their designated box, the silence of the vast throne room amplifying their footsteps. The grandeur of the space, with its high ceilings and ornate decorations, felt almost oppressive, a fitting arena for the battle of words and wills that was about to unfold.

Slowly, the room began to fill. First came the representatives of the Azure Alliance, their faces marked with hope and concern. Soon to follow was the Crimson Order, appearing both concerned and calm about the situation. Two robed figures sat in their mist that Kriegon pointed out, but Garthen paid it little mind. Then, members of the public, nobles, and curious onlookers trickled in, their whispers creating a soft undercurrent of noise. The tension in the air grew palpable.

Finally, the arrival of King Abraham, escorted by an entourage that included the jury members, shifted the atmosphere entirely. The king's presence was commanding, his expression unreadable, yet his eyes scanned the room with an intensity that missed nothing. Beside him, the jury members took their seats, their faces aa assortment of solemnity and curiosity.

Lord Denither, known for his stern judgments, sat with a composed demeanor, while Ryoma, with his relation among the Guardians, offered them a nod, a small gesture of acknowledgment.

As the room settled, the Lawbringers positioned themselves with military precision, their armor clinking softly, a reminder of the order they were there to maintain. The air was thick with anticipation, every eye on the throne where King Abraham stood, his gaze sweeping over the assembled crowd before settling on the Guardians.

The silence in the throne room was deep, a cloak of anticipation draped over every soul present. King Abraham, his regal presence commanding the space, initiated the proceedings with a voice that carried the weight of authority. "Let this trial be officially underway," he declared, his tone as deep and sober as the severity of the occasion demanded.

Garthen, sitting among his fellow Guardians, felt a surge of tension at the king's words. The room, filled with the kingdom's elite and the curious, seemed to hold its breath, waiting for the unfolding drama.

Abraham continued, "Today, I will act as the mediating judge between the Crimson Order and the Guardians, supported by the Azure Alliance. Accusations of traitorous acts have been levied by both camps, and it falls upon this esteemed jury, led by none other than Duke Denither, to render the final verdict."

At this, Duke Denither rose, his posture rigid, his eyes scanning the room with an intensity that spoke of his reputation for fairness yet sternness. "As the king has said, I am Duke Denither. To my right, Viscountess Adelisa Cabal, Baron Frank Tolas, and Viscount Helain Bold. On my left, Baron Ryoma Yasumoto and the honorable Seers of the Ever Watcher, Lucius," he introduced, each name adding to the importance of the trial.

As Denither took his seat again, leaning forward with a hawk-like focus on the proceedings, King Abraham gestured towards Tom Cabal of the Crimson Order, signaling the commencement of the opening statements.

Tom Cabal, dressed in his striking red suit with dark trimmings, stepped forward with a grim determination. His presence was like a dark cloud, his words a storm brewing on the horizon. "The kingdom has suffered unspeakable losses with the destruction of Windmontley and Malgrave," he began, his voice a slow, deliberate cadence. "While not the direct cause, these so-called Guardians have exploited this tragedy, sowing chaos, undermining our noble hierarchy, all under the guise of fulfilling a prophecy they've twisted to their own ends."

Garthen's hands clenched at his sides, his heart pounding with the truth only he knew. Every word from Tom felt like a personal assault, each accusation a dagger aimed at the very essence of what Garthen had lost and everything he fought for now. The urge to leap forward, to challenge Tom's words with action, was a fire in his veins, but he held back, knowing the battlefield today was not of swords but of words.

Tom's statement, though lengthy, was crafted to sound reasonable, yet to Garthen, it was a distortion of reality, a manipulation of events to fit a narrative of deceit. The pain of betrayal, the sting of accusations, all of it coursed through him, demanding a response he knew must wait for the right moment.

As Tom concluded, the room seemed to exhale, the tension momentarily easing before the storm of rebuttals and testimonies that was sure to follow. King Abraham, his face an unreadable guise, nodded solemnly. "We will now proceed with the opening statement from the Guardians, followed by testimonies," he announced, his voice a calm contrast to the charged atmosphere.

Garthen felt all eyes turn towards him and his companions, the load of expectation hard on his shoulders. He took a deep breath, his mind racing through the countless hours of preparation, the many scenarios they had discussed. Now was not the time for anger or rash decisions; it was a time for clarity, for truth.

Garthen, his voice steady despite the turmoil within, addressed the assembly. "Your Majesty, esteemed Duke, members of the jury, and all gathered here, I stand before you not just as a Guardian, but as a man who has known loss, a pain that sears both flesh and spirit. My family, like so many others, fell to the chaos that now threatens our lands. This pain, this void, is my daily companion, a reminder of what I fight against."

He paused, letting his words sink in, his gaze sweeping over the faces before him, seeking understanding, perhaps empathy. "We, the Guardians, were not chosen; we were called. Called by a need greater than ourselves, to stand as a bulwark against the darkness that seeks to engulf our world. We took up this mantle not for glory, not for power, but to protect others from the agony I endure each day. We fight so that no more families are torn apart, so that the light of hope is not extinguished."

Garthen's eyes hardened as he turned his attention towards the Crimson Order's box, where Tom Cabal had made his accusations. "While we have faced the Black Crop Gang, those who would sow discord and chaos, directly confronting them to protect our realm, the Crimson Order chooses to see us as enemies. They align themselves, perhaps unwittingly, with forces that would see this kingdom burn, with demons from the depths of hell itself."

His voice rose, filled with a conviction born of his experiences, of battles fought with both sword and with heart. "We stand accused of using the chaos for our gain, yet it is we who have bled for this land, who have faced the true enemies of peace and order. The prophecy we follow is not one of conquest but of salvation, a beacon in the darkness we all face."

Garthen's opening statement, charged with emotion yet delivered with the precision of a seasoned warrior, left the room in a profound silence. The pain he spoke of was profound, a shared heaviness among those who had lost. As he stepped back, the room seemed to breathe again, the air thick with the weight of his words, the truth of his burden laid bare for all to see.

The silence was broken by the rustle of parchment, the clearing of throats, as the members of the jury exchanged glances, some with expressions of contemplation, others with a newfound respect for the man who had just shown the depth of his pain.

King Abraham, his voice tinged with a sorrow known only to those who had lost everything, acknowledged Garthen's pain with a nod. "I, too, know the void left by loss. My family, taken at Windmontley Keep, haunts me still. Let us proceed, in search of truth and in the pursuit of justice, for all who have suffered."

The atmosphere shifted as Tom Cabal of the Crimson Order stood, his demeanor shifting from accuser to advocate. "Your Majesty, we will begin with our testimonies, starting with evidence of the Guardians' actions that have led to this trial."

The first witness called was a young investigator, his hands slightly trembling as he approached the stand in front of the still Lawbringers. He introduced himself as Jorin, tasked with reviewing communications related to the Guardians' activities.

Tom Cabal began his questioning with calm precision. "Investigator Jorin, in your review of the communications, did you come across any messages from Garthen himself that could shed light on the Guardians' methods?"

Jorin, clearing his throat, replied, "Yes, sir. I reviewed several messages, but one in particular stood out due to its ... directive nature."

"And what was the nature of this directive?" Tom pressed, leaning forward slightly, his eyes sharp.

"It was a message to one Artemin, instructing her to show no mercy at Neil Paris's town. The context suggested a harsh crackdown, possibly on innocents caught in the crossfire," Jorin explained, his voice gaining steadiness as he spoke.

Tom turned to the jury, his expression concerned. "And how do you interpret this message, in the light of our kingdom's values of justice and mercy?"

Jorin hesitated, then said, "It suggests a willingness to use force without regard for the collateral damage, which could be seen as ... reckless, if not outright malicious."

The room buzzed with whispers, the implications of Jorin's words hanging heavy. Garthen's face tightened, his mind racing to recall that moment, the context of that message, knowing the consequence it carried now.

Tom, satisfied with the impact of this revelation, moved to conclude his questioning. "Thank you, Investigator Jorin. No further questions."

Bracus, taking the floor with a confident stride, replaced Tom at the forefront of the Crimson Order's table. His gaze was sharp, his demeanor that of a seasoned debater ready to weave his narrative. "Next, I'd like to call to the stand Miss Elara Voss, an accountant from Orris

Felix's estate," he announced, his voice carrying an edge of anticipation.

Elara Voss, a young woman with an air of meticulousness, approached the stage, her ledger in hand. Her nervousness was evident, yet her eyes held a determination that spoke of her commitment to truth.

"Miss Voss," Bracus began, his tone almost cordial, "please tell the court about the financial transactions you've discovered related to the Guardians' stay at Orris Felix's estate."

Elara nodded, opening her ledger. "Upon reviewing the estate's accounts, I noticed several irregularities. At first, the sums were minor, barely noticeable. But as time progressed, the amounts grew significantly, reaching sums that could comfortably sustain a family for over a year. Offset by an increased funding from the crown."

"And can you specify the nature of these transactions?" Bracus inquired, his interest piqued.

"They were payments to unknown individuals, or rather, entities with no clear identity within the estate's usual dealings. The entries were marked with codes, not names, which is unusual for Orris Felix, known for her clear recordkeeping."

Bracus paused, letting the information sink in before he continued. "And how do these transactions relate to the Guardians?"

Elara hesitated, her fingers tracing the lines of numbers. "It's speculative, but given the timeline and the sudden increase in these transactions, it suggests that these payments could be linked to the Guardians' activities or influence during their stay."

Bracus, turning to address the jury, his voice rising slightly, concluded, "Ladies and gentlemen of the jury, what we have here is not just financial mismanagement but a clear indication of manipulation and deceit. The Guardians, under the guise of protection, have seemingly used their position to funnel money, to hoodwink the estate and its resources for their personal gain."

In the shining light of the chamber, where the air was thick with tension, Garthen leaned closer, overhearing whispers among Rei, Kriegon, and Vittel. They were discussing the validity of these accounting claims that had been brought to light. Their conversation was hushed but earnest, centered on the financial discrepancies that had become a focal point of contention.

Vittel, with a stern look, raised his voice just enough to be heard by Abraham, who was overseeing the proceedings. "I wish to review the witnesses' records," Vittel stated, his tone firm yet respectful, a request that was more an assertion of right than a plea.

King Abraham, after a moment's contemplation, nodded. "As this is a matter of considerable importance to the case, I grant this request. The records will be made available for review."

Without hesitation, Vittel, Kriegon, and Rei moved to examine the ledgers presented by Miss Voss. Their scrutiny was meticulous, comparing each entry against the records they had brought with them, documents that detailed the estate's usual expenditures and the recent increases.

Kriegon, with a keen eye for numbers, was the first to speak up, his voice carried through the chamber as he addressed the court. "Upon review, there is indeed an increase in expenditure noted. However, these increases correspond directly with the estate's heightened costs for food supplies."

He paused, allowing his words to settle before continuing, his gaze shifting between the king and the jury. "The estate has been hosting the Guardians, some of which have a... considerable appetite, such as Zenmore, whose dietary needs alone could account for a significant portion of these increased costs."

Vittel, holding up the ledger, added, "Furthermore, if we examine the records more closely, we see that these large sums are not hidden transactions but rather payments for bulk food supplies, which have seen a price surge due to market instability and increased demand from the influx of guests and the estate's own staff."

Rei, standing beside them, chimed in with a quiet authority. "These expenditures, when put in context, do not reflect deceit or personal gain. They are the natural consequence of increased activity and responsibility at the estate, a responsibility that Miss Orris took on to assist in our mission to help the kingdom at large."

King Abraham, listening intently, turned his attention back to Bracus. "Do you have any rebuttal to this explanation of the financial discrepancies presented?"

Bracus, momentarily thrown off by the detailed counterevidence, managed a composed response. "While these explanations provide context, the method of recording these transactions remains unconventional and raises questions about transparency."

Abraham, considering both sides, addressed the jury. "You have heard the testimonies and the explanations. It is now your duty to weigh the evidence, considering both the accusations and the defenses provided. The records will be provided to you upon concluding statements."

As the trio and Bracus took their seats, the air in the courtroom was thick with anticipation. Tom Cabal, sensing the shift in momentum, stood resolutely, ready to request his next witness. "I call upon Seris, a former servant of the late count of Neil Paris's town," he announced, his voice echoing with an authoritative tone.

Seris, an older man with weary eyes, approached the stand, his steps hesitant, his demeanor that of someone who had seen too much. Tom began his questioning with a calm, almost sympathetic approach. "Seris, please tell the court what you witnessed when the Guardians entered the mansion you served in."

Seris, his voice trembling slightly, recounted, "It was a night of terror. I watched as these ... these animals, the Guardians, stormed through the mansion. They killed without mercy, without even a word. It was as if they were not there to defend but to destroy."

Tom, nodding solemnly, pressed further, "And were these actions unprovoked? Did anyone in the mansion raise a weapon against them?"

Seris shook his head, his expression despairing. "No, sir. Not a single sword was raised in defense. They attacked as if possessed by demons, leaving a trail of blood behind them."

Garthen, seated among his companions, felt a surge of frustration at the falseness of Seris's words. He remembered that night vividly—every encounter, every loosed shot, was in response to an immediate threat. Each person they had confronted was armed, some even in the act of attacking first.

Tom, concluding his questioning with a dramatic flourish, turned to the jury. "What you've heard today, ladies and gentlemen, is not the tale of heroes but of men who have lost their way, who have become what they claim to fight against. These are not Guardians; they are usurpers, bloodthirsty and deceitful. With this, I rest this set of first testimonies."

As Tom sat down, the courtroom buzzed with whispers, the narrative of the trial now heavily laden with accusations of brutality. Garthen shifted, feeling their reputations tarnished by these claims. Vittel, standing, prepared to call their first witness, aiming to dismantle the web of lies spun around them.

The echo of Vittel's cane was the only sound in the grand courtroom as he moved with deliberate steps back to the speaking area. His voice, firm and resonant, broke the silence. "Ladies and Lords," he began, his tone imbued with enormity, "I stand before you not just as an advocate, but as a witness to truth. Before I call forth my first witness, allow me to recount a moment that shifted my perspective forever. When Kriegon first revealed his staff, declaring himself a Guardian amidst a crowd that could have turned hostile at any moment, I felt a stir in my soul. It was as if the ancient prophecy were unfolding before my eyes."

He paused, letting his words sink into the hearts of those assembled. "But today, we are not here to speak of the prophecy alone. We are here to expose the true adversaries of peace, those who act under the guise of the Crimson Order. To illuminate their dark intentions, I now call upon a crucial witness, one who has seen the worst of this conflict."

A murmur rippled through the room as a Lawbringer, his armor clanking with authority, escorted a figure forward. The woman, known as Miss Kanah, was visibly shaken, her spirit dimmed and dragging, just like the iron of her chains. Garthen could see the change in her demeanor, which once shone with sorrow just after they had saved her. Now it resembled the nature he had experienced before Ryoma had found him. Broken.

As she approached the stand, Vittel's voice softened yet retained its command. "Miss Kanah, you were once part of the Black Crop Gang, is that correct?"

She nodded, her voice barely above a whisper. "Yes, I was."

"And can you tell the court your role within this gang?" Vittel prompted, his gaze steady.

"I ... I was involved in operations, errands. I did what was asked of me," Kanah replied, her hands wringing together in the confines of her shackles.

Vittel, leaning forward, his gaze piercing yet not unkind, asked, "Miss Kanah, why would someone like you join such a reprehensible group as the Black Crop Gang?"

Kanah's voice trembled as she answered, "We were desperate, my husband and I. We needed food; we were trying to survive. As part of an impoverished town near Lord Neil's, most of our crops were transferred to him. When the Black Crop came recruiting, there was no other choice for us."

Before Vittel could continue, Tom Cabal rose sharply from his seat, his voice cutting through the room. "Objection! This line of questioning seeks only to smear the name of the late Neil Paris, a man of honor and a leader within our order!"

King Abraham raised his hand for silence. After a brief pause, he spoke in a tone that brooked no argument. "Overruled. Let her speak. The truth of Neil Paris's actions and associations is pertinent to this trial."

Vittel, acknowledging the king's decision with a nod, turned back to Kanah. "Please, continue, Miss Kanah. Did you have any knowledge of the Crimson Order's interactions with the gang beyond Neil Paris?"

Kanah, her resolve strengthening, nodded. "Yes, my husband, when he was acting as a bodyguard, saw Neil conversing with a large person, always under a cloak, in the shadows of the mountain. Neil often spoke of receiving orders from those above him, allowing these cloaked figures into the sewers."

"And these cloaked figures, did you learn anything about them?" Vittel pressed, allowing interest into his tone.

"After they started appearing, some of our gang members vanished. We began to see large shadows at night, flying towards the mountains. It was ... unsettling," she admitted, her voice dropping to a whisper.

Vittel, sensing the import of her testimony, asked gently, "And why are you here now, willing to give this testimony?"

Kanah raised her shackled hand to her mouth, a gesture of her deep sorrow. "One of Neil's men killed my husband, and Neil nearly killed me too. But that shadowy figure — Garthen, and the huge brute, Zenmore, they saved me. I owe them my life, and this is my way of repaying that debt."

Vittel paused briefly, letting Kanah catch her breath as the court watched her seemingly close to breaking down. Once she was settled again, he continued pointedly, "Kanah, I need you to go back to that painful night. Tell us why the Guardians needed to save you."

Kanah shaking voice started again, "My husband and I were ordered to Lord Neil's side, as added personal guards. Neil was nervous, going on about the troops' encampment outside possibly invading at any second. His nerves put everyone on edge; the spear I carried was pointed at the door with my husband. But hours passed and nothing happened. While we were still nervous, night fell. Then the three Guardians burst in, and the fight started without a word. When my husband and I watched the others beaten easily, we threw down our weapons hoping for mercy. That was when Neil and another gang member turned on us." She paused, taking in a large, shaking breath again before continuing. "I held my husband as he choked on his own blood and watched as a purple light snuffed out Neil's life."

Vittel pressed one last time, "This purple light, what was it from?"

Kanah shook her head. "It was something branded on his chest ...

from where, I have no idea."

The courtroom was silent, the somberness of Kanah's words hanging gravely in the air. Vittel, satisfied with her revelation, stepped back, allowing the court to digest the information he had brought to light.

As Kanah was led back to the doors of the throne room, her steps difficult with the burden of her chains and her revelations, a soft, sorrowful sob broke from her, echoing through the stone chamber. The sound was haunting, a reminder of the human cost behind the political and magical machinations being discussed. The room fell into a brief, respectful silence, acknowledging her pain.

Once Kanah had been escorted out, Rei, with a composed grace, stepped forward to take her place at the speaking area. Her presence was like a breath of calm after the storm of emotion that had just passed.

Rei stood before the assembly, her posture both confident and composed. "Magic," she began, her voice steady, "is fundamentally understood through the lens of Runes and Psychic Energy. A mage must visualize with precision, for the clarity of the image directly influences the manifestation of the spell."

With a graceful motion, she presented her scythe, the weapon gleaming under the light of the courtroom's windows. "However, the weapons granted to us Guardians transcend these established rules of magic. They operate on a level that defies conventional understanding."

Rei's eyes swept over the room, ensuring she held the attention of all present. "These weapons facilitate communication across languages, cultures, even species, without the slightest effort on our part. Imagine the complexity of such magic, and yet, here it is, accomplished without a rune in sight."

She demonstrated the scythe's ability to transform, shifting it into a poleaxe and back with a fluid, almost effortless motion. "And this transformation, this manipulation of form, again, requires no rune. Indeed, I wouldn't even know where to begin with runes to achieve such feats. This is not magic as you know it; this is something bestowed upon us by a power far beyond our realms."

Rei's voice took on a tone of reverence as she continued, "This can only be the work of a being of immense power, like the Archangel Saforus, whose name I've heard whispered in awe. Only such a divine entity could summon individuals from different worlds, like Kriegon, Saphire, Zenmore, and myself, to aid in this world's time of need. These weapons, these gifts, are proof of our destiny, a destiny not crafted by mortal hands but by the will of the divine, to heal, to protect, and to unite."

Rei concluded her testimony with a deep, respectful bow to the king and the jury, her words echoing in the solemn chamber. "Let us not mistake divine intervention for mere magic. Our purpose here is guided by a higher will, and these weapons are our testament."

As she stepped down, Kriegon, his fist clenched on his staff, approached the front of the court. His voice, full of pride, filled the room. "Having heard the unjust besmirchment of our great leader, Garthen, I now call up to the witness stand not just any man, but Garthen himself."

Tom stood immediately, objecting with a hint of frustration, "Your Majesty, it is unprecedented for an accused to serve as a witness in their own trial."

Kriegon, unyielding, responded, "Who better to speak on Garthen's actions and intentions than the man himself? His words are not just his defense, but the truth we seek."

The king, after a moment of contemplation, nodded. "Let Garthen take the stand. His testimony might shed light on this complex matter."

Garthen, with measured steps, ascended to the witness stand, his demeanor calm yet authoritative. Kriegon, now standing before him, began, "Garthen, tell us, why did you venture into Neil Paris's territory?"

Garthen, his gaze steady, answered, "My forces, led by Lady Artemin, were in relentless pursuit of the Black Crop Gang across the eastern side of Riversong. Despite our efforts, we were consistently outmaneuvered, unable to capture them as per Your Majesty's orders."

He paused, gathering his thoughts. "Realizing the need for a new strategy, I decided on a two-pronged approach. I led a smaller team, consisting of Ellena, Saphire, Zenmore, and Rei, to track the gang covertly. Meanwhile, I sent my main force farther east to seek assistance from Neil Paris, hoping to encircle the gang."

Garthen's voice grew more somber. "However, when our tracking efforts led us back to Neil's very city, and Lady Artemin was denied access with her forces, I made the decision to infiltrate the city under the cover of night. It was not an act of aggression but one of desperation to fulfill the king's command and bring order to the chaos wrought by the gang."

Kriegon, his tone now one of solemn curiosity, asked, "And what did your team discover within the city?"

Garthen's expression darkened as he recounted their findings. "We entered the city through the sewers, moving silently to avoid detection. But as we ventured deeper, I felt a formidable presence, a darkness that I've only encountered once before."

He paused and then, with a deliberate motion, pulled back his hood, revealing the scarred, blackened skin—a testament to a past encounter with the demons of Windmontley. The court gasped. "I had this done to me when Windmontley was captured. Demons burned me alive and killed countless others."

After allowing a moment for the severity of his appearance to settle, Garthen raised his hood once more, his voice steady but filled with a quiet fury. "That familiar presence led us to a hidden chamber beneath the city, where three mages were engaged in a dark ritual. They were transforming a human into a wyvern, a creature whose head now lies before this court, brought by Rei as evidence."

The room was thick with tension as Garthen described the scene. "The transformation was grotesque, a violation of nature. We intervened, stopping the mages and the abomination they created. In the aftermath, we discovered cells filled with hostages, innocents caught in the maelstrom of this dark evil magic. Likely to share the same fate as

122

the man we failed to save."

Kriegon, absorbing the importance of Garthen's words, nodded solemnly. "Your actions, then, were not only to pursue the gang but to thwart a greater evil beneath Neil Paris's own city."

Garthen affirmed, "Yes. Our mission was to protect, to serve justice, not just against the gang but against any who would distort the natural order for their gain."

Kriegon, leaning forward, asked, "And what justice did you seek after saving those you could?"

Garthen, his voice now carrying an authority of resolve, responded, "Our next objective was Neil Paris himself. We needed to determine if he was aware of the dark magic being practiced under his nose or if he was coerced into allowing it. When we entered his mansion, our suspicions were confirmed. We encountered two gang members, fully armed as if preparing for battle, not mere guards but warriors ready for conflict."

He took a moment, the memory of that night vivid in his mind. "Zenmore, Ellena, and I confronted Neil in his study. He was surrounded by more of these gang members, indicating his deep involvement. The moment of truth came when he turned his blade on Kanah, the woman you've just heard from, and her husband, who had surrendered. That act of aggression, in the face of submission, left no doubt of his guilt."

Kriegon pressed, "And what of Neil Paris's fate? Did you execute him on the spot?"

"No," Garthen replied, his tone somber. "We intended to capture him, to bring him before the king for judgment. However, as we subdued him, a dark magic rune, unfamiliar even to Rei, activated. Before our eyes, it killed Neil Paris. It was a magic beyond our comprehension, suggesting forces at play far greater than mere gang activities. Perhaps connected to the demonic magic we had stopped earlier in the sewers."

As Garthen concluded his statement, Kriegon turned to face the king and the jury, his posture solemnly respectful. "Your Majesty, esteemed members of the jury, what we've unveiled today is but the tip of the iceberg concerning the dark forces at play. The Guardians, along with the Azure Alliance, are at the forefront of uncovering these malevolent influences. However, for the moment, let us return to the matters at hand concerning the Crimson Order."

The king, observing the hour, interjected with a tone that carried both authority and a touch of warmth. "It seems the hour approaches noon by my reckoning, and while the testimonies presented have been enlightening, they do not satiate our hunger. We shall break for a meal prepared in the courtyard."

A murmur of relief and anticipation rippled through the room. The king continued, "Let us reconvene after lunch to hear the next round of testimonies from the Crimson Order. Court is adjourned for now."

Garthen started to move back to the box to join his comrades, the relief washing over him. Out of the corner of his eye, he caught the odd movements of two cloaked figures heading into the middle of the court instead of out toward the courtyard. Turning at the gate of their box, Garthen watched as one of the figures stopped in front of the Lawbringers, right where he had just vacated, while the other moved into the middle of the speaking area.

Garthen realized now that Kriegon had mentioned these individuals before they sat with the Crimson Order group. Garthen looked around at their box, Tom appearing frustrated but watched on without a word, whereas Bracus seemed to be holding back a smirk.

Just as he turned back to the individual now standing before the king, the hood of the cloak fell away to reveal a strange sight. It appeared to be an identical twin to Kriegon, who stood before them but with midnight black hair and striking blue eyes. The assembly gasped, and murmurs fluttered through the room like disturbed leaves. Unlike Kriegon, he had a nasty smile on his face as he spoke.

"Noble King Abraham, esteemed Lawbringers, and all who bear witness today, I stand before you not as an enemy, but as a seeker of truths." The Lawbringers exchanged uneasy glances, their stoic faces betraying a hint of concern. King Abraham's expression remained unreadable, his gaze fixed on Kriegon's doppelgänger, as if trying to decipher an ancient script.

"Speak your piece, stranger. But be warned, this court does not tolerate deceit." The king sounded wary but firm.

The stranger's smile turned toward the rest of the quiet and watching court, a chilling thing, devoid of warmth but full of intent. "Deceit, Your Majesty, is often in the eye of the beholder. I am here to offer a perspective, a truth perhaps overlooked by those in attendance today. But first, you know my brother and his friends, the Guardians. And so should you know my name, Vladmir. It is a good name, is it not …?" Vladmir paused as if waiting for acknowledgment that didn't come. "Be that as it may, back to the topic at hand. Truth is a defined term, yet this kingdom has stretched and altered its true meaning to keep those like dear Kanah from succeeding." A minor uproar came from Denither and Tom, but Vladmir raised his voice, seeming to drown out all the others. "I am here to tear down that injustice of a system for the Guardians and my brother!"

Then, in a swift, fluid motion, Vladmir reached beneath his cloak and pulled out what to Garthen looked like a black relic, a double tube connected to a strange wooden handle, pointing it at Tom Cabal. "Gun!" Kriegon screamed. Garthen was pulled off to the side. The blast was deafening, the smoke thick. Tom fell, shock frozen on his face.

As if by the force of the blast, Vladmir fell back into the king, who was too shocked by the scene and the noise. In a flash, the gun, as Kriegon had called it, turned on Duke Denither, and another fireball seemed to completely obstruct the throne briefly. When the smoke cleared, Denither lay on the ground in front of the other jury members, bleeding. Vladmir and King Abraham were gone, the plate glass window to the side of the throne smashed.

The ringing in Garthen's ears started to fade as he heard Zenmore yelling at Rei to go after them. Garthen went to turn and instruct the same of Rei, if possible, to carry him to the base of the cliff, which he knew was just on the other side of the window, when his heart seemed to stop for the second time.

His daughter, Beatrice, stood before him. Skin ice-white with a tear streak frozen on her cheek below terrified eyes. As he struggled against the hand holding him back, Garthen watched his daughter's face twisted into an inhuman smile of pure cruelty. The Lawbringers behind her reached toward her so slowly they might have been stuck in a bog. Like lightning, Beatrice swung a blade made of ice from under her cloak and severed a Lawbringer's hand, which had nearly caught ahold of her. The cloak fell away, and Garthen could now see his daughter's body had been distorted as well, with shards of glass like ice jammed into the shoulder of the arm wielding her deadly blade. With one last look into the nightmare scene of a throne room, Beatrice backflipped out the very same window Vladmir had pulled the king through.

Chapter 11: The Divide and Retreat

The throne room was gripped by supreme chaos, its air hectic with betrayal and the smell of gunpowder. Kriegon watched in disbelief as his doppelgänger, Vladmir, vanished with King Abraham through the shattered window, leaving behind a tableau of destruction. The once ordered and majestic room now echoed with cries of fear and cries for justice Rei, in a flash, followed the girl with the ice blade out the window as the Lawbringer with a missing hand fell to his knees, ice slowly encasing the arm.

"Arrest them!" The voice of Adelisa, sharp and accusatory, cut through the tumult. Her finger, like a dagger, pointed at Kriegon and his fellow Guardians.

To his shock, Helain joined her, his voice rising in panic. "Kill them if you must! They have taken the king!"

Kriegon's heart raced—this was not the plan. They were supposed to be heroes, not fugitives. He pulled Garthen's arm, which he still had hold of; however, Garthen was trying hard to follow Rei out the window. "Garthen! We need to go!" Kriegon knew one thing as the Lawbringers were trying to bring order back to the room: they needed to get out of here.

"I need to go after my daughter." Garthen's heartbroken explanation gave Kriegon a shock he didn't need at this time. Before Garthen could slip away, Zenmore, with his formidable strength, scooped him up, his struggles futile against the giant's grasp.

Saphire called to the others with Vittel standing next to her. "Where are we to go?"

Ryoma appeared then. "Denither is dead. You all need to escape. Quickly, back to the Felix mansion."

Vittel, his voice a beacon amidst the storm, commanded, "Go now; we have been betrayed. I will try to get things under control."

Kriegon took charge of the escape. He pushed through the crowd, treating any who got in his team's way as an enemy, Coolgen following his example next to him. The air outside was no less charged, but the path to the mansion was momentarily clear.

Quickly making their way into the front hall, Kriegon turned to see Rei land just outside and follow the group in. "The trees are too thick at the base of the cliff. But we have a bigger issue. A mob is making its way here, chanting 'down with the false Guardians.'"

"That is too quick. What do we do? Where can we go?" Ellena's concern reflected Kriegon's. He looked to Garthen, but he was limp under Zenmore's arm, a defeated man.

They needed a leader now more than ever, and he tried to step into it. "We need to get out of here now. Do we have a secret tunnel or those magic runes?"

Ryoma was rummaging through a satchel that blended into his black robe and walking over to Rei. "Found it. Rei, you know what to do." He handed Rei a flat stone slab with a rune on the surface. Rei seemed to recognize the object, grabbed it, and quickly ran outside and took to the sky. Everyone looked at Ryoma, who already had an identical slab out of the bag and was setting it on the ground.

"So do you just carry around those teleportation slabs everywhere?" asked Kriegon, who had realized what the device was after watching Rei use it before.

Ryoma's smile was thin, his focus on the task at hand. "In times of need, yes. These slabs are our ticket out of here." The group gathered around, their eyes on Ryoma, who now seemed their only link to salvation. "This isn't just a simple escape," he explained, his voice steady despite the chaos encroaching upon their sanctuary. "The rune will light up when Rei channels the magic from the other side. It's our signal. Make sure you have everything you need; this journey isn't reversible once the last of us are through."

The gravity of his words spurred the group into action. Kriegon, feeling the significance of their precarious situation, ordered Ellena and Saphire to grab anything they might need before following them in a mad dash through the corridors of the Felix mansion. His room yielded little in the way of essentials, but he grabbed what clothes he could, his hands moving with a purpose he hadn't known in this world until now.

In Rei's study, Saphire was a whirlwind of activity, stuffing items into a burlap sack with no regard for order. Kriegon joined her, adding his clothes to the pile, then grabbing whatever seemed useful or valuable—books, herbs, scrolls, and an odd, pulsing stone that caught his eye. Together, they hurried back to the front, the sounds of the mob growing louder, more insistent.

Back in the entrance hall, the air was thick with tension. The mob was at the gates, their chants a cacophony of anger. Some of their companions had already vanished through the magic. Saphire raced over with the sack and placed one hoof on the slab. With a rush of wind, she was gone.

"How many more?" Kriegon's voice was tight, his gaze flicking between the courtyard and Ryoma, who was now visibly strained from the magic's toll.

"Just Ellena," Ryoma replied, his face etched with the effort of maintaining the spell. "But we can't wait much longer."

Kriegon didn't need to be told twice and raced back upstairs, calling for Ellena. He found her in Garthen's study, her arms overloaded with items she couldn't bear to leave behind. Without a word, he scooped her up with everything she carried, ignoring her protests, and hurried back to Ryoma. The urgency was unmistakable; the mob's advance was relentless.

"We all go now!" Kriegon declared, stepping onto the slab, Ellena still in his arms. The world around them blurred into a whirl of colors as Ryoma activated the rune. For a moment, Kriegon felt as if he were being pulled in all directions, his stomach lurching with the disorienting sensation. Then, as abruptly as it began, it ended, and they were standing in a forest, the distant walls of Riversong visible through the trees.

With a slight cough, Ellena asked, "You mind?"

He looked down and flushed slightly while placing the red-faced Ellena on her feet.

Rei was leaning against a tree, panting just as heavily as Ryoma.

"Cabitha ran off to get us a carriage from near the gate."

Zenmore, attempting to lighten the mood with a half-hearted joke, remarked, "Good, because hoofing it would be a real pain."

Saphire, however, was in no mood for levity. "This isn't the time, Zenmore!" she snapped, her frustration evident.

Ignoring the bickering, Zenmore adjusted Garthen, still under his arm, and began walking towards the road.

Ryoma, his face still marked by the strain of the teleportation, spoke up. "I need to return to Riversong. My guild needs to be moved to safety. We can't leave them to face whatever comes next alone."

The group exchanged looks of disbelief and concern. Kriegon couldn't hide his surprise. "You're going back? Now?"

Ryoma nodded, his decision firm. "My guild ... they're not just magicians; they're like my family. They need to know where to find us, and I need to ensure they get there safely."

Kriegon understood the emphasis of loyalty and duty in Ryoma's voice. It mirrored his own feelings towards his new companions in this strange world. "What about us? What do we do?"

"You head south," Ryoma instructed, his gaze sweeping over the group. "Orris's father's domain is well fortified and secluded. It should be safe enough for now. I'll join you there once I've done what I can."

Rei, still catching her breath, added, "The carriage should be here soon. Cabitha should have enough coin."

As if on cue, the sound of wheels crunching over forest underbrush announced Cabitha's arrival. The horse-drawn carriage, modest but sturdy, pulled up beside them.

"Everyone, let's move!" Kriegon urged, his voice full of command and concern.

The group began to load into the carriage, their movements coordinated yet tinged with the silent understanding of their precarious situation. Zenmore, with Garthen slung over his shoulder, was the last to board, his massive frame making the carriage creak slightly under the added bulk.

Kriegon, standing by the door, looked back at Ryoma one last time. "Be careful," he said, the words carrying more weight than he intended.

Ryoma managed a small, reassuring smile. "I will. Keep them safe, Kriegon."

With that, Kriegon climbed into the carriage, and through a flick of the reins, they were moving. The forest around them was silent, save for the rhythmic clatter of the carriage wheels and the occasional rustle of leaves in the gentle breeze. Inside, the atmosphere was tense; each member of the group was lost in their thoughts, the stress of their escape from Riversong hard upon them.

Ellena, seated beside Kriegon, leaned in slightly. "Do you think he'll make it back?" Her voice was a whisper, meant only for him.

Kriegon met her gaze, his own expression a mask of concern. "Ryoma's resourceful. If anyone can navigate through chaos, it's him." His words were meant to comfort, but he hoped the uncertainty in his heart didn't betray the confidence he tried to show.

The journey through the dense forest, the path south winding and occasionally rough. Orris, sitting opposite Kriegon, seemed lost in thought, her fingers nervously twirling a strand of her hair. "My father's domain is several days' journey from here," she finally said, her voice steady but carrying an undercurrent of worry. "We'll have to be cautious. The roads aren't safe with the unrest."

Cabitha, who was driving, called back, "We'll take the lesser-known paths for a couple days. Less chance of running into trouble that way."

As the day waned, the forest around them began to thin, revealing glimpses of the open fields. The sun dipped below the horizon, casting long shadows and bathing the landscape in a soft, golden light.

Zenmore, who had been silent, spoke up, his deep voice rumbling through the carriage. "We should set up camp soon. It's not safe to travel at night, especially not now."

Kriegon agreed with the suggestion, calling to Cabitha to find a small clearing as soon as possible. For the first time he reflected on what had just happened. How could there be another him? It had used his joke call sign when in the military, the bantered name now twisted with murder. Looking at the others, he could see each of them reflecting, not meeting his gaze. This worried him; they needed to be united now more than ever, but unlike his fellow soldiers before, he didn't know how to lift their spirits now. Or if their spirits should be lifted.

As the carriage slowed and stopped, Kriegon helped Ellena down, feeling the cool evening air against his skin. They set about making camp, the tasks of gathering wood for a fire and setting up a simple perimeter around their resting spot providing a momentary distraction from their worries.

Zenmore and Garthen, who now walked almost zombielike on his own, headed off into the forest. Kriegon could see them leaning against a nearby tree but isolated from the rest of the group.

Saphire, with a newfound cheerfulness in Zenmore's absence, took charge of organizing the supplies, her usual stern demeanor softened by the night's tranquility. "We'll need to keep watch," she reminded everyone, her voice carrying authority yet kindness.

Kriegon found himself sitting by the fire, the flames casting dancing shadows across the ground. He watched as Ellena tended to the food, her brow furrowed, her concern evident. He couldn't help but feel a deepening connection to her, throughout the training at Felix mansion, and now, she seemed unwavering. It reminded him of his mother and his friends' tough wives, always putting their best foot forward. He admired that now more than ever as the dark settled around them.

In the night, the forest came alive with the sounds of nocturnal creatures. The group took turns at watch, the quiet hours stretching into the early morning. Kriegon's turn came, and he sat vigil, twisting his staff in his hands, wishing more than ever he had his service rifle back. The potential futures passed through his mind, the uncertainty in this situation where there was no safety net, no higher command structure giving him a directive. They were out on their own, and he couldn't think of the best move to keep their mission alive both in actions and in heart.

As the first light of dawn cast its gentle glow over the camp, the Guardians found themselves at a crossroads, both literally and metaphorically. The peace of the morning opposed the internal turmoil brewing within the group as they prepared to journey on. However, the packing was interrupted when Garthen called a private meeting with the Guardians, away from the others.

"I'm going back," Garthen declared, his voice ladened with resolve, yet it sparked an immediate uproar among Ellena and Rei. Their protests were fierce, a mix of concern and frustration. Kriegon had thought this might happen but stayed silent from his own objections.

Garthen raised his hand, a silent plea for calm. The protests died down, but the air was thick with dissent. "I must return, not to reclaim my role as a Guardian, but as a father. My daughter needs me, now more than ever."

Ellena's response was sharp, her pain intense. "And what about us, Garthen? We need you too." Her words must have been a dagger to his heart, yet his resolve did not waver.

"My duty to my daughter supersedes all," Garthen replied, his face, uncovered from the normal disguise, marked by the scars of his past and present anguish.

In a moment of raw emotion, Ellena's hand met Garthen's cheek with a slap that echoed through the quiet morning. Tears streaked down her face as she walked away, her words trailing behind her. "Go then, but remember, chasing ghosts won't heal you."

The silence that followed was thick, laden with unspoken thoughts and emotions. Garthen turned to Kriegon. Expecting a word of wisdom or the passing of leadership, Kriegon straightened. "Kriegon, about your brother's weapon yesterday ... Can you tell me how to defend against such a thing?"

Kriegon, momentarily taken aback, shook his head. "That wasn't my brother. I don't know who that person was or where they came from. And the gun is useless; the gun must have fallen through the portal into this world with me, and I only had two shots."

"Then who was that? What aren't you telling us?" Saphire pushed.

Kriegon swallowed dryly, watching the people he trusted look back in suspicion. "I truly don't know what happened to me … When Lucifer touched me … He was in my place. I wish I knew more, but I really don't."

Everyone continued to look at him with various levels of distrust before Rei cleared her throat and interrupted the silence with her motherly tone. "Well, until we understand better, we just need to be mindful who Vladmir is to us. Kriegon, can he make more of those shots?"

Kriegon shook his head, thinking back to his own world. He hadn't learned how to load bullets, and the technology here wouldn't be accurate enough to produce the shells needed. "Let's just say that this world has a long way to go before catching up to that particular device."

Satisfied with this explanation, Garthen turned to Zenmore, his plea barely concealed. "Please, come with me. Your tracking skills are unmatched."

Zenmore, initially reluctant, grumbled. "But the rest of the clan …" He looked towards Kriegon and then to Rei.

Rei touched him on the arm. "If we can't convince him not to go, it would be safer if he wasn't alone." With a deep sigh, Zenmore nodded.

Garthen, turning back to Rei, asked, "Do we have communication scrolls? We need to stay in touch."

Rei nodded, disappearing with Saphire to fetch the scrolls. Kriegon looked to Garthen, waiting for something … anything, but the man he now looked up to just waited silently. The wait was tense, each second stretching into an eternity. When they returned, Rei handed Garthen a scroll, embracing him in a heartfelt hug. Saphire, with less ceremony but equal concern, threw a pack at Zenmore, loaded with supplies.

Kriegon watched, emotions swirling inside him. Garthen, without another word or glance back, set off north through the woods, Zenmore following with a toothy grin aimed at Kriegon and Rei. The forest swallowed them, leaving the rest of the group to head back to the carriage. Kriegon felt the disappearance of Garthen in such a way that it left an empty spot in his heart. One without a leader to trust or look to.

The days following Garthen and Zenmore's departure were marked by a profound shift within the group. The carriage rides were filled with a silence that spoke volumes, the group grappling with the void left by their comrades. Saphire's mood seemed to lighten, her usual stern demeanor softening in Zenmore's absence, but Ellena's spirit appeared to dim compared to the strong person he had seen, her eyes often distant, her laughter rare.

Kriegon, who found himself increasingly the silent confidant, felt Ellena's weight against him more often, her head resting on his shoulder or lap as if seeking comfort in his proximity. He couldn't deny the warmth her presence brought, yet his mind was elsewhere, tormented by the sudden appearance of his doppelgänger, Vladmir, and Garthen's apparent disregard for his trust or potential leadership. Kriegon's thoughts were a tumultuous sea of frustration and confusion. His knowledge of a more advanced society, his readiness to step up, seemed to be ignored, leaving him feeling both undervalued and oddly disconnected from his own emotions.

On the fifth night since parting ways, Kriegon took the first watch. The group had crossed into Felix territory, and a sense of tentative peace had settled over them. Seizing the opportunity for solitude, Kriegon excused himself for a walk, the forest's edge calling to him as the sun dipped low, casting long shadows across their path.

As he ventured deeper, the forest enveloped him in its quiet embrace, the soft rustle of leaves underfoot a counterpoint to his racing thoughts. His frustration with Garthen's departure, the lack of acknowledgment, and his own inexplicable emotional fluctuations created a storm within him. Just as he was about to give in to the urge to vent his anger on the nearest tree, the feeling abruptly dissipated, leaving him bewildered.

"What is happening to me?" he muttered, his gaze falling on his staff as if seeking answers within its metal.

Then, from the shadows, a voice, chillingly familiar yet utterly foreign, responded, "Did I get our intelligence in the split?"

Kriegon spun around, his heart racing, to find Vladmir, his doppelgänger, leaning against a tree, the shotgun casually aimed at him. The sight of himself, or rather, this other version, was jarring, a mirror reflecting not just his face but a twisted version of his soul.

"What the hell are you?" Kriegon demanded, his voice a mix of fear and anger.

Vladmir's smile was cold, his eyes calculating. "The better half, it seems. Remember Lucifer splitting us when we first arrived in this world?"

The memory was foggy, fragmented by shock and pain, but Vladmir's words triggered a recollection of that moment of division. Kriegon's mind raced, trying to reconcile this reality with his fragmented memories. Anger rose again in Kriegon like it used to when he was gearing up for a fight, but then … it was gone, pulled away as if it were never there.

Vladmir sucked in a sharp breath. "Aw, that's the stuff." He smiled demonically as Kriegon tried to piece things together.

"What have you done to me?"

Vladmir's next move was swift; he closed the distance between them, pressing the gun's barrel under Kriegon's chin. "I take what makes us stronger," he whispered, his breath cold against Kriegon's skin. "And they have made me a much stronger man than if we were still stuck in the same body." Then, with a swift motion, he struck Kriegon with the gun's butt in the face, sending him sprawling against the roots of a tree, his staff dropping at Vladmir's feet.

As Kriegon struggled to rise and looking up at the smirking face, Kriegon asked, "How is this even possible?"

"Well, that would give away too much fun, wouldn't it? All I will say is Lucifer and the angels know magic to a far better extent than any world can hope to know. After all, it is their language that God bestowed on them in the beginning of all things. It's a language of creation, of power."

Kriegon's mind reeled at the casual revelation of cosmic truths from Vladmir's lips, truths that seemed to unravel the very fabric of his understanding of good and evil, of power and knowledge. "Why would Lucifer tell you this?"

Bending down and picking up Kriegon's staff, Vladmir casually dropped the gun, discarding it as if it were nothing but a toy. The proximity showed a bruise forming on Vladmir's face, as he had just been struck as well. "Such an interesting bit of metal. You must be like me right now and want to study it so much further." He stepped away and held the staff up with an academic curiosity to one of the last rays of light shining through the trees.

Kriegon watched closely while slowly shifting toward the discarded gun. Vladmir didn't turn or answer him but continued to examine the metal staff with hard eyes until the ray of light faded. As it did, Kriegon's fingers wrapped around the wooden handle and trigger, a sharp feeling of normalcy in this strange world.

Vladmir, absorbed in his examination of the staff, didn't notice Kriegon's movement until the moment Kriegon aimed and pulled the trigger. The click of the firing pin was a hollow sound, echoing the emptiness of the gun and Kriegon's hope. Vladmir's smirk widened as he turned, his eyes mocking.

"You asked why Lucifer would share such knowledge," Vladmir began, his voice smooth, almost reasonable. "He offers power, the kind that reshapes worlds. Knowledge has always been his currency, from Eden to the ends of the cosmos. Why resist? What he offers could bring order, peace, a new world paradise."

Kriegon's rebuttal was fierce, his voice shaking not from fear but from anger. "Peace? At what cost? Look around! This land is bleeding because of his influence, his manipulations."

Vladmir's laugh was cold, devoid of warmth or humor. "Humans, mortals, bleed themselves. They invited chaos, sought power beyond their grasp. Lucifer merely answered their call. But you…" He paused, pressing the staff against Kriegon's chest. "You have a choice. Join us. Help us build a realm where peace isn't just a dream but a reality. A place where we can shape destiny."

The proposal hung in the air, heavy with implications. Kriegon's mind raced, torn between his duty as a Guardian and the allure of an ultimate peace, one that might justify the means, however dark. Could joining forces with Vladmir and Lucifer be the path to fulfilling the prophecy? The idea was seductive, the thought of two halves reuniting to bring about a new era.

Vladmir stepped back, placing the staff against a nearby tree, his movements deliberate, as if giving Kriegon space to think, to breathe. "Time is a luxury you no longer have," he said, his voice now carrying a note of urgency. "Your friends will start to worry. Here," he said, tossing a small scroll towards Kriegon, who caught it instinctively. "This will allow you to contact me when you decide. We move towards Asceriate soon, within two months by this world's calendar."

The scroll felt dense in Kriegon's hand, not the mass but the burden of decision it represented. As Vladmir's figure began to dissolve into the shadows of the forest, his final words lingered. "Don't take too long, Kriegon. Destiny waits for no one."

When Kriegon was left alone, the forest seemed to close in around him, the trees whispering secrets of the universe, of power and choice. His mind was a whirlwind of thoughts. Could working with Vladmir and Lucifer truly bring peace? Was the prophecy speaking of him and Vladmir reuniting as one? The questions were endless, each more daunting than the last.

Returning to the camp, Kriegon's steps were slow, his mind far from the physical path he trod. When he entered the camp, his companions turned toward him with a mixture of concern and curiosity. The scroll burned in his pocket, a silent testament to the crossroads at which he now stood.

As Kriegon settled himself a short distance from the fire's glow,

Ellena came, her form barely visible in the dim light, her steps quiet against the forest floor. She must have noticed the shadow of a bruise forming on his cheek, as she touched it lightly. Concern etched her features as she sat beside him, her presence a silent question.

Kriegon, feeling the weight of her gaze, whispered the tale of his meeting with Vladmir, his voice low, the words thick with the gravity of the situation. He spoke of the offer, the choice laid before him, and the scroll now hidden away, a secret burden he chose not to share with the group. "Keep this between us," he implored, his eyes searching hers for understanding, for secrecy. "I need time to think, to decide our path."

Ellena's eyes hardened. "Why? You aren't alone in this, and the group should know about Vladmir if he is aligned with Lucifer."

Kriegon exhaled heavily before answering. "I know myself pretty well ... even my darker side. If I am doing something like aligning with Lucifer, I must truly believe that's what is best. Who knows? That line in the prophecy about a villain guiding us and the two halves becoming whole. It's a lot to think about, to question how to go about it."

Ellena shook her head. "But you are still putting all this on yourself. Maybe talking with me puts a little on me, but I can tell you're trying to carry a burden we all should share."

Kriegon looked into her fierce eyes as he answered her. "It's what is best. In this case, I know not to burden others with this kind of choice. I will make it for us, if or when the time comes. So please, keep this between us until the time is right. I'll make the best choice."

Ellena looked into his eyes for a long moment before nodding, her face a mask of worry and resolve. "Your secret is safe with me, Kriegon. We'll face whatever comes, together."

The night deepened around them, the fire's crackle a distant comfort as they sat in silence, Kriegon lost in thought, the significance of the future pressing down like the darkness of the forest itself.

Come morning, with the first light casting a soft glow through the trees, Kriegon rose before the others. His mind was restless, his decision unmade. He ventured back to where the confrontation had occurred, his steps retracing the path of his turmoil. The gun lay where it had fallen, a silent relic of another world, another life. He picked it up, feeling its cold heft, a reminder of his vulnerability, of the potential power that would make this journey so much easier.

With a sense of purpose, Kriegon found a secluded spot, a tree with roots exposed like the veins of the earth. Here, he hid the gun, covering it with leaves and soil, a secret to be kept or revealed when the time was right. As he walked back to camp, the morning air crisp against his face, he felt the burden of secrecy, of decisions yet to be made, weighing heavily upon him.

His companions were stirring now, the camp coming to life with the soft sounds of morning routines. Ellena caught his eye, her look one of silent support. Kriegon nodded slightly, a silent acknowledgment of their shared secrecy. Today, life in the camp would go on as usual, but beneath the surface, Kriegon's mind was a battlefield, his heart divided between duty, desire, and the daunting unknown that lay ahead.

A few days later, the group found themselves in a bustling town. As they unloaded from the carriage, Orris seemed to come to light. "The Crossroads at last! This is the center of my father's domain, offering the best routes north, south, east, and west. With this we are merely a day away from Swiftswallow, where my father's estate is." She paused, looking back at the group shuffling near the carriage.

Kriegon could tell Rei and Saphire were nervous about being seen. Even Ellena flicked up her hood and seemed to shrink from passing villagers. However, Orris came over with a smile. "No need to worry here. Since you are with me, and everyone knows me from past visits, you are safe. I even know a great little inn with the best food!"

The inn they chose for their repast was alive with the sounds of travelers and locals alike, making conversation an endeavor of raised voices. The group, including Kriegon, was slightly cautious of being called out for being so different. Orris was right, however; a majority of people that greeted them knew she was the Earl's daughter and gave them comfort. As they sat at a large table to fit the entire group, no one seemed to look twice at their odd group as they drank and ate.

Kriegon, with the weight of Vladmir's proposition still pressing on his thoughts, sought to grasp any detail that might sway his decision. He leaned towards Cabitha, his voice louder than intended to cut through the tavern's din. "Cabitha, I've been meaning to ask, how does the calendar work here?"

Cabitha, momentarily puzzled, responded with the simplicity of someone explaining the obvious. "It's just days, weeks, and months. Isn't it the same where you're from?"

Kriegon nodded, though his mind was elsewhere. "Yes, but I heard something that makes me think time might flow differently here."

Ellena, catching the drift, gave Kriegon a look that asked more questions than it answered, but the rest of the group remained oblivious to the undercurrent of their exchange.

Cabitha, taking a moment to think, elaborated, "A day here is defined by our sun and moon cycles. A week is seven days, a month is four weeks, and we count twelve months for a year. We're in the year six hundred and thirty-eight AF. Or After Flood."

Kriegon's mind raced, piecing together the implications. "So, each month has exactly twenty-eight days? That would make your year only three hundred and thirty-six days."

"That's correct," Cabitha confirmed, a hint of confusion tinting her voice. "Is there an issue with that?"

Before Kriegon could delve deeper into the discrepancies between their worlds' timekeeping, Rei interjected with her own perspective, her voice carrying a fusion of fascination and academic interest. "That's quite peculiar. My world cycles through forty to forty-five days per month, with ten months to a year."

Kriegon added, "And back home, we had months ranging from twenty-eight to thirty-one days, with twelve months making up a year. It's interesting how time is perceived so differently across worlds."

The conversation naturally turned towards Saphire, who found herself suddenly the focus of everyone's attention. Her expression shifted from surprise to slight discomfort. "What?" she asked, her tone defensive as she set down the flagon.

Ellena, with a gentle curiosity, prodded, "What about your world? How do you measure time there?"

Saphire's response was tinged with bitterness, a reflection of her world's hardships. "We didn't have the luxury of such detailed timekeeping. Day and night, seasons like winter or summer—that's all that mattered. Time was ... less about numbers and more about survival."

The revelation brought a profound silence over the group, as it was a harsh reminder of the diverse realities each member hailed from. Saphire's world, constantly at war, had no place for the leisurely tracking of days.

After a moment to digest this, Kriegon, seeking to shift the mood, turned the conversation towards their immediate future. "Rei, you mentioned teaching us magic. Could we start once we reach Swiftwallow?"

Rei's eyes lit up, her toothy grin returning. "Of course! There's nothing quite like sharing knowledge, especially something as personal as magic. It'll be my pleasure to introduce you all to the wonders of my world's magic."

Chapter 12: Garthen's Hunt and Blood

As Garthen and Zenmore made their way back around Riversong, the initial ease of their journey gave in to a growing tension. The days spent circling the base of the cliff where Vladmir, Abraham, and Beatrice had vanished were fruitless, and the forest, once a place of solace, now teemed with the presence of roving gang members.

From his vantage point among the trees, Garthen observed a particularly brutal scene. A group of Black Crop Gang members, emboldened by the absence of the city's guards, was capturing fleeing citizens. His heart raced as he listened to their vile conversation, their laughter echoing through the forest.

"It sure does make hunting easier with all them guard folk sent north," one gang member sneered, pressing a knife against a young woman's throat.

"Watch it, idiot. Don't damage the goods. We might not have to deal with soldiers, but I don't want to get my pay cut if you kill more slaves," another warned, his tone cold and calculating.

The first gang member's laugh was cut short as Garthen's arrows found their marks, each shot a silent testament to his resolve. As the gang members fell, Garthen descended from the canopy, his movements swift and purposeful.

"Thank you, thank you so much!" the captives exclaimed, their relief plain as Garthen freed them from their bonds.

Ignoring their gratitude, Garthen pressed for information. "What news from the city? They mentioned something about the guards leaving."

A middle-aged man, still trembling with fear, spoke up. "Three days ago, the entire city militia was ordered to reinforce Commander Flavius in the White Woods to take back Windmontley and Malgrave. My son was among them. Then, the gangs and pirates took over, imposing fake taxes. We were trying to escape when they caught us."

"Who's raising these taxes now, with the king missing?" Garthen asked, retrieving his arrows from the fallen gang members.

"The remaining nobles. Lady Cabal and some wealthy noble whose name escapes me," the man replied.

Garthen's mind raced. Could Vladmir or his daughter be connected to this upheaval? Before he could ponder further, Zenmore's voice broke through his thoughts.

"You know, leaving me behind is rather rude," Zenmore said, emerging from the shadows.

The captives, startled by Zenmore's sudden appearance, whispered among themselves. "Wait ... could you two be the Usurpers? The ones accused of kidnapping the king?"

Zenmore's laughter shook the trees, contrasted heavily by Garthen's stern silence. "That's the lie they're spreading now?" Garthen remarked, his gaze fierce.

The group, sensing the danger, quickly apologized and fled into the forest.

Back at their camp, Garthen let his frustration boil over.

"I didn't find anything again today. It's as if those three never landed on the forest floor. There's glass around, but nothing else," Zenmore reported, his tone filled with curiosity and concern.

"It might not be surprising. It's been nearly two weeks since they fell from the throne room," Garthen mused, his thoughts dark and swirling with possibilities. If the gangs and pirates were now openly asserting themselves in Riversong, it was plausible that Vladmir and Beatrice could be hiding within the city's shadows, perhaps even orchestrating these events from the inside.

The notion that the Crimson Order was now openly aligning with the criminal underbelly of the kingdom filled Garthen with a cold dread. His personal quest for Beatrice, now tangled with comforting the corrupt nobles, pushed his patience at the situation.

"What do you think about hunting in the city?" asked Garthen, almost to himself as much as Zenmore next to him.

Zenmore smiled. "Well, it would be a show for all who witness us striding back into the city after what happened last time."

Garthen shook his head. Zenmore clearly didn't understand his thoughts on the situation. "If the gang and pirates are now helping to control the city, we will be walking into intense fighting. We need to be stealthy about this so we can find King Abraham … and my daughter, without a threat to their lives."

Zenmore got up and walked southeast along the cliff face bordering the city. "Either way, it'll be one hell of a story and get me away from this boring standby we have been in."

Quickly getting up and jumping into the trees, Garthen leaped ahead of Zenmore while scouting. Again, for the hundredth time since starting this hunt with Zenmore, Garthen marveled at his new ability to jump through the trees like a shadow. While he had been agile before whatever those cursed mages had done, this was completely on another tier for his speed.

They reached the edge of Riversong just as dusk painted the sky in shades of purple and orange. Climbing the rocky cliff face next to the easternmost wall, they were able to get on top of the battlements with some effort. Luckily, the once watchful wall had been abandoned by the new rulers of the city.

From their elevated position, they could see the city below, its streets teeming with the chaos of gang rule. The once-vibrant markets were now shadowed corners where fear walked openly, and the laughter of children was replaced by the cries of the oppressed.

Garthen's heart ached at the sight. This was once a breathtaking city, now a shell of its former self, overrun by those who sought only profit in its misery. He turned to Zenmore, his resolve hardening. "We move at night. The cover of darkness will be our shield."

Zenmore nodded, his expression serious for once. "Lead the way, Garthen."

As night fell, Garthen and Zenmore, amidst their stealthy pursuit through the shadowed alleys of the city, stumbled upon another group of gang members herding a new batch of slaves. Concealed by the darkness, they observed the gang interacting with a figure whose attire screamed "pirate leader," busy dividing the captives with remarks that were as crass as they were dehumanizing, focusing on the physical attributes and supposed market value of each individual.

Zenmore, tensed and ready to leap from their hiding spot, was halted by Garthen's firm grip. "Wait," Garthen whispered, his voice barely audible. "This could lead us to the others." The pirate leader, with an air of authority, split the slaves into two groups, directing them down different paths through the city.

The decision of whom to follow was agonizing for Garthen, but the sight of the unmistakable large build of Lawbringers, known for their brute strength, in one of the groups tipped the scales. "We follow them," Garthen decided, signaling Zenmore, whose eagerness to engage was unmistakable.

Their pursuit led them to a shipbuilding warehouse, now repurposed as a grim holding pen for the enslaved. Garthen opted for a high window entry, silently dispatching four gang members as he infiltrated. Below, the sound of Zenmore's more direct approach echoed through the warehouse as he charged in, his war hammer-axe combo weapon making short work of his opponents.

Inside, Garthen quickly swept the area, ensuring no more threats lurked in the shadows, and descended to meet Zenmore, who stood over a makeshift card table, now splattered with blood. Five bodies, evidence of Zenmore's brutal efficiency, lay around it, each cut down by his formidable weapon.

"We need to get these people out," Garthen said, urgency in his voice as he began searching the fallen gang members for keys. Zenmore, without a word, started hacking at the locks of the cages with his weapon, the sound of metal yielding to his strength filling the air.

Among the captives, Garthen found Kristin Collin, her face marked by the hardships she'd endured. "Garthen," she gasped, relief evident in her voice, "the Crimson Order, they've taken over. With traitors within our ranks, they've installed themselves as rulers. Bracus has emerged as their leader after accusing Vittel Hero of treachery and executing him.

Stability is crumbling."

Garthen absorbed the information, his mind racing. "What of the other group? The ones taken in a different direction?" he asked, his concern for his daughter and the king clear.

Kristin's face darkened. "I overheard whispers about a chilling place in the slums, something about a 'frosty girl.' It's where they might be taking them," she said, her voice full of fear.

Garthen nodded, the pieces of the puzzle slowly coming together, though the picture was far from complete. "We'll free everyone here first. Then, we find this 'frosty girl' and anyone else they've taken," he declared, attempting to put resolve in his voice for all who could hear him.

Kristin, her face a veneer of determination, rallied the freed prisoners with a commanding presence that showed her noble upbringing. "Alright, listen up," she began, her voice firm. "We're not out of the woods yet. But if we stick together, we'll make it through."

Garthen, watching the scene unfold, couldn't help but admire her leadership. "You've got quite the knack for this, Kristin," he remarked, a hint of respect in his tone.

She flashed him a brief, grim smile. "Years of managing the Azure's affairs. Never thought it would come in handy in a situation like this," she replied, her voice tinged with irony.

Zenmore, itching for action, stepped in. "Garthen, while they organize here, I think it's time we stir the pot elsewhere. If we draw some heat, it might give them a clearer path out," he suggested, his hand already gripping his weapon tighter.

Garthen considered this, nodding slowly. "A distraction could work. But we'll need to be careful not to become the main event," he added, his mind calculating the risks.

Zenmore grinned, a spark of excitement in his eyes. "Oh, let them try to catch us. It'll be one hell of a story to tell!" he said, his tone laced with anticipation.

As they stepped out into the night, Zenmore immediately spotted a group of gang members loitering near the shipbuilding warehouse, their laughter and crude jokes carrying through the air. Without hesitation, he charged, his war hammer-axe combo weapon gleaming ominously in the dim light.

"Zenmore, wait—" Garthen started, but it was too late. Zenmore was already upon them, his weapon swinging with deadly precision. "Or maybe not," Garthen muttered, drawing his bow and preparing to cover his friend.

Zenmore's reasoning for the immediate attack was clear as he fought. "If we can draw their attention here, it'll give Kristin and the others a better chance to slip away unnoticed. Besides, nothing like a good fight to get the blood pumping, right?" he called, his voice booming over the clash and shattering of steel.

Garthen couldn't help but agree, even as he released arrows with practiced ease, each finding its mark. "Just make sure you don't get yourself killed doing it," he shouted back, covering Zenmore's flank as they moved through the gang members like a scythe through a wheat field.

Their strategy worked. The chaos they created outside the shipbuilding warehouse drew more gang members towards them, away from the main escape route Kristin and the others would need. The fighting was fierce, but Garthen and Zenmore were a well-oiled machine, their movements synchronized as if from years of fighting side by side, instead of a few weeks together.

As the last of the immediate threats fell, Garthen looked around, scanning for any sign of the dark magic's influence or the other group of captives. "We should head toward the slums. If there's any place where dark magic could be hiding, it's there," he suggested, his voice serious.

Zenmore, catching his breath, nodded. "Lead on, Garthen. Let's find your daughter and put an end to this nightmare," he said, determination etched in every line of his face.

With that, they set off into the night, their path lit by the faint glow of the moon, their hearts steeled for what lay ahead in the slums of Riversong, where shadows whispered of unseen evils and the air was thick with the promise of a confrontation that could change everything.

Their journey through the darkened streets of Riversong was tense, each step taking them closer to the heart of the city's rat-infested district. The slums loomed ahead, a labyrinth of despair where the air seemed to thrum with a malevolent energy.

Garthen kept his eyes and senses peeled for any sign of the dark magic that had once plagued Neil Paris's city and Windmontley. "It's here, I can feel it," he muttered, his voice barely above a whisper yet carrying the stress of his concern.

Zenmore, walking alongside him, cracked his knuckles, ready for whatever might come their way. "Let's hope this magic has a face we can punch," he quipped, trying to lighten the mood, though his eyes were hard, scanning for danger.

As they neared a particularly decrepit building, the source of the ominous feeling became undeniable. The air around it was colder, the shadows deeper, as if the structure itself were a conduit for the dark energies at play.

Before they could plan their approach, a shadow moved across the two moons, momentarily eclipsing its light. Both Garthen and Zenmore looked up in time to see the silhouette of a wyvern, its wings casting a chilling shadow over the slums. It let out a piercing cry before gliding eastward, disappearing into the night sky.

"That's our sign," Garthen said, his voice low with determination and dread. "Whatever's happening, it's connected to that creature."

Zenmore nodded, his expression grim. "Time to crash the party then," he said, moving towards the building with purpose.

With Zenmore leading, they approached the entrance. Before Garthen could suggest a stealthier infiltration, Zenmore, in his characteristic style, decided action was the best plan. He kicked the door open with a force that sent it crashing against the wall inside. Immediately, they were met with resistance.

Inside, the scene was chaotic. Three figures cloaked in dark robes, reminiscent of the mages they'd encountered before, were preparing some dark rite. But what caught Garthen's breath was the sight of Beatrice, her face seeming devoid of any emotion or understanding of what was happening around her.

Garthen's heart skipped a beat, his resolve faltering for a moment as he nocked an arrow, aimed not at an enemy, but at his own daughter, now a puppet of the dark forces at play.

Zenmore, noticing Garthen's hesitation, took the lead, charging at the mages with his weapon swinging. "Garthen, now's not the time to freeze up!" he yelled, his voice cutting through the haze of Garthen's shock.

The battle was swift but brutal. Zenmore's sheer force and Garthen's precise archery took down the mages and others that appeared from shadowy back rooms, but the presence of Beatrice left Garthen in a state of turmoil.

"Beatrice," Garthen whispered, his voice breaking as he lowered his bow, unable to take the shot. The room seemed to close in around him, the weight of the situation pressing on his shoulders.

Zenmore, his chest heaving with the exertion of battle, stood amidst the fallen, his gaze shifting between Garthen and Beatrice that of concern. The air was thick with the aftermath of violence, every breath they took tinged with the metallic scent of blood and the cold, dank smell of decay that seemed to seep from the walls of the dilapidated building.

Garthen, his heart a tumultuous storm of hope, fear, and an unbearable pain of loss, let his bow clatter to the ground. The sound echoed in the silent room, a call of the battle's end and the personal war that was just beginning. He approached Beatrice, his steps heavy with dread, each one a silent plea for the return of his daughter from whatever dark abyss had claimed her.

"Beatrice, love." Garthen's voice broke the silence, his tone a blend of fatherly affection and desperate hope. As he neared, her face, once so familiar and full of life, now bore the twisted, unnatural smile of someone lost to themselves, her eyes reflecting a cold, icy void.

A two-tone voice emanated from her, a chilling harmony of her own sweet one and something else, something that sounded like the grinding of ice against stone. "O Father, how you've changed." The words were a dagger to his heart, yet he reached out, his hands finding her shoulders, ignoring the sharp bite of the ice that seemed to grow from her very skin.

"Please, come back to me," Garthen whispered, his voice a command and plea. "Fight whatever's inside you. I know you're in there, Beatrice."

But his plea was met with a cold defiance. An ice sword materialized in her hand, its tip finding its way to his chest, then sliding upwards to rest against his throat. "What if I don't want to come back? This power … this freedom is amazing," the chilling voice declared, a complete contrast to the warmth he remembered in her soul.

Garthen's response was desperate, his voice cracking under the strain of his emotions. "You must. It's only you and me in this world now. Your mom, she's gone. I need you, just as much as you need me."

A crack appeared in the icy facade. Beatrice blinked, tears like frost melting on her cheeks, and her voice, now unmistakably her own, trembled with fear and recognition. "Dad?"

That single word, filled with all the vulnerability of the child he once knew, broke through Garthen's resolve. He pulled her into a tight embrace, feeling her drop the sword with a dull thud, a symbol of her return from the brink. If he could have wept, his tears would have fallen then, mingling with hers, but relief was a fleeting guest in the cold room.

Zenmore, standing guard by the door, coughed to draw attention. "This isn't good," he muttered, his voice severe with foreboding. Outside, the threat was far from over; a gruff voice demanded surrender, promising a quick end if they complied, followed by cheers and jeers that spoke of a bloodthirsty mob.

Garthen, reluctantly releasing his daughter, turned to assess their situation with Zenmore, who was peering through a crack in the wall. "How many are there?" Garthen's voice was tense, his mind racing for a plan.

"Too many," Zenmore replied, his usual battle-ready demeanor replaced by an admission of dire odds. This was not the Zenmore Garthen knew, the fighter who never backed down from a challenge, which meant their situation was dire indeed. Without a word, Zenmore quickly moved to the door and put his shoulder against it. A second later, something slammed into the door, but Zenmore's strength held. "You take her out through the roof, my friend. I'll find another way."

Garthen shook his head as he stepped away from his daughter. "No, we will find a way out together." He wasn't about to leave someone who felt as close to him as a brother.

Garthen's refusal to leave anyone behind, especially not his daughter or Zenmore, was met with the harsh reality of their circumstances. He thought desperately for a plan, but fate dealt a cruel hand.

"Dad …" Beatrices voice came from behind him, a desperate moan. He turned back to see her quickly snatch up the ice blade and lunge at him. Garthen, with reflexes honed by years of combat and the new agility born of his cursed body, dodged her attack, his heart breaking with each desperate call to his daughter to fight the darkness within.

"I can't! I can't! I can't!" Beatrice's voice, an amalgamation of her own terror and the control of the magic, echoed through the decaying room. Garthen, in a desperate move, slid across the blood-soaked floor to his fallen bow. With a quick twist, he pinned her blade between them so he could reach out, wiping a frozen tear from her cheek.

Just as he thought he might reach the part of her that was still fighting, a cold wind blasted through the room, pushing Garthen back. Beatrice became the eye of a swirling vortex of ice, her control slipping further away.

"I'm sorry, Father! I can't contain it!" she screamed, the center of chaos.

Garthen, fighting against the gale, reached out to her, his voice a beacon in the storm. "Please! You can!" But as he extended his hand, he watched in horror as Beatrice turned the blade on herself, aiming it at her heart. His cry of "NO!" was swallowed by the wind, the blade finding its mark before he could intervene.

The storm ceased as quickly as it had begun, leaving Beatrice kneeling, the frost and ice spreading from the buried blade in her body. Garthen was there in an instant, cradling her as she whispered her last words. "I ... love ..." The ice consumed her, and with her last breath, she was gone, leaving Garthen with a void no amount of warmth could fill.

"No, please God, no." He stroked her face as frost moved across her. In the silence that followed, a rage unlike any he had known before took hold of Garthen. He carefully laid Beatrice down, her body now a frozen monument to his failure and loss. He reached for his bow, for once wishing he held blades in his hands again as he trembled with pure hate. His bow split into two at the hand grip, forming long, curved, wicked blades.

"Move," he commanded, his voice a low growl, his eyes burning with the fire of retribution as he looked at a stunned, terrified Zenmore. On the other side of that door stood his enemies, who had sided with the disgusting demons. They took everything from him ... He was going to return the favor.

Zenmore slowly shook his head, eyes wide. But the depth of Garthen's despair and rage would not be contained. Garthen launched himself through a hole in the roof, his new weapons gleaming with a deadly promise.

From above, Garthen surveyed the mob below, his mind no longer on survival but on destruction. He descended upon them like a vengeful spirit, his blades singing through the air, a dance of death that left none standing in its wake. The streets became a canvas of his grief, painted with the blood of those who had dared to stand against him.

Zenmore, following Garthen, tried to reach him, to pull him back from the brink of madness, but Garthen was beyond reach, his actions fueled by a need to destroy what had destroyed his world. It was only when Zenmore physically blocked a strike, his hand pierced by

153

Garthen's blade, that the red haze of vengeance began to lift.

"Garthen, stop! You're about to hurt yourself further," Zenmore pleaded, his voice breaking through the fog of rage.

Garthen, looking around, saw the terrified faces of the captured citizens he had nearly slaughtered, their fear a mirror to his own internal turmoil. The realization of what he had almost done, what he had become in his grief, was a cold splash of reality. He pulled back, his blades lowering, the fire in his eyes dimming into a smoldering ember of sorrow.

Zenmore, his hand still bleeding, placed it on Garthen's shoulder, a gesture of solidarity and understanding. "You're hurt. Let's get back to Kristin and the others. They can help get this group to safety, and we can go," he suggested, his voice a calming force amidst the chaos.

Garthen nodded numbly, attempting to wipe away the blood that stained his cracked skin, a futile effort against the evidence of his rage. He looked around once more, the bodies of his enemies a grim reminder of the price of vengeance. "Take them. I'll follow soon," he managed, his voice hollow.

As Zenmore led the survivors away, Garthen returned to the house, to Beatrice. He knelt beside her frozen form, his hand hovering over her face, not daring to touch the ice that had claimed her. "Goodbye, my love," he whispered, a promise of vengeance left unsaid.

Chapter 13: Learning Magic

Swiftwallow bustled with the vibrant chaos typical of a lively metropolis at the peak of the afternoon. The city's heart, where Felix Zella's mansion stood, was not just the family residence but also a hub for government officials, making it a nexus of power and activity. The main square, a mosaic of stalls and voices, was alive with the barter and banter of merchants and commoners.

The Guardians' carriage, Coolgen navigating through this lively scene, halted abruptly. A well-dressed man, with an air of authority, clambered onto the driver's seat next to Coolgen. "Hello there, friend. We can't allow passage carriages through this way. Surprising you've made it this far without the guard stopping you."

Kriegon, peering through a small carriage window, noticed Coolgen's discomfort. This was the third such encounter on their journey through to the city's heart. Orris, with her usual assertiveness, leaned out, her voice sharp enough to cut through the din. "Perhaps, instead of interrogating my friend, you could inform my father of our imminent arrival."

Her command sent the man scurrying away, his earlier confidence replaced by urgency. Ellena, seated next to Kriegon, chuckled. "I guess we won't be surprising your dad after all."

Orris shrugged, settling back into her seat. "Ryoma probably sent word ahead with one of his scrolls."

The carriage moved slowly, weaving through the crowd, until they finally reached the mansion's steps. Descending from the carriage, the group stretched and murmured about the comfort of a bed after their long journey. As they ascended the steps, they were met with a line of men and women, all pausing in the mansion's grand entryway.

The atmosphere was thick with anticipation, not the quiet return Kriegon had imagined. Before he could ponder further, a voice boomed from the staircase, "So, Ryoma wasn't spinning tales, unlike the rest of the reports!"

"Hello, Father!" Orris beamed, pushing through the crowd towards him with the group in tow.

Felix Zella stood at the top of the stairs, a robust man in his middle age, his black hair laced with streaks of gray. His face lit up with a broad smile as he enveloped Orris in a bear hug, lifting her off her feet. "Come now, let's not stand here. I've had the maids prepare your favorite tea."

Leading them down the hall, with Orris still in his side embrace, Felix was both commanding and welcoming. The mansion's interior was as grand as its exterior promised, with high ceilings and walls adorned with portraits and tapestries that spoke of the Zella family's long-standing influence. The group followed Felix, their footsteps echoing softly against the polished marble floors.

As they walked, Felix's voice carried a warmth that filled the expansive hallway. "I've heard tales of your journey, though I'm eager to receive them all from you directly. And your timing couldn't be better; we have much to discuss."

The room they entered was a blend of opulence and comfort, with plush seating arranged around a large fireplace, above which hung a portrait of a younger Felix with his family. The windows allowed natural light to flood the space, highlighting the intricate woodwork and the rich fabrics of the furnishings.

Felix gestured for everyone to sit as a maid entered with a silver tray laden with a teapot and cups. "Tea for everyone, and then we can talk strategy. Ryoma has told me much, but I want to hear from each of you," Felix said, his gaze sweeping over the group as he took his seat, still holding Orris close.

"Well, sir," Kriegon began, his voice betraying a hint of nervousness, reminiscent of awkward introductions on Earth with a girl's overprotective father, "the trial involving us and the Crimson Order seems to have been a diversion, a ploy to sideline us and King Abraham."

The room's atmosphere shifted as a military official entered, his uniform impeccable, his posture rigid. "Sire, I have come at your request."

"Perfect timing, Dunstan!" Felix exclaimed, gesturing towards the newcomer. "Everyone, this is Commander Dunstan." Nods and murmurs of greeting filled the room as Dunstan stood beside Felix's chair, his gaze sweeping over the group. "Ah, Kriegon, correct?" Felix pointed to him, receiving a nod in acknowledgment. "Ryoma has mentioned you extensively. Given your travels without communication scrolls, you might not have heard—the Crimson Order has seized Riversong and claims dominion over the kingdom."

Orris gasped, covering her mouth, while the others exchanged looks of dismay. Rei leaned forward, concern etching her features. "What of Ryoma and the magic guild?"

Felix's smile was tinged with pride. "He moved the entire guild here overnight a couple of days ago. The new regime didn't sit well with him. I'm sure they're none too pleased to lose such a strategic asset in this unfolding conflict."

The room fell into a stunned silence at Felix's revelation. Orris broke the quiet with a single, incredulous word. "War?"

Dunstan nodded, his expression grim. "Indeed, war. The Crimson Order has usurped the throne and dealt ruthlessly with any nobility that opposed them. We cannot stand idly by while such travesty unfolds."

Ellena, puzzled, looked between Felix and Dunstan. "Is this solely for the kingdom? Or do you realize they're also in league with the Black Crop Gang and the Blood Sail Pirates? Perhaps even connections with the demons from the Windmontley and Malgrave incidents?"

Felix's face darkened at the mention. "Ryoma's reports confirmed much of that, especially regarding Neil Paris's operations. The movements of the gang and pirates corroborate your suspicions about their alliances. My scouts report daily of refugees fleeing Riversong and the surrounding areas due to the gang's increased activity, exacerbated by Commander Wells being pulled north to aid Flavius."

"So, the city is left undefended? How much farther can they push?" Cabitha interjected, her voice laced with worry.

Felix's grimace deepened. "It's worse. The refugees speak of the

157

gang rounding up people for the pirates to sell into slavery in Uthos."

At this, Saphire shot to her hooves, her eyes alight with a fierce glow. "They're engaging in slave trade?" Her voice was venomous, her stance combative.

As Dunstan moved to intervene, stepping between Saphire and Felix, Felix's voice carried a note of both regret and determination. "Yes, the slave trade was abolished by King Abraham's grandfather. It's a significant reason behind the Crimson Order's disdain for the royal lineage; their commerce relied heavily on such dark practices. Uthos's neutrality during our last conflict with Asceriate also stems from this very issue."

Saphire's eyes, burning with a fierce light, swept across the room before she turned sharply, the sound of her hooves echoing down the marble corridor as she stormed out, leaving a gloomy silence in her wake.

Kriegon leaned forward and broke the silence. "How can the Guardians be of service?"

Felix's smile was one of relief and machinations. "There are a couple things we need. We're currently conscripting citizens to bolster our ranks, but our recruitment efforts are falling short of our needs. I propose an open-air rally where the Guardians of the fabled prophecy can make an appearance. Your presence alone will significantly boost morale and recruitment. Following that, maintain a public presence, gather your strength. Your insights and power will be invaluable in our strategic meetings and when we march to reclaim what has been lost."

The night of Felix's impassioned speech to the crowded town square had proven effective from Kriegon's perspective. A surge of enlistments followed, with people eager to join the military ranks under Dunstan's command. Coolgen and Cabitha, leveraging their military lineage and noble estate management, seamlessly integrated into Dunstan's leadership, leaving the Guardians to navigate their path independently.

Later that evening, amidst the afterglow of the city's revived spirit,

Ryoma sought them out, his relief intense upon seeing them unscathed from their journey. "But what of Zenmore and Garthen?" he inquired, his concern evident.

Rei, with a hint of regret, explained, "They ventured back to Riversong, in search of King Abraham and Garthen's daughter."

Ryoma, visibly troubled, massaged his temples. "I wish I had been aware. I could have offered assistance during my time there."

Kriegon, understanding the importance of Ryoma's responsibilities, reassured him. "Don't dwell on it. Your focus was rightfully on relocating your guild. Did everything transfer smoothly?"

"Yes, though the effort nearly broke some of us. Two of my guild members were out cold for an entire day afterward. They lack the psychic energy reserves that Rei or I possess," Ryoma confessed.

Rei, her nails scraping thoughtfully at her neck, interjected, "Do you have them regularly expend their psychic energy?" Seeing Ryoma's puzzled look, she continued, "Like any muscle, psychic reserves grow stronger with use. If you don't push them, they won't develop."

Ryoma, struck by the simplicity of her insight, slapped his forehead in frustration. "Of course! I've been overlooking the basics. Everyone strengthens with practice!" His gaze turned to Rei, filled with admiration and a plea. "I need your expertise in training my people."

Rei, already considering this, nodded. "I was hoping you'd say that. Plus, I'm eager to delve deeper into your magical devices."

Their conversation veered into the intricacies of magic, leaving Ellena and Kriegon to their own devices. The crisp night air enveloped them as they strolled through the bustling streets, her hand finding his in a silent gesture of companionship.

Ellena's voice broke through the quiet. "Are you still haunted by Vladmir's words?"

The question made the scroll in Kriegon's pocket feel like a lead weight. "It's always lurking in my thoughts," he confessed, his eyes drifting to the dual moons hanging in the sky.

She gave his hand a reassuring squeeze. "Have you decided what to do?"

Shaking his head, Kriegon answered, "Not yet. Every time I consider accepting his offer, something feels amiss. It's as if the idea of aligning with him is fundamentally wrong, a betrayal of our purpose, our quest."

Ellena nodded, her expression thoughtful. "It's like we're meant to chart our own course, not just follow someone else's directives. Vladmir's offer might seem like a shortcut, but at what cost?" Her words were gentle, yet they carried the burden of their secret. "Have you thought about at least telling Rei? I'm sure she would be understanding."

Kriegon sighed, the complexity of their situation weighing on him. "I can't. Not yet at least. I need to gain back their trust. I feel as if I lost it for the others after Vladmir's stunt in the throne room."

He could see Ellena look up at him with worry but remained quick. He was unsure if that was enough of a reason to keep her silence, but he desperately hoped so. He wanted to find his own way with this evil side of himself.

As they walked, the streets began to thin, the crowd dispersing into the night. Their steps led them towards a quaint restaurant, its warm lights a beacon in the cool evening air. The aroma of spiced dishes wafted out, inviting them in. Kriegon's stomach rumbled, breaking the contemplative silence between them.

Ellena laughed softly, the sound light and refreshing. "Seems like your body has made one decision for us tonight," she teased, pulling him gently towards the entrance.

Inside, the restaurant was bustling yet cozy, with wooden tables and chairs that spoke of tradition and history. They found a secluded corner, away from the main throng, where they could talk more freely.

Once seated, Kriegon leaned in, his voice low. "And what of us, Ellena? Beyond the prophecy, where do we stand?"

Her eyes met his, filled with resolve and tenderness. "We stand together, Kriegon. Whatever comes, we face it side by side. Our journey isn't just about the destinations we reach but the bonds we forge along

160

the way."

In the days that followed, Kriegon clung to a newfound hope, a beacon through the rigorous training sessions led by Rei. These sessions were less like the gentle guidance one might expect from a mentor and more akin to the harsh discipline of a military drill sergeant, pushing both Kriegon and Ellena to their limits in mastering the magical arts. The days blurred into a rigorous cycle of physical exertion and intellectual challenge, reminiscent of college semesters and military basic training tied together but with the added dimension of magical practice.

Kriegon, despite his adeptness at manipulating imagery to give form to magic, struggled profoundly with channeling his psychic energy through runes. This particular aspect of magic seemed alien to him, an obstacle that drained his reserves faster than his peers, leading to sessions where his frustration was substantial. Ellena, on the other hand, found summoning her psychic energy effortless, but her control over its form was lacking. Her first attempt at creating a water sphere resulted in a misshapen blob that quickly burst, an incident Rei used to highlight the dangers of uncontrolled magic, especially with elements as volatile as fire or earth.

Evenings away from Rei's extreme training sessions often found Kriegon and Ellena observing Saphire as she led new recruits in physical combat drills alongside other military leaders. Attempts to discuss integrating magic into her training or to revisit the sensitive topic of slavery were met with Saphire's cold dismissal. She seemed to view magic as secondary to the immediate need for physical combat readiness, her responses to their concerns about slavery terse and dismissive, suggesting a future where everyone would "know their place."

Two weeks into this grueling regimen, Kriegon, though still battling with the nuances of rune-based magic, had made considerable progress in controlling his psychic energy. This improvement earned him and a few others the privilege of after-hours lessons with Rei, where the complexities of magic unfolded in layers.

During one such session, Rei posed a question to the group about healing, prompting a discussion that went beyond the basics. "Healing isn't just about mending the visible," Rei began, drawing everyone's attention. "For example, consider a fractured leg. What's the first step in using magic to heal it?"

An energetic young man named Ronald, eager to participate, raised his hand. "You'd activate the healing rune, right?"

"Correct, but that's merely the beginning." Rei nodded and pointed to a crudely drawn human leg on the board. "Now, imagine this leg is broken. Simply activating the rune won't suffice. You must envision the bones aligning correctly first. If you fuse them improperly, you're setting up the patient for lifelong issues."

The class listened intently as Rei detailed the process. "After alignment, you must gather any bone fragments, ensuring they're positioned correctly. Only then can you focus on fusing these pieces together. But we're not done. The area where the bone was broken remains weak. Strengthening it is crucial for full recovery."

The room fell into a thoughtful silence, the complexity of what they'd thought was a simple healing process dawning on them. A woman, about Kriegon's age, raised her hand, her voice filled with curiosity. "What if the bone is protruding through the skin?"

"Ah, now that's a more complex scenario, Asselin." Rei smiled, pleased with the question. "Let's explore that together. First, you'd need to handle the immediate threat of infection, which means cleaning the wound magically or physically, then carefully realigning the bone without causing further damage, which requires not just magic but also a steady hand and a calm mind."

The class delved deeper into the discussion, imagining scenarios and solutions, their understanding of healing magic expanding with each question and answer. When Rei finally called an end to the session, Kriegon stayed behind to help clean up, his mind buzzing with new insights.

"Your world's approach to healing is fascinating," Rei remarked as they tidied up. "While you did not have magic, the understanding of the body's needs might exceed my own. Through I will say, human bodies are slightly different than dragonkin."

"I'm nowhere near as knowledgeable as true doctors or healers, either from my world or yours," Kriegon admitted with a humble smile.

Rei chuckled, ruffling his hair with her scaled hand. "Don't underestimate yourself. Every step you take in learning adds to our collective strength."

Their conversation was interrupted by a knock at the door. Saphire stepped in, her presence commanding. "There's a military demanding meeting at Felix's mansion. Dunstan has updates on recruitment and enemy movements along the coast. Thought you'd like to join."

Rei, hands on her hips, faced Saphire with a stern look. "And what of your training? When will you consider learning about magic? It's not just about brute force out there."

Saphire's annoyance was evident, her posture stiffening. "My focus is on leading from the front. If the troops don't see me as a competent leader, how can we expect them to follow us into battle?"

"But how do you plan to keep them safe from threats like the wyverns or potential demonic incursions without magic?" Rei pressed, her voice firm yet concerned. "Magic could offer protection that physical combat alone cannot."

Saphire's expression soured. "I won't coddle them with magic. We'll face whatever comes our way, together."

Rei shook her head, not backing down. "Ignoring magic is like going into battle without armor. You have the potential to be one of the most powerful assets to our forces with your natural psychic reserves, Saphire. Yet, you choose to ignore it. Imagine the difference you could make, as a leader on the battlefield and as a protector of your troops."

Saphire, clearly uncomfortable with the confrontation, turned towards the door. "I'll consider it," she said, though her tone suggested reluctance rather than conviction.

As Saphire marched out, Kriegon and Rei hurried to catch up. The walk to Felix's mansion was filled with a tense silence, each step echoing the unresolved debate between physical might and magical prowess. The cool night air did little to quench the heated atmosphere from the discussion that had filled the room moments before.

The mansion was alive with activity, its halls echoing with the footsteps and voices of officials and workers darting between desks and boards in the front hall, each engaged in their own piece of the larger puzzle of war and governance. Kriegon, Rei, and Saphire navigated through this organized chaos, their steps purposeful as they ascended the staircase not to the familiar lounge but to an office that served as both a study and a war room. The walls were lined with bookshelves, but the center was dominated by a large map, detailed with figures representing military units and, notably, a crudely crafted wyvern positioned over what had once been Neil Paris's town.

As they entered, the military faction's presence was evident, with Coolgen approaching them, his face lighting up with recognition. "It's always good to see you three. I must apologize for not being around more; Cabitha and I have been swamped with Commander Dunstan's directives."

Kriegon, with a reassuring pat on Coolgen's shoulder, responded, "No need to apologize, Coolgen. Everyone's role is crucial here, and it sounds like yours is more critical than most."

Coolgen's smile was grateful before he excused himself to assist Dunstan, who was deeply engrossed in a scroll, with Cabitha nearby, managing several more documents.

Finding seats among the few available, the trio settled just as Ellena appeared, almost ghost-like in her quietude. Her eyes were fixed on Dunstan with an intensity that Kriegon couldn't ignore. When he caught her eye, she simply mouthed "later," her jaw set in a line of determination.

Felix, ever the composed leader, opened the meeting. "Thank you all for coming on such short notice. Dunstan will lead tonight's briefing on our current situation."

Dunstan stood, placing his scroll on the table with a decisive thud. "First off, the pirates we've been tracking have moved south, showing no signs of making landfall in our territory. Our scouts are having trouble keeping up, but for now, they're not our immediate concern."

Murmurs of relief and discussion rippled through the room before Saphire cut through with her question. "And do we know if these pirates are holding slaves?"

Dunstan's response was curt, his eyebrow raised in mild surprise at her focus. "We have no information on that front, and frankly, it's not our primary concern right now." He paused, allowing for any follow-ups before he continued. "On another note, there's been an uptick in wyvern activity near the mountains. Thanks to the information provided by Rei on these creatures, we're prepared to handle them should they decide to venture out. However, for now, they seem content in their domain."

The room filled with concerned whispers, the threat of wyverns a new, looming shadow over their plans.

"Lastly, we've noticed a significant reduction in gang activity along our northern borders. This coincides with a large influx of refugees moving south. Among them, a group led by Kristin Collin of the Azure Alliance, along with Garthen and Zenmore of the Guardians, which should be of particular interest to us."

All eyes turned to the present Guardians, their expressions a sea of shock and curiosity. Kriegon leaned towards Rei, whispering, "Did you get any word from Garthen?"

Rei shook her head, her face showing her surprise.

Dunstan continued, "Apparently, Garthen and Zenmore managed to free Kristin and several others from slavery. They are currently about a week's journey from Swiftwallow, hindered by the muddy autumn roads and their large group."

The room erupted into a buzz of conversation, with Saphire turning to the other Guardians with a mix of shock and a hint of respect. "I never pegged Zenmore for the type to lead such an endeavor."

Rei, with a knowing smile, replied, "There's more to everyone than meets the eye, Saphire. You might learn something from this."

Dunstan, seeking to refocus the room, raised his hand for silence. "Now, on to the less favorable news. Despite our recruitment drive following the Guardians' announcement, we're still short on manpower for an effective assault on Riversong and its surrounding areas. Therefore, we will have to resort to conscription from the general populace."

This announcement sparked immediate debate. Representatives from various guilds—merchants, farmers, ranchers—voiced their concerns, arguing how the military's increasing demands had already stretched their workforce thin, impacting productivity and livelihood. The discussion grew heated, with concerns about the sustainability of such measures.

Felix, standing to address the room, brought a moment of quiet with his authoritative tone. "Consider that no supplies will be sent to Riversong. Along with the influx of refugees to fill the workforce, this should alleviate some of your concerns regarding manpower."

One by one, the guild representatives sat back down, their expressions shifting from defiance to contemplation.

Then, Ellena stood, her voice cutting through the room with a sharpness born of frustration. "And what of those who cannot fight? What of those without the heart to even hold a shield? Are we just sending them to their deaths?"

Dunstan met her challenge with a steely gaze. "Miss Rona, as we've discussed, not everyone conscripted will be on the front lines. Many will support in other capacities, from logistics to supply transport."

Ellena's retort was halted by Felix. "The decision has been made, and I've signed off on it. Conscription is necessary for our defense."

The meeting transitioned into logistics, discussing supply costs, troop movements, and other tactical considerations. As it concluded,

Ellena approached Felix with a request that must have been on her mind throughout the session. "I want permission to go to the Crossroads. If Garthen and Zenmore are nearly here, I should be there to greet them."

Kriegon, sensing the urgency in her voice, added, "It could be beneficial for us. I also need practical experience in command for this world, not just in magic."

Felix, after a brief consultation with Dunstan, nodded. "It's within our borders, and the troops there are disciplined. It could be a good opportunity for both of you."

With their course set, they left the mansion into the crisp night, discussing their plans under the starlit sky. Rei was the first to speak. "So, you two are going to leave your magic studies behind with us?" A scolding, motherly tone.

"Not exactly. Ellena and I can work on magic training between us while getting a new experience," Kriegon reiterated.

Saphire added jokingly, "So you two will finally take on some leadership after all."

"Oh, no you don't, missy. We are continuing this conversation about bailing on magic training." Rei turned on Saphire. Kriegon and Ellena made their escape.

As they walked towards their lodgings, Ellena's voice was soft but sincere. "Thank you for backing me up."

Kriegon smiled, feeling a sense of unity. "We stand together, right?"

Her grin was all the confirmation he needed.

Chapter 14: Sieged

"Lieutenant Artemin Hill, good to meet you." The words were delivered in a voice as rough as the terrain they were set to march through. A woman of striking presence, her skin a rich, deep hue indicative of the harsh sun, approached Kriegon and Ellena as they prepared to mount their horses. Her build was powerful, her posture commanding, speaking volumes of her military background.

Kriegon extended his hand, his gesture one of respect and curiosity. After all, this was the first Black person he had seen since coming to this world, Garthen excluded. "It's good to meet you as well," he said, his voice steady but tinged with intrigue.

Artemin's handshake was firm, a brief but telling interaction that spoke of her strength. Turning to Ellena, she repeated the gesture with equal firmness. Ellena, with a hint of curiosity in her tone, couldn't help but inquire, "Why is an Uthos human here in Transcendent?"

Kriegon was both confused and intrigued at Ellena's question; his gaze shifted between Ellena and Artemin, seeking clarity.

Artemin, unfazed by the question, provided a straightforward answer, her voice carrying the weight of her history. "My brother and I came to seek further military knowledge during the last conflict. King Abraham saw fit to retain our services."

An awkward silence followed, filled only by the rustling of their gear and the distant commands of the soldiers. Ellena managed a polite smile, though it felt out of place in the harsh quiet. Artemin, seemingly indifferent to the social undercurrents, turned to her horse, leaving Kriegon and Ellena to exchange glances.

As they mounted their horses, blending into the column of soldiers moving north from Swiftwallow, Kriegon leaned closer to Ellena. "Uthos?"

"Yes." Ellena nodded, her voice low enough for only him to hear. "A land of conflicts, with both fertile plains and deserts. It's south of Asceriate."

Their conversation drifted from geography to personal anecdotes, their voices a soft counterpoint to the rhythmic clatter of hooves on the muddy path. Before long, they found themselves riding alongside Artemin again, their horses keeping pace naturally.

Artemin's raspy voice broke into their discussion, her words laced with a hint of amusement. "You two are rather close for companions of the old prophecy." She was puffing on a pipe, the smoke curling into the gray, overcast sky.

Kriegon, slightly embarrassed, responded with what he hoped was nonchalance. "Isn't it good for a tight-knit group to face evil forces together?"

Artemin let out a short huff, her smoke briefly enveloping Kriegon, reminding him of college days spent in smoky rooms but with only the smell of burning cider filling his nostrils. The memory brought a wry smile to his face, though the current smoke made him cough slightly. "Close as comrades, perhaps," she continued, her tone suggesting she saw right through their attempt at casualness, "but you two are obviously more than that."

The remark hung in the air, ladened with implication. Kriegon felt his cheeks warm with a flush of embarrassment. He glanced around, noting that none of the soldiers marching behind them met his gaze. Instead, they seemed engrossed in the mundane—watching the backs of horses, the sky, or their own boots.

The realization dawned on Kriegon: perhaps their relationship wasn't as discreet as they had believed. He exchanged a look with Ellena, her eyes reflecting amusement and a touch of concern.

Artemin, perhaps sensing the shift in mood or simply moving on, tapped her pipe, letting the ash fall to the ground as she urged her horse forward. "We've got ground to cover before nightfall," she said, her voice now all business.

Kriegon and Ellena followed, their horses stepping in sync, the muddy road squelching under their hooves. The conversation shifted to lighter topics, the tension easing as they discussed their plans for the Crossroads, their strategies for fortification, and their hopes for the arrival of Garthen and his group.

The rain began its gentle descent just as the last light of day faded, casting a gray curtain over the small town. The column of soldiers, weary and alert, trudged through the mud towards the town, their boots squelching with each step. Kriegon, Ellena, and the imposing figure of Artemin led the way, their horses' hooves splashing through puddles as they approached the stable on the northern edge of the main square.

Artemin, with her commanding presence, dismounted first, her movements precise despite the slick ground. Kriegon and Ellena followed suit. Kriegon felt his cloak weigh him down with rain, and his hands were cold from the air. He looked to Ellena to see if she was fine, but the neko didn't acknowledge the discomforts, so he pushed them aside as well. The stable was a refuge from the rain, its wooden beams smelling of hay and the comforting scent of horses. They handed their horses over to a stable hand who looked curiously at the trio before leading the animals inside.

Artemin gestured for them to follow her to a modest building just off the square, its wooden facade weathered by many storms. Inside, the air was thick with the scent of wet wool and leather, mingling with the underlying aroma of stew from the kitchen. The soldiers inside snapped to attention at the sight of Artemin, their respect palpable.

"Enough of that," Artemin's voice boomed, silencing the rustle of movement. "Where's your captain?"

A man, slightly shorter than Artemin but with a stature that spoke of authority, stepped forward. "Lieutenant, we were informed of your arrival. I am Captain Siomon. How long do you plan to stay at the Crossroads?"

"Just a couple of nights," Artemin replied, her tone brisk. "Once the rain eases, we'll head to the eastern villages to bolster their defenses."

Siomon nodded, leading them to a large table where a detailed map of the region lay. "These two villages," he said, pointing, "are about a three-day march from here, close to the border."

"Just as Dunstan and Cabitha briefed us," Artemin said, her eyes scanning the map, her mind likely calculating distances and potential threats.

"How might we assist you and your companions during your stay?" Siomon inquired, his gaze shifting to Kriegon and Ellena.

Artemin, lighting her pipe, used it to gesture towards Kriegon and Ellena. "These two are Guardians, not under my direct command. They're here to assist with your operations. I just need a place to bunk down for the night."

The room fell silent for a moment, the soldiers' eyes turning towards Kriegon and Ellena with curiosity and surprise. Kriegon felt a slight flush creep up his neck and tried to stand taller, to embody the stature of a Guardian as Artemin did so effortlessly.

Captain Siomon's eyes narrowed slightly, appraising them. "Well, we did hear rumors about the arrival of the Guardians. Some of the men had a little wager going on whether you'd actually show up." His tone was light, but there was an undercurrent of challenge in his words.

Kriegon, feeling the weight of their gaze grow heavier, managed a confident smile, though he felt anything but. "We're here to help out however we can, and truly, we're eager to learn from you."

Siomon seemed to ponder this for a moment before turning to a soldier who was mopping the floor. "Torcall, prepare a couple of bunks for our guests." He gestured for the trio to follow him outside, leading them towards an open area that served as the kitchen.

The kitchen was bustling with activity, the air thick with the aroma of stew and fresh bread. Two cooks were at work, their movements synchronized from years of shared labor. One of them, noticing the new arrivals, quickly grabbed four bowls, filling each with a hearty serving of stew before slamming them down on the counter.

"You keep bringing more folks, Siomon, and I'm going to have to start questioning our food budget!" the cook grumbled, but his eyes twinkled with mirth.

"Thank you, my friend," Siomon replied with a laugh. "The usual time?" The cook nodded, turning back to his pots and leaving the group to their meal.

The stew was simple, a combination of root vegetables and meat. They ate standing, the bowl warming Kriegon's cold hands, the steam mingling with their breath in the cool air.

As they ate, Siomon's curiosity couldn't be contained any longer. "So, why did Dunstan really send you two here?" he asked, his voice casual but his eyes sharp with interest.

Ellena, who had been quietly observing, finally spoke up. "He didn't send us. We requested to come here. We need to understand the ground realities, learn from those who are actually defending these lands and how to lead them."

Kriegon nodded. "Right, for instance, the world I came from had quite a different military. For me, I'd like to learn the difference and see how to improve."

Siomon raised an eyebrow at this, the skepticism clear on his face. "Guardians needing to learn, huh? That's not something I ever thought I'd hear."

"We're still human, or should I say, mortal," Kriegon chimed in, giving Ellena a half-smile. "We believe our strength lies not just in our abilities but in what we can learn from others, from real warriors like yourselves."

The captain looked between the two, his expression softening slightly. "Well, if you're here to learn, you can start by following me around tomorrow. I'll go through the daily routines, show you the ropes. But," he added, his tone firming, "if there comes a time when I need to leave, I expect you to step up, to take charge where needed."

Both Kriegon and Ellena nodded, their eagerness plain. Siomon chuckled at their enthusiasm, shaking his head slightly. "Might finally get some rest if you two prove yourselves capable. But remember, this isn't about magic or prophecies; it's about leadership, moral strategy, and, sometimes, just sheer grit."

Kriegon nodded as he downed the last of his stew, setting the bowl back on the counter. The rain started to pick up as the night fell. Kriegon thought of the monsoon season in Tucson, where a soft rain could turn into a downpour in seconds without warning. The kitchen staff began cleaning up then, drowning out any further talking the group might have had there.

Siomon was a man of his word, and from the outset, the work was a relentless grind. Kriegon and Ellena, under Siomon's watchful eye, quickly immersed themselves in whatever duties he thought they could manage after just a couple of days. By the end of the first week, they had established a new routine where each of them took turns leading the town's forces for a few hours, a system that was not only practical but also educational. For Kriegon, this arrangement served dual purposes. It not only allowed him to spend time alone with Ellena, practicing their magic in the quiet moments between their duties, but it also provided him with invaluable insights into leadership. Leadership wasn't merely about issuing commands or reprimanding failures; it was about understanding each soldier's unique capabilities and how to effectively guide them. Despite not remembering half of their names, Kriegon learned to recognize faces and tailor his instructions to fit each individual's strengths during various tasks.

What Kriegon truly cherished during this time was the opportunity to be alone with Ellena. Amid the constant drizzle that seemed to define the rain-soaked town, they honed their magical skills and engaged in mock battles to test their physical abilities. Compared to the grueling basic training on earth, this was a cakewalk but no less fulfilling. Each day spent in Ellena's company deepened their connection, not just as fellow Guardians but as individuals. Kriegon found himself joining Ellena during her shifts as the acting captain, observing her command style and trying to emulate her approach to leadership rather than just following the examples of the captains he had known before all of this.

However, magic remained a tricky subject for both. Ellena struggled with visualization, often needing Kriegon's help to picture the forms she needed to conjure, a process sometimes disrupted by the slightest distraction. Meanwhile, Kriegon still found it challenging to manifest magic, the energy feeling like a stubborn, tangled thread within him, resisting his efforts to manipulate it into spells.

Days turned into a week and a half in this manner, a time Kriegon would later recall with a sense of dreamlike quality. An extraordinary woman stood by his side, the challenge of leadership became increasingly rewarding and manageable in this fantasy life, yet he felt frustrated with his magical practice.

During a rare dry morning, as they sat eating, Ellena's voice cut through Kriegon's thoughts. "Do you think Garthen's group will show up soon?" she asked, her gaze distant, watching the mist that hadn't yet lifted from the morning's early chill.

Kriegon, considering the question after swallowing his last bite, thought out loud. "They should be close. I can't imagine that so many refugees would be ahead of them."

They ended the conversation abruptly when they noticed the hurried approach of a scout, his leather armor light but his steps heavy with urgency. "Kriegon, sir, we have a scouting party that's late returning from their morning rounds," he reported, his voice tinged with worry.

Kriegon, used to such delays, initially dismissed the concern. "I'm sure it's just the fog," he suggested, trying to hide his annoyance.

But the scout shook his head, his expression serious. "This time, it feels different, sir. One of the horses returned without its rider, in a state of panic."

Kriegon grimaced, the thought of an accident crossing his mind. "Perhaps someone caught a branch."

Ellena, standing beside him, nudged him sharply. "Send another party out, just in case they need help with whoever fell off the horse."

The scout nodded, bowing slightly, and rushed off to organize the search party. Kriegon watched him leave before turning his attention to a group of soldiers starting the construction of a wooden watchtower.

"You should take these reports more seriously," Ellena chided him gently.

"It's usually nothing," Kriegon replied. After all, it wasn't like the terrorists he had to worry about during his deployment. "The worst we've had was a shadow panther, and the soldiers handled it without issue."

Just then, the southern gate was called to open, and both Kriegon and Ellena moved towards it, curiosity piqued about the new arrivals. To their surprise, it was Coolgen, his wide smile breaking through the morning mist as he approached on horseback, his assistant trailing behind.

"Hey there! Good to see you both again!" Coolgen greeted them cheerfully.

"And it's good to see you too, Coolgen. What brings you to the Crossroads today?" Kriegon inquired, moving alongside Ellena towards the stables, where another scouting party was being dispatched. Coolgen's assistant rode straight over to the military barracks.

Coolgen, still atop his horse, answered with a casual shrug, "Commander Dunstan believes we're now ready to commence the main march north towards Riversong."

"But what about Garthen and Zenmore? They haven't returned yet. Are we not waiting for them?" Ellena's voice carried surprise and concern.

Coolgen dismounted, handing off his reins to a stable hand who had approached. "Seems the commander thinks we'll just pick them up on the way. My assistant's gone to deliver new orders to Captain Siomon. After today, you two are to join the main company in the march. Siomon's reports to Dunstan have been nothing but praise for your progress."

Kriegon and Ellena exchanged looks of astonishment. "Since when did he start sending reports?" Ellena asked. Her tone held curiosity and a bit of betrayal.

"Almost immediately after you arrived. At first, Dunstan was skeptical about your roles as military leaders, but I had no doubts; after all, Lord Saforus chose you," Coolgen said. He sniffed the air. "I've been on the move since before dawn. Any chance there's a kitchen nearby?"

They led Coolgen to the kitchen, where the warmth of the hearth and the smell of cooking food offered a welcome contrast to the cool morning outside. As they walked, Coolgen filled them in on the latest developments. "Rei and her students are also joining the campaign. She's trained some skilled healers now, and that was the final piece to push Dunstan into starting the march."

"Just healers? What about their combat readiness?" Kriegon asked, his curiosity piqued about the capabilities of Rei's students.

"You'll have to ask Rei when she gets here. I've been too caught up in logistics to get the full details," Coolgen replied, his mouth full, indicating his immediate preoccupation with the hearty meal before him.

Their conversation was interrupted by the sound of a bell from the northern gate, a signal that was both familiar and urgent, calling for the attention of the acting captain, which was Kriegon at that moment. He glanced at Ellena and Coolgen. "Let's see who's arrived. It's always good to welcome newcomers or deal with any new issues."

As they approached the gate, the guard's voice cut through the early morning mist. "It appears to be another refugee caravan coming down the road!"

Kriegon responded with a nod, his voice firm. "Thanks, we'll go greet them!" He turned to Ellena, whose eyes were already scanning the road with anticipation and caution, and Coolgen, who was buried in his hurried breakfast. "Could be Garthen's group, or perhaps more refugees from south of Riversong?"

Ellena, with a thoughtful shrug, replied, "Let's not assume. We'll greet and inspect as usual. Better safe than sorry." Her words, practical and calm, were a reminder of the protocols they'd established alongside Captain Siomon to prevent any surprises.

As they walked towards the stables, the rain started to fall gently, a soft patter against the cobblestones, urging Kriegon to pull his hood over his head. The caravan wasn't far, its approach marked by the creaking of wooden wheels and the soft whinnies of horses, a sound that had become familiar over the past weeks.

The only other sounds were the distant rumbles of thunder and the occasional squelch of mud underfoot. As Kriegon led his horse out, something caught his eye—a fleeting movement towards the trees to the west. It was quick, almost too quick to notice, but it set his senses on high alert.

They positioned themselves to intercept the caravan, Kriegon's voice carrying over the rain. "Hey there! Identify yourselves! We live in troubled times, after all!"

The lead driver, a man whose face bore the marks of recent hardships, raised his hand in a wary greeting. "Hail! We're from a town south of Riversong, fleeing from the Black Crop's terror. We've little but our lives to offer if you seek payment."

Kriegon's heart sank at the familiar tale of loss and displacement. He nodded, understanding all too well the plight of those fleeing conflict. "No payment needed here, friend. We only ask to check your carriages for our safety. Can't be too careful these days."

The driver, with a resigned sigh, signaled his agreement and relayed the message back to the other carriages. As Kriegon dismounted to begin the inspection, a small voice, tinged with curiosity and innocence, broke the somber mood. "Mommy! Mommy! Look, a cat lady is here!"

A woman, her face lined with worry, quickly pulled her daughter back. "I'm sorry, she hasn't seen much beyond our village before."

Ellena, with a warm, disarming smile that could melt even the coldest of hearts, leaned towards the carriage. Her feline ears twitched slightly, capturing the young girl's attention. "It's quite alright," she reassured the mother, before engaging the child with a gentle tone, allowing her to touch the soft fur of her ears. It was a moment of pure connection amidst the dark times, a reminder for Kriegon of the innocence they were all fighting to protect.

In short order, Kriegon moved to methodically check the second carriage, his mind half on the task at hand and half on the peculiar movement he had seen earlier. Finding nothing but personal belongings and the remnants of lives uprooted, he moved to the third carriage, his thoughts interrupted by Ellena's concerned voice. "Is Rei supposed to be around here?"

Kriegon, momentarily confused, shook his head. "Not that I heard." But his attention was quickly drawn to where Ellena was pointing. Above the tree line, a figure soared, one that could only be Rei. Yet, the scene took a dark turn as a raptor-like shriek filled the air, not from Rei but from something far more menacing.

"Do you think that's a wyvern?" Kriegon's voice was barely a whisper, his earlier unease turning into dread as the creature circled ominously and dropped a lifeless body into the trees with a sickening thud.

Ellena galloped back to the front, her voice urgent, and commanded the drivers, "Everyone, head to the crossroads now. Move with all speed, something's coming!"

The young girl, still peering out from the safety of her mother's arms, pointed excitedly. "Momma, what kind of bird is that? I haven't seen it before."

As Kriegon glanced back the way the creature had come, a chill of foreboding swept through him. The sky was darkening, not with clouds, but with the silhouettes of more wyverns, at least two dozen, their wings slicing through the air with ominous purpose. The carriages, mired deeply in the thick, clinging mud at the crossroads, struggled under the frantic, desperate urging of their drivers. Horses, their muscles straining against the clinging mud, whinnied in distress, their hooves sinking with each attempt to move.

Kriegon's voice was a command, sharp and clear, cutting through the rising panic. "Coolgen, back to the gate! Get everyone unarmed under cover. Grab all the bows; if there aren't enough, hand out spears to defend the archers. Use your judgment before attacking!" His words were orders that he now feared weren't enough for what they faced.

With a single, sharp nod, Coolgen turned and galloped away, his cloak billowing behind him like a dark flag of urgency, racing off down the road. The carriages, now gaining momentum, moved with a reckless speed, their wheels churning the mud into a treacherous slurry, the drivers no longer caring for the safety of their horses in their blind rush to escape the unknown terror.

Kriegon, walking his horse slowly, kept his gaze fixed on the advancing wyverns, their shrieks, which seemed to echo the despair of the moment, sent cold shivers racing up his spine. As the first carriage reached the crossroads' gate, its passengers erupted into a frantic dash towards the nearest refuge, the stables, their fear profound in the air.

Now dismounted, Kriegon could see the wyverns in grim detail. Their leathery skin, a dull, almost golden sheen under the clouded light, stretched over long necks and tails, their bodies designed for flight and battle. Their faces, however, were the stuff of nightmares, unlike any he had seen before, even the one Rei had brought into the throne room for the council. Their mouths were wide, filled with sharp, uneven teeth pointing in all directions and a forked tongue that flicked out, tasting the air with a sinister intelligence.

Kriegon, his heart pounding, moved past the bunched-up carriages, his eyes locked on the diving monsters. A flight of arrows, loosed by the archers, met the leading beasts head-on, their shafts piercing through wings and necks in a deadly rain. Yet the remaining wyverns, undeterred by the death of their kin, dove with a ferocity born of desperation or madness, their eyes fixed on the defenders below.

Leaping into action, Kriegon joined the couple hundred men, some of whom were barely dressed for battle, their attire more suited for the tavern than for war. The air cracked with distant lightning, momentarily illuminating the scene as three wyverns met their end on the spears of the defenders. Some spearmen managed solid hits, driving back the beasts with a grim satisfaction, while others were lifted or thrown aside, their screams swallowed by the pounding rain.

Kriegon, transforming his staff into a lance with practiced ease, aimed for the heart of the nearest wyvern. His thrust was precise, the lance piercing the creature's chest. The wyvern let out a dying shriek, its body crashing down, the impact throwing Kriegon back into the mud. Around him, the battle was chaos, with wyverns circling and diving, some landing to attack at random. With the aid of his men, Kriegon fought to bring down one after another, his commands echoing through the tumult. "Hold the line! Protect the archers!"

Suddenly, Ellena's desperate cry, "KRIEGON! HELP ME!" cut through the noise. Turning, he saw her, now the lone protector before the overfull stables, with women and children huddled in fear behind her. The ground around her was a grim tableau of fallen men and soldiers, their bodies a silent testament to the battle's ferocity with two wyverns looming down on her.

Without hesitation, Kriegon shouted, "Coolgen, whoever can, with me now!" His feet pounded the mud as he sprinted towards her, his heart racing with the fear of what might happen if he was too late. He could hear Coolgen rallying more men behind him, his voice a steady beacon amidst the chaos.

Ellena, her face etched with determination, was fending off the wyverns with her whip sword, her movements a blur as she targeted their vulnerable points, but she didn't hold them off for long. Knowing he wouldn't reach her in time, Kriegon hurled his staff, now imbued with icy magic through a water rune, at the nearest wyvern. The staff, now a lance of ice, struck deep, and with a mental command, Kriegon triggered the ice to explode outward, catching the second wyvern in the face and chest. Seizing the moment, Ellena whipped her sword around, decapitating the beast as the other fell, mortally wounded.

The psychic drain from his magic hit Kriegon like a ton of bricks, and his knees buckled, his vision blurring at the edges as he fell in the mud. Ellena, catching her breath, turned towards him, her expression shifting from relief to sheer terror. Following her gaze, Kriegon saw why: another wyvern, its wings spread wide, was descending upon him, its talons extended like the grim reapers of death itself.

181

Time seemed to slow as Kriegon struggled against the psychic backlash, his movements sluggish in the thick mud.

Just as Kriegon braced for his end, a sudden, forceful shove sent him sprawling into the cold, unforgiving mud. The sensation of something hot and wet splashing across his face was immediate; turning with a mix of horror and disbelief, he saw Coolgen hoisted into the air by the taloned feet of a wyvern. The creature's grasp twisted Coolgen's limbs into grotesque angles before it violently jerked its feet, tearing him into pieces that fell to the ground with a sickening thud.

Kriegon, his body numb from the psychic drain and shock, struggled to his feet, his movements weighed by grief and mud. Ellena, rushing to his side, quickly handed him back his staff and checked him over for injuries with urgent hands. The battlefield around them was quieting, the last of the wyverns either fleeing or falling, but the horror was far from over.

A wyvern, its body a pincushion of arrows, shrieked one last time before plummeting from the sky. Its massive body crashed into the already weakened roof of the stables with a sound like thunder, sending up a cloud of dust and splinters. From within the wreckage, cries of pain and desperation echoed as Ellena, ignoring her own bleeding cuts, desperately began tearing at the debris, her face set with determination and fear.

Kriegon, moving as if through a fog, joined her, his mind barely registering the chaos. They pulled at the rubble, uncovering bodies— some alive, some not. Each discovery was a blow to his already battered spirit, a hard reminder of the cost of this battle.

The aftermath saw villagers emerging from their hiding spots, their faces etched with shock and sorrow, rushing to help Ellena. Her hands, red with her own blood from the sharp edges of the collapsed roof, worked tirelessly. Kriegon, trying to shake off his daze, realized the need for leadership amidst the chaos and directionless soldiers.

Facing the remaining soldiers that had wandered, his voice was rough but commanding. "Alright, men, we need to organize. First, gather the wounded and the dead near the barracks. We'll count our losses there. Double the watch on all roads and keep an eye on the skies. Any movement, signal the alarm. And get those wyvern carcasses piled up by the north gate; clear the carriages from the road."

The soldiers moved with an assortment of weariness and purpose, their faces reflecting the recent battle's toll. One soldier, his expression hard with resentment, challenged Kriegon, "Why didn't you warn us about these wyverns? We've never heard of them until now."

Kriegon, feeling the consequence of his oversight, answered heavily. "I assumed you were all briefed from the reports of other Guardians and Dunstan's scouts. My mistake. We must be united and prepared; evil like this is unpredictable. Now, to your tasks." He assigned leaders for each group, including the soldier who had spoken out, hoping to channel their discontent into action.

With orders given, Kriegon felt a profound drain, not just physically but mentally and psychically. He made his way back to Ellena, who stood beside the uncovered bodies, her gaze fixed on a small form—the little girl from one of the carriages, still cradled by her lifeless mother. Blood dripped from Ellena's hands, unnoticed in her grief.

Kriegon, the sight before him a reminder of their failure, sat heavily beside her, his legs no longer able to hold him. The battlefield around them was a tableau of devastation, with the remains of the wyverns, the broken carriages, and the scattered bodies of men, women, and children.

Ellena's voice, thick with emotion, broke the oppressive silence. "Do we deserve the title Guardians?"

Her question hung in the air, a mirror to the doubts that plagued Kriegon's own mind. They were supposed to be protectors, soldiers against the darkness, yet here they were, amidst the ruins of what should have been a safe haven, surrounded by the consequences of either their failure to anticipate such an attack or simply the cruel whims of fate.

He looked at Ellena, her face a veil of sorrow, streaked with dirt and tears, her eyes reflecting a turmoil that mirrored his own. "I don't know," he admitted, his voice barely a whisper, rough with unshed tears.

Chapter 15: Marching Forward

Garthen led the weary refugees alongside Kristin and Zenmore through the blood-soaked mud of Crossroads. This wasn't their first encounter with devastation since leaving Riversong for Swiftwallow, but here, for the first time, he witnessed a community not fleeing but rallying to rebuild amidst the ruins. Many in his group had joined seeking the protection of Garthen, Zenmore, and the Lawbringers, running from devastation to safety behind them.

As they approached, a soldier, his armor dulled by the recent battle, spotted them and dashed into a still-standing structure. Moments later, a group emerged, their faces etched with the grime of conflict and their hands on their swords, ready for yet another challenge.

The leader, a stern man whose eyes spoke of a sleepless night, called out, "What do you want? We have no room to house anyone at the moment."

Garthen, maintaining his composure despite the drizzle that softened the ground beneath them, replied, "I am Garthen, leader of the Guardians. I've heard Felix Zella shelters my comrades. I seek only to place these refugees under his care."

The man's response was a sneer. "So, the famed Garthen arrives. Ellena and Kriegon spoke of you with reverence, yet here you stand, a shadow of your former glory, a burnt walking corpse."

Garthen, momentarily forestalled by the hostility, felt a surge of anger but quelled it. He had done away with his hood and mask, intent on showing the world his pain after his daughter had been snatched from him for a second time. "Appearances may deceive, but my purpose remains unchanged. Are Ellena and Kriegon here? I'd like to speak with them."

With a dismissive wave towards the chaotic western part of town, the man said, "They're over there, nursing their wounds while I try to piece this town back together. Ensure your refugees move on before nightfall. We're stretched thin as it is." He turned and barked orders, his voice carrying over the patter of rain.

Turning to Kristin, Zenmore, and the vast caravan of refugees, Garthen directed, "Kristin, take them south of the town. Zenmore and I will find out what's amiss here. You'll be safer with this town between us and further attacks." He referred to the sporadic assaults they'd faced—bandits, rogue gang members, even wyverns.

Kristin nodded, her resolve firm. "Understood. Swiftwallow is close. If memory serves, this is Crossroads, a day's march from there." She began organizing the group, her commands clear and calm, despite the murmurs of fatigue and reluctance from the refugees.

As the procession moved towards the south gate, which opened with a mechanical eagerness to be rid of them, Zenmore, kneeling to match Garthen's eye level, asked, "What could have soured that man's opinion of you so quickly?"

Garthen, scanning the remains of the town, replied, "A question for when we find Ellena and Kriegon."

With most of the refugees past the city, their thanks a soft murmur in the air, an alarm suddenly blared from the south gate, slicing through the quiet departure.

Garthen and Zenmore, their steps quick and purposeful, hurried toward the south gate, where soldiers stood ready, their bows aimed at the gray, drizzling sky. The rain made the ground beneath them slick, but their urgency was unmistakable. As they approached, the soldiers, their faces filled with fear and resolve, pointed skyward, their hands trembling slightly with the heft of their weapons.

From the mist and rain, Rei descended, her wings beating powerfully, creating a spray of mud and water as she landed. In her talons, she carried Saphire, her grip releasing just off the ground. Their sudden appearance startled the soldiers, who instinctively drew back, their weapons raised in defense.

"Is this another wyvern?" A soldier's voice cut through the drizzle, laced with both fear and aggression.

Rei, folding her wings with grace, and Saphire both raised their hands in a gesture meant to calm and reassure. "No, we're here on Lord Felix's

186

orders to assist with the aftermath of the attack." Saphire's voice was calm, yet it carried the authority needed to pierce through the tension.

The stress filled atmosphere didn't fully dissolve, but some soldiers lowered their bows, their curiosity piqued but their wariness remained. It was then that the same man who had greeted them with disdain earlier made his way through the crowd, his face a guise of irritation. "Stand down, they're with us," he barked, his voice cutting through the drizzle like a knife. "I got a message about their arrival, though it seems the timing's off." His mood was as sour as the weather, his gaze sweeping over the Guardians before he turned away, leaving an awkward silence in his wake.

Rei, her scales shimmering faintly under the dim light, approached Garthen and Zenmore. Her embrace was warm, briefly staving off the cold rain. "Not the best of times for a reunion, but it's good to see you both unscathed," she said, her voice carrying both relief and concern.

Garthen, feeling the significance of the new scar on his heart, nodded without correcting Rei's belief. "Ellena and Kriegon should be around here. Let's find them and get to the bottom of what's happened," he suggested, trying to sound concerned for their fellow Guardians.

Saphire, her expression serious, nodded in agreement. "It's crucial we regroup. They came here to learn leadership, not to wallow in defeat."

Zenmore, with a forced chuckle that didn't quite reach his eyes, added, "If I know Ellena, she's plotting our next move, and Kriegon's got one hell of a strategic mind."

The group made their way through the town, their boots, hooves, and talons squelching in the mud, asking after their comrades. They were eventually directed to a small inn, where an elderly woman, her face etched with the lines of worry and years, greeted them with a sad smile. "They're upstairs. It'll do them good to see you," she said, her voice soft, leading them to a room on the second floor.

The door was slightly ajar, revealing Kriegon slumped against the wall, his eyes empty, his clothes stained with blood and mud. Ellena lay curled in his lap, her face buried in his chest, her body language speaking volumes of their shared sorrow. The room was dimly lit, the only light coming from a small window, casting long shadows that seemed to echo their despair.

Zenmore, unable to restrain his urgency, gently pushed the door open wider.

"What happened to you two?" said Rei the second she caught sight of them, her motherly concern evident as she moved past Zenmore to their sides, her healing rune glowing faintly on her scales as she reached out to them.

Ellena, at the sight of Rei, withdrew further into Kriegon's embrace, her body tense with unspoken grief. Kriegon, his voice a hollow echo of its usual strength, began to recount the events of the wyvern attack, each word laden with regret and self-blame. He spoke of their desperate defense, the chaos, and the tragic death of Coolgen, a moment that seemed to haunt him most.

"I can't get the image of how Coolgen was killed out of my head. I can't make the nightmare end," Kriegon confessed, his gaze lost in the ceiling as if seeing past it to the scene he described. Saphire, moving silently to sit beside him, offered her shoulder, brushing what they now knew was Coolgen's blood from his face.

As Kriegon's narrative unfolded, Ellena's soft sobs filled the room, a mournful sound that seemed to seep into the very walls. She finally allowed Rei to check her wounds, her resistance melting away under Rei's gentle insistence. The deep gashes on her arms reflected the story of the fierce desperation to save those she could. Rei's hands moved with practiced ease, her healing rune casting a soft glow over Ellena's injuries, while her words, spoken in a soothing tone, offered comfort that transcended mere physical healing.

Garthen, standing in the doorway, watched this scene unfold with a strange detachment and a growing sense of responsibility. His mind was racing with thoughts of how to channel this group's pain, their loss, into something more, something productive for their cause. Yet he couldn't help but feel a pang of isolation, the unity displayed before him almost distant.

In that moment, Garthen realized two things: first, that the group before him was far more compassionate than he, their immediate response to tragedy being comfort and healing rather than his instinctual drive for revenge; second, that this group could be so much better than they were now, but he had no idea how to bridge the gap between their current state and that potential. This realization left him feeling disconnected, uncertain of his place among them, yet determined to find a way to lead them through the darkness that loomed ahead.

As Zenmore, with his massive frame, settled before the bed, the floorboards beneath him groaned under his bulk, a sound that seemed to echo the hefty mood in the room. Garthen, standing next to him, his stature barely taller than Zenmore's even while seated, decided it was time to rally his group, to transform their despair into determination.

"Kriegon, Ellena," Garthen began, his voice firm yet not without warmth, "you're burdening yourselves with too much guilt, too much sorrow. Look around you," he urged, gesturing to the faces that watched them with concern and empathy. "No, really look. These aren't just your friends. This is your family, here to lift you up when you fall. You did everything you could. Coolgen would be proud, not disappointed."

The room fell into a contemplative silence, the importance of Garthen's words hanging in the air, mingling with the scent of rain from outside. Ellena, released from Rei's healing touch, moved into her arms, seeking solace in the embrace, her tears silently acknowledging the comfort found there.

Rei whispered words of comfort, her voice a soft murmur against the backdrop of the storm outside, as she gently rocked Ellena, her hands still aglow with healing magic, though now it seemed more to soothe the soul than the body.

Garthen, seeing the need for more than just physical healing, continued, his voice growing more impassioned. "We walk on the edge of a razor every day. We're at war, not just with flesh and blood, but with darkness itself. I've faced my own battles, lost my first family to this very war," he confessed, his eyes meeting each of theirs in turn, sharing a piece of his own pain.

"But we're still here, still breathing, still fighting," he said, extending his hand towards Kriegon, his gesture an invitation, a bridge back to standing. "This pain…" He paused, his voice dropping to a whisper. "It's not a curse. It's a gift, a reminder that we're alive, that we still have a purpose. Use it, don't let it use you. Stand up, remember what you've lost, but let that memory drive you to prevent more loss, to fight against the cause of that pain."

Kriegon, his gaze fixed on Garthen's outstretched hand, hesitated for a moment, his eyes reflecting the turmoil within. Then, with a deep breath that seemed to draw strength from the very air, he grasped Garthen's hand. The contact was firm, a silent agreement of trust and mutual support. With a heave that spoke volumes of their shared resolve, Garthen pulled Kriegon to his feet. Though visibly shaken, Kriegon's posture straightened, a spark of life returning to his eyes as he faced his companions.

Ellena, inspired by the exchange, reached out to Garthen. He approached and, with the same strength that had lifted Kriegon, helped Ellena to stand. Her face, though streaked with tears, held a new determination, a refusal to be defined by her grief.

Rei, ever the caretaker, broke the tension with a gentle smile, her voice light as she guided Ellena towards the door. "Well, it's settled then. Let's get you two cleaned up. You've had enough of the mud and blood for one day."

Zenmore, his rough laughter filling the room, added, "Right, they do smell worse than usual after a battle."

Saphire, with a playful kick to Zenmore's side, retorted with her typical irritation, "No more than you always do, you big oaf." Her words, though normally an attempted stab, carried an undertone of the lightness that was slowly returning to the group, a sign that despite their losses, they were not broken.

As the group filed out of the dimly lit room, Garthen remained for a moment, watching them go with pride and an unspoken, lingering sorrow. The scene before him was one of unity, of a group finding strength in each other's company, spurred on by words he had just spoken—words meant to inspire but which felt hollow in the cavern of his own heart.

He stood there, the silence of the room enveloping him, the flurry of activity and emotion that had just filled it seeming to deepen the isolation. The walls seemed to close in, the shadows lengthening as if to swallow him whole, a fitting metaphor for the darkness that had taken his first family. The Guardians were his duty now, his charge, but they could never fill the void left by those he'd lost.

Yet, as he watched the last of them disappear through the doorway, Garthen felt a resolve hardening within him. His pain, a constant companion, was a burden but also a catalyst. If his own loss could transform into something that pushed others to stand, to fight, to be better than the despair they felt, then maybe, just maybe, his suffering had a purpose beyond his own torment.

As the night folded over the town, its gloom deepening with each passing moment, a solemn procession made its way to the mass funeral held just beyond the south gate. Garthen, with his group of Guardians, moved through the mist, their presence a quiet strength amidst the sorrow that hung in the cool autumn air. The event's somberness was blatant, the chill of the night seeping into their very souls, a fitting companion to the sorrow they bore.

Rows of graves stretched before them, bodies shrouded in white, displaying the town's losses. Some headstones stood proudly with names etched into them, while others lay blank, a silent testament to lives lost too suddenly, their identities swallowed by the chaos. Garthen's gaze fell upon Coolgen's grave, the body beneath the cloth contorted in an unnatural way, a grim reminder of the violence that had claimed him. Beside him, Kriegon's face twisted in pain, the memory of Coolgen's death haunting him anew.

Garthen reached out, his hand a firm presence on Kriegon's shoulder, while Zenmore mirrored the gesture, offering silent support. Their actions spoke of camaraderie, a shared burden in the face of overwhelming grief. It was then that a priest from the Seers of the Ever Watcher approached, his robes whispering against the grass as he began his solemn address to the gathered crowd.

"For all those who stand here today, understand that this tragedy will live in our hearts," he intoned, his voice a beacon in the night, speaking of loss, of memory, and of a future where these sacrifices would not be forgotten. His words, intended to comfort, wove through the air, mingling with the mist, touching each soul present with the emphasis of shared sorrow and the promise of remembrance.

"And for all to remember," the priest concluded, his voice rising slightly, "the fight against the darkness will continue. Until the Ever Watcher Saforus comes for us, we must protect and grow in our lives. Now go forth and speak of the joys and stories of those who lie before you now. Let the night be a celebration of the lives now with the angels."

As the priest stepped back, signaling the end of his eulogy, soldiers moved forward, beginning the solemn task of covering the graves. The townsfolk, their faces etched with grief, slowly dispersed, some heading back into the town, while others lingered, lost in their thoughts or prayers.

The Guardians, however, did not follow the townsfolk into the taverns for solace or distraction. Led by Kriegon, they turned toward what he identified as the main military barracks, now transformed into a makeshift hospital for the wounded from the battle.

Inside, the atmosphere was one of organized chaos. Beds and the floor were occupied by injured soldiers and citizens, their groans and the occasional sharp cry of pain filling the air. The man, the original sore soldier who had greeted Garthen earlier, noticed the Guardians' arrival. He paused in directing the efforts to care for the wounded.

"So, you all have come to finally help out?" His voice carried expectation and annoyance.

Kriegon, struggling with his words, managed to reply, "I'm sorry, Siomon. We weren't—"

Siomon's expression softened, understanding dawning in his eyes. "It's fine. You've been through enough. But let's move forward."

With a brief, comforting embrace for both Kriegon and Ellena, Siomon directed them towards the back of the barracks to help with bandaging the less severely wounded. It was then that Rei stepped forward, her presence drawing attention.

"Siomon, was it? I can help direct Kriegon, Saphire, and Ellena to heal those with the worst injuries. Where are they?"

Siomon looked at Rei, skepticism evident in his gaze, but he pointed towards the bunks on the left side. "Those in the bunks are most injured. I'm worried they won't last the week without intervention."

Rei, with a determined nod, gathered Saphire, Ellena, and Kriegon and moved towards the indicated area, her knowledge of healing from another world now put to the test in this one. Siomon watched them go, his skepticism slowly giving way to a cautious hope, his eyes following their movements with curiosity and doubt.

Garthen, observing the exchange, leaned in to speak to Siomon. "She's from a world where healing magic is far advanced. You're in good hands."

Siomon's eyebrows lifted, his interest piqued. "I thought our own Ryoma was the authority on magical arts."

"He is, for artifacts and tools," Garthen agreed, his voice carrying a note of pride for Rei's capabilities. "But Rei's world focused on the direct application of magic for healing. It's ... different, more personal, you could say."

"Well, if you vouch for her," Siomon said, his tone shifting from skeptical to cautiously optimistic, "then I'll trust your judgment, Commander of the Guardians. And what about you two? Interested in the wyverns?"

Zenmore, his deep voice resonating in the confined space of the barracks, nodded. "From what we heard, they were larger than any we've encountered before. Their behavior was ... unusual. We haven't encountered any that attacked in such a large group."

Without further ado, Siomon led Garthen and Zenmore out of the barracks and into the night. The air outside was crisper, carrying the scent of rain-soaked earth and the distant toll of a bell, perhaps from the church or a memorial for the fallen. The night was alive with whispers of the wind, a somber symphony to the events of the day.

As they walked, Siomon's steps were brisk, his mind clearly racing with the implications of what they had faced. "The wyverns," he began, his voice that of concern and intrigue, "weren't just attacking randomly. There was a purpose, a coordination that's unnatural for beasts of their kind."

Garthen, walking beside him, nodded. His thoughts aligned Siomon's observations with Kriegon's account. "Do you think someone's controlling them?"

"Or something," Siomon corrected, his gaze fixed on the path ahead as if he could see through the darkness to the answers they sought. "We've found strange secondary stomachs. Some filled with metals. But the stomachs led nowhere else into the body's system."

Zenmore, his deep voice a rumble in the night, added, "And the metals you mentioned earlier, found in their stomachs?"

"Precious metals," Siomon confirmed. "It's as if they were being used as couriers, perhaps for some ritual or construction far beyond our understanding."

The trio reached the outskirts of the town, where the silhouette of a fallen wyvern lay, a remnant of the days before terror. Its eyes, even in death, seemed to hold a lingering malice, a testament to the unnatural force that had driven it.

Garthen approached, reaching out to touch the creature's cold, rough scales, feeling for any residual magic that might cling to them like a dark aura. "If they're being controlled, then we're not just fighting beasts. We're up against someone, or something, with the power to bend nature to its will."

"And that," Siomon interjected, his voice filled with the grimness of the night, "means we're facing a war on multiple fronts. Not only do we combat these creatures physically, but we must also confront the dark arts that command them."

Garthen, pondering the complexity of their situation, mused aloud, "Perhaps a prince from the prophecy?" His skepticism was flagrant, the idea of ancient prophecies intertwining with their current predicament adding layers of mystery and doubt.

As if to underscore the surreal nature of their discussion, Zenmore, with a grunt of effort, began to cut into the chest of the fallen wyvern. The sound of tearing flesh was disturbingly loud in the quiet night, a grim necessity for the reality they faced. After a few tense minutes, he extracted a gluey sack from the creature's body. Ripping it open with a decisive movement, he revealed the expected iron remnants of armor or tools and also a single gold necklace, its luster dulled by the creature's insides.

"Well, that is very odd indeed, but exactly as you described," Garthen remarked, his voice a combination of fascination and concern.

Zenmore, attempting to clean his hands on the wing of the wyvern, paused, his brows furrowing. "Hey, why does this look so familiar?" He reached for the edge of the wing, stretching it towards the flickering light of a nearby torch. The light played across the membrane, revealing a slightly deformed symbol that Garthen instantly recognized as the tattoo of the Black Crop Gang.

Moving closer to inspect the symbol, Siomon muttered, "Guess we now know that the gang was betrayed by the forces that originally partnered with them."

Garthen's gaze hardened as he considered the implications. "Maybe these multiple fronts are only one head," he suggested, the pieces of a larger puzzle starting to align in his mind.

Days after the initial chaos, Felix, Dunstan, and their entourage, including nobles rescued by Garthen and Zenmore from Riversong, approached the town. Their arrival was marked by the sleek lines of Felix's clean military suit, highlighting Dunstan's traditional, sharply imposing armor. Among them, Ryoma, dressed in neat, tight-fitting mage's robes, carried an air of quiet power, his presence a reminder of the potential of his magic guild.

The barracks, now a hub of strategy rather than healing, greeted them with an air of anticipation. Inside, the room was set up for a war council, maps and documents littering the tables, each one a silent testament to Cabitha's forward arrival and impeccable work ethic. The atmosphere was charged with the burden of decisions yet to be made.

Felix initiated the conversation after a brief exchange of greetings around the room, his voice carrying the weight of the kingdom's plight. "Thank you all for being here in this time of great sorrow for our realm. We've all felt the sting of this war against the shadows. But with the might of the Guardians, Dunstan's military strength and Ryoma's mastery over the arcane, we stand a chance to reclaim Transcendent from the darkness." His attempt at a smile was grim, a silent acknowledgment of the battles ahead. "Now, I'll hand over the floor to Commander Dunstan to outline our strategy for victory."

As Dunstan rose with the grace of a seasoned warrior, Garthen stood to interject, his voice firm yet respectful. "I must object, Felix. I believe I should lead this campaign."

Dunstan's expression, composed to this point, flickered with anger. "And what right do you have to usurp my command and the loyalty of my soldiers?"

Garthen, shaking his head, replied, "It's not about taking away your duty or your forces, Dunstan. I'm suggesting that I'm better suited to face what's happening in Riversong, which is turning into something far more sinister than we've encountered before. The wyverns are just the beginning. Have you faced these threats as I have, along with the other Guardians and Artemin?"

"That sounds like you're undermining all the effort I've put into rallying our forces for the nation's recovery," Dunstan countered, his voice rising with each word, his face flushing red.

"I need your expertise, Dunstan, not to sideline you. Your strategic mind was renowned even when I commanded at Windmontley. I intend for you to be at the forefront, and I assure you, once Riversong is secure, your troops will be returned."

Felix stood tension with the riding tension, his expression one of displeasure. "Garthen, while you and the Guardians saved many here, including my own daughter, your failure at Windmontley casts a shadow over your leadership for this crucial campaign."

Garthen's face tightened, the pain of past losses flashing quickly through his mind. "The failures I've endured are lessons you can't possibly comprehend from the safety of your council chambers. I've witnessed horrors no one should, like pulling my wife from a mountain of bodies or watching my daughter take her own life to rid herself of a demonic possession." He put all the struggle and pain in his soul to bear in his words. "These failures have not weakened me; they've forged me into someone who understands the enemy's deceitful ways better than anyone here."

Before Dunstan could retort, the room was engulfed in a blinding light. Everyone shielded their eyes, the sudden illumination blinding against the dimness of the barracks. As their vision adjusted, they saw a softly glowing orb hovering in the center of the room. Mark, the priest, fell to his knees, whispering in reverence, "Watcher Saforus!"

The light pulsed, and a voice resonating with power and clarity spoke. "You bicker while the world decays around you. Know this: the Almighty has chosen the Guardians to lead this world from the brink. This war is not merely against flesh and blood but against nightmares unleashed upon our reality. While you may not eradicate these horrors entirely, when the one who leads them is sent back to the depths of hell, this small section of the world can begin to heal. Garthen, of all here, understands this burden."

The room fell into a stunned silence as the light dimmed and vanished. Dunstan, his face full of resignation and respect, finally spoke. "As the Ever Watcher commands, I will step aside."

Garthen, with a nod of acknowledgment towards the now-gone light, turned to the assembled leaders. "Thank you, Dunstan. Now, let's review the strategy I've devised." He unrolled a large map on the table, detailing the known movements of the wyverns. "With the knowledge that the wyverns have been using the Sky Peak Mountains as their gateway across the continent," Garthen began, his finger tracing a path on the map, "we must divide our forces strategically. Dunstan, along with Kriegon, Ellena, and Zenmore, will command a quarter of our troops. They'll advance from the curve of the forest road, aiming towards Neil Paris's old territory. Your path shouldn't meet the bulk of the enemy forces directly, but it will serve to distract and flank them, allowing you to strike at Riversong from the east."

The room buzzed with the logistics of troop distribution, the allocation of magic guild members to the secondary force, and the timing of supplies across the dual fronts. The discussion stretched into the night, each detail meticulously planned to ensure every group understood their role in the upcoming march and battle. The burden of the impending conflict hung in the air, yet there was a profound sense of unity and resolve among them.

As the meeting drew to a close, Garthen turned to his fellow Guardians, his voice hoarse from hours of strategizing. "Thank you all for standing by me."

Kriegon, with a weary smile, placed a hand on Garthen's shoulder. "You were there for Ellena and me in our darkest time. We couldn't do less for you now, especially after everything."

The camaraderie was definite as Garthen clapped the shoulders of his comrades, each gesture a silent promise of mutual support. They dispersed, each to their rest, the night air cool against their tired faces, carrying whispers of the challenges ahead. Garthen looked to the rare clear night sky for the season, the dual moons rising high, and thought soon his promise would be fulfilled. In the morning, Garthen would start his march toward his vengeance, unhindered by those who would hold him back from doing what he needed to do.

Vladmir lounged in the dim light of Riversong castle, his eyes occasionally flickering with irritation as he watched the magic scroll connected to Kriegon's, a tether to a blank sheet he found increasingly frustrating. Beside him, the Shadow Panther that Lucifer had tamed for him lay sprawled, its purrs a low, comforting rumble in the otherwise silent room. The night had fully claimed the sky outside, and with a heavy sigh, Vladmir stood, his movements fluid yet charged with a simmering discontent. There was a meeting scheduled in the now-bare throne room, and with nothing else demanding his attention, he decided to make his way there.

The Shadow Panther rose silently, its sleek form a shadow trailing Vladmir through the deserted corridors of the castle. The emptiness of the halls was a reminder of the isolation his ambitions had cultivated. As they approached the throne room, the grandeur that had once marked this place was noticeably absent; the banners, the opulent decor, even the throne itself had been stripped away, leaving the space as cold and uninviting as the heart of its current ruler.

Inside, a single figure stood by the shattered remnants of what was once a grand window, gently caressing a wyvern that perched precariously on the castle's exterior. The creature's eyes glowed faintly in the dim light, a mirror to the unsettling changes in its master.

"Still coddling your pets, I see?" Vladmir's voice was laced with disdain as he settled onto the Shadow Panther, using it as an impromptu throne in the corner of the vast, echoing room.

The figure, Bracus—or what remained of him, now a vessel for the demon Mammon—turned slightly, his golden-tinged face catching the moonlight, his features twisted into something both majestic and grotesque. "They are more than pets, Vladmir. They are symbols of power, of control."

The silence that followed was thick, oppressive, broken only by the distant clatter of footsteps approaching. Moments later, Adelisa Cabal and Helain Bold entered, their steps hesitant, their gazes flickering nervously between Vladmir and Mammon before they knelt.

"We've come as you requested." Adelisa's voice trembled slightly, betraying her fear.

Mammon's laughter was a deep, rumbling sound, like the shifting of ancient stones. "Good. I'm pleased you've chosen to honor your commitments rather than flee."

Lucifer, a silent sentinel, stepped forward, his presence a dark omen. "Their greed is too profound for them to abandon the treasure you've amassed, Mammon."

"Is that so?" Mammon's smile was chilling, his eyes gleaming with a predatory light. "Then they will serve me well."

With a swift motion, Lucifer placed a hand on each of their heads, and the room seemed to hold its breath. The nobles convulsed, their bodies wracked with an unseen force, before slumping to the floor, unconscious or worse. Golden lions, ethereal and terrifying, entered the room, their jaws gently but firmly taking the nobles and carrying them away.

Mammon, the demon wearing Bracus's form like an ill-fitting suit, walked slowly towards the exit, his movements deliberate. "It will be liberating to shed this human guise for a little while. My power has finally transferred enough for my reign to really begin."

Lucifer's smile was a mere twist of lips. "As you say. Our deal is concluded, with a bonus, it seems."

"Just ensure you uphold your part of the bargain," Vladmir interjected, his voice sharp with authority, his eyes narrowing as he watched Mammon's retreat.

Mammon paused, turning back with a nod that was almost a bow, though it lacked any semblance of respect. "The pirate ships will be laden with the treasure as promised. Not a coin more, Vladmir. Remember, our alliance is one of convenience, not loyalty."

Lucifer approached Vladmir with what looked to be a true smile. "I am proud, as you far exceeded my expectations. If you keep your word, I will have to get you another gift once we arrive in Uthos."

Vladmir smiled widely. "Your gifts have always been amazing. I truly look forward to it."

Chapter 16: Rotted Counterattack

Kriegon looked at the scroll as they rode, wondering if he should keep it or burn it. He now knew that no matter what Valdmir had said or could say in the future, nothing justified the devastation he had witnessed. While the experience had left him hollow, Garthen and the others pushed him back from sending a message.

He had wanted to escape in the dark room, bring Ellena with him away from the terror they had witnessed. When talking with the others the following nights, he found a new resolve, and while he wasn't sure if he was an effective leader like everyone told him, he would try his best to live up to their standards.

The path they took was slow, a deliberate march through the dense forest, each soldier carving a new trail where none had existed before. Beside him, Dunstan's presence was a steady reassurance, his armor occasionally clinking as they moved. The forest's quiet was an absolute difference to the turmoil within Kriegon's thoughts. Kriegon looked to Dunstan again, as he often did now, and tucked away the scroll.

Dunstan glanced over and noticed Kriegon's look. "Just ask if you have another question."

Kriegon, feeling his cheeks warm at the thought of pestering the seasoned warrior again, ventured, "Do you think we'll reach Riversong in time for the siege?"

Dunstan pondered, his face a front of concentration as he calculated distances in his head. "Unlikely. This path might lead us into open conflict in the fields, and at night, with those creatures ... it's not ideal."

Ryoma, on Dunstan's other side, flashed a mischievous smile. "I might have something up my sleeve that could give us an edge at night."

"Another artifact?" Kriegon's interest was piqued. The prospect of discussing magical creations with Ryoma was always a highlight of their journey.

With a wink, Ryoma confirmed, "Indeed, inspired by Archangel Saforus's second appearance."

Dunstan's surprise was evident. "Second time?"

"Yes, the first was when he delivered the prophecy slabs in the king's war chamber. Less blinding this time, but no less awe-inspiring," Ryoma explained, his voice tinged with reverence.

Dunstan's demeanor was one of stoic resolve as they trudged through the forest, the column's progress painfully slow against the dense undergrowth. His commands, when issued, were brief and to the point, his voice cutting through the fatigue that hung over the soldiers like a oppressive cloak. The day seemed to stretch interminably, each step forward a battle against nature's resistance.

As dusk began to settle, the forest cooled, shadows lengthening across the ground where tents were pitched. Servants moved with practiced ease, setting up shelters for the night, their actions a familiar ritual against the backdrop of the untamed wilderness. Zenmore and Ellena had already moved over to the servants they had been assigned. Zenmore walked the entire time due to the troubles he had with the "tiny horses." The larger ones were reserved for provision transport.

Ellena, having dismounted, approached Kriegon with a question in her eyes. "You're going to stay with us tonight, right?"

Kriegon, momentarily torn, glanced towards Ryoma, who was already engaged with his magic guild, discussing the evening's plans. "Give me a moment; let me see if they need any help first," he replied, giving her hand a reassuring squeeze before moving towards Ryoma's tent.

Inside, the scene was one of focused chaos. The tent was cluttered with animal bones, scrolls, and carving tools, each item a crucial component in the creation of magical artifacts. Two mages were diligently working at a small table, their quills dancing over parchment, summarizing the day's communications for Ryoma's later use.

Ryoma, catching sight of Kriegon, waved him over with a knowing smile. "Ah, the curiosity of an inventor, today we are working on rebuilding our communication scroll pile." He chuckled, handing Kriegon a long ox bone, two scrolls, and an etching file. They moved to a side bench, separate from the bustling activity where others were deep into their work.

"Now, remind me, how do we start the process of creating a magic artifact?" Ryoma asked, his tone light yet expectant.

"With a clear intention of the purpose we wish to imbue into the medium when carving the rune," Kriegon responded, his voice steady with the knowledge he'd absorbed from recent, countless discussions with Ryoma.

"Exactly." Ryoma nodded, his eyes gleaming with approval. "And in this case, our medium is this ox bone. It's particularly suitable because of its length, which allows for more intricate runework and a stronger connection between the scrolls." He demonstrated how the scrolls would be attached to the bone with dowels. "Once I'm done, I'll rewrap the scrolls around the bone. Our goal is for these scrolls to communicate with each other, mirroring any writing from one to the other."

Kriegon, intrigued, posed a question. "What about using a mirroring rune? Wouldn't that also work to reflect the information from one scroll to the other?"

Ryoma paused, considering. "Mirroring could indeed be an approach, but there's a snag. First, information truly mirrored often comes out reversed, which isn't practical for our needs. Second, I'm not familiar with a rune specifically for mirroring that could be used as a base for this purpose."

"Ah, I see," Kriegon conceded, watching intently as Ryoma began to carve. The air was filled with the soft sound of the file against bone, each stroke deliberate and precise. Ryoma's focus was absolute, his hands steady as he etched the rune that would bind the scrolls in magical communication.

Once the carving was complete, Ryoma looked up, his expression one of satisfaction underlined with fatigue. "Now, all that's left is to split the bone, and we'll have our pair of communication scrolls."

As Ryoma prepared to cut the bone, Kriegon voiced another thought. "Why do we need the devices to be connected initially? Could we not create them to communicate directly with others of the same magical intention, without this physical link?"

Ryoma paused, saw in hand, and thought for a moment. "That's an intriguing idea. The truth is, we've always done it this way because it's how I developed the technique. It's possible there's a way to bypass this step, but it would require experimentation, perhaps a new kind of rune or method of imbuing."

Before Kriegon could delve further into the theoretical possibilities, Ryoma held up a finger, signaling him to wait, and then gestured towards the materials Kriegon held. "Let's focus on this for now. You've got everything you need to try your hand at creating your first communication scroll. Let's see what you can do."

Kriegon nodded, setting aside his burgeoning questions for another time. He settled onto the bench, his focus narrowing to the task at hand. The ox bone lay before him, its surface smooth from Ryoma's initial preparations. With careful hands, he began to etch, his movements slow but deliberate, each stroke an attempt to channel his intent into the very marrow of the bone.

Ryoma, meanwhile, moved around the tent, checking on the progress of his guild members, offering guidance or corrections where needed. The tent was alive with the hum of focused activity, the air charged with the potential of magic being woven into physical form.

As Kriegon worked, the complexity of the task became apparent. The runes needed to be precise, their lines clean, their forms exact to ensure the magic would take hold correctly. He found himself lost in the process, the world outside the tent fading as he concentrated on the bone, the file, and the runes. His mind started to meld with the driving magic, as it often did. He intended to push the nightmarish images away and develop a skill to prevent them from ever happening again.

Time passed unnoticed, marked only by the gradual dimming of light outside as night fully claimed the forest. When Kriegon finally looked up, his hands aching from the effort, Ryoma was there, observing with quiet pride.

"You've done well," Ryoma said, examining Kriegon's work. "Now, let's see if it activates."

They prepared to test the scroll, the anticipation palpable. Ryoma wrote a simple message on one scroll, and they watched with bated breath as the other, still blank, began to glow faintly. Slowly, the same message appeared, a testament to Kriegon's successful enchantment.

A grin spread across Kriegon's face, his fatigue momentarily forgotten in the thrill of success. "It worked," he said, almost in disbelief, but also with excitement and pride.

Ryoma clapped him on the shoulder, his own smile wide. "Indeed, it did. You're a natural, Kriegon. I've been thinking about what you had proposed. The idea could open up new avenues for how we create these devices. It's worth exploring."

As they discussed the implications and potential of Kriegon's work, the night deepened around them. The forest outside was a symphony of nocturnal sounds, a backdrop to the energetic talk within the tent.

Ellena peeked in, searching for Kriegon. "Are you coming?" she asked, her voice soft yet carrying a note of impatience.

Kriegon looked up, caught between his fascination with the magical work and his promise to Ellena. "Just a moment," he called back, then turned to Ryoma. "We should definitely look into this further, perhaps during our next rest."

Ryoma nodded in agreement. "Absolutely. For now, let's pack this up. You've earned your rest."

Kriegon, his tools and newly crafted scrolls packed away, stepped into the night, the cool air sharp on his face compared to the warmth of the tent. The forest around him transformed under the moonlight, shadows dancing where once there was light, creating a world both familiar and alien.

Ellena was there, her posture radiating impatience and concern. She seized his hand, her grip firm as she led him towards their shared tent. Her urgency was conspicuous, a silent rebuke for his prolonged absence.

Near the fire, Zenmore sat, his massive form silhouetted against the flickering flames. With a casual flick of his axe, he sent sparks soaring into the night sky, a mundane yet mesmerizing display of brute force meeting art.

Ellena, having guided Kriegon to a log by the fire, handed him his now-cold dinner. "Eat," she commanded, her tone brooking no argument. "You've been neglecting yourself, running off to Dunstan or Ryoma every evening."

Kriegon, feeling the weight of her gaze, began to eat, the food a mere afterthought to the evening's earlier successes in magic.

Zenmore, leaning back with a groan of boredom, questioned, "How much longer with this dull march?"

Kriegon, swallowing a mouthful, responded with what little he knew. "According to Dunstan's maps, we should reach the open fields near the mountain lake in a day or two. Then the pace will pick up quite a bit."

Zenmore's response was a huff, as he reclined fully, staring up at the stars, his interest clearly waning.

Ellena's silence was thick with worry, her eyes not on the fire but on Kriegon. When he tried to reassure her about the potential reduction of encounters with wyverns once they pass the lake, her response was sharp, her frustration boiling over.

"It's not the wyverns that worry me, Kriegon," she snapped, her eyes fierce. "You've been with Dunstan or Ryoma since we left Crossroads. Every night, you prioritize them over us, over me."

Kriegon, caught off guard, tried to shovel food into his mouth, a futile attempt to delay the confrontation. But Ellena's words hung gloomy in the air, demanding attention.

"I didn't expect this, Kriegon. You're preparing, yes, but you're leaving us behind. Zenmore wants to learn about magic, our weapon-changing abilities, but he needs both of our guidance. And I ... I thought we would train together, like before."

Her voice softened, a hint of vulnerability seeping through. "I want to protect you too, Kriegon. But I need your help to protect myself."

The food forgotten, Kriegon set it aside, his heart heavy with realization. He thought about their interaction and his neglect, a stone filling his stomach rather than the food. The desperation to spare his comrades the potential pain he and Ellena had felt had instead isolated those most important to him.

Ellena's hands were gentle on his face, her touch contrasting her earlier irritation. Her kiss was soft, a silent plea for connection, before she turned away, her steps frenetic as she moved towards their tent, brushing away tears that glistened in the firelight.

Kriegon sat, stunned by the depth of Ellena's emotions, by the kiss, their first, which had shifted something fundamental between them. The forest seemed to hold its breath, the night sounds fading into the background as he processed her words, her touch, her kiss.

Zenmore, who had been watching the exchange with amusement and concern, chuckled deeply, his voice a low rumble in the quiet night. "You two make quite the pair," he said, his eyes reflecting the firelight as he looked at Kriegon. "But she's right, you know. You can't just dive into your own world, leaving everyone else to fend for themselves. Especially not when you have people who care about you, who want to be part of your journey."

Kriegon nodded slowly, his gaze following Ellena's retreating form. Zenmore's words were a mirror to his own growing realization. This was a tipping point for them, he knew it. If he continued down this road, he would end up alone like before. He hated the idea, the feeling he had burned into his mind after his military brothers died. Now was the chance to correct his mistake before it took root again.

Standing, he felt the importance of the balance he needed to strike. He walked over to where Ellena had disappeared into their tent, pausing at the entrance. Inside, he could see her silhouette, her back to him, shoulders shaking slightly.

"Ellena," he started, his voice low, filled with a newfound determination. "I'm sorry. You're right. I've been so caught up in everything else that I forgot that we're here together, fighting together."

She turned, her face illuminated by the dim light inside the tent, her eyes searching his for sincerity. "It's not just about the journey or the magic, Kriegon. It's about us, about supporting each other."

Kriegon stepped inside, closing the distance between them. "Let's train together, learn together. I want to be there for you, just as much as you've been there for me. We can face whatever comes next, together."

Ellena's expression softened, a small smile breaking through her earlier sadness. "Together," she echoed, her hand finding his in the dim light. "That's how it should be."

The dense forest canopy finally gave way to the open fields after four grueling days, much to Zenmore's relief. The troops, feeling the consequence of their delay, pushed forward with renewed vigor, hoping to catch up to the main column progress. Initially, the absence of wyvern attacks seemed like a stroke of luck, a brief respite from the constant threat they had anticipated.

However, this illusion of safety shattered abruptly when five smaller wyverns swooped down from the sky, their screeches piercing the quiet. Dunstan barked orders, his voice cutting through the chaos. His captains relayed his command with precision, and the archers responded with a volley that deterred most of the aerial assailants. One wyvern managed to break through, but it was quickly dispatched, its threat ended before it could cause any harm among the troops.

Ellena and Kriegon, momentarily paralyzed by the sudden attack, found themselves reliving the terror of the Crossroads. Their horses stood still as statues, mirroring their riders' shock. Kriegon reached out, his hand finding Ellena's, both seeking solace in the shared moment of fear, a silent support in the face of their shared waking nightmare.

As they moved through the fields towards the lake at the mountain's base, each encounter with the wyverns became a repeated chisel to their fear. By the end of the second day, both Kriegon and Ellena had found their footing, assisting Dunstan in directing the troops, their voices steady as they called out orders amidst the chaos.

That evening, around the campfire, Ellena's voice was a soft murmur against the night. "I fear that is going to haunt my dreams for my whole life," she confessed, her eyes reflecting the flickering flames.

Kriegon, with his arm around her, tried to inject a bit of humor into the intense atmosphere. "I thought you were here to chase away my nightmares," he said, his tone light.

Ellena gave him a reluctant smile from behind her shaking hands and switched topics. "I guess we don't have to worry about the gang attacking anymore. None of the reports from Garthen's group show they have encountered any."

Kriegon looked into the fading light. "It is strange how quickly the gang attacks just cut off with the increased wyvern attacks. But the ritual you all described would take a huge amount of manpower to change all the gang members, and I doubt they'd just lie down and take it."

Ellena shrugged under his arm. "Maybe the gang joined the pirates on the ships. Garthen's scouts did say that a rather large fleet headed south from Riversong. I'm sure they got their fill of gold from Riversong and left. Those greedy bastards."

Kriegon thought about it, humming randomly for a little bit. "Wait, greedy ... Lucifer said he was the Prince of Pride. What if the next prince is Greed?"

Ellena, intrigued by the shift in his demeanor, asked, "What's that got to do with our current predicament?"

Kriegon stood and strode around the fire as Zenmore and the servants came over with food. "What's up with him? Didn't get enough movement today?" joked Zenmore, sitting heavily on the ground.

Kriegon was thinking back to all the seemingly pointless videos he had watched growing up and in barracks or college. "Back on my old world, we had videos that told people about different things."

Ellena watched him as she started to eat. "This going back to your gamertag thing?"

Kriegon shook his head but then paused. "Well, it is related, but not important. Anyway, I used those videos to watch hypothetical, made-up, or religious stories about demons at some point." It was actually rather rare he watched those videos, but he did remember parts of one in particular about Solomon's kings of hell, now that he focused on it. "I do remember now about Lucifer being the Prince of Pride, but there are other princes for each of the sins."

The trio was silent while Kriegon thought quickly. Zenmore asked, "So how many are there?"

Kriegon looked at him, surprised. "Wait, do you not know about the seven deadly sins? It's basic school stuff." Zenmore just shrugged as he ate, only seeming to partly listen. "Well, you know about Lucifer for Pride, but there's more of them. Sloth, Gluttony, Envy, Lust, Wrath, and Greed each have their own dark overseer, commanding legions of lesser demons."

"So, seven things to kill. Easy enough to remember," Zenmore remarked with a smirk, his voice echoing slightly against the backdrop of the crackling fire. His eyes glinted with amusement and anticipation, the firelight casting dancing shadows across his rugged features.

Ellena, her brow furrowed in deep thought, chewed her food with deliberate slowness. "When you mention legions of lesser demons, are you talking about ..."

"Yes," Kriegon interrupted, his voice tinged with a hopeful edge. "These wyverns we've been encountering, they must be underlings of one of these princes. What if it's the Prince of Greed we're up against? If we could somehow defeat this prince, maybe the wyverns would cease their coordinated attacks."

Zenmore, his expression skeptical, shook his head slowly. "Kriegon, remember, Rei mentioned wyverns were part of her world, too. Don't start dreaming of a world where slaying one demon prince fixes everything. It's not that simple."

Kriegon's hopeful feeling faltered, a sigh escaping him as reality set in. "I know, it's just ... it would be a significant blow, wouldn't it? To their organization."

A moment of silence fell over them. Zenmore's hand slowly reached for Kriegon's untouched plate. Kriegon, catching the movement from the corner of his eye, dashed back to his spot, snatching the plate away just in time, which caused Zenmore to laugh loudly into the calm night. "Not so fast, Zenmore," Kriegon said, a playful warning in his tone.

As Kriegon quickly consumed his meal, shoveling food into his mouth with less grace than intended, Ellena turned to him with a question that had been brewing in her mind. "Do you know who these princes are, what they look like?"

Kriegon paused, his fork halfway to his mouth, then set it down with a slight frown. "I wish I could give you a definitive answer, Ellena. There are so many versions of these tales, so many names thrown around. Some say Mammon for Greed, others Asmodeus for Lust, but there's no consensus. It's like everyone had a story or theory to throw around."

Ellena nodded, her expression one of understanding and disappointment. "So, we're essentially in the dark, fighting shadows without a clear target."

"Yeah," Kriegon admitted, "but knowing there's a structure to their chaos, that's something. It means there's a head to this beast, or at least, heads. We might not know their faces or names for certain, but we can start unraveling their influence, starting with these wyverns."

The night had deepened to an inky blackness, the only light coming from the ethereal glow of two ever-present full moons, casting an eerie sheen over the landscape through the light cloud cover. Kriegon, momentarily caught in the beauty of the celestial bodies, was about to voice a question about them when a sudden outcry broke from the camp's northern edge.

The trio rose with a start, their eyes scanning the dark, their hearts pounding with the onset of adrenaline. Around them, the camp was stirring, soldiers waking from their slumber, their faces a jumble of confusion and fear. A call to arms echoed through the lines, sharp and urgent, slicing through the night.

"Is it another wyvern attack?" Kriegon's voice carried his urgency and disbelief, his hand instinctively reaching for his weapon.

Zenmore, his vision piercing the darkness better than any human's could, shook his head. "No, these are not wyverns. They're about the size of ... well, humans, but there's something off about them."

With no time to lose, they grabbed their weapons. Ellena and Kriegon mounted their horses, hastily resaddled by their servants, while Zenmore, his massive frame a shadow moving through the night, led the way towards the commotion. As they approached, they could see Dunstan, still in the process of donning his armor, his voice booming over the chaos, orchestrating the defense.

Spotting the trio, Dunstan waved them closer. "I need you three now. Kriegon, take the left flank; Ellena, the right. Organize the troops, form a line. Zenmore, you and I will hold the center where it's thickest."

Kriegon, confusion knitting his brow, asked, "But what enemies? We didn't see anything from the fields or the sky."

Dunstan's expression was grim. "I don't know how they approached so silently, but they're humans ... or were, I suppose. They've already torn through ten of my men."

Zenmore, his voice a low rumble of thunder, concluded, "Then it's undead we face." Without waiting for further explanation, he forged through the ranks, his size and presence making a path to the front.

Dunstan nodded at Kriegon and Ellena before spurring his horse forward, his commands slicing through the night air.

Kriegon, sharing a last determined look with Ellena, directed his horse to the left flank. The soldiers there were half-ready, their fear severe as they tried to form ranks. Kriegon began issuing orders, his voice strained with the need to be heard over the rising din, urging the men to form a spear wall to support the shield line that was beginning to waver under the pressure of the advancing undead.

Ryoma rode up beside him, his horse neighing in the confusion, and asked, "What's going on? Who's attacking us?"

Already hoarse from shouting, Kriegon replied, "Not sure, and I can't tell how many. They keep coming, wrapping around our flanks."

As Ryoma rummaged through his horse's pack, he pulled out a small tube. "Let's see what we're dealing with," he said, activating the device.

214

A bright flare shot into the sky, illuminating the battlefield with an unnatural light.

The scene that unfolded under the stark light was horrific. The attackers were indeed human in form but moved with a grotesque, unnatural gait. Their eyes were empty, their skin had a ghastly pallor, and their movements were devoid of any human emotion or strategy. They wore remnants of what could have once been armor or clothing, now tattered and decayed, moving inexorably forward like a tide of death.

From his vantage point amidst the chaos, Kriegon watched as Zenmore, a towering behemoth of muscle and metal, swung his colossal weapon with devastating force. Each arc of his blade was like a scythe through wheat, cutting down swaths of the undead with an almost brutal efficiency. His presence was a beacon of hope and fear, a giant amidst the fray, his every movement a testament to the power of the living against the relentless dead.

On the other side of the battlefield, Ellena was a different kind of storm. Her sword whip, a gleaming arc of silver in the moonlight, danced through the air with lethal precision. Its movement was fluid, a serpent of steel that struck with the speed of lightning, slicing through any undead that dared approach her flank. Her command over her weapon was mesmerizing, a deadly ballet against the backdrop of war.

The battle raged on, the night air thick with the clash of steel, the grunts of soldiers, and the eerie silence of the undead, who neither screamed nor cried out when struck. Their bodies fell only to be replaced by more emerging from the darkness, their numbers seemingly endless.

The sheer mass of the undead was overwhelming. They were like a dark sea, endless and unyielding, their tide seeming to grow with each fallen soldier. Kriegon, his heart tight with the impossibility of their predicament, exchanged a glance of despair with Ryoma. The light from Ryoma's device, though bright, was not enough to stem the tide, and as it dimmed, the reality of their situation grew all the more dire.

Kriegon's mind raced back to simpler times, to games where the undead were mere pixels on a screen, easily dispatched with the click of a button. Here, in the cold grasp of reality, there were no respawns, no easy victories, no guns to mow them down. The undead before him were relentless, their numbers daunting. He turned to Ryoma, desperation in his eyes. "Do you have anything in that bag that can send fire over the enemy?"

Ryoma, fumbling through his satchel, shook his head in regret. "Nothing that can do that," he replied, his voice tinged with frustration.

Kriegon, his resolve hardening, knew he had to act. He pointed to the nearest captain, his voice firm despite the uncertainty in his heart. "If something goes wrong, you're taking my place."

Before Ryoma could voice his concern, Kriegon was already channeling his psychic energy, focusing it into the newly formed rune on his staff. The energy crackled, a storm of power in the night, and from it, a fireball began to form. It started small, a mere spark of light and heat, but as Kriegon poured more of his will into it, the fireball grew, its flames dancing with an almost sentient fury.

With a gesture that mirrored the one Ryoma had used to launch his light, Kriegon raised his staff high. The fireball, now a roaring inferno above the battlefield, cast an eerie glow over the undead horde. Just as he felt his energy wane, his strength nearly at its breaking point, he released the fireball with a shout that was half defiance, half exhaustion.

The fireball soared, a comet of destruction, before exploding in a wide arc over the undead. The flames spread like wildfire, consuming the decayed flesh of the zombies, their forms shriveling under the onslaught of fire. The heat was intense, the light blinding, turning night into a semblance of day.

Kriegon's vision blurred as the last of his energy was spent. His body, unable to endure the strain any longer, gave in to the darkness at the edges of his consciousness. He slumped forward, his grip on his staff loosening, but not before he saw the flames doing their deadly work, the undead ranks thinning under the fiery assault.

As he passed out, his last thought was a hope that his sacrifice would tip the scales, that his friends would hold the line, and that somehow, they would all see the dawn together.

No sooner had the darkness of unconsciousness claimed him than Kriegon was jolted awake by a sharp movement. The world spun as he opened his eyes, the harsh light of early morning slicing through the slit in the tent's fabric, casting a bright line across his face. His head throbbed with a pain that felt like the aftermath of a heavy night's drink, his throat raw as if he'd swallowed sand.

Ellena's face, framed by the golden light of dawn, was the first thing he saw. Her smile, both comforting and mischievous, was a welcome sight compared to the chaos of battle he'd last remembered. His head rested gently on her lap, her fingers combing through his hair in a soothing rhythm.

"What happened?" Kriegon managed, his voice a hoarse whisper, the effort of speaking sending a fresh wave of pain through his skull.

"Your magic, that's what happened," Ellena replied, her voice a blend of admiration and pride. "You turned the tide out there. Without that fireball, we would've been overrun for sure." Her expression turned to mocking severity. "But why haven't you taught me that kind of magic? Were you trying to keep all the heroics to yourself?"

Kriegon's chuckle was weak but genuine, his laughter cut short by the throbbing in his head. "As if. I just ... pushed too hard."

"But it was necessary," Ellena conceded, her voice dropping to a whisper, her eyes darkening with the memory of the battle. "I thought about breaking the line, coming to get you, and just ... running."

Kriegon, understanding all too well, reached up to touch her face, his fingers brushing against her cheek. "It's okay. We all face fear in battle."

Ellena sighed, her frustration clear. "Except Zenmore. He was boasting about another 'Guardian achievement' but then grumbled about not getting to kill more undead himself." Her voice carried exasperation and amusement as she mimicked Zenmore's deep, rumbling tone. "He was actually disappointed he didn't have more to fight."

Kriegon's laughter, though painful, was hearty. "That sounds like him. Always looking for the next challenge, even in the midst of a fight." His hand fell back to his side, the strain of even this small gesture evident through his aching muscles.

Ellena's gaze softened as she looked down at him, her fingers still playing with his hair absentmindedly. "You did well, Kriegon. Better than well. You saved us out there." Her voice was sincere, carrying the emphasis of gratitude and respect.

Kriegon managed a weak smile. "We all did. It's what we do, right? Protect each other, no matter the cost."

She nodded, her eyes misting slightly. "Yes, that's exactly what we do." There was a pause, a moment of silence that felt filled with unspoken words and shared memories of battles fought and lives that hadn't been saved.

Finally, Ellena spoke, her tone lightening, trying to lift the mood. "But next time, maybe let's try not to push ourselves to the brink, huh? We might not be so lucky."

Kriegon's eyes narrowed, and he met her gaze with a smirk. "I'll try to remember that. But when have we ever done things the easy way?"

Ellena laughed, the sound like a melody in the quiet of the tent. "Never, it seems. But hey, at least we're consistent." Their laughter mingled, a brief respite from the harsh realities of their world. Sighing softly, she rested one hand over his eyes. "Go back to sleep now. I'll wake you if anything comes up."

The journey across the plains had morphed into a relentless cycle of rest and readiness, with skirmishes becoming a grim routine. Yet, the ferocity of the initial onslaughts by wyverns and the undead had somewhat abated, allowing the company to press on with relative ease, their defenses now well-honed against such threats. Kriegon felt the weight of the constant assaults, but the support of Ellena and Zenmore carrying the load with him kept his head high.

As they approached the first village, a tangible tension hung in the air, presenting a dilemma for Dunstan and his command. On Zenmore's counsel, a scouting mission was quickly organized, with Zenmore himself leading the foray. His return was met with a council of war, where Kriegon, Ellena, Dunstan, and his captains gathered in the command tent, thick with the pungent smoke of Artemin's favored blend—a habit shared by many in the camp.

Inside the tent, the atmosphere was one of strategic urgency. Kriegon and Ellena stood opposite Dunstan, poring over maps laid on a makeshift table.

"Our current pace will necessitate a resupply before we skirt the lake," one of the captains remarked, his finger tracing their route on the map, eyes squinting at the numbers on his scroll.

Dunstan, with a nod, absorbed this information. "And the towns along our path? Can we draw supplies from them?"

Another captain leaned in, pointing to several small, unnamed towns dotted around the lake and up the river. "These settlements are minor, hardly more than hamlets. The nearest city, substantial enough for our needs, lies far off our projected path. We might have to make do with what little these villages can offer."

The discussion was abruptly punctuated by a commotion outside. All eyes turned towards the tent's entrance, anticipation hanging thick. Zenmore ducked in, his massive frame barely fitting under the tent's canopy. He was a grim figure, smeared with the blood and viscera of battle, methodically cleaning his weapon with a piece of cloth torn from the dead.

"The tales from my world, the darkest ones, have nothing on this," Zenmore's voice boomed, onerous with the weight of what he had seen. "The village ... it's been utterly consumed by the undead. There's nothing left there that breathes life."

The gravity of his words settled over the group like a cold fog. The realization dawned that this was no isolated incident; every town, every village from here to Riversong might be a mirror of the horror Zenmore described. The campaign, already fraught with peril, now faced the grim prospect of purging entire communities that had turned necrotic.

Dunstan's face hardened, the lines of command and worry etching deeper. "Then we prepare for what must be done. We cannot afford to let this plague spread unchecked."

Chapter 17: Riversong's Hive

The news of the undead's existence had reached Garthen's troops days prior, yet the reality of facing them, when it finally came, struck a chord of fear and uncertainty through the ranks. Now, as the sun dipped below the horizon, casting long shadows over the battlefield, Garthen, Saphire, and the battalion leaders, including Artemin, gathered around a massive pyre where the bodies of the fallen undead were being consigned to flames. The air was thick with the acrid smell of burning flesh, a grim reminder of the battle.

Rei closely examined a couple of the bodies before they too were tossed on the raging inferno of decay. She approached Garthen with a furrowed brow. "I couldn't find any magical runes I recognize. It's just like with the wyverns," she reported, her voice laced with concern. The implications were clear: whatever force animated these undead was beyond their current understanding, possibly linked to the same dark magic that had corrupted the wyverns.

Garthen, taking in the grim expressions of his leaders, issued his orders with a steely resolve. "Double the night watches. We move out at dawn as planned. Consider this a test of our readiness and resilience. Tonight, grant each soldier an extra ration of ale. They've earned it."

Murmurs of agreement and relief passed among the group as they dispersed, leaving Garthen, Saphire, and Rei alone by the pyre. The flames danced, casting flickering light on their faces, each lost in thought.

Saphire, her gaze fixed on the inferno, seemed to be grappling with memories she'd rather forget. Rei, sensing the import of the moment, ventured a question that was on her mind. "You've dealt with undead before, haven't you, Saphire? Zenmore mentioned the undead before all this really started."

Saphire's nod was almost imperceptible, her voice barely above a whisper. "After battles or massacres, sometimes the dead wouldn't stay down. We'd have to burn them, like now." Her eyes, usually bright with determination, dimmed as she spoke. "My village ... after an orc raid, it wasn't just the living who suffered. I had to ... re-kill my family. The ones not taken into slavery, that is."

The revelation cast a somber shadow over them. Rei, moved by Saphire's pain, reached out to offer comfort, but Saphire, with a shake of her head, walked away, her stride filled with grief, towards her troops.

Rei turned to Garthen, her expression troubled. "No wonder she has such animosity towards Zenmore."

Garthen, his gaze following Saphire's retreating figure, nodded slowly. "Yet, Zenmore claims his tribe never acted against her race. It's a complex web of hatred and history."

Rei's expression hardened. "History or not, the pain is real. And for Saphire, it's personal. The source of her vendetta doesn't erase the scars it's left."

Garthen, understanding the depth of such personal disputes, especially in the context of this conflict, agreed. "True. And in this war, any who align with the demons, or embody their cruelty, are marked for death in my book."

They walked in silence away from the pyre, the heat of the flames still warming their backs. Garthen, feeling the need to bridge the gap between the mages and the rest of the troops, broached a sensitive topic as they approached the Magic Guild's section of the camp.

"Rei, your use of magic has been invaluable to our efforts. Do you think some of your mages could engage more directly in the battles, perhaps to reduce the need for so much healing afterward?"

Rei's gaze swept over her students, who were busily engaged in their own tasks, from crafting magical artifacts to tending the wounded. Her concern was clear. "I'm not sure, Garthen. Few of them possess the psychic reserves like the Guardians do. Even with some training, most barely match what you've shown, and that's after years of study compared to your days."

Garthen was disappointed, but he pressed on, hoping for a compromise. "Their healing is crucial, yes. But if they could help stem the tide of battle, perhaps fewer would need healing in the first place."

Rei, clearly deep in thought as she considered possibilities, offered a hesitant nod. "I'll consider it, Garthen. But we must be cautious. Their lives are not just tools of war; they're young, eager, but not yet seasoned."

As they parted ways, the night air around them was filled with the sounds of preparation and the soft glow of magical lights from the mage's tents.

Over the following weeks, as the relentless siege of wyverns and undead bogged down their advance, Garthen's patience wore thin. Each day that passed with little progress towards Riversong only deepened his frustration, especially with Rei, whom he believed was too protective of her mages.

As Riversong loomed on the horizon, its silhouette marred by the constant aerial threat of wyverns, Garthen's strategy had to adapt. The undead had ceased their ground assaults, but the air was now dominated by wyverns, forcing the camp into the dense cover of the forest for any semblance of safety. The situation grew direr with each passing day, their movement towards the city's southern gate painfully slow, only picking up pace as Dunstan's forces approached from the east, splitting the wyverns' attention.

At the edge of the forest, amidst the cacophony of battle cries and the beating of wings, Garthen's voice boomed over the noise. "Rei, are your mages ready to fight, or what?" His tone was edged with irritation, a reflection of weeks of pent-up frustration.

Rei soared above, her scythe a whirlwind of motion, slicing through the air with precision. Despite her effectiveness, each swing was a reminder of the limits of her endurance. Landing next to Garthen after dispatching another pair of wyverns, she was visibly drained. "They're exhausted, Garthen. All they can manage now is healing, and even that's a stretch."

Garthen's response was a grimace, his features hardening as he released another arrow, felling a juvenile wyvern. "You're still babying them, Rei. We need that gate down, and magic is our only shot at this point."

Their attempts to bring down the gate with a battering ram had been met with fierce resistance from the wyverns, always quick to dive-bomb the ram as soon as it emerged from the tree line.

Rei's retort was sharp, her patience with Garthen's criticism worn thin. "I'm not babying them. I'm ensuring they're ready, not throwing them into the fray unprepared!" Her words carried the weight of her convictions, a fierce protectiveness over her mages. Without waiting for Garthen's reply, she launched into the air towards the gate, her scythe now glowing with a bright green light.

Garthen watched, his skepticism morphing into reluctant admiration as Rei's scythe, with each powerful swing, manifested as violent gashes in the gate. Upon reaching it, Rei's scythe transformed into a colossal hammer, its head glowing with radiant light. With a powerful arc, she struck the gate, the impact echoing like thunder. The gate, unable to withstand such force, began to crumble, its iron bands snapping and wood splintering under the magical assault.

As Rei retreated, the gate gave way, revealing not just the path into Riversong but also a new challenge. From the breach, a swarm of young wyverns, their scales not yet fully hardened, poured out. Their cries were high-pitched and frantic, a terrible prelude to the deep, menacing roars of their adult counterparts.

Garthen, witnessing the unfolding scene, couldn't help but feel a mix of triumph and dread. "Shields up! Form a defensive line! Archers, keep those beasts at bay!" His commands cut through the chaos, his troops responding with the discipline of seasoned warriors, despite the unexpected onslaught.

Rei, landing beside Garthen, her chest heaving from the exertion, shot him a look that fused exhaustion with defiance. "The gate's down, but look at what's coming through. We need to be strategic, not reckless."

Garthen, his annoyance at Rei's perceived overprotectiveness of her mages not entirely quelled, nodded curtly. "I see it. But we can't afford to be gentle now. We need every advantage. Can your mages help, or are they too precious for this fight?"

Rei's departure from the conversation was abrupt, her figure disappearing into the dense underbrush towards the camp, her movements marked by exhaustion and irritation. Garthen's question hung unanswered in the air, a testament to the growing rift between their strategies and perspectives.

As the day wore on, Garthen's troops found themselves embroiled in skirmishes with the juvenile wyverns that emerged from the city. These creatures, though less formidable than their mature counterparts, were numerous and relentless, their presence adding an unexpected layer of complexity to the siege. The fall of the southern gate, however, was a pivotal moment, allowing Dunstan's forces to approach the eastern gate by nightfall, setting the stage for a coordinated assault on Riversong.

In the seclusion of Garthen's tent, illuminated by flickering lanterns, a makeshift table bore a detailed map of Riversong. The leaders of Garthen's company gathered around, their faces etched with the gravity of the impending battle. Garthen's gaze was penetrating as he studied the map, his mind racing through possibilities. "With these new wyverns, expect fierce resistance within the city walls," he cautioned, his voice steady yet filled with an undercurrent of tension.

Artemin, her voice as rough as ever, chimed in, "And don't forget, we lose the advantage of forest cover once inside."

The tent fell silent, save for the distant clash of battle and the occasional screech of a wyvern, as each leader pondered the implications. It was Saphire who broke the silence, her question cutting through the tension, "Could the city's buildings offer us the cover we need?"

Garthen, a spark of inspiration igniting in his eyes, remembered the large shipyard structures, reminiscent of those he and Zenmore had once navigated to rescue Kristin and the others. Pointing to their location on the map, he outlined his plan. "These shipyards can serve as our primary bases. They're spacious enough to shelter troops and could be fortified."

Agreement rippled through the group as they began to strategize, detailing who would lead which faction and how they would spearhead their assault into the city. Cabitha was tasked with relaying these plans to Dunstan's group, ensuring coordination between the two forces.

As the meeting concluded with plans set for the next day's midday assault, Garthen approached Rei, who had been observing from a distance. Her presence was marked by the visible toll of the day's events, her usually vibrant scales now shadowed with fatigue.

"I've arranged for my group and Saphire's to provide direct protection for your mages," Garthen began, his tone carefully neutral, attempting to bridge the gap that had formed between them.

Rei's response was a nod, her weariness evident in the droop of her scales. "With luck, taking their territory might discourage the wyverns," she mused, her voice tinged with hope despite her exhaustion.

Garthen, recognizing the logic in her words yet feeling the weight of his own skepticism, continued, "We can convert one of those shipyards into a field hospital and kitchen. It'll help keep your team operational."

Rei, leaning heavily on her scythe, seemed to struggle against sleep. Garthen watched, concern flickering in his hollow heart, as she nearly nodded off standing up. "You need rest, Rei. No duties until tomorrow's assault," he advised, his voice softening.

Without a word, Rei succumbed to her fatigue, her head resting against the handle of her scythe, asleep where she stood. Garthen turned to Saphire, who had approached, her expression filled with concern and resignation. "Maybe we just leave her here," Saphire suggested, a grim smile playing on her lips. "If we move her near the mages now, she'll find some task to busy herself with."

Garthen nodded, understanding all too well Rei's tendency to push herself beyond limits, especially when it came to her mages. "Let her rest," he decided, his gaze lingering on Rei's sleeping form, a silent acknowledgment of the battles she fought against both the wyverns and balancing leadership with care.

As Saphire brought Rei a makeshift bed, Garthen stepped away to his private sleeping area to catch what little sleep he was likely to get with all that weighed on his mind.

The first snow of the season began to fall, delicate flakes that seemed almost out of place against the backdrop of war. The air was crisp, carrying the scent of impending conflict and the cold promise of winter. Dunstan's group, inspired by Rei's earlier display of power, unleashed their own brand of magic on the eastern gate of Riversong. The distant explosion echoed like thunder, a booming testament to their success, as the gate crumbled under their spell.

As the immature wyverns, previously relentless in their attacks, began to falter, Garthen seized the moment. With a commanding gesture, he called his soldiers forward. Artemin's group took the lead, their assault as precise and forceful as a ship cutting through choppy seas. They sliced through the wyverns' disorder, their movements a dance of death, clearing a path for the main forces.

Saphire, Rei, and Garthen's troops advanced behind Artemin's vanguard, their path littered with the aftermath of the battle. Mature wyverns, their scales glinting even in the dim light of the overcast, snowy day, dove from above, their attacks desperate and fierce. The ground was a macabre tapestry of baby wyvern corpses, their once-threatening presence now reduced to obstacles underfoot.

Inside the city, the scene was one of devastation. The northern section of Riversong lay in ruins, buildings either crushed as if by a giant's fist or ravaged by fire. The wall of the nobles' quarter, once a symbol of opulence and status, was marred by what appeared to be molten gold, a grotesque decoration of destruction.

Amid this chaos, the unexpected presence of civilians emerged. Gaunt, their eyes wide with fear and hunger, they stumbled from the shadows of the city, seeking escape. Garthen, his heart heavy with the burden of war's victims, ordered guards to escort these non-combatants out of the war zone, directing others to push forward into the heart of the city.

The shipyards became their haven, where Rei's mages, despite their exhaustion, began to set up a makeshift field hospital. But as they settled, the ground beneath them seemed to tremble with an ominous prelude to what was to come.

An explosion drew Garthen's gaze towards the castle, where two figures, majestic and terrifying, clawed at the spires. Dragons, not wyverns, their presence undeniable by their size, their four legs, and the sheen of their scales. One was a brilliant blue, the other a deep, blood red, both dwarfing any wyvern seen before.

Then, from the ashes of the inner gate rose a third dragon, its scales gleaming like molten gold in the firelight. With a deep, resonant inhale, it exhaled a stream of liquid fire, a river of melted metal that set ablaze the remaining northern structures, its laughter a deep, earth-shaking rumble that filled the city.

"Fools who come for what I have gained and amassed, despair! You will never have the glorious treasure I am sitting atop. Though, if you so desire, become my underling and join my hordes of wealth," it declared, its voice boasting a challenge and mockery.

The golden dragon's chuckle was like the rumble of distant thunder, reverberating through the air as it retreated behind the flames and rubble, its presence a looming threat over the city. Garthen, rooted to the spot, was caught in the magnitude of the moment, his eyes locked with those of the dragons, feeling the authority of their challenge resonate in his very soul.

Garthen, shaking off the initial shock of the dragons' appearance, rallied his voice with a confidence he scarcely felt. "Do not falter! Look, they retreat behind their walls, cowering from our might!" His words were meant to bolster the spirits of his troops, to cover his own uncertainty about facing such formidable creatures as dragons. Yet, his stance was unwavering, his gaze steady, as if the dragons were nothing more than another obstacle in their path.

The southern part of Riversong fell under their control with surprising ease. Amid the captured territory, they discovered houses and storage buildings filled with wyvern eggs. Without hesitation, Garthen's soldiers crushed every egg they found, a grim but necessary task to prevent further threats. By the time Dunstan's forces rejoined the main company, the sun was dipping towards the horizon, casting long shadows over the city and bathing the scene in a dusky glow.

It was amidst this strategic regrouping that Rei approached Garthen, her expression filled with urgency and concern. "Two of my mages are missing, Tristan and Ninette. They spoke of seeking glory and might be off on a fool's errand."

Garthen, already burdened with the authority of command and the looming threat of the dragons, waved off her concern. "Rei, we have soldiers unaccounted for as well. We'll find your mages after securing the city."

But Rei's insistence was clear in the frantic shake of her head. "No, you don't understand. These two are headstrong, likely chasing danger for the sake of valor or some misguided sense of heroism."

Garthen, recognizing the determination in Rei's eyes, sighed, knowing full well she wouldn't let this go. "Fine. Has anyone seen any robed figures wandering off?" he asked, turning to the council for answers.

The room was silent, the air thick with the tension of war, until a captain in the back, previously unnoticed, shifted uncomfortably. His movement caught Rei's sharp gaze, and she was upon him in an instant. "What do you know?" she demanded, her tone brooking no argument.

The captain, visibly swallowing his fear, spoke up. "I saw ... some figures in robes heading towards the easternmost bridge not long ago. Wasn't sure if they were ours or ..."

That was enough for Rei. Without another word, she was airborne, her scythe gleaming under the fading light as she launched herself in the direction the captain indicated. Garthen watched her go with irritation, wondering how she managed to care so deeply for each of her mages.

Kriegon turned to Garthen. "We're going after her, aren't we?" His voice challenged Garthen in a way he hadn't done before.

Garthen, still processing his own thoughts, replied, "She's capable, but those dragons ..." His voice trailed off, the unspoken worry hanging in the air.

Ellena added, "Those dragons could be too much for anyone alone. What if they decide to engage her?"

Zenmore, with his characteristic bravado, chimed in, "We could take 'em, if we're together. Why not make sure we're all there when it happens?"

Relenting, Garthen nodded. "Alright. The Guardians will follow Rei, just in case she walks into something bigger than herself."

The same captain who had pointed out Rei's mages raised his hand again, this time with a request. "Sire, I would like my battalion to join as well. Rei and her mages have saved many of us. It's only right we return the favor."

Garthen's annoyance was self-evident, the strain of leadership making him brusque. "Why would we split our forces now, especially with dragons in play?"

The captain stood his ground, his loyalty to Rei and her mages evident. "Sir, it's a matter of honor. We owe them, and I won't sit by while they might be in danger. If we're going, let us go in strength."

Noticing the resolve in the captain's eyes and understanding that the bond between soldiers was often forged in such moments of mutual aid, Garthen softened his expression slightly. "Very well. Your battalion can join the Guardians. But remember, our primary goal remains to secure the city. We engage the dragons only if absolutely necessary."

The preparations were made swiftly under the veil of the ever-darkening night as the battalion headed into the northern section of the city. The streets, choked with the rubble of countless destroyed buildings, barely allowed passage, yet the troops pressed on with grim determination. Ryoma and Kriegon took turns launching what they referred to as flares, their bright light cutting through the darkness, guiding their path. Garthen, with hope in his heart, prayed that Rei would see these signals and understand that rescue was on its way.

However, as they traversed roughly halfway through the northern district, disaster struck. A sound like a torrential river suddenly erupted, followed by flames that licked the inner walls of the keep to the castle's left. The sinister laughter from the keep's new master, a chilling echo in the night, preceded a booming command: "So you insult me by sending such pitiful resistance. Worry not, for you shall taste this prince's mercy. GO, BRIRDAN AND YDDRU. END THESE THIEVES!"

The call to action was immediate. Garthen's heart raced as he commanded his troops into a defensive formation. "Shields up! Archers, ready!" His voice, a beacon amidst the chaos, steadied his men as they braced for the inevitable onslaught. The air itself seemed to vibrate with the anticipation of the dragons' next move, a tension so deep it felt like the very ground was holding its breath.

Then, without warning, a jet of fire, as if from the bowels of hell itself, swept across the left flank of their formation. The screams of men and the smell of burning flesh galvanized Garthen. His horse, sensing its rider's urgency, surged forward as he shouted to the mages, "Quickly! Fire something into the sky! We need eyes on the enemy!"

Kriegon and Ryoma, their faces set in fierce concentration, complied. "You got it, Garthen!" Their voices were nearly lost in the cacophony of the raging fire. Their flares soared into the night sky like comets, illuminating pockets of darkness around them.

Garthen, his own bow drawn to its limit, searched frantically amidst the fleeting light for any sign of the dragons. The air vibrated again with the ominous sound of approaching danger, and as one of the flares found its mark, Garthen loosed his arrow, signaling his archers to follow suit.

The sky was briefly lit by the fiery trail of the dragon's breath, consuming the right flank of the army. Now caught between two fires, the arrows and Kriegon's hastily cast magic struck true. The dragon, hit and floundering, crashed onto the street, its wings riddled with holes, its body thrashing in an attempt to right itself.

Garthen, seeing an opportunity, turned back to Kriegon and Ryoma.

"Can you do something about its flame attack? At this rate, we'll be reduced to ash."

Kriegon, his breath coming in arduous gasps, nodded. "We can try, but it's a gamble. We need to turn its own fire against it."

The plan, as mad as it was, was all they had. Garthen quickly relayed instructions to Zenmore and Saphire. "Kriegon and Ellena will create an opening. Zenmore, Saphire, you know what to do."

As the second dragon plummeted to the ground, shaking the earth like a falling titan, the first dragon, seeing its companion's fate, roared and prepared another fiery assault. The intensity of the flames was such that even from a distance, Garthen could feel the heat sear his already burned skin.

Kriegon, Ryoma, and Ellena sprinted forward, their plan echoing in the air. "We need to turn those flames back into its mouth!"

The trio halted just before the front lines, where the dragon's attack had caused disarray. Garthen watched as their weapons, glowing with the runes of magic, prepared to cast. The dragon, now in a frenzy, whipped its head, spewing flames wildly. But then, something miraculous happened—the fire stopped midair, as if caught by an invisible hand, and was drawn back towards the dragon. The head lowered, nearly touching the ground, and its body convulsed like someone hiccupping.

Seizing the moment, Zenmore charged with a roar, swinging his axe with all his might towards the dragon's vulnerable snout. But the dragon's scales were like armor; even Zenmore's powerful strikes barely scratched the surface. Ellena, with a grace born of desperation, leaped, her sword aimed at the dragon's eye. The blade found its mark, sinking deep, and the dragon's scream of agony tore at Garthen's ears.

The beast, in its recoil, flung Ellena aside, its one remaining eye locking onto her with a hatred that was almost tangible. Garthen, his heart in his throat, spurred his horse forward, knowing he was too far, too late. The dragon's next breath was a column of fire aimed directly at Ellena, who was still lying knocked out. The heat felt like his skin was roasting off again.

The horse bucked and slid to a stop, throwing Garthen from its back. Rolling out of the fall, Garthen could only watch as the flames bathed the area Ellena had been. Falling to his knees, he felt the pain of loss all over again, refreshed and sharp in his heart. However, this time all the strength left his body, it was like he was in a block of ice, unable to move.

When the flames did go out, something unbelievable was in its place. A bright orange sphere was over the spot Ellena had been. As Garthen watched, the sphere fell away, and he saw Kriegon lying next to Ellena. The staff, which had been the sphere, was glowing orange a few feet from Kriegon's hands.

Revived by the sight of his friends' bravery, Garthen turned his attention back to the dragon, now vulnerable and attempting to claw the sword from its eye. Noting a difference in the scales under its leg, Garthen saw a chance. "Let's end this now! I'll distract it from the damaged eye side," he shouted, his voice rallying the remaining fighters.

He put everything into this sprint, his legs screaming from how hard he pushed them, and the dragon took up his entire view. Garthen slid beneath the dragon, his bow's sharp edge aimed at the creature's armpit. The dragon's roar of pain was his cue; he dodged out, using its blind spot to stay alive. Garthen, using every ounce of agility he possessed, dodged around the beast frantic attacks hoping someone had gotten the message about his distraction

As the dragon reeled for another attack, Saphire, with a warrior's precision, drove her sword into its other eye. Zenmore, following her lead, used his hammer to drive the blade deep into the dragon's skull. The beast convulsed, its head rising briefly before crashing lifelessly to the ground.

Climbing atop the fallen dragon's head, Garthen, exhausted yet triumphant, called for silence among the cheering troops. "Gather the wounded; we need them treated by the mages. To those not occupied, spread out and find Rei. Let's return to camp, victorious over these odds!"

Chapter 18: The Black Death Wave

Kriegon awoke with a throbbing headache that felt like a relentless drumbeat inside his skull, the wooden beams of the shipyard ceiling above him reminiscent of his disorientation upon first arriving in this world. His body ached as if he'd been through a maelstrom, the ground beneath him offering little comfort. Flashes of the battle replayed in his mind: Ellena in peril, his desperate move, and then darkness as the dragon prepared to unleash its fiery breath.

With effort, he pushed himself into a sitting position, his vision swimming slightly with the movement. Around him, the other Guardians were scattered, some sitting, others lying on makeshift stretchers. The relief was deep when he saw Ellena, safe beside Rei, both under the care of Ronald, Rei's most dedicated student. Ronald's focus was intense, his wand glowing with a blue light as he worked over Rei's leg, sweat beading his forehead from the effort.

Kriegon, every step a significant effort, made his way to Ronald, waiting patiently as the young mage completed his healing spell. The air was thick with the scent of burnt wood and healing herbs, a backdrop to the quiet concentration of the scene.

"How are they?" Kriegon's voice was hoarse, betraying his concern.

Asselin, who had just entered the room, answered with her usual calm. "Everyone here is stable. No severe injuries, thankfully." She had kept up with Ronald, a narrow second for Rei's teachings.

The memory of the dragon's devastating power lingered in Kriegon's mind, prompting him to ask the question he dreaded most. "And how many didn't return?"

There was a moment of shared silence between Asselin and Ronald before Asselin responded, her voice carrying a weight of sorrow. "Twenty-eight."

Kriegon's heart sank, the number echoing in his mind like a tolling bell for the lost. He looked around, the absence of Garthen suddenly noticeable. "Garthen?" he inquired, a hint of panic in his tone.

Ronald, voice filled with admiration and concern, replied, "He hasn't taken a break since he got back. Last I heard, he's planning the next move against the remaining dragon."

Reassured by the news of Garthen's safety, Kriegon allowed himself a moment of relief. The room fell silent again, save for the soft murmurs of those being tended to. Asselin moved to begin her own healing work on Rei, and Kriegon, sensing the need for quiet, decided to give them space.

As he walked through the makeshift medical ward, the reality of the battle's aftermath hit him hard. Soldiers lay bandaged, some with missing limbs, others with burns or bite wounds, their faces etched with the pain of survival. The air was thick with the scent of healing herbs and the quiet resilience of those who had faced death and lived.

As Kriegon made his way across the bustling shipyard, the air was suddenly filled with the savory scent of cooking food. The familiar figure of the chef from Crossroads was there, his hands busy at the grill and stew pot, a beacon of normalcy amidst the chaos they'd endured. Spotting Kriegon, the chef's face lit up with a broad, toothy grin. "So, I hear y'all have upgraded from wyvern slayers to dragon killers?" he teased, his voice carrying a warmth that felt like a balm to Kriegon's weary soul.

Kriegon couldn't help but return the smile, albeit tiredly. "I'm not sure I'd claim that title."

With a deft movement, the chef flipped a steak onto a wooden cutting board and ladled a hearty bowl of stew, handing them to Kriegon. "Nonsense," the chef said, his voice carrying over the sizzle of the grill. "The soldiers can't stop talking about how you and your lass made that dragon choke on its own fire. You're practically legends now."

Kriegon chuckled, accepting the food with a nod of thanks. "I'm just glad we're all still standing."

The chef winked, a knowing look in his eyes, before turning back to serve the next soldier in line. Kriegon, feeling the stress of the recent battles lift slightly with each step, found a quiet corner outside the main building. There, he settled onto a makeshift seat—a sturdy wooden crate—and began to eat, savoring the simple yet profound comfort of a warm meal.

The morning sun climbed higher, casting long shadows across the shipyard. Kriegon watched as soldiers, some still bearing the marks of yesterday's fight, moved with purpose, clearing out the remaining wyvern nests and preparing for another push into the northern section. The absence of any wyvern attacks today was as unexpected as it was unsettling, lending the morning an eerie calm.

"Rather strange, isn't it?" The voice was quiet but startling enough to make Kriegon jump. He turned to find Garthen beside him, his burnt face still giving Kriegon the chills, his presence as sudden as if conjured by the morning mist.

"How long have you been there?" Kriegon asked, trying to camoflage his surprise.

Garthen, without answering, reached over and cut himself a chunk of Kriegon's steak, biting into it thoughtfully. "It's too quiet," he finally said, voicing the unease that hung in the air like the morning fog.

Kriegon nodded, the peace of the moment tinged with a growing sense of foreboding. "Yeah, it's like we're in the eye of the storm," he mused, his gaze drifting over the city. "And the undead ... they should have shown themselves by now."

Garthen's expression darkened at the mention of the undead, a reminder of the threats that still loomed over them. "We've had no word from Commander Wells," he said, his voice filled with concern. "Wells's communication scroll went dark a week ago, and Commander Flavius reports nothing out of the ordinary. Wells's troops should have reached the White Pine Forest by now but instead vanished into thin air."

Kriegon's brow furrowed, the puzzle pieces not fitting together as they should. "Why would Wells follow orders to march north, taking all of Riversong's troops? He must have known it was a trap set by the Crimson Order."

Garthen shook his head, his gaze distant, lost in thought. "Wells was always one for following orders to the letter. His loyalty was to the chain of command, not necessarily to the crown or its current bearer. When the command shifted, he didn't question it. I tried to reach him, to sway his decision and have him turn back, but his adherence to protocol was ... unyielding."

Kriegon grimaced, the complexity of military loyalty and the rigidity of command structures a bitter pill to swallow. Would his brothers-in-arms have done the same on Earth? He liked to think they had better sense. "That's a dangerous way to think in times like these."

Garthen shrugged, a wry smile playing on his lips. "I was the same once, before all this madness began. But my loyalty was to Abraham, not just the structure of command. Wells, perhaps, hasn't learned that distinction yet."

Their conversation ceased abruptly as a deep, resonant rumbling vibrated through the city of Riversong. Soldiers, mages, and Guardians alike froze, their activities halting mid-motion as they sought the source of the disturbance. The morning, until then a deceptive calm, now brimmed with a unmistakable tension.

The golden dragon, its scales shimmering under the first light of dawn, ascended above the walls of the keep. It perched with an imposing presence, its massive front feet resting atop the battlements, surveying the city below with an air of superiority that silenced all.

The dragon's voice, when it came, was a deep, earth-shaking rumble. "I didn't think they would be brought low here. You mortals have truly surprised the Prince of Greed and earned the right to know my name." The air seemed to contract, drawn in by the dragon's immense inhale, before expelling in a roar that could be felt in one's very bones. "I AM MAMMON! REMEMBER IT WELL, AS ONE DAY MY WORTH WILL BE YOUR UNDOING!"

With a sudden drop, Mammon disappeared behind the walls only to re-emerge, his vast wings unfurling with a grace that belied their size. Each powerful flap sent ripples through the air, and as he ascended, Kriegon could see the glint of gold falling from his claws, a mocking gesture of wealth that could not be held. Turning eastward, toward the rising sun, Mammon soared away, a symbol of greed and power fleeing from the battlefield.

Following Mammon's lead, several wyverns, smaller but no less menacing, scooped up what treasure they could carry and trailed after their master into the horizon, their silhouettes fading against the morning sky.

A collective sigh of relief swept through Riversong as the last of the dragon's form vanished from sight. Kriegon, still processing the surreal encounter, turned to Garthen. "That was unexpected."

Garthen, with a nod of acknowledgment, leaped off his crate with urgency. "I need to meet with Dunstan and the others immediately; this changes everything about our strategy." Without waiting for a response, he dashed into the crowd of soldiers, his figure a blur of purpose.

Kriegon, feeling his relief tangle with the meal now sitting heavily in his stomach, returned the borrowed dishes to the kitchen before navigating back through the makeshift medical ward to where the other Guardians were gathered. Zenmore, Saphire, and Ellena, now awake, looked up at his approach, their expressions an assembly of exhaustion and anticipation.

Zenmore, always the first to break the silence, leaned forward, his voice low with disbelief and curiosity, "Did we just hear what we think we heard?"

Kriegon, managing a tired smile, nodded. "Yes, Mammon, the dragon and Prince of Greed, has retreated to the east. The city's safe, for now."

Saphire and Ellena exhaled deeply, a sound of relief echoing through the room as they processed the news of Mammon's retreat.

Zenmore, however, couldn't hide his disappointment. "So, the prince got away before I could fight it?" he grumbled, his tone laced with the frustration of an unfinished battle.

Kriegon, with a wry smile, shrugged. "I think you'd have been facing that challenge solo if the prince decided to act today, buddy."

Zenmore glanced around at his fellow Guardians, all showing signs of their recent ordeal. He let out a resigned sigh. "Well, guess it's something to look forward to in the future then!"

Laughter filled the room, a brief respite from the burden of their reality. As they chuckled, servants and members of the magic guild entered, bearing trays of food meant to nourish the weary heroes. The aroma of freshly cooked stew and warm bread wafted through the air, inviting a sense of normalcy back into their lives, if only for a moment. Kriegon passed his over to Zenmore, knowing full well that he would never turn down extras.

As they began to eat, their conversation lightened, filled with the camaraderie that he hadn't expected. Kriegon feeling a wholeness he hadn't had since his last deployment, the friends around him letting something profound fall in place. Rei, stirring from her slumber, sat up with a groan that cut through the joviality.

"And she returns to the land of the living!" Zenmore boomed, his voice carrying both jest and admiration. "Got to admit, taking out your own dragon when it took all of us to fight one... You're something else, Rei."

Rei, wincing at the noise, motioned for quiet before accepting a bowl of stew from Roland with a grateful nod. "Thank you, Roland," she murmured, her voice soft, weary from her ordeal. "And I didn't do anything special, just happened to outsmart my predator."

The group watched, waiting for her to elaborate, but she focused on her meal, taking small, deliberate sips. Zenmore, impatient, lobbed a bread roll at her. "Come on, spill it! You're killing me with suspense here!"

With a tired sigh, Rei set down her bowl. "Alright, from the beginning. I went after Tristan and Ninette, my two mages who sought heroism on their own. The idiots. When I caught up, they must've thought I was a wyvern or something, because they hit me with a stone spell. By the time I shook it off, they were crossing into the nobles' district, right where the dragons were."

Kriegon winced, connecting the dots. "That's what Mammon meant by 'pitiful resistance.'"

Rei paused, her brow furrowing. "Mammon?"

Quickly, Kriegon recounted the morning's events, describing Mammon's dramatic departure.

Rei absorbed this, nodding slowly. "Interesting. We were chasing a prince all along. Anyway, back to my tale. I saw the siblings enter the nobles' quarter. I didn't follow but heard their screams when one of the dragons attacked with fire. After Mammon's declaration, I was ambushed by one that used ice breath. I relied on wind magic to be more agile, dodging its attacks, but my scythe couldn't penetrate its scales."

Zenmore nodded, understanding her predicament. "Same here. My axe was useless against the scales. We had to aim for the eyes."

Rei's face lit up with curiosity before she continued. "I needed an opening. Since this dragon was so fond of its ice breath, I thought its mouth might be vulnerable. I pretended to flee, diving toward the ground to make it seem like an easy target. When I felt the chill of its breath coming, I stopped mid-dive and swung my scythe towards where I guessed its head would be. I missed, but the force of my swing hit the dragon's wing joint, severing it. The momentum sent me spinning, and I nearly crashed as hard as the dragon did, but I managed to slow down just enough to survive."

The Guardians listened, their meals momentarily forgotten, as they visualized Rei's daring and desperate gamble.

Rei, noticing the awe in everyone's eyes, looked embarrassed and quickly redirected the conversation. "So, how did the other one go down?"

Zenmore, never one to shy away from recounting heroics, launched into the tale with gusto. His narrative was filled with exaggerated valor and the undying spirit of the soldiers and Guardians who fought alongside him. As he spoke, the room filled with the echoes of their battle cries, the flight of arrows, and the roar of the dragon. Kriegon listened, half amused, half in disbelief at how the story grew in

Zenmore's retelling.

When Zenmore reached the part where Kriegon heroically intervened to save Ellena, she herself couldn't resist joining the moment. She walked over to Kriegon, wrapping her arms around him from behind. Her presence was warm, a nice contrast to the cold weather seeping into the building. Leaning in, she whispered into his ear, her voice a playful tease that sent a shiver down his spine, "I guess I owe you a big one." The soft laughter that followed was a balm to the tension that had gripped them all.

Zenmore, energized by his own storytelling, continued with even more fervor, detailing how he and Saphire had managed to drive her sword into the dragon's skull, a feat he described with the dramatic flair of a bard. His hands moved animatedly, mimicking the action of the sword piercing through the dragon's thick skull as if it were nothing but soft earth.

As his tale concluded with a grandiose bow, the room erupted in chuckles, not just at the story but at Zenmore's evident delight in being the center of attention. Even Saphire, usually quick to dismiss such bravado, let out a chuckle, her grimace softening into something resembling affection or at least tolerance for Zenmore.

"I'm sure this won't be the only time this tale is told," Saphire remarked, her tone a mix of resignation and amusement. It was clear that while she might not always approve of Zenmore, she couldn't deny the effectiveness of his storytelling in lifting their spirits, even if just for a moment.

Kriegon looked at the present Guardians scattered around, some sitting on crates, others leaning against the makeshift barriers of their camp, their conversation light, filled with the relief of survival. He joined in with enthusiasm when they started tossing around ideas about their next steps, his laughter joining them when a jest was made about a prince crumpling under their combined might.

Then, Garthen's figure came into view, his approach subtle but his presence immediately sobering the atmosphere. His face, with charred skin, mirrored the heaviness of his thoughts, the burns nearly hiding the emotions he was repressing.

He paused, taking in the sight of his team before speaking. "It's good to see everyone here, safe and sound," he started, his voice hinting at an underlying sorrow. His eyes met each of theirs in turn, settling with a particular heaviness on Ellena.

"I've left the main force under Dunstan's command," Garthen announced, his voice carrying a slight tremor that showed his usual steadfastness cracking. "He's starting the restoration of Riversong. We'll have the nobles, including Felix and Orris, joining us soon to plan our next moves."

The room fell silent, the lightness of their previous talk dissipating under the substance of Garthen's next words. "Funerals have been arranged," he said, his voice cracking under the strain of his next revelation. "Among them, my daughter."

Kriegon, alongside Zenmore and Saphire, bore the weight of the ice coffin that encased the still form of Garthen's daughter, Beatrice. The ice had preserved her body in the moment she had stabbed herself, a statue to forever show the struggle she lost. The journey through Riversong's shattered streets was a somber procession, each step ladened with the burden of loss amidst the ruins of what once was a bustling city. The snow fell silently, blanketing the destruction in a cold, white shroud, yet it could not cover the pain etched on every face nor the silence that spoke louder than any words.

As they moved toward the newly consecrated cemetery outside the eastern gates, the streets filled with soldiers, each carrying their fallen comrades on makeshift biers. Kriegon felt the air, thick with grief, drawing him back to Coolgen and even earlier funerals. They never got easier, but in this case, the death had achieved something profound. The only sounds as Kriegon followed Zenmore's broad back were the soft crunch of snow underfoot and the occasional muffled sob. The procession was a river of sorrow, flowing toward its final resting place.

Dunstan's captains, with solemn efficiency, directed the groups of soldiers to their designated plots, organizing the chaos of death into orderly rows. The trio carrying Beatrice was led to a prominent spot beneath a massive headstone, a silent sentinel over the graves. Here, the ground had been magically prepared, the graves deep and precise, a testament to the skill of Rei, Ryoma, and the magic guild. Kriegon's shoulders screamed from the load of the icy tomb, but he ignored it right up to the edge of the spot to which they had been directed. He would never dishonor or disgrace his team's leader by lowering his daughter's body prematurely.

Zenmore, with a gentleness that contradicted his usual boisterous nature, lowered Beatrice into her grave. The depth of it seemed excessive to Kriegon, but as Zenmore stepped in to place her, it was clear it was designed with respect, not haste. With a salute that echoed through the silent cemetery, Zenmore climbed out, leaving Beatrice to her eternal slumber.

A call to order drew Kriegon's gaze up to the entrance of the graveyard. Garthen, flanked by Dunstan, the nobles like Felix, and the same priest who had seen them through darker times at Crossroads, walked slowly among the graves. Each step was measured, each glance filled with unspoken words. Kriegon, moving to stand beside Garthen, placed a hand on his shoulder, feeling the tremor of suppressed emotion before it stilled under the power of Garthen's resolve.

The priest, his robe billowing slightly in the chill wind, approached the monolith, its surface blank yet destined to bear the weight of memory. His hand rested on the stone, a gesture of connection to all those beneath the earth. His voice, when he spoke, carried a substance that seemed to draw the very air to silence.

"Grief," he began, his voice steady, "is the shadow cast by the light of valor. Today, as we stand here, we are reminded that our battles, our wars, they carve deep into the fabric of our lives, leaving marks of sorrow but also of honor. The Ever Watcher Archangel Saforus, in his celestial vigil, surely weeps with us, yet he also rejoices for the brave souls who have ascended to join him."

The priest's words hung in the frosty air, mingling with the breath of the gathered crowd. "Each of you here, each standing figure, carries stories of those now silent beneath us. These fallen are not merely bodies returned to the earth; they are legends, tales of courage that will outlive the stones that mark their graves. It falls upon us, the living, to speak their names, to share their deeds, ensuring that the memory of their sacrifice ignites the hearts of those who come after us. In the light of their legacy, we must stand firm, for them and for each other."

As the priest stepped back from the monolith, intending to conclude his solemn address, the stone beneath his hand began to emit a soft, ethereal glow. The light was gentle, like the first dawn breaking through the night. Kriegon watched in awe and confusion as the stone seemed to come alive with light.

Then, as if by some divine or magical intervention, pieces of the stone's surface began to flake away, revealing inscriptions beneath. The names of the fallen, etched in glowing runes, appeared one by one, a luminous testament to their sacrifice. The magic at work was subtle yet profound, a final tribute that transcended mere remembrance.

Kriegon, his eyes scanning the illuminated stone, found the name of Coolgen Hero among the others. The name stuck out sharply compared to others because of his dedication to memorizing the symbols representing the man who saved him. The realization that this act of remembrance included all who had given their lives in this war, regardless of their origin or status, brought a lump to his throat. The magic had not only recorded names but had woven a tapestry of light that connected every soul present to those lost.

The mourners, carrying the weight of their grief, started to share tales of the fallen, their voices a low rumble of sorrow and pride, creating a tapestry of memories that wove through the crowd. The air was filled with the soft murmur of stories, each word a stitch in the fabric of remembrance.

However, Garthen remained rooted to the spot, his gaze fixed on the monolith. Kriegon, along with the other Guardians, stayed by his side, a silent vigil in the face of their leader's deep mourning. The snow continued to fall, each flake a silent witness to their collective loss.

Garthen's steps were slow, almost reluctant, as he approached the stone monument. His eyes, usually so sharp and commanding, were now dim as if the fire went out from pain that seemed to deepen the cracks of his burned skin. He reached out with a trembling hand, his fingers brushing against the names etched in light, whispering them—Beatrice Brus and Bella Brus. The realization hit Kriegon like a cold wave: Bella must have been Garthen's wife, a detail he had never thought to ask about, overshadowed by the immediacy of war and survival.

The significance of this oversight pressed on Kriegon, a reminder of how war had not only claimed lives but had also stolen the space for personal stories, for knowing the depths of one's comrades. Garthen's murmur was almost lost in the gentle whisper of the wind, a sound so faint that Kriegon felt privileged and burdened to overhear. "I'll avenge you both. Please wait for me."

Life in Riversong's ruins found a new rhythm, blending sorrow with resilience. The scarred city crept toward recovery, driven by nobles directing supplies and Guardians trading swords for shovels. Kriegon worked alongside his fellow soldiers, clearing debris and laying stones—each one a step toward healing the city and himself.

Ryoma tackled the sewers with fervor, his magic reshaping the underground. Felix, when Kriegon asked about the city's future, gestured confidently. "Core services and nobles' homes first. The rest? Up to the people. Let them rebuild Riversong in their image."

Kriegon and Ellena grew closer, their evenings a quiet refuge—though Zenmore's jabs about their "hand-holding" never ceased. But Garthen troubled him most. The leader was pulling away, drifting from the group, often spotted alone by his daughter's grave. Rei left tea, Zenmore brought ale, yet Garthen remained distant. One evening, with Kriegon nearby, Ellena sat with him. Garthen's voice cracked as he spoke. "You remind me of Beatrice, Ellena—too much sometimes." Kriegon caught her eye, seeing the weight of it land.

He stayed silent, thoughts drifting to his own dark days before the Guardians—alone, hollow, wishing for a group like this to pull him through. Now, he and the others meant to be that for Garthen, though the man seemed to slip beyond their reach

Three weeks after the last echoes of battle had faded, the gates to the noble district and castle finally gave way, breached with caution. The walls, once fortified by Mammon's greed in molten gold, had become precarious, necessitating a meticulous clearance to prevent a catastrophic collapse.

The nobles, alongside Dunstan and the Guardians, were the initial party to traverse the desecrated halls of the castle. Kriegon's gaze swept over the grandeur turned to ruin, a testament to Mammon's avarice. The throne room, a sanctuary from the winter's chill, was their next stop. Snow had claimed parts of the floor, creating a strange feeling this was an ancient ruin rather than the opulence that once defined this space mere months prior.

As Felix began delegating tasks, his voice barely rising above the crunch of snow under their boots, the Guardians gravitated towards Garthen, who stood by a shattered window. The vista beyond, a forest blanketed in white, offered a moment of serene beauty amidst the devastation. They stood in silence, absorbing the tranquility, a counterpoint to Felix's pragmatic discussion of repairs and defenses.

This quiet was shattered by the frantic arrival of a scout, his breath visible in the cold air as he burst into the throne room. "Sire!" he gasped, his urgency palpable. "Terrible news! The undead are marching from the north towards us."

Kriegon turned to see Dunstan met his captains' eyes, a silent command passing between them. "We've faced them before. We'll crush them again," he declared, his voice steady.

But the scout's next words doused the room in cold dread. "No, sir, this is different. They're numbering in the hundreds of thousands, by our estimates."

A harsh silence fell over the room, the burden of potential annihilation pressing down on all present. Dunstan's initial confidence wavered. "That can't be right. Our forces are nowhere near prepared to face an enemy ten times our number."

Felix, turning towards the Guardians, his expression filled with hope and desperation, asked, "Can we call upon your aid once more?"

Garthen, stepping forward with a resolve that seemed to steel the very air around him, spoke with a severity that matched the man Kriegon remembered from before. "We would have joined the fight even without your request."

The Guardians, each in their own way, nodded in agreement, their faces set with determination. For Kriegon, he felt the call, the mission that drove him further than any other before. This was not just about defending Riversong; it was about finding the cause of this darkness and sending it back to hell, and he looked forward to that moment.

Dunstan, regaining some of his composure, addressed his captains. "Prepare our defenses. We'll need every able body, every weapon we can muster. And..." He paused, looking at the Guardians. "We'll need strategy. We can't face them head-on; we must outthink them."

The meeting that followed was passionate, with maps spread across the snow-dusted floor of the throne room. Plans were drawn, escape routes considered, and siege weapons drawn up. The Guardians contributed their insights, their experience from different worlds helping to fortify the city from the undead.

As the discussion waned, Kriegon found himself by the window again, looking out at the forest. The snow continued to fall, a silent reminder of the purity they fought to preserve amidst the encroaching death.

Zenmore approached the window, his usual swagger replaced by a somber reflection. He peered into the forest, his gaze distant, as if searching for an answer in the falling snow. Behind him, Rei's voice broke the quiet. "What is it, Zenmore?"

Zenmore's response came intense with a rare seriousness, his voice devoid of its characteristic lightness. "There's no honor in fighting the dead," he muttered, his words hanging in the cold air.

Saphire, quick to challenge him, retorted with her usual sharpness, "Honor doesn't choose its battles, Zenmore. Sometimes, survival is the only honor there is."

Their exchange left a silence in its wake, a contemplative pause that seemed to echo through the room. The strategic discussions continued in the background, a murmur of plans and possibilities, until Garthen approached, drawing the group's attention.

Kriegon turned, expecting the authority of command, ready to act on his leader's orders. Garthen's eyes met each of theirs, a silent acknowledgment of the seriousness of their situation.

"Rei," Garthen began, his voice steady, "we need you to scout. We must gather as much information as possible about their numbers, their pace, and any unusual threats among them."

Without a word, Rei nodded and stepped towards the window, her wings unfurling. With a powerful leap, she was airborne, disappearing into the cloudy sky, a silhouette against the snowfall.

Garthen turned to the remaining Guardians. "The rest of us will focus on those siege engines Kriegon, Rei, and Zenmore have relayed from their worlds. If we can complete them in time, we might just have a fighting chance against this horde."

Rei returned that night to a team worn thin by their relentless efforts. The others, save for Zenmore, felt as if their arms might detach from their bodies after chopping down countless trees to fortify their defenses. The familiar Zella mansion, thankfully still standing, offered them some semblance of shelter. Zenmore had rearranged the sleeping quarters, merging two rooms for the group's use. As he led Rei inside, she collapsed face-first onto the nearest bed, her exhaustion plain.

"It's like seeing Riversong covered with wyverns all over again." Her voice came through muffled by the mattress. The room waited in silence, too tired to press for details, until Rei lifted her head, her expression grim. "There's at least a hundred thousand of them, and they're moving fast. They'll be upon Riversong in a couple of days. I couldn't get close enough to spot any leaders or ... princes among them," she added, a hint of uncertainty in her voice. "But there were these strange, human-like creatures with wings that chased me. They were fast, faster than I expected."

Kriegon, intrigued, leaned forward. "Anything else stand out about them?"

Rei shook her head. "Just their taunts as they pursued me. Nothing I could grasp beyond that."

"Liches, maybe?" Kriegon speculated, lying back as he pondered creatures of legend or games that could speak and fly.

Zenmore snorted. "Liches, smiches. As long as I can cut 'em or bash 'em, I don't care what they're called."

Garthen, without a trace of amusement, interjected, "With what's coming, you'll likely get your chance to do both."

Their conversation turned out to be more prescient than they realized, for the undead's relentless advance meant they would reach Riversong sooner than Rei had anticipated. The very next day, the leaders found themselves on the northern edge of the cleared forest, facing the eerie stillness of the undead army. They stood as if rooted to the spot by the snow, an unnatural tableau of death.

Felix, breaking the silence, turned to Dunstan. "How close are we with those siege engines?"

Dunstan signaled to his captains for a status report. The first captain approached, his voice brisk. "The five Zenmore advised on will be operational by tomorrow."

The second captain, consulting his notes, added, "Kriegon's catapult design needs at least another two days, if not more. As for Rei's engine..." He paused, glancing towards Rei. "We're still gathering the materials. It's a complex setup, requiring significant magical preparation."

Rei murmured, "I knew it was ambitious."

Garthen, placing a reassuring hand on her shoulder, stood beside Felix. "Don't fret. This might turn into a prolonged siege. We'll have time to bring everything online."

The group watched in tense anticipation as the undead ranks began to stir, a rider emerging from their midst and moving towards them. As the rider approached, the air seemed to thicken with an ominous dread. Kriegon couldn't shake the surreal feeling of watching an ancient horror unfold before his very eyes, reminiscent of the chilling tales of the Headless Horseman from Earth's folklore. The figure, astride a spectral steed, moved with a purposeful dread, its form shrouded in an eerie, almost tangible darkness. The horse's hooves made no sound on the snow, adding to the ghostly spectacle.

Coming to a sudden halt before the gate, the rider lifted its severed head, its eyes empty sockets and its mouth agape in a perpetual scream. With a voice that gurgled like death itself, it demanded, "Who goes there that has taken the palace of the great Mammon?"

Garthen, standing tall upon the battlements, his silhouette against the winter sky, responded with a booming voice that carried the emphasis of his defiance. "It was never that prick's palace to begin with. Who are you to question my comrades?"

The head, held in the rider's hand, let out a sound that could have been mistaken for laughter had it not been so devoid of life. "So, the nameless will fall and be lost to our great history then. However, I will answer you. I am Alvun, Speaker for the Gluttonous glory of Beelzebub."

Kriegon felt a chill run through him at the name, one he knew from tales of rebellion and fall from grace. Beelzebub, not just a demon but a fallen angel, once part of the celestial host, now a figure of dread and power in the infernal realms.

Unaware of Kriegon's silent recognition, Garthen pressed on, "I did not realize there was another monstrous being lurking in our kingdom.

If he commands the undead, he should bury himself and let those bodies rest in peace. If not, we Guardians will dig his grave for him."

The head's laugh, a grotesque sound that echoed through the cold air, was clear and mocking. "You have no idea what you've stirred, tiny man. I will relay your impudence to my master, and his response will be swift and terrible."

With that, the rider turned his undead steed, spurring it back into the ranks of the undead, which seemed to part and then close like a dark, flowing river around him. Felix turned to Dunstan and Garthen. "I should leave you to your preparations. May the Watcher guide us."

As Felix departed, Dunstan and Garthen began to organize the defenses, their commands crisp in the cold air. Kriegon, still processing their situation, felt Zenmore's hand clap him on the back, a gesture meant to be reassuring but so forceful it almost knocked him over.

"Don't let it get to you," Zenmore said, his voice attempting to lighten the mood. "This Beelzebub can't be worse than that dragon we faced, right?"

Kriegon, his gaze fixed on the shifting mass of undead below, replied somberly, "No, he's much worse." The other Guardians gathered closer, sensing the depth of his concern.

Taking a deep breath, Kriegon shared what he knew, his voice low and steady against the backdrop of their preparations. "Beelzebub isn't just any demon. He's one of the fallen angels, Lucifer's right-hand man when they rebelled against Heaven. He was among the first to be cast out. His fall from grace wasn't just a descent into darkness; it was a plunge into the deepest pits of malice and power. If he's behind this, we're facing an enemy force driven by millennia of corruption and destruction."

The Guardians listened, their faces a mix of determination and unease. The name Beelzebub conjured images of ancient evils, tales of a being whose very name meant 'Lord of Flies,' a title that spoke of decay and the devouring of the living by the dead.

Garthen, absorbing the importance of Kriegon's words, nodded slowly. "Then we fight not just for Riversong, but for the very essence of life against corruption. We'll need every ounce of our strength. Go and wait to be called. The Guardians are a trump card to be used at the right time."

The group dispersed, each to their tasks, their movements imbued with a sense of urgency and purpose. The battlements became a hive of activity as orders were shouted, weapons checked, and the built siege engines were prepared. The air was thick with the tension of impending doom, yet all soldiers looked to the Guardians with hope against this darkness.

Kriegon and the other Guardians, apart from Garthen, went to the first inner wall before the nobles' section to watch. Before they reached the top to get a vantage point, the sound of battle roared through the city. Looking out over the northern wall, Kriegon watched the barrels of oil thrown over the wall explode on the churning mass of bodies slamming against it.

Chapter 19: The Prince of Gluttony

The relentless assault on the northern wall of Riversong's stronghold had turned the city into a macabre theater of war. Every glance over the battlements revealed a fresh wave of the undead, their decayed forms clashing against the fortifications like a grim tide. The soldiers, under the command of Garthen and Dunstan, fought with grim efficiency, their shifts perfectly coordinated to repel the unending horde.

The undead, in their grotesque ingenuity, began constructing ladders from their own fallen, a macabre stairway of flesh and bone reaching towards the heavens of Riversong's walls. However, these grim structures were met with fiery retribution; barrels of oil, ignited and hurled from the battlements, or the searing magic of Rei and Ryoma ensured that no ladder could stand for long.

Two days had passed in this grim dance, the city's defenders holding strong, their morale bolstered by the absence of casualties among their ranks. But as the sun dipped below the horizon on the third day, a profound shift in the air heralded a new phase of the siege.

Kriegon, alongside Rei, surveyed the siege engines, a discussion on their efficacy turning into a moment of levity. "The engines I spoke of could hurl stones the size of houses," Kriegon mused, his voice carrying a note of nostalgia. "These seem almost quaint in comparison."

Rei, her attention divided between the conversation and her own siege engine, which resembled nothing more than an oversized child's toy, nodded in agreement. "Size isn't everything in battle," she quipped, her eyes scanning the horizon for any sign of the enemy's next move.

Garthen chimed in. "As long as they outperform Zenmore's makeshift stick throwers, we're in good stead."

Zenmore kicked one of his engines with mock disdain. "These were designed by orcs for orcs. No surprise they barely function for humans."

Their moment of respite was shattered by the arrival of a messenger, his face etched with panic. "Commander Garthen, Dunstan requests your presence at the northern gate, urgently.

You and the Guardians, now!"

Without hesitation, the Guardians grabbed their weapons, their movements fluid with the urgency of battle. As they sprinted towards the gate, Garthen demanded, "What's happening?"

"The undead have brought forth new monstrosities," the messenger gasped out between breaths. "Giants, wielding weapons like tree trunks. Arrows barely slow them."

The sounds of their approach grew louder, a rhythmic pounding against the gate that spoke of immense strength. Dunstan, atop his horse, directed the formation of a shield wall, a last line of defense should the gate fail. His voice, hoarse from days of command, carried over the din of battle. "Good, we'll need your strength. Ryoma couldn't reach his position in time for a spell barrage."

"I've ordered the barricading of the bridges to the southern district and the nobles' quarter. If we must fall back, that's our rally point."

Zenmore, stepping through the shield wall, called back, "Then let's not let them in at all. Let's give them a spectacle they won't forget!"

The Guardians, steeling themselves, moved into position, ready to face the new threat. The gate, now visibly straining under the assault, creaked ominously as the first of the monstrous figures began to force their way through. Their appearance was nothing short of terrifying: towering over men, their skin a patchwork of decay and muscle, eyes glowing with a malevolent light, and weapons that looked as if they could smash through stone.

Kriegon, alongside his fellow Guardians, braced for impact. The air was thick with anticipation, the snow beneath their feet crunching as they shifted, ready for the onslaught. The first of the giants broke through, its weapon swinging wildly, knocking aside defenders like a child scattering toys.

Rei, quick on her feet, unleashed a bolt of powerful fire magic, her spellcraft precise and devastating. The giant staggered and fell back, its weapon arm now a smoldering ruin, but another took its place, undeterred by the fate of its predecessor.

As Zenmore let out a battle cry that seemed to shake the very foundations of the city, he charged, his axe a silver arc against the backdrop of the night, meeting the giant's massive club with a clash that echoed like thunder. The impact sent shockwaves through the air, a physical manifestation of the power on display.

Saphire, her movements a blur of grace and deadly precision, danced around the giants, her blade slicing through their thick hides as if they were mere parchment. Each strike was a study in lethal ballet, her sword finding its mark with the ease of a seasoned warrior.

Ellena positioned herself behind Zenmore, her whip sword lashing out at the lesser undead, clearing a path for Zenmore to focus on the larger threats. Her weapon snapped like a living thing, each crack sending another undead to its final rest.

Meanwhile, Garthen and Rei, positioned slightly back, unleashed a barrage of arrows and spells into the throng of undead that continued to pour through the breached gate. Garthen's arrows found skulls with unerring accuracy, while Rei's magic, a fiery tempest, incinerated swathes of the enemy, her spells casting an eerie glow over the battlefield.

Kriegon sought his place in this dance of death. He moved behind Saphire, his mind racing for a strategy. As he advanced, he noticed that while the elite of the undead had breached the gate, the bulk of their forces still lingered outside, a dark tide waiting to flood in.

Turning to Garthen and Rei, he shouted over the din, "We need to seal the gate!"

Garthen, his voice strained, replied, "It's beyond repair now. The wall has likely fallen at this point."

That sparked an idea in Kriegon. "Great idea, Garthen! Then we'll bring it down ourselves! Call Dunstan to pull his men back from above the gate!"

"That wasn't an idea!" Garthen called back as Kriegon turned to the gate, a rune of stone forming on his metallic staff.

Rei stepped beside him, her scythe already forming the same rune.

"What's the plan?"

"Collapse the gate. Cut off the undead outside," Kriegon replied, his voice calm despite the urgency.

Rei nodded and shouted, "Ellena, Zenmore, Saphire, cover us!"

Kriegon, deep in concentration, visualized the structure of the gate, the stones, and the potential points of weakness. With a mental command, he began to manipulate the energy within the stones, loosening their bonds, initiating the collapse from within.

Rei, her power complementing his, pulled at the side structures, ensuring the collapse would be complete, sealing off the undead's access to the city. The ground trembled as the gateway began to crumble, the once proud archway now a pile of rubble, effectively blocking the path.

Amid the dust and debris, Zenmore, having just dispatched the last of the giants, turned with awe and disbelief. "Wasn't expecting a demolition show," he quipped.

The action paused momentarily, as if the world itself took a breath, the Guardians and soldiers alike looking at the collapsed gate. The undead outside, now cut off, pressed against the new barrier, their numbers a sea of decayed flesh unable to breach the makeshift wall of stone and rubble.

Kriegon, his energy drained, leaned on his staff, watching as the last of the immediate threat was contained. "It's not a permanent solution," he panted, "but it buys us time."

Garthen, clapping a hand on Kriegon's shoulder, nodded in agreement. "Time enough to regroup, perhaps even to plan a counterattack with those siege weapons. Well done."

Rei, gaze fixed on the sealed gate, added, "We've stemmed the tide, but we must prepare for what comes next. They'll find another way, or they'll send something else after us."

Ellena, her whip sword retracted, walked over. "For now, though, we've stemmed the tide. Let's use this respite wisely."

The brief calm was shattered as quickly as it had come. The next day, as the siege engines thundered to life, hurling fiery destruction into the ranks of the undead amidst the swirling snow, a new terror descended from the skies. Kriegon, overseeing the operation of his own creation, felt his heart sink as he watched three figures, human-like but with wings, land near the Orc-type engines.

The ensuing chaos was apocalyptic, reminiscent of the dragon's fury they had faced before. The orc engines and their operators were decimated in mere moments, their structures collapsing into splinters and ruin. Kriegon, with Rei not far behind, charged toward the destruction.

From the wreckage, Zenmore emerged, engaged in a brutal test of strength with one of the winged beings, who, despite being half his size, matched him blow for blow. The creature's wings flapped aggressively, adding to its otherworldly menace.

The other two-winged assailants launched themselves at Kriegon and Rei. Rei managed to divert one of the creatures, leaving Kriegon to face his attacker alone. His staff met the creature's twin rapier-like swords in a desperate parry, the impact driving him to a knee in the snow.

Kriegon looked up in horror at the creature towering over him, its face a grotesque mockery of humanity, with fanged teeth bared in a sinister grin below eyes that glowed a cold red. "Oh, are you like us? What pretty eyes you have."

"I'm not like any of you bastards!" Kriegon shouted back, his arms trembling under the strain of holding back what must be a vampire's relentless assault. Just as his strength was about to falter, four soldiers appeared, their swords swinging. However, the creature's speed was supernatural, dodging and counterattacking with deadly precision, slicing through the soldiers as if they were nothing but paper.

Kriegon, now on his feet, regrouped with the remaining soldiers, signaling a coordinated attack. They lunged forward together, but the vampire moved like a shadow, evading their strikes and countering with lethal force cutting through the soldiers' blades, armor, and bone.

Each of the vampire's strikes was a blur, leaving cuts across

Kriegon's chest and face as he struggled to dodge and parry the silver flashes of its blades. When the vampire lunged with a particularly vicious stab, Kriegon managed to sidestep, but the effort left him sprawled in the snow, quickly scrambling up.

The vampire, watching him with that eerie smile, hissed, "You know, you're the first in this world to last this long against me. The others were merely ... appetizers."

"Sorry, but I'm off the menu today," Kriegon retorted, wiping blood from his eye.

An arrow, expertly shot by Garthen, pierced the vampire's arm, momentarily disrupting its attack. Seizing the moment, Kriegon transformed his staff into a bladed edge, aiming for the creature's head. The vampire, however, managed to block with its still-functional arm, the other pinned by the arrow.

Garthen, attempting to exploit the distraction, charged from behind but was kicked aside, leaving the fight a desperate two-on-one. Garthen continued to fire arrows, each one narrowly missed or deflected by the vampire's blade.

Finally, as both Kriegon and Garthen were nearly at their limit, Ellena entered the fray. Her whip sword, with a fluid motion, wrapped around the vampire's neck, and with a swift, decisive pull, she decapitated the creature.

Panting, Kriegon looked around for the others. Zenmore and Saphire were finishing off their foe with brutal efficiency, while Rei had already grounded her opponent with the removal of one of its wings.

Kriegon pointed towards Rei, urgency in his voice despite his exhaustion. "Help her finish this!"

Garthen, nodding, nocked another arrow, aiming carefully as the vampire struggled against Rei. His shot pierced the creature's heart, a merciful end to its unholy existence.

Rei, landing gracefully, looked around at the devastation, her scythe resting by her side, its blade still dripping with the remnants of the fight. The ground was littered with the fallen, the snow was stained with blood, and the remnants of the siege engines.

The Guardians gathered, their breaths visible in the freezing air, their clothes torn, their faces set with the grim reality of what they faced. Zenmore wiped blood from a cut on his cheek, his expression one of fierce determination combined with a hint of respect for their adversaries. "We're far from done. These abominations are merely the harbingers. There's bound to be more."

Garthen, shaking his head in frustration, countered, "We can't keep playing defense. We need to strike at the source, at Beelzebub, if we're to have any chance of ending this."

Kriegon agreed. "Every strategy we come up with gets dismantled. We're running out of options fast."

The others nodded, the gravity of their choice settling in as the military and mages gathered around. Garthen quickly dispatched a soldier to fetch Dunstan and the captains, urgency lacing his command.

As noon approached, the sun managed to pierce through the cloud cover, casting a weak light over the snow-covered battlefield. Inside the warmth of a shipyard building, the leaders met, the fire crackling in the hearth providing the only warmth against the cold dread of their situation. Garthen took the floor and told them of the latest attack. "We need to strike back. The defensive line won't hold if we're constantly surprised by new threats."

Dunstan nodded solemnly. "Agreed, but how? Even with all the damage we've inflicted, they outnumber us by a large margin."

Garthen answered quickly. "The Guardians are going to go hunting. Beelzebub has to be one of the princes named in the prophecy. We will achieve that goal and prevent further destruction of the undead by killing the ringleader."

The room filled with a murmur of agreement, the direness of their situation making the desperate plan seem almost rational. Dunstan, after a moment of contemplation, extended his hand to Garthen. "If it is what was foretold, who am I to object? Not that I would have at this point anyway."

With a grim smile, Garthen shook Dunstan's hand. "We'll return victorious."

Dunstan answered, "If you don't, I'm sure we will meet you in the afterlife soon enough."

The group moved out through the eastern gate, an area inexplicably free from the undead's assault. This oddity did not escape Kriegon, but he chose not to question their stroke of luck. Rei scouted ahead, her silhouette a fleeting shadow against the snowy sky.

As they maneuvered through the woods, skirting the cliff face of Riversong, Kriegon approached Garthen with a nagging question. "Why didn't you shoot to kill the enemy I was fighting back there?"

Garthen, his expression mildly annoyed, explained, "Now is not the time for this, but if you want to know, I was aiming to make sure if the creature dodged, I wouldn't hit you."

Kriegon, realizing he might have just been in Garthen's way during that battle, just nodded in silent thankfulness.

In a clearing where the cliff turned westward, Rei landed. "I saw something unusual." She pointed northeast. "Looked like the messenger we encountered, with someone large in a clearing that way."

Saphire, confused, asked, "Why would a commander be so far from his troops, and in the open?"

Zenmore, his voice a low rumble, said, "Either it's a trap or sheer arrogance. Both mean trouble for us."

Ellena whispered, "This reeks of a setup."

Garthen, resolute, directed them towards the northeast. "We've come too far to turn back now. Let's proceed, but eyes open."

As they approached the designated clearing, they noticed the ground was strangely warm, the snow melted away, which made Kriegon wary. Yet, he followed the group forward, each step deliberate, mindful of the silence around them. The clearing opened up as they laid eyes on the grotesque scene. The space was dominated by a massive figure, its back turned to them, sitting upon a throne constructed from writhing, tormented bodies. The air was thick with the stench of decay and fear.

A headless messenger on horseback, its own steed trembling, stood guard beside this monstrous entity. The ground around them seemed to pulse with malevolent energy, as if the very earth was alive with dread.

Garthen, his voice a low whisper, rallied the group. "Okay, I'll signal the charge with the first arrow. Let's end this before it begins. Zenmore, Saphire, front line. Defend, distract. Ellena and I will cover from a distance with our ranged attacks. Rei, Kriegon," he said, pausing, locking eyes with Kriegon, "watch for any disruptions. Stay sharp."

Kriegon, feeling the sting of being sidelined, nodded. The others, with a synthesis of determination and trepidation, readied their weapons. Garthen, standing in the shadow of the trees, drew his bow with a tension that could be felt in the air. His arrow, when released, flew with deadly precision, striking the large figure with a force that seemed to echo through the clearing.

The figure's head exploded in a spray of dark ichor, but the grotesque spectacle didn't end there. The headless horseman beside it received a similar fate, an arrow piercing through the skull it carried. Zenmore and Saphire charged forward, their weapons gleaming under the sparse light that managed to pierce the canopy above, with Garthen and Ellena following.

As they advanced, something bizarre occurred. The figure's head, which had paused mid-obliteration, began to regenerate in reverse, like a film played backward. Laughter, deep and guttural, filled the air as the creature stood, placing a golden helm atop its now fully formed head. Turning, it revealed not two but four thick arms. Each of them moved with a life of its own, wielding weapons that seemed too large for any normal combatant, yet he manipulated them with a terrifying grace.

The creature's form was a nightmare made flesh. Its chest was armored in gold, but above and below, its body morphed into something out of a horror tale. Its head was a mass of human-like features, distorted and twisted into a grotesque mask. Below the waist, where one might expect legs, there were instead thick, hairy appendages ending in sharp talons, resembling those of a monstrous spider.

As Zenmore and Saphire engaged, their strikes met with a clang against the creature's massive swords. Beelzebub's retaliation was swift, his hammers swinging with force enough to split the air, requiring both warriors to dodge or face a crushing blow. Zenmore, with a desperate swing, managed to sever one of the spider-like legs, but the creature's laugh only grew.

"You really think the great Beelzebub can be felled so easily?" it boomed, its voice echoing unnaturally through the clearing. A rune on its sash around the thick neck glowed with a sinister black light, and where the leg had been severed, another began to grow, as if the creature was merely inconvenienced rather than injured.

Kriegon, feeling a shiver trace the length of his spine, watched in a mix of awe and horror. Beelzebub, a figure from the darkest recesses of legend, an embodiment of ancient fears. The creature's next action was as terrifying as it was strategic: he raised his hammers, and another rune on the sash ignited with a malevolent glow. The ground beneath them quaked violently as he struck it, the force of his blow sending shockwaves that knocked the Guardians to their knees, the earth itself seeming to cry out in pain.

Rei soared into the air to escape the upheaval. Kriegon, struggling to his feet, his mind a whirlwind of potential tactics and desperation, found no immediate solution. He moved in tandem with Ellena, who, in a display of both bravery and futility, lashed out at Beelzebub with her sword-whip. The weapon merely glanced off the creature's golden breastplate.

Zenmore and Saphire, meanwhile, were locked in a deadly dance with Beelzebub, their movements a blur as they dodged and parried. Each weapon in Beelzebub's hands dancing with an autonomy that defied natural law, as if the weapons themselves were sentient, each blow a calculated action in this macabre ballet of death.

Garthen attempted to exploit any weakness he could find. Darting to the side, he unleashed a barrage of arrows, each one aimed with precision. Yet, like Ellena's whip, the arrows could not penetrate the breastplate or helm, only managing to embed themselves into the less protected joints of the armor, offering a momentary hindrance rather than a decisive blow.

In a moment of desperation, Kriegon conjured a fireball. He hurled it towards Beelzebub's face, hoping to blind or at least disorient the creature. But Beelzebub, with a grotesque display of power, opened his mouth wide and consumed the fireball, his laughter echoing mockingly across the clearing as if savoring the taste of magic itself.

Rei, seizing the moment, darted in from above, her attack swift and aimed at the creature's back. But even her strikes, though fierce, seemed to do little more than irritate the beast, its wounds healing with an unnatural speed, the psychic energy emanating from it a demonstrable force that seemed to defy the very laws of nature.

Saphire, amidst the chaos, called out to her companions, "Take his attacks! I have an idea. Rei, follow me!" With that, she dashed back. Ellena and Kriegon, understanding the need for distraction, replaced her on the front line, their efforts aimed at drawing Beelzebub's attention away from Zenmore, who was now the focal point of the creature's fury.

Garthen's earlier efforts, though seemingly futile at the time, now bore unexpected fruit. The arrows he had embedded into one of Beelzebub's shoulder joints had effectively immobilized his upper right arm, reducing the onslaught of attacks. This slight advantage allowed the group to focus on defending against the remaining three.

As the trio remained engaged in the fierce battle, their movements a blur of steel against the monstrous form of Beelzebub, a sharp whistle pierced the chaotic air. It was a sound that seemed out of place in the heat of combat, almost surreal. Then, from above, Saphire descended like a meteor, her sword seeming attached to her hooves, slicing through the air with precision.

Her descent was a spectacle, her blade aimed not at Beelzebub's armored torso or head but at the vulnerable neck, where the sash of runes lay exposed. The sword met its mark with a force that seemed to shake the very ground beneath them, cutting through the sash and deep into the creature's neck, disabling the upper left arm. The impact was monumental, a moment of triumph amidst the chaos.

But triumph came with its price. The impact sent Saphire to the ground among Beelzebub's many legs. Beelzebub, in a fit of rage, swung one of his massive hammers with the precision of a golfer. The blow connected with a sickening crunch, sending Saphire flying through the air to crash into Garthen, who had been momentarily distracted by something in the forest. Both were hurled into the underbrush, disappearing from view, their fate momentarily unknown.

Zenmore, witnessing the fall of his comrade, was consumed by a berserker's rage. With Beelzebub hindered by the loss of his magical regeneration and two upper arms, Zenmore's attacks became a torrent of fury, each strike aimed at the vulnerable joints and legs of the creature. The fight, though still titanic, seemed to tilt ever so slightly in their favor due to Saphire's bold move.

Kriegon and Ellena, though eager to assist, found themselves momentarily sidelined, the intensity of Zenmore's engagement with Beelzebub making direct intervention risky. As Kriegon scanned the battlefield for any sign of Rei, he spotted her amidst the underbrush where Saphire and Garthen had landed, her form illuminated by a soft green glow, indicative of her healing magic at work. However, the situation quickly deteriorated as undead, likely summoned or controlled by Beelzebub's dark powers, began to emerge from the forest's edge, their movements slow but relentless.

Kriegon, realizing the dire situation, transformed his staff into a sword with a swift motion as he ran to back up Rei, engaging the undead with a fierce fear and determination. Each swing of his blade was a desperate bid to keep the tide at bay, to give his comrades a fighting chance. Ellena, understanding the need to protect Zenmore's back, joined the fray, her own weapon a blur as she fought off the encroaching undead.

Amid this chaos, Kriegon called without turning, "Rei, you need to finish this. Zenmore's got his attention; you can end what Saphire started!"

Out of the corner of his eye, he could see Rei, torn between her duty to heal and the necessity to fight. She looked at the scene before her, her eyes wide with the shock of their precarious situation. "But what about these two?" she asked.

Kriegon turned and gripped her arm, pulling her to her feet, his voice a blending of command and plea. "I will watch over them. The sooner we defeat him, the sooner we can ensure their safety and ours."

With a final look around the clearing, Rei's resolve wavered slightly. "What could I even do?" she asked, her voice small against the backdrop of battle.

Kriegon pointed towards the gaping wound Saphire had inflicted on Beelzebub. "There. Use your scythe like it was meant to be used—take off that bastard's head."

With a nod, Rei took to the skies once more, her blade gleaming with a purpose. Her ascent was swift, allowing Kriegon to turn back to the incoming death.

Realizing the futility of his efforts against the relentless tide of undead with mere sword strikes, Kriegon swiftly reverted his weapon back to its staff form, his mind racing through the potential ways to protect his friends. With a quick visualization, he summoned a barrier of fire, the rune glowing intensely on his staff. The air rushed around him, a prelude to the fiery spectacle that erupted, a wall of flames that stood between them and the encroaching horror. The magic, while powerful, sapped his reserves of psychic energy, each flicker of flame a testament to his dwindling strength.

As the undead met their fiery demise, their forms turning to ash upon contact with the inferno, Kriegon's gaze swept across the battlefield to Ellena and Zenmore. They were now fighting back-to-back, a desperate last stand against an unending wave of death, their movements growing sluggish with exhaustion. Beelzebub, watching from a distance, let out a booming laugh, his form slowly retreating, perhaps to regroup or summon more of his dark forces. But his laughter was abruptly silenced.

With a sound like the crack of doom, Rei descended from the heavens, her scythe aimed with lethal precision. Her strike was perfect, a blur of motion that ended with Beelzebub's head severed from his shoulders, flying through the air to land with a thud near Kriegon. The undead, as if puppets with their strings suddenly cut, halted their advance, their forms rigid, eyes vacant. The battlefield fell into an eerie silence, broken only by the soft crackling of Kriegon's fire barrier and the labored breathing of the Guardians.

Kriegon let the flames die down, the barrier dissipating into the cold air. Rei landed heavily beside him with the exertion of her final act, her chest heaving as she tried to catch her breath.

Together, they moved towards the severed head of Beelzebub, its laughter still echoing in the air, an unnatural sound that seemed to defy death itself. The head, lying on the ground, began to morph before their eyes, the demonic features gradually giving way to a more human appearance, though not entirely. It was a face that Kriegon recognized with a jolt of horror—Tom Cabal.

As the Guardians gathered around, the head's eyes flickered with a malevolent light, and it spoke, its voice a chilling echo of its former self. "You might have won today's battle, but I have given you an unending war. My essence, my minions, are now part of this mortal plane. Enjoy your brief victory."

Zenmore, his face a mask of fury and disgust, stepped forward, his weapon raised. With a decisive swing, he crushed the head.

Chapter 20: A Lone Road

Garthen, amidst the pain and the bulk of Saphire's body pressing him into the cold, damp earth, heard the chilling echo of Beelzebub's final words. The sound of the creature's head being crushed under Zenmore's weapon was like a signal, a release. The undead, momentarily frozen, began to move again, but not in attack. Instead, they retreated into the shadows of the forest, as if repelled by the weak rays of sunlight piercing through the overcast sky.

Rei, along with Kriegon and Ellena, approached to offer aid. Saphire's condition was dire, her injuries severe, while Garthen, though battered, could manage a limp on his own. Rei, her face etched with concentration and fatigue, worked tirelessly until the sun dipped below the horizon, her hands glowing with healing magic as she stabilized Saphire. The effort left her visibly drained, her breath onerous and her movements slower.

A oppressive silence had fallen over the group. Garthen, like the others, was lost in thought, processing the day's events. It wasn't until Rei, with a sigh of relief, asked Zenmore to carry Saphire back to Riversong that the quiet was broken. Ellena, her voice filled with disbelief, whispered, "We defeated one of the princes." Her words hung in the air, a testament to their incredible feat.

Zenmore's response was immediate, his stoicism replaced by his usual wide grin. "Oh yeah, we did! Talk about a battle for the ages!" He let out a triumphant howl into the night sky before carefully lifting Saphire into his arms, cradling her with a gentleness that contrasted sharply with his warrior's exterior.

Garthen, supported by Kriegon and Ellena, limped alongside. The path back to the city was eerily quiet, the threat of the undead absent. Garthen's mind replayed the battle relentlessly, each decision, each move scrutinized for flaws. He berated himself for the moment's distraction that had led to Beelzebub's vicious counterattack.

The journey back to Riversong felt endless without the adrenaline of battle to spur them on. The moons cast a pale light over the landscape, and as they approached the city, the collapsed northern gate came into view, illuminated by torches. The guards, spotting the group, erupted into cheers that echoed off the stone walls, breaking the icy silence of the forest they had just left.

Rei, carefully lifting Saphire from Zenmore's arms, prepared to take her to the mage guild for further healing. Meanwhile, Garthen, reaching the top of the rope ladder, was immediately enveloped in a bear hug by Dunstan, whose usually stern facade had melted away in his relief and joy. "I can't believe you all pulled it off. It was so strange to see the undead retreat; we feared the worst."

As Garthen pushed away gently, his body protested with pain. "Honestly, I'm surprised we made it, too. But let Zenmore recount the tale; he enjoys the limelight more than I do."

Dunstan's concern was conspicuous. "Are you okay? Should I call for a mage to heal you?"

Garthen shook his head. "No need, I'll go myself. Just get me a cloak to slip through the crowd unnoticed."

Without hesitation, Dunstan removed his own thick winter cloak and draped it over Garthen's shoulders. Garthen pulled the hood over his head, a gesture that felt symbolic, hiding from the celebration, from the eyes of those who might see him not as a hero but as a man still haunted by loss.

The others stayed atop the wall, basking in the adulation of the crowd, their figures silhouetted against the torchlight, while Garthen found a quieter path, slipping away from the spotlight. Without the immediate threat and action hanging over him now, his thoughts slipped back into pain and the ever-present shadow of grief. He thought about going back to his daughter's grave again but decided against it. If he knew Rei, she would be out looking for him quickly if he didn't arrive at the magic guild's base for healing.

He quickly made his way through the crowd. The revelers, caught up in their own celebrations, barely noticed him as he ducked into the large tent that had once served as his command center. Now repurposed by the magic guild for treating the wounded near the city walls, it was quiet inside, save for the soft murmurs of healing spells and the occasional instruction from Rei.

Inside, Garthen found an empty cot and lay down, pulling Dunstan's cloak over him like a makeshift blanket. Though the fabric was hefty, meant to ward off the chill of the night, Garthen felt no discomfort from the cold. His body had become numb to such discomforts, a fact he kept to himself, not wanting to burden his companions further with his personal afflictions.

At the back of the tent, the mages were gathered around Saphire, attempting to mend her wounds with their magic. Garthen could hear Rei's voice, firm and clear, directing the efforts of her apprentices, guiding their hands with precision to ensure Saphire received the best care possible.

Left to his own devices, Garthen's mind wandered, the day's events replaying in his head, each moment of the battle dissected for what could have gone differently. His thoughts were interrupted by the sensation of warmth spreading across his chest—a healing spell. He opened his eyes to see one of Rei's students standing over him, her concentration evident as Rei observed, occasionally offering quick, sharp instructions.

"Are you ever going to let them handle things on their own?" Garthen asked, intending it as a lighthearted tease, but his voice carried more of an edge than he'd meant.

Rei's response was swift, her lips pursing slightly. "When I return home, maybe." Her tone suggested exasperation and affection for her students, a mother worried over their development.

A silence fell over the trio as the apprentice continued her work, the warmth of the healing magic fading as she completed her task. Garthen gave a nod of gratitude, then stood, draping the cloak over his shoulders and pulling the hood up to shield himself from the world outside.

Rei stepped closer, her expression softening. "Are you going to join the celebration outside?"

Garthen shook his head, his voice low. "It's not for me to join. I think

I'll go visit my daughter again."

Rei's disappointment was flagrant, her eyes reflecting understanding and sorrow as she let him pass. Garthen stepped into the night, the sounds of celebration muted in his ears, his thoughts turning inward as he walked towards the place where memories of his daughter lingered, seeking solace in the quiet of the night.

The next morning, the atmosphere within the Zella mansion was one of both triumph and tension as the Guardians and the nobles of Riversong gathered around a large dining table. Garthen sat among them, his presence more physical than mental, his thoughts adrift towards his daughter's grave, where he yearned to find some semblance of peace or perhaps a path forward in his grief.

Felix, who had taken a leadership role in the absence of evident governance, called for attention with a clearing of his throat, his hand raised for silence. "Guardians, your efforts have not only liberated Riversong but have also saved countless lives by defeating Beelzebub," he began, his voice filled with gratitude. The room erupted in cheers once again, though Felix quickly sought to steer the conversation towards the future. "However, we must now look forward. What comes next for our kingdom is crucial."

He unveiled a scroll, the paper crackling as it unrolled, revealing its contents to the assembly. "I propose that the Guardians join forces with Commander Flavius to address the situation in Malgrave." The mention of Malgrave brought a hush over the room, the gravity of its implications not lost on anyone.

"First, I must inform you all, Commander Wells's forces are missing. We fear they've been absorbed by the undead army before they could even glimpse the shadow of the White Pine Forest. It would account for the swollen ranks of that ghastly horde. This ill news, coupled with a scouting report I've withheld for months, underscores the dire need for the Guardians' intervention."

Silence, heavy and expectant, as if the very walls of the hall leaned in to hear more.

"Flavius," Felix continued, his gaze sweeping over the crowd, "reports that a majority of the ships once docked at Malgrave have set sail, their hulls cutting through the icy waters before the frost could claim the harbor entirely. But more chilling are the sightings of humans, not as they should be, but marred with strange, icy spikes protruding from their flesh, as if the cold itself sought to claim them for its own. These … creatures, for they can hardly be called men any longer, have been seen in large numbers, leaving Windmontley, their path set northwards into the wild, untamed lands of the Barbarians."

Garthen's attention, previously distant, snapped back to the present at the mention of beings with ice-like spikes, a detail that eerily echoed the fate of his daughter. His heart raced with dread and a rekindled desire for vengeance.

Felix, with a grave expression, passed around the communications scroll. The parchment was handed from one set of hands to another, each person's face growing more somber with each word they read. He opened another scroll and started again. "We have also received word that the pirate's fleet has rounded the Cape of Transcendent and sailed east, with potential destinations being Uthos and Hammerforged."

Kriegon, his brow furrowing, leaned forward, his chair creaking under his shift. "What could be their motive for heading to those two countries?" he asked, his voice laced with concern.

Felix, tapping his fingers rhythmically on the table, speculated with a hint of disdain, "Most likely to unload their ill-gotten gains, including slaves. It's rumored that Asceriate has little taste for human slaves, so they're unlikely to land there."

Saphire, her eyes flaring with indignation, stood abruptly, her chair scraping loudly against the stone floor. "This vile practice must be abolished! I wager that's where they've taken your king," she declared, her voice echoing off the high ceilings.

Felix nodded, his expression grim. "Indeed, if we are to restore any semblance of peace here, we need our king returned. But confronting

Uthos or the dwarves of Hammerforged to demand they cease such a profitable endeavor is akin to trying to stop a river with a dam made of twigs. We would require considerable leverage, something only the support from Asceriate territories could provide."

As the room erupted into a heated debate, with voices rising in defense of Saphire's impassioned plea, and others, like Ellena and Felix, advocating for a more diplomatic approach through Asceriate, Garthen found himself detached from the fray. His gaze was fixed on the scroll before him, the words blurring as his mind replayed the harrowing images of his daughter, transformed into something terrible by the same icy corruption described in the reports. The numbers of these corrupted beings, their direction northwards, it all felt too personal, too close to his own tragedy. To close to a mission yet unfulfilled.

The meeting's end was marked by the scraping of chairs and the shuffle of feet, but Garthen remained still, lost in thought. It was Zenmore's nudge that finally broke his reverie.

"What's on your mind, friend?" Zenmore's deep voice rumbled, cutting through the noise of departure.

Garthen sighed, his eyes still distant. "Just pondering which path to tread," he murmured, though his thoughts were far from the strategic debates still simmering around him. His path was clear in his mind; it lay not with political negotiations or military strategies but with a journey into the cold, merciless heart of the north, where he might find answers or at least confront the darkness that had taken his daughter.

As the last echoes of the nobles' footsteps faded down the grand corridor of the Zella mansion, Zenmore, with a voice as rough as gravel, grumbled to Garthen, "Can I borrow you for a second?"

Garthen, surprised by the rare unease in the orc's demeanor, decided to heed his request. He had planned to part ways soon, but one last heart-to-heart with each companion seemed fitting. "What's on your mind?" Garthen asked, careful to ensure he seemed properly concerned.

Leaning against the cool stone wall, Zenmore crossed his massive arms, his posture betraying his discomfort. "It's about Orris ... you know how I've always bragged to her. Last night, during the revelry, she came up to me and suggested we could be a couple."

Garthen's eyebrows shot up in surprise; this was a turn he hadn't anticipated. "And Felix? Where does he stand in all this?" he inquired, curious about the dynamics.

With a shrug that seemed too casual for the magnitude of the conversation, Zenmore replied, "He was there, like they had it all planned out."

Despite the dark cloud of vengeance that hung over his thoughts, Garthen couldn't suppress a chuckle at the absurdity of the situation. "So, what was your response?"

"I told them I'd think about it and then drowned my shock in ale," Zenmore confessed, his voice a jumble of regret and confusion. "But just before the meeting, Felix hinted they were still waiting on my answer."

Garthen offered a smile tinged with empathy. "Do you care for her?" At Zenmore's nod, he continued, "Then why not say yes? Courting isn't marriage. Look at Kriegon and Ellena; they're happy without rushing into anything formal."

With a grimace that spoke volumes of his inner turmoil, Zenmore nodded again. "Guess I should talk to her then." He pushed off from the wall, his steps heavy as he made his way down the corridor.

Left alone, Garthen let the immensity of his own loss wash over him. He saw the harsh irony of counseling his friend into a happiness he himself could no longer have and could never reclaim. The mansion's grandeur seemed to mock his solitude, its walls echoing with the laughter of others, the warmth of potential love stories unfolding.

The room where Rei had once lived was now filled with the quiet rustle of dried herbs and the soft clink of medical tools. Saphire, lying on a makeshift bed, grimaced slightly as she stretched under Rei's watchful eye, her body still healing from the recent ordeal.

Garthen entered, his presence a sudden shift in the room's

atmosphere, his voice light but carrying an undercurrent of concern. "Hey, you two. Everything healing up good?" he asked, trying to inject a bit of normalcy into the air thick with recovery.

Saphire, attempting to comply with Rei's instructions, stretched again, wincing at the tightness in her muscles. "Yes, just a bit tight," she managed to say, her tone strained.

Rei tapped Saphire gently on a horn, a gesture meant to be reassuring. "You'll be fine. Your muscles are just recovering from all the stress we went through. I could barely lift my scythe this morning," she admitted, her voice a combination of exhaustion and humor.

The room was momentarily silent, save for the soft rustle of herbs as Rei reached up to retrieve some from where they hung drying from the ceiling. Her movements were precise, each herb selected with care for its healing properties.

"What's your stance on the path forward, Garthen?" Saphire asked, her voice serious, her mind clearly on the larger issues at hand as she sat up.

As Rei began to grind the herbs in the mortar, her movements forceful, Garthen responded with a measured tone, "The path isn't for one person to decide here. Maybe it will take multiple paths for us all to achieve the prophecy."

Rei slammed the mortar down on the table with a bit more force than necessary, her frustration evident. "No, we should stick together. It's clear we barely stood a chance against a prince with all of us. Imagine if even one of us was absent during the fight with Beelzebub."

Saphire countered, trying to keep her frustration down. "But we aren't talking about princes now. We're discussing a trade that's likely bolstering their strength."

Garthen, trying to soothe the rising tension, added, "And if we keep in touch with communication scrolls and have teleportation slabs, would the group really be that divided?"

Rei's response was sharp, her teeth bared in a snarl of frustration. "I still don't like it. It's not a perfect solution. What if one group gets ambushed?"

Saphire, sensing the need to diffuse the escalating tension, sighed deeply. "We can't cower at the potential of something bad happening. We need to take risks sometimes."

Garthen, trying to lighten the mood, chuckled softly. "Yes, it's kind of like Zenmore agreeing to date Orris. A little risk for him to find happiness."

The room fell silent, both women staring at Garthen with expressions of sheer bewilderment. The revelation had slipped out unintentionally, and Garthen realized too late that this was news to them.

Saphire opened and closed her mouth several times, words failing her, but Rei quickly found her voice, her tone laced with incredulity and a hint of rage. "He is doing what now? He is going to … date?"

Garthen, backpedaling, tried to explain, "Hey, don't be angry. He was approached by Orris, with Felix right there, asking him to date. I thought he would have sought your advice before mine."

Rei exploded, "So he gets to find something in this world?! Kriegon and Ellena I can understand, but …" Rei's frustration was overt as she became lost for words. Quickly, she thrust the ground herbs towards Saphire. "Here, mix this with your food today. I need to have a word with that meathead." Her speech clipped, her movements abrupt as she stormed out of the room, leaving a trail of anger in her wake.

Saphire, still in shock, looked after Rei, then back at Garthen. She took the herbs mechanically, her mind clearly racing to process this new development. Garthen, feeling the consequence of his unintended disclosure, watched Saphire as she began to follow Rei.

Garthen's footsteps echoed softly as he ascended the weathered stone stairs leading to the top of the nobles' border wall. The air was cooler here, the wind carrying a whisper of the distant forest. As he reached the summit, he paused, his breath catching at the sight before him.

Ellena and Kriegon stood at the edge, their figures silhouetted against the vast expanse of the horizon. Their voices were low, intimate, lost in the gentle gust that swept over the wall. Garthen watched, unnoticed, as Ellena's tail flicked with a life of its own, a sign of her animated conversation. Then, in a tender moment that seemed to pause time itself, Ellena stood on her toes, her lips pressing a kiss to Kriegon's cheek.

The scene struck a deep, resonant chord within Garthen. Ellena, with her youthful exuberance and fierce spirit, was so reminiscent of his own daughter before the darkness had taken her. Witnessing this display of affection, of life continuing unabated, was a sharp reminder of all the years, the moments, his daughter had been denied.

His heart, a tumult of emotions, clenched with a clash of joy for his friends and a renewed, fierce anger at the fate that had befallen his child. Then, as if he had been thrown into the past, a scene mirrored the couples before him. He and Bella atop a wall in Windmontley just before a proposal, the distant mountains to the north snowcapped and calling him. For a moment, he stood frozen, the contrast between the living, breathing love before him and the silent memory of his family too painful to bear.

Realizing there was nothing he could say, no final words that would bridge the gap between his sorrow and their happiness, Garthen turned away. His steps were careful, almost silent, as he descended the stairs, leaving the couple to their private world.

With each step, Garthen's resolve hardened. He had his path, a lonely journey driven by a need for vengeance, for understanding, a path that now felt even more solitary after witnessing such a moment of connection. As he walked away, his mind was set on the preparations needed for his departure, the finality of his decision echoing in the quiet of his heart.

Chapter 21: The Parting of Ways

The snow fell like silent whispers from a sky darkened by the approaching night. Kriegon and Ellena, their steps muffled by the fresh snow, made their way back to the mansion. The tranquility of the moment felt like a stolen breath amidst the relentless storm of their duties and battles. It was as if, for a brief time, they had been granted a reprieve, a Christmas vacation in the midst of chaos.

As they approached the mansion, the peace was shattered by the unmistakable sense of urgency that greeted them. Servants and guards moved with purpose, their faces etched with concern. Rei, her form a blur of motion, descended from the second story, landing softly before them.

"Have you seen Garthen?" she demanded, her eyes scanning their faces.

Kriegon, taken aback by the sudden question, shook his head, his concern growing. "No, we haven't seen him since the meeting this morning. Why? What's happened?"

Rei's voice trembled slightly, revealing her distress. "He's gone. Left a note saying he's off to seek his own path."

The words hit Kriegon and Ellena like a physical blow. They exchanged a look of shock, their brief respite forgotten in the wake of this new development. Before they could react, the sounds of hurried footsteps announced the arrival of Zenmore and Saphire, their expressions a torrent of anger and disappointment as they converged in the dining hall.

Zenmore, his voice booming with frustration, slammed a fist into his palm. "How could he just leave us like that? Without a word!"

Saphire, pulling Garthen's note from her pocket, handed it to Kriegon, who struggled to read the hastily scrawled message. Ellena, reading over his shoulder, whispered aloud, "Comrades in arms. I am off to seek out the being who took everything from me. I will not tell you where, but know that when I am done, I will return to help finish what we started. Don't look for me, but instead move on in whatever paths you feel are best to achieve the mission. I will miss you all, Garthen."

Kriegon turned the paper over, hoping for more, for anything that might give them a clue or a semblance of hope. But there was nothing. Just the cold, hard reality of Garthen's departure, his intentions as clear as the winter's chill.

Felix entered, his face grim. "Garthen wasn't spotted leaving the city, but Dunstan has the guards on alert."

The room fell silent, the pain of Garthen's decision hanging heavily in the air. Kriegon, feeling the obligation of speaking an uncomfortable truth, spoke with a resolve that surprised even himself. "No, we should respect his wish. Don't pursue him."

The reaction was mixed: shock painted on some faces, anger on others. Zenmore, his voice rising in protest, argued, "We can't just leave a member of our clan to the cold!"

Kriegon, his decision firm, shook his head. "We aren't abandoning him. We respect our leader's decision. After the argument this morning, it's clear the clan won't stay intact anyway."

Zenmore's retort caught in his throat as Felix, with a somberness that seemed to pull the room's attention, moved to the head of the table. His eyes, sharp and searching, fixed on Kriegon. "What are you saying, Kriegon?"

Kriegon sighed deeply, the sound echoing in the vast, cold room. "Ellena and I, we've decided to head to Malgrave, then on to Asceriate. It's where we feel we can make the most difference." His gaze shifted to Saphire, her face set like stone, her eyes a storm of resolve. "But Saphire, she's set on Uthos or Hammerforged, no matter our counsel."

Saphire, her nod crisp, confirmed, "That's right. And if it weren't for Garthen's departure, I would've already been discussing with Felix about securing passage on one of the remaining ships."

Rei, her features etched with deepening sorrow, looked between them, her voice barely above a whisper. "So, Zenmore and I must choose between you two now?"

Zenmore, his grunt of displeasure filling the room, admitted, "I've made my choice. I'm with Saphire. Not just for the debt I owe her but because we need to stick together."

Saphire's surprise was obvious, her eyes widening slightly, while Felix managed a half-smile. "And that aligns with my original strategy," Felix continued, his tone shifting quickly. "I was planning to send a delegation to Uthos anyway, aiming to locate King Abraham if indeed he was taken there, and to strengthen our ties for some much-needed aid. With Zenmore going, it makes sense for Orris to join you as well."

Zenmore, taken aback but accepting, reached out to shake Felix's hand, the gesture sealing their mutual agreement.

Rei stepped away from the table, her back to them. The silence stretched until she turned, her eyes glistening but her voice firm. "I'll go with Ellena and Kriegon then. But let's remember what Garthen said this morning: we all carry communication scrolls and teleportation slabs. If anything goes awry, we need to be able to assist each other swiftly."

Saphire, a grim smile touching her lips, nodded. From there, the group dispersed into action. Felix returned to Dunstan, ensuring the news of Garthen's departure was kept under wraps. Saphire and Zenmore set off to find Orris, to share the plan and gather what they'd need for their journey. Meanwhile, Rei, Ellena, and Kriegon made their way to Ryoma and the magic guild, the air thick with the urgency of their mission to secure magical artifacts vital for their respective quests.

Kriegon thought through his choice again as he walked along with the other two. As Ellena squeezed his hand, he looked to her. He knew the choice was right, and they needed more allies to combat the demonic forces. Ellena was sure of her tribe's choice if the Guardians came to them seeking aid. Beyond that, the conclave of the beastkin and elves would be within reach once Ellena's tribe came to the table.

Days of relentless preparation culminated in a flurry of activity at the docks of Riversong. The ship destined for Uthos was a hive of anticipation, its deck crowded with those who would accompany

Saphire, Zenmore, and Orris on their quest. The city, awakening from winter's grasp, saw the snow melting into the rising river, its waters now a pathway to new adventures.

The farewells were of solemnity and excitement, the air thick with unspoken emotions and the worry of departure. Kriegon, his voice a blend of command and care, simply said, "Be safe," as he embraced Zenmore and Saphire amidst the cheers of a gathered crowd, all eager to witness the Guardians' departure.

Both Zenmore and Saphire, towering figures of strength and resolve, had to stoop to return Kriegon's hug, their embrace a testament to the bond they shared. When they stood to hug Rei, her face was streaked with tears, a common display from her these past couple days. Her voice trembled as she implored, "You two had better message me if anything comes up, you promise?"

Their nods were solemn, but Kriegon couldn't help but chuckle softly, turning away to hide his amusement. He knew, and it seemed Rei had momentarily forgotten, that neither Zenmore nor Saphire could read or write. The responsibility of communication would fall to Orris or another literate member of their crew.

The urgency of the captain's call for departure spurred the group forward, their steps quickening as they ascended the gangway. The ship, eager to embrace the river's generous flow, was set for a swift exit from the harbor, its sails catching the wind of change.

Kriegon watched, his heart filled with pride and sorrow, as his friends waved their goodbyes, their figures shrinking with distance as the ship began its journey. The ties to the dock were released, and the vessel started to drift, carried by the river's current.

Beside him, Ellena's hands found his, her grip tight, seeking comfort in the choice of their shared path. He looked down at her, her face mirroring his own emotions—a sad smile that spoke volumes of their shared resolve and the unspoken fears of separation from their comrades.

"We will be alright," Kriegon assured her, his voice steady despite the turmoil within. A new feeling of belonging in a world full of darkness, his presence with the other Guardians a method to drive it back.

Ellena's response was soft, her smile tinged with the same melancholy. "As long as we are together," she said, her words a quiet vow that they would face whatever lay ahead, side by side.

Vladmir stood at the very prow of the ship, the cold sea spray lashing against his face as the vessel carved its relentless path through the frothy waves. The salt air filled his lungs, invigorating him with a sense of freedom and purpose he hadn't felt since long before coming to this world. As the ship surged forward, he felt an immense thrill, the kind that came from venturing into the unknown, into a land of wonders and terrors alike.

Beside him, the intense, almost palpable presence of Lucifer, the Morning Star, loomed like a shadow cast by the sun at noon. Vladmir sensed him, not just as a physical entity but as an aura of power and subtle menace, long before any words were spoken.

Lucifer's voice broke the silence with a hint of amusement. "I must confess, they've surpassed our wildest anticipations. Their resilience, their ingenuity—it's something to behold, isn't it?"

Vladmir turned slightly, his lips curling into a knowing smile. "Indeed, especially Mammon's return with his pride swallowed whole. A sight I never thought I'd see."

A low, rumbling chuckle escaped Lucifer. "True, the sight of Mammon humbled is rare. But there's more." He paused, his expression hardening. "Beelzebub has been ousted from the game. A rather shocking update to my status board for the world."

Vladmir's eyes widened in genuine surprise. "Ousted? He was always the strategist, or so he thought."

Lucifer nodded, his gaze distant. "He was, in his own way. Yet his vision was too narrow, too focused on immediate gains without seeing the broader tapestry of our plans. It was one of our biggest flaws when rebelling in heaven."

As they spoke, Mammon, clad in his resplendent golden human form, emerged from below deck, his steps heavy with the weight of his recent defeat. He didn't acknowledge them as he made his way to the stern, perhaps to brood over his loss.

Vladmir watched him for a moment before turning back to Lucifer, curiosity piqued. "What of the others? Are they still in play?"

Lucifer's response was non-committal, a shrug that seemed to carry the magnitude of ages. "Their status remains as it was. Their utility in our grand design? That's yet to be seen. We must focus on our own path, on the prize that awaits us."

The conversation shifted as Vladmir's attention turned to a more personal matter. "And the gift you promised upon our arrival in Uthos?" he inquired, a hint of anticipation in his voice.

Lucifer turned to him, his eyebrow arched in a silent challenge. "That, my friend, was contingent upon your success. Have you succeeded, then?"

Vladmir's smile was confident, almost triumphant, as he unrolled a scroll he had kept hidden beneath his cloak. In clear, bold English, the words read, "We are going to Asceriate. Prepare yourself."

About the Author

Chance Fribbs is a manufacturing engineer by trade, with experience spanning from the high-stakes world of missile and submarine technology to the precision of medical devices. Now, Fribbs embarks on a new journey as an author, bringing his love for intricate systems and problem-solving into the realm of fantasy with his debut novel, The Guardians Trilogy: Rise of Vice.

Become Part of the Community

The adventure doesn't end with the last page. Dive deeper into the world of Maeglover, share your theories, and connect with fellow adventurers at betweenrealmspublishing.com. Join a community where fans discuss, debate, and celebrate the intricate tapestry of these new realms.

Embark on this journey with us, where every chapter is an invitation to explore, imagine, and belong.

A Request from the Author

If you enjoyed The Guardians Trilogy: Rise of Vice, I'd be incredibly grateful if you could take a moment to leave a review on your favorite platform—whether it's Amazon, Goodreads, or elsewhere. Your feedback not only helps other readers discover the book but also means the world to me as I continue this storytelling journey. Thank you for your support!